# Bound By

# Honor

## BORN IN CRIME

## BOOK 1

### AN ARRANGED MARRIAGE MAFIA ROMANCE

# KELSEY DAWSON

Bound by Honor

Copyright © 2021 Kelsey Dawson

ISBN: 978-1-8384515-0-9


**CREDITS:**

Cover Model: Valerio Logrieco

Photographer: Roberto Viccaro

Editing: Jennifer Collins

Proofreading: Christine LePorte

# TABLE OF CONTENTS

# PLAYLIST

Red Right Hand - Nick Cave & The Bad Seeds

The Fear - The Score

Boulevard of Broken Dreams & Wonderwall - Green Day feat. Oasis

Undiscovered - Laura Welsh

You don't Own Me - Grace ft G-Eazy

Welcome to Wonderland - Anson Seabra

The Heart Wants what it Wants - Selena Gomez

Jar of Hearts - Christina Perri

Teardrop - Massive Attack

Now or Never - Halsey

Peaches - Milk & Bone

Vienna - Billy Joel

# Chapter 1

## John

People who say money can't buy happiness have clearly never lived.

I chose my Midtown Manhattan penthouse primarily for the view, and from the forty-eighth floor, what a view it was. Staring out at the sparkling city lights from my living room, I could see the whole city laid out at my feet. Glittering lights pierced a black that was never totally dark. It seemed to me, sometimes, that the sprawling city below twinkled just for me. One day, it would all be mine, but in the meantime, money had bought me quite a bit of what I certainly deemed to be happiness.

Anyone would be envious of what I had, but that's not the reason I wanted it all. At twenty-nine years old, not many men could afford my lifestyle. Not many men of any age could live the way I do, in fact, and I'm not just talking about the money.

The ice in my glass clinked when I took a sip of Widow Jane, my favorite whiskey. Aged for twelve years, the Brooklyn-sourced bourbon tasted of orange peel and burnt sugar. It seared my throat.

At the moment, I was content to be an underboss, second-in-command after my uncle, but one day I'd run the entirety of the Colombo family's enterprises. Everyone could already see my talent as well as my ambition, as I handled the "entrepreneurial" pursuits of the family, and I handled them well. Even though most mafia family heirs didn't go the college route, I'd made sure to get a good education, earning a degree in business.

I used that knowledge to increase revenues across the board. Legitimate businesses were, after all, a great way to launder money.

One day, I would be in control of the Colombo family's destiny. Becoming the don of the Colombo family was my birthright. My Uncle Leone had safeguarded it for me since I'd been nine years old, when my parents had been killed in a boating accident.

That was the official report, of course. A boating accident. Hard to believe, and harder still when you look at the paperwork involved—truly, it was a story full of loopholes and bullshit. One day, I *would* find out what really happened to my parents, and I would make whoever was responsible pay. And if they were no longer walking the right side of the turf, I'd be sure that their descendants paid the price for their crimes.

I was getting there, too, though I wasn't there yet. Retribution would come when I had full control of my birthright.

When the so-called accident happened, I was obviously nowhere near ready to be at the head of the family. My uncle stepped in, filling my father's shoes. I'd been waiting to take my rightful place for years now, though. Waiting, and waiting some more. Seething with vengeance.

Of course, I'd learned how to be patient. It helped, too, that I had more money and more power than most of the people who legally ran the city. One day, I'd have even more. One day.

The sound of the doorbell interrupted my reverie. My fingers curled tighter around the glass in my hand and I turned away from the window. My condo being twice the size of the houses that the wealthy could afford, it was a long way to the door, but since the place was totally open—with floor to ceiling windows on one side, and the loft on the other—I could see the door easily.

My housekeeper, Mary, scuttled across the room from out of nowhere, as if the walls at the far side had just birthed her. How someone could move so silently, and be so unobtrusive, I would never know. I was about to call out to her to leave the door, but she hustled over on her stick-thin legs and yanked it open before I could utter a word.

Mary was a good housekeeper. She was loyal, and had been with me for years. Even though she was pushing sixty, she was in no hurry to retire—and I was in no hurry to ask her to. As fit as a woman in her twenties, she was so trim and compact that she could easily be mistaken for a much younger woman from the back. The only problem with Mary was that she was too trusting. She'd open the door for anyone. And while it was true that not just anyone could gain access to the penthouse, that was a worry. The security downstairs ensured that I had a high degree of privacy, but one day, I knew her kindness and trust could bite us both in the ass.

Fortunately, I knew who was on the other side this time. I looked at my watch and saw that Piero and my brother Dario were early. *Good*. I wanted to handle whatever they needed quickly and get them out the door again. I'd been feeling unsettled all week, and I didn't like dealing with petty crap right now. That was why I'd been willing to make them wait on me opening the door myself, but this was just as well.

I cautioned myself to have patience as I turned back to the window and took another sip of my whiskey. Not only was Dario my younger brother, but he was slowly coming into his own. At twenty-seven, he was gradually shucking off the irresponsibility of youth, and I had to admit it was a relief. He had a carefree nature that bothered me. In the past, he'd relied on wit and sarcasm to get what he wanted, and when that had failed, charm alone; anything he could slide by with rather than force. As a capo—a man who worked below me, a man who had growing responsibility as well as command of many of our soldiers—he needed to take his duties more seriously. *I needed him* to take his duties more seriously.

Piero Bruno, on the other hand, was far more reliable. He was a short, squat man who had worked for our family for forty years, and as a second cousin to my Uncle Leone, no one doubted his loyalty. I had hoped for years that Dario would learn something about commanding our soldiers from the older, grizzled veteran, but it had been a slow process, at best.

"Oh. Um, hello…" I heard Mary stammer. I'd looked away, meaning to take my brother's entrance casually, but now my attention was immediately drawn back to the door.

I barely repressed a groan when I saw who stood at the entrance, and had to resist the urge to hurl my glass at the nearest wall as a stunning model sashayed through the door. She slammed it shut after her and glared Mary down.

Mary cast one look at me and scurried off down the hall. I didn't particularly blame her.

Raquel, whose birth name was Eloise Hunter, grinned at me like she had a right to be here. I supposed she had spent a shit ton of time at my condo, but that didn't mean I wanted her there now. Definitely not when I was expecting my brother and Piero.

She leered at me now, and I was reminded that Raquel was a stunning woman of rare beauty... on the outside. She had raven black hair that cascaded down her back in soft waves, eyes so light blue that they shone like sea glass, and full, sensual lips, as well as a lithe body. Inside, however, she was no different than any other girl I'd fucked—or maybe she was worse. Raquel was all about money and fame. She liked to wait and watch until she was certain of how she could exploit a situation to her advantage. Nothing else penetrated her tiny brain.

Lately, she'd been angling for more from our relationship, which had so far only consisted of kinky sex and dirty talk. She seemed to believe that making our relationship official, meaning *public*, would be mutually beneficial. She would gain the prestige of dating me along with access to my wealth and connections, and she believed I would obtain my heart's desire. She'd somehow gotten the notion that she could make me fall in love with her, and have me wrapped around her little finger for as long as she wished. She couldn't have been more wrong.

I'd learned to hate my enemies a very long time ago, but I'd *never* learned to love.

"What are you doing here?" I barked from across the room, refusing to give her the satisfaction of a real greeting. "I didn't invite you here tonight, Raquel, and I've got other business."

Instead of apologizing, she ignored my point entirely and smirked at me. "I was in the area." She shook her black leather jacket off and angled to the side, giving me a full view of her voluptuous breasts. Tonight, they were just barely crammed into a tight black dress that was short enough to have been a shirt stretched down over her sensual curves. "I

4

just finished up with a photo shoot and thought I'd check in. It doesn't *always* have to be you calling the shots. I can come by and see you if I want to." She batted long, fake eyelashes at me.

"That's not how it works, sweetheart." Even patronizing her didn't put her off. "I've got shit to do tonight."

"No, you don't. You're the boss." Her hands rested on her hips and she winked playfully at me, still not absorbing my tone. "You sit here with me and get everyone else to do your work for you. That's how it works. That's how it's always worked for you. Don't think I don't see that."

A shiver of revulsion crawled up my spine. Raquel suspected what I did, but she didn't know for sure. Even so, suspicions of my activity would have bothered a better person, and she only cared to take advantage of it all. But tonight was important, and having her around wasn't an option. I hadn't gotten to be the underboss of the Colombo crime family by spilling family secrets. That was some "need to know" shit right there, and she did *not* need to know.

I shook my head at her, looking pointedly to her discarded jacket before I met her eyes. "Look, this isn't a normal Friday night for me. When I say that I'm busy, I mean I'm *busy*."

"You didn't call because you're getting bored of me." Her plump lips jutted out in an unsexy pout. "You *never* call me anymore."

That was true, though I hadn't thought she'd noticed. It had been a while since I'd put in a booty call to Raquel, but I sure as fuck wasn't in the mood for her now.

"It has nothing to do with you. It's work." I pointed to the door. "Out."

"No, spend time with me!" She actually stomped her foot like a little kid. My desire for her had already been waning, and her childish actions just killed it completely. "I want to see you, John-John, and you never want to let me in anymore. We should be moving forward," she wheedled, sidling closer and leaning over the couch to give a better, more directed, view of her breasts.

*For the love of fucking fuck.*

But regardless of her particular attributes, I wasn't moving forward—or anything remotely close to that—with her, or with anyone. Not a chance

5

in hell. The suggestion was such a turn-off that I barely even noticed the way she'd called me "John-John" again. I fucking hated that stupid nickname, and she knew it. Before I could let off steam and unleash some of my anger, though, Raquel scurried across the room and dropped to her knees in front of me. Her hands worked quickly, unzipping my pants even though she knew that Mary was in the other room. Unfortunately, Raquel had been here enough times that she also knew Mary would stay hidden in her own room, making as much noise as possible so as not to overhear anything we did. Hell, Raquel probably didn't even care when her mind was this set on what she wanted.

Much as I didn't want to deal with Raquel anymore, I supposed this wouldn't be the worst thing to come out of her unwelcome visit. Maybe I could release some tension and be done with her, with any luck. Besides that, my brother wasn't here yet, and she was offering. I didn't know many guys who would refuse a blowjob, especially one from someone as talented as Raquel. If that made me a bastard, then I guessed I'd earned the title fair and square, although I preferred to use the term *realist*.

Still, I set my glass to the side and resolved to enjoy this. Then, I'd make it clear I was done with her.

My hard cock burst free and Raquel wrapped her lips around me hungrily, taking extra encouragement from the fact that I was no longer trying to kick her out. The wet heat of her mouth surrounded me as she took me in as deeply as she could before nearly gagging. She slowly ran her mouth back up to the head, swirling her tongue around it. Normally, I'd already have been pumping my hips to fuck her mouth as I yanked on her silky hair, but today something was off. I found that I wasn't into it—which wasn't *exactly* a surprise, given that I wanted her out of here, but had given in to a second of weakness where my dick was concerned. Apparently, my brain wasn't on board with the idea.

"Stop," I told her quietly. She moved her hands around my balls and took me deeper, refusing to listen. "I said to stop!" I yelled more forcefully as I pushed her head back, my cock falling out her mouth. "Get off your knees and get out!"

"Why are you doing this?" Raquel whimpered. She shoved herself to her feet, wobbling on her towering black heels as she tried to pull her dress back down to a semi-respectable length. She pushed stray strands of hair from her face. Even though she was no longer on her knees, begging me, she still looked pathetic. Did she really think such a display would do it for me?

"I told you I don't need you tonight." I offered her a one-shouldered shrug as I tucked myself back into my pants. "I have shit to do. As I've said. *Repeatedly.* You need to go. As I've said. *Repeatedly.* There's a reason I haven't invited you over, Raquel. There's a reason I haven't called you. I won't be doing so again." The words hung in the air, and I waited for her to storm off, but she only stared back at me.

"You won't be calling me again?"

Holy shit, was her bottom lip trembling? Damn, her acting skills were improving.

"Why aren't you going to call me again?" she demanded. "I thought that we had something here. I thought we might be together—"

"No, Raquel. It's time for you to go," I told her, nodding toward the door. "We were *never* going to be together. I don't know why you would even think that. You need to go, Raquel. We're done here."

From the look on her face, and the start of this teary-eyed act, I realized she wasn't going to go unless I led her to the door—so that's exactly what I did. I grasped her, quite gently, underneath her shoulder, but made sure I held her with enough force to get her moving. Near the door, I stooped and swiped her leather jacket off the expensive, hand-scraped hardwood before I handed it to her. Then I marched her directly to the door, opening it and, without another word, nudging her out before I closed it firmly behind her.

I slid the lock home and ignored her fist landing on the other side of the door, as well as the banging that ensued. Thank fuck the thing was thick, because it drowned out most of the expletives coming from the other side. By the time Raquel started screaming about regrets and me, I was already walking away and didn't catch the rest. God, I didn't need this shit. I should have blocked her number and been done with it a while ago. Told security at the front desk not to let her up. Ever again. Things had clearly gone too far.

Now that I'd thrown her out like this, though, I *would* have to make sure I called down and made my orders clear.

I was halfway to retrieving my abandoned glass when a rough knock sounded on the door. The banging had stopped a few seconds before, and I'd thought she'd given up, but apparently not. I was about to change my mind about ignoring her and give her a lecture she wouldn't forget when a second rap penetrated through the fog of anger clouding my brain.

My brother could have had better timing.

I walked over and forced myself to approach the door with more calm than I felt. I composed my face, wiping away any trace of impatience and anger that might have been there. Emotion was a weakness. I never allowed myself to betray anything. Least of all to my brother, who needed to learn his own control.

Dario grinned at me from the hall. He was just over six feet tall and built like a natural athlete—which was fitting since he'd played football in college for years. He would have made a career of it if he hadn't blown out his knee. But that injury had meant Dario, at twenty-two years old, knew his football dreams were over. He'd handled it with more courage and humor than I would have if I'd been in his place. Even now, I knew how badly he'd wanted to make it big. Working for the family instead hadn't dried up the wit that always seemed to run just underneath his confident exterior, though. Dario still looked every inch the jock he'd used to be, and most of the time, he acted like that was his persona now, too, even though he hadn't been on the field for years. Part of who he was, I guessed.

Women had always loved my brother, and it was easy to see why. He had enough jet black hair, burning dark eyes, and olive-skinned charm to subdue half the female population.

With Raquel nowhere to be seen, Dario grinned at me easily, flashing perfect white teeth. He was a direct contrast to Piero. Standing right beside Dario, Piero looked every inch the goon he was. While Dario was tall, Piero was squat and thickly built. He was about as ugly as they came, too, but Piero was effective because people feared him. He had thick brows made thicker because he wore a perpetual frown. A long scar on his left cheek stood out in contrast to his dark olive skin. He also wore a perpetual sneer, and since he was missing teeth, it just leant itself to his sinister air. He was the same age as Mary, nearly sixty, but he looked more like two hundred. He was her opposite in other ways, as well. A person never knew what they were going to get with Piero—or, at least, what level of nastiness they were going to have to endure.

"Passed your company in the hallway," Dario said. "She was clearly pissed about something. You never did know how to treat the ladies, John." He paused, grinning as he leaned on the doorframe. "But, hey, since you're obviously not going to be enjoying her fine company any longer, would you mind passing her number on to me? It shouldn't go to waste, after all."

Piero let out a custom snarl in response to Dario's tasteless humor, and I let that end the discussion. They were here to talk about business, not my fucking personal life.

I led them into the expansive living room, heading over to retrieve my whiskey. Maybe the gravity of the setting would get my brother settled down. The entire condo had been furnished by a leading interior designer when I'd bought the place years ago. Most of the furniture was imported, and that meant expensive. The sprawling leather couch that wrapped around in a U-shape was as uncomfortable as it looked. There were also token items of stature in the condo. Rugs, artwork, statues. It all set the scene, but I didn't give a fuck about any of it. I hadn't picked it out and it didn't matter to me. Each item was just another symbol of my wealth, of my status in the world. I surrounded myself with it.

I mentioned earlier that I never learned to love, but that was something of a lie. I had two real loves in my life. My family, and vengeance. Everything else was just a minor distraction or a stepping stone in my path.

Piero took a seat on the far side of the couch. He looked uncomfortable, as he always did when he had to pay a visit anywhere but to one of our warehouses. Out of place. A turd in the middle of luxury.

Dario was far more at home. He sat down on the opposite end of the couch, crossed one heel over his knee, and slung his arms behind his head and leaned back like the hard couch was a fucking divan at the side of a pool at a luxury fucking resort. He grinned at me obnoxiously.

"Got anything to drink? Have to say that I'm parched."

I bit back an instant retort and instead offered him the same bourbon that I'd been enjoying before Raquel's untimely interruption. Piero shook his head. I'd known he would. He didn't drink while on duty. Another thing Dario could learn from him. As per usual, however, my brother ignored Piero and accepted the bourbon straight-up. When I handed him a glass, he tipped it back, but knew better than to ask me for another. Instead, he settled in, cupped his empty glass in one big hand, and stared at me.

I remained standing. Silent, waiting.

I wanted a report, and I wanted Dario to give it to me. Piero was just there to keep my brother honest. Piero was good at his job, and we all knew that. He was always able to find one lucrative source after another. Just one icy look from him, missing teeth and scar included, and men who liked to walk the straight and narrow were shaking in their buffed shoes the same way Piero's soldiers did.

Dario, on the other hand, wasn't much of a capo at all. He had yet to fine-tune the small details of intimidation. Or any details at all, if we were being honest with each other. He enjoyed running smaller operations—dealing with stolen cars on the black market, money exchanges, and other jobs that wouldn't matter so much in the long run if he happened to fuck them up. He was known for being impulsive, and his dick or his love of a good drink could easily distract him.

Still, he was my brother, and for me, family had always come first. Despite his faults, we were close. It was more than blood for us. Tragedy did that to people. Pulled them together and sewed them up tight with unshakeable bonds.

"Tell me," I urged my brother, when he was clearly getting too comfortable with the silence.

"Everything's under control," Dario declared, which was a token thing to say.

I glared at Piero, and he nodded slightly to confirm that this was the case. Almost imperceptibly, I felt myself relaxing. I waited some more, and Dario finally continued. He'd obviously been working himself up to a real story, but because Piero was there, he couldn't exaggerate as he normally did.

"The workers at the warehouse have their money," he said simply. "They filed the theft report for the cigars. What do you know, shit sometimes goes missing during shipping. The goods are on the way to our warehouse right now." Dario reached into his black suit jacket and produced a thick cigar. "I took the liberty of bringing some of the product here for you to inspect."

Piero grunted—his version of an eye roll. Piero might look like a thug, but he always dressed immaculately. He preferred the same black suits and expensive shoes that Dario wore. And while it made Dario look even younger and more charming, it somehow made Piero that much more fearsome.

The effect produced by the contradiction between a tasteful, expensive suit and a rough man could never be underestimated.

I took the cigar from my brother and held it up to my nose. The rich, smoky scent flooded my nostrils, and I tucked it away in my own suit jacket. Our taste in clothes was probably the only thing the three of us shared. I had a custom tailor who hand-made all of my suits for me, but black was always my color of choice. I rarely deviated from it, and I hadn't today.

The cigars were a new venture for us, which was one reason I needed to keep tabs on them especially carefully. It was an idea for business that Dario had brought to us and championed, so of course I was nervous about the details and even more so about the men involved. They were variables, new ones, and variables had to be controlled at all times.

"Are they trustworthy?" I asked—not for the first time.

Dario nodded slowly. For once, he wasn't smiling.

"Good."

Piero looked more hesitant when my eyes tracked to him. Piero preferred violence over words at all times. He was a smart man. But I nodded in his direction, forcing him to speak.

"I'm not as confident as Dario that the parties will be loyal and live up to their word," he ground out.

Dario started to protest, but I held up my hand to stop him. I trusted Piero's judgment, whereas Dario's was questionable. "If that's the case," I asked, "what do you suggest we do about it, Piero?"

He paused for a moment and looked at Dario, who didn't look happy, but wasn't unduly angry. Dario knew who was boss, and he also had a healthy amount of respect for Piero. By *respect*, I meant *fear*.

"I suggest bringing in some muscle to have a nice chat with anyone we don't think can be trusted. I'm not talking rats—just the guys who might think they could skim a little off for themselves, or anyone thinking they could be a fucking hero."

I thought about that for a moment, then looked pointedly at my brother. "Dario, it's your call. This was your idea, so I want you to decide if these guys can be trusted. And if they can't, then I want you to take care of it."

"I said I have everything under control." This time, there was an edge to Dario's voice, but it disappointed me that I heard petulance, not certainty.

Piero looked like he wanted to say something else, but he evidently changed his mind and fell back into his sneering silence. He didn't want to give Dario the benefit of the doubt, I knew. I also knew, though, that he would keep an eye on the situation and apprise me of the situation if something more needed to be done. And then I'd have to remind Dario that it was his mess, and that I'd suggested here that we get ahead of it.

I wouldn't undermine my brother on the venture that he'd dug out for himself, despite my misgivings. I wanted to give him the chance to succeed, but I would watch how it went. I needed to see that he could nurture an idea and make it a reality. Maybe one successful job would light a spark in him and he'd then take our business, and himself, more seriously in the future.

I sipped my whiskey and stalked back to the window, thinking over where we were. It was always on the back of my mind that Dario hadn't wanted to do this for the rest of his life. He'd had much bigger aspirations. Ones that should have worked out. I'd never seen a kid more talented at football. He'd been born with a head for that, for plays, for the field, for the game, and a body built to match. The fact that he was working for the family instead of playing for a living wasn't fair, and we both knew it—but that was all the more reason that I needed to see him succeed in our ventures.

And he was trying. He'd spent years training with our soldiers, though it wasn't the same kind of grooming that I'd received from my uncle. As a first-born son, I'd been born into this life. Dario had had a choice. It had been when that choice was taken from him that he'd had to abruptly switch gears.

Now, in the face of this disconnect between him and Piero, and between my seriousness and his immaturity, I reminded myself to have patience. Dario might have been at this for five years, but his experience was different from my own. Our personalities couldn't have been more different, either. We might have looked similar, as brothers, but that was about where *sameness* ended. I lacked Dario's easygoing nature, his humor, and his ability to rebound no matter what shit life demanded that he eat, or how much circumstance liked to piss on his breakfast.

With nothing else to discuss, Piero glanced at me and I cleared my throat, signaling that he was excused. He didn't wait for Dario. Clearly, they hadn't come together. Piero had probably arrived first, even before Raquel, and waited like a gargoyle for my brother to show up.

He let himself out without a backwards glance.

Dario didn't move, but I also didn't offer him anything else to drink. I wanted him clear-headed. I turned back to the tall windows and looked out over the city again, but the view had lost its earlier charm. Something restless shifted and chafed under my skin, like a sliver that had been there too long and putrefied.

It bothered me that I couldn't figure out what the fuck this feeling was. The darker, asshole part of me said that maybe I should have just

13

let Raquel suck me off. But no. Getting her out of my hair for good was worth an abbreviated blowjob.

I didn't normally feel like this, however. *Restless.* I hated being out of control, which meant that I was an expert at remaining centered, doing what needed to be done and compartmentalizing anything else. In fact, my life had been framed around always being in control. In control of my men. In control of myself. My life. My future. I didn't *get* restless.

I poured myself another drink, forgetting about Dario for a moment while I tossed the bourbon back. I was waiting for the familiar buzz, the warmth that drowned out the sensation of unease crawling under my skin, when Dario's phone went off, shattering what little peace I had just started to feel.

I whirled and watched him take the device out of his pocket. As he looked at the screen, his handsome face twisted and my insides went with them. I knew that, whatever this message was, it centered on another thing that he hadn't managed properly.

"Fuck," Dario swore, "I need to go. Money exchange. Fucking hell, I forgot about it. Has to just be me, too, I guess," he added with a frown. "Piero's not here anymore and I don't have time to get someone else to go with me."

He and I both knew these things were better done with a partner. Someone to intimidate. Someone to keep everyone honest.

Dario started scrolling through a list of contacts on his phone, muttering to himself, and I guessed he was unwilling to call Piero at this point. That would mean he'd have to admit that he'd forgotten about this part of his night's schedule.

Annoyed, I nearly crushed my empty glass in my hand. I needed yet another reminder to be patient with my brother, but they were getting harder to come by.

Swallowing down my frustration, I turned away from him, back to the window into darkness. An image of us as kids, running around our backyard, came to mind unbidden. Dario two years younger than me, but way the hell faster than me. Dario, with his head thrown back in laughter because I couldn't catch him, no matter how hard I tried.

When I grew frustrated and angry, he slowed down some and let me get within reach before he darted away. Eventually, he'd just collapse on the grass, even though he could have run for hours, and then he'd look up at the sky.

I remembered lying down beside him on that day out of the past, all of my frustration and anger forgotten. He'd pointed out the shapes in the clouds and I'd laughed along.

Back then, we'd been free to be kids. Back before our parents had been taken from us and we'd aged a thousand years overnight.

I turned back to the couch and blinked at Dario, an idea forming. It had been too long since I'd observed my brother in action. I'd put my trust in him, but he clearly needed a different kind of guidance than what Piero or our soldiers offered. With us being adults now, this was one of the only ways that I could allow myself to spend time with him. The other things my brother enjoyed—friends, beers, clubs, going to a game or just watching it at home—were things that I didn't allow myself. Control mattered in everything.

"There has to be someone close," Dario muttered.

"I'll come with you."

Dario's head jerked up in surprise. "You will?" He stared at me like I'd just sprouted a nut sack on my forehead. "You never come out for things like this. It's not...it's not what you do," he finished simply.

"I know it's not what I do," I bit out. The words sounded like I was grinding my own teeth to dust. "Tonight, I'll make an exception."

Dario looked at me for another second. "That's fine with me." He stood and headed for the door, but he'd clearly determined that I had a reason for going—and it wasn't that I wanted to be brotherly.

I choked back anything I could have said to his swagger as he walked over to the door. I could have told him that I just wanted to help, that I didn't want to test him or challenge him. That I missed him. That I missed that closeness we'd shared as kids. But things like that were better left unsaid. There was no room in our lives for sentimentality. I knew that even if he didn't.

15

"Where are we going?" I asked, and then I tossed back the rest of my drink, purposely taking my time.

"A little grocery store in Brooklyn." Dario turned. His bored tone didn't bely his unease at having me come along as a supervisor. "I don't know what it's called, but I know where it is."

*For fuck's sake.*

I stalked across the living room, over to the kitchen. Just like everything else in the condo, it had cost a fortune. The granite had been imported straight from Italy. It was golden with brown grains running through it. I personally found it ugly as shit and couldn't understand the sixty-thousand-dollar price tag it had carried, but the designer had liked it, and what the fuck did I actually care? The cupboards were dark, custom-made for the space. They stretched on in a long, linear line across the entire far side of the condo. The island stretched right along with them. The appliances had cost another fuck-ton of money, but I'd handed it over in order to get all the perks I desired. The designer had furnished me with the latest technology, as requested. The fridge had a goddamn tablet built into the front of it, while the dishwasher looked like just another cabinet.

The one feature that I truly enjoyed was that the double stainless steel sink had a garbage disposal installed. I imagined that, one day, it would come in handy.

I pulled open the cupboard above the gas stove and grabbed a set of Glocks. I shouldered them quickly, adjusting my suit jacket over the top of them.

Dario just rolled his eyes at me. I could only hope that he himself had come prepared. Generally, though, that wasn't one area I needed to worry about where my brother was concerned. He had an arsenal hidden away that could rival the supplies of some of our arms dealers.

We left the condo together, going down the impressive elevator in silence. One of the building's security guards, Phil, was sitting at the desk at the front. He might have had a token, shit name and looked like the token security guard who ate half a box of doughnuts every single day and hated his life, but he was a good man, and when I told him something, he listened.

I approached the desk with a smile. I could be warm—when the situation called for it. I'd learned more than just business over the years. For one thing, I'd learned how to present a face to the world that the world wanted to see. I even knew men who would call me a people person, and while that made me want to laugh, it was true only because I wanted it to be true.

"Phil. I hope you're having a good evening."

"I am, Mr. Colombo. Thank you." Phil smiled back just as warmly. He had a thick black moustache that stood out in stark contrast to his shiny bald head. His massive belly protruded over the lip of the desk he sat behind.

I nodded. "Can you do me a favor and ensure that the woman who was here earlier is never allowed up again?"

Phil's eyes widened, but he wiped the look of surprise off of his face and gave me a professional nod. "Yes. Of course, sir. Will do."

"Thank you. Have a great night."

I then joined my brother, who snorted at me as soon as we walked through the double glass doors and out into the cool April night.

"If I had a woman like that who wanted to come up, I'd let her come up. In fact, I'd let her come just about any way she pleased."

I remained silent until we reached Dario's black '67 Mustang Shelby. The windows were tinted in the front and back, in a concession to the updated sedans our family normally used, but I didn't feel secure sliding in beside him. I didn't normally ride in the front seat of a vehicle. In fact, I didn't normally ride at all. I preferred driving to being a passenger, and not just because I would never dream of letting anyone touch the cars I owned. They might look like nondescript, imported luxury vehicles, but they were mine, and no one touched what was mine. They weren't fancy because I didn't want to call attention to myself, but the bulletproof windows and extra reinforcement in the side panels could one day save my life.

17

Dario would have been driving an expensive, flashy car if I'd allowed it, but he'd gotten this classic car a while back as a gift from me, in hopes he'd embrace his role with more seriousness if he at least liked his ride, given how much he loved cars. It wasn't much like the token black vehicle that most of us drove; his car wasn't armored because Dario didn't want to modify a classic '67 Mustang. At the moment, I wasn't pushing him on the compromise, but soon he'd have to implement bulletproof glass and reinforce the rest.

I continued my silent streak while Dario drove us to the meeting spot. Staring out the window, I ground my teeth at his obnoxious driving. I hadn't expected anything less. To Dario, unfortunately, the roads were always a racetrack.

When I realized that the neighborhood we'd entered was as seedy as pond sludge, my skin prickled, but I said nothing at first. I wanted to see our destination. Dario finally parked the car alongside a darkened street, and it was obvious from the looming, black brick building a hundred feet away that we weren't at a fucking grocery store.

"What is this?" I snapped to Dario as he cut the engine. "That's a fucking nightclub over there."

"I'm not going in there. The meet-up is over there by the grocery store," Dario responded, gesturing to the small building across from the nightclub. "The club is just… there."

"You know how the family feels about this!" I snapped. "What are you thinking?"

Dario shrugged. Why did he do shit like this? I *needed* him to care about this stuff. To think. As my brother, as a blood member of the Colombo family, he was *supposed* to care, and to think about what made sense—not just for him, but for the family.

An icy tendril churned in my gut as I stared down the building Dario had pointed out. It did look to be a shitty grocery store, open late since it was across the street from a seedy-looking club. I couldn't imagine what kind of clientele they'd get in there. They would have been better off closing up early. At least they'd had enough sense to put bars on the windows.

"This doesn't feel right," I told him quietly. My fingers hovered over one of my hidden Glocks.

"I'll only be a minute." Dario waved his hand dismissively. "Don't worry so much, bro. You really need to loosen up."

He got out of the car before I could tell him that I didn't need to loosen up, but he needed to grow up. Or that if he called me "bro" again, ever, there would be good reason for my Glock to make an appearance. My brother could use a good fucking whipping with the butt end.

I might have been Dario's backup, but he obviously felt he had something to prove. I could only sit there and grind what was left of my molars to dust as I watched him cross the street to the dilapidated little grocery store. Did he always come to places like this to do his business? Why schedule an exchange right in front of a nightclub? That was just asking for trouble. Guys with our status were not supposed to be seen meeting with the lower ranks by a seedy club.

All interactions needed to be planned, preferably in places where there was no alcohol present to cloud judgment or give fuel to latent hostilities.

Dario was far too lax with the rules, though, and I knew it. I'd hoped he'd gotten smarter, but I'd seen enough after just a few minutes.

This just wasn't acceptable.

Watching the darkness, which was watered down by a few flickering streetlights, I tried to figure out what to say to my brother that he would actually fucking listen to for a change.

# Chapter 2

## Elisa

"Is dancing making you feel any better?" I called over the music as loudly as I could, but I wasn't sure if my cousin, Sara, could hear me. The thumping of the base line overshadowed every single word either of us spoke.

Sara nodded so hard that her thick, dark hair fluttered around her shoulders. She was rocking a tight red dress that made her normally average body sizzle. Sara's dark eyes were huge, too. They looked darker than ever now, framed by thick black lashes and lined with heavy black liner and dark eyeshadow. Her pupils were dilated, and when she tried to focus on me, it was pretty apparent that she was drunker than she let on. She wavered a little in her tall red pumps. Pumps she didn't need, either, because at five-nine, she was already a few inches taller than I was, and had an intensity that made her stand out even in a crowd.

I sighed as I watched my cousin sip her drink—vodka with soda—and gyrate her hips to the thumping music.

This wasn't my idea of a good time. Clubbing had never been my thing. I might have just graduated from college, but I'd skipped out on the whole partying scene. Even if I would have liked to be a part of it, though, I had taken a nursing track, and mine was such an intense program that I'd had almost no free time. Sometimes I could hardly believe that I was only twenty-two. Places like this, packed and teeming with writhing, drunken, sweaty bodies all gyrating madly to music that pulsed and pounded far too loudly, made me feel ancient.

Once again, I had to remind myself that I was doing this for Sara.

Sara made an effort to smile at me and reassure me that she was fine, but I knew better. Sara *was* suffering from her recent break-up, no question. There wasn't a chance in hell that being inside this crazy nightclub was helping her get over anything, either, much as she'd have liked that to be true.

"You sure?" I basically had to scream to get her to hear me.

Sara nodded, but as she went to take another sip of her drink, her eyes wandered, and then fixated on something off in the distance. "Ooh, there's that guy!" She pinched my side playfully as she screamed in my ear. "The one I was dancing with before!"

*Ugh. God.*

That could mean any number of things. Sara had danced with a variety of guys tonight. Five or six who I had counted, but there might have been more when I'd had my back turned.

Her eyes twinkled with delight over this one, though, which caused me to take a little step backwards. If Sara wanted to dance and flirt with some hot guy to help her get over her ex, then so be it. I wasn't going to stand in her way.

Sure enough, Mr. Hot Guy spotted Sara looking at him from across the dance floor and honed in on her like an actual hound dog chasing after downed birds. He was taller than her by a few inches—broad, with sandy blond hair and dark blue eyes. But while I could admit he was fairly attractive, he was also wasted.

I stepped aside when his hands landed on Sara's hips, and she ground against him in time to the beat. She gave me a reassuring smile as she threw back her head and leaned into her new dance partner, but I just shook my head at her and forced a smile for her benefit.

I kept dancing a few feet away, watching to make sure that the guy didn't take any liberties with Sara. Hurting from a break-up, she might not be in the right frame of mind when it came to making decisions. Booze didn't help.

I danced awkwardly by myself, not really thinking about what I was doing—beyond babysitting—while I went full-on mother hen with Sara. I didn't even have a drink to keep my hands busy. They felt awkward, so I tucked them onto my hips. I was dressed in a shorter dress than I would have liked. It was Sara's since I didn't own anything appropriate for clubbing. I had a pair of black heels on to match the sparkly little dress. When I glanced downward, the sequins caught the light as I moved, making me slightly dizzy. The rough fabric also chafed against my palms annoyingly.

As usual, I was wary of what was going on around me. The club was huge, and too dark for my liking, with sketchy booths lining both sides of the dance floor. There were two bars in the front, one huge one in the back, and various stands set up around the place to sell beer. With all the bars, I had no idea why there was any need for waitresses and shooter girls, but they walked around, too, showing off their bodies in little black skirts and tight white shirts.

I was so busy scanning the place that I failed to see the real threat until it was right behind me.

"Hey there, girl." Someone grabbed onto my hips from behind me and yanked my body flush against his. Before I could react, he slowly moved his hips against my ass.

I tried to swing around to face him, disgust crawling up my throat, but I wasn't fast enough to step away. A forceful arm came around my shoulders, pulling me closer to an unrelenting wall of a chest before I could even get a good look at the guy.

He leaned down and placed his mouth close to my ear. "I've been watching you for ages. The way your body moves, the way you get lost in the music. It's so fucking hot. I'm Jason, and you're gorgeous. What do you say about going to one of the private booths and getting to know each other?"

"No, thank you," I said loudly, and pushed my hands against his arm, giving him an assertive shove to get him out of my space. "I'm here with my friend and I'm certainly not looking to get to know anyone tonight."

I was free for just long enough to try to signal to Sara that I needed help, but she was gone. I glanced around frantically, but she'd gotten lost somewhere in the undulating crowd.

Intending to look for her, I tried to step away, but the first-rate creeper grabbed my wrist and kept me where I was. His fingers curled into me painfully, and I wanted him to leave me alone, but I also wanted to keep calm. That was the best way to deal with a situation, or things could get ugly. The last thing I wanted was more drama. The crowd was writhing around us, but apparently everyone was too drunk to notice one random girl getting moved in on.

"Nah, come on," the creep cajoled, pulling on my arm and moving closer—I could feel him behind me, pulling me into his personal space again. "At least dance with me. Looks like your friend has ditched you for some guy anyway."

He reached out to take me in his arms all the way and I smacked his hand away forcefully before whirling to face him. I finally looked up into his face, already taking a step back. He could have been handsome if his features hadn't been so twisted with lust, not to mention warped from being completely tanked. He had shaggy dark hair, flashing green eyes that wouldn't totally focus, and a bone structure that made his features chiseled without being hard. He was tall and lanky, too, with striated muscle and enough shoulders to have played football when he was younger. He looked like a jock, and he had the typical frat-boy jock attitude to match.

"I already said no thank you," I hissed, trying to tug my hand away from his grip. "I'm not interested. I'm sure there are plenty of other women who'd like to dance with you tonight, so why bother wasting your time on someone who clearly wants to be alone?"

I attempted to turn away from him again, but his other hand slammed down on my shoulder. "I like the challenge." His face hovered near mine when I half-turned.

My nose instantly screwed up in disgust while my stomach heaved. The guy's breath smelled like stale beer. "I'm not a challenge. I'm not here for your pleasure. Now, will you please get your fucking hands off me before I break one of them?" There was unmistakable venom in my voice, and I only hoped he was sober enough to hear it. I was done being polite.

His hand moved from my shoulder to cup my breast. Fucking hell, he just wouldn't quit.

*Oh, fuck no, this is not happening.*

I tried to push him away, but he just pulled me against his chest, his arms holding me tightly as he started to move his way through the crowd, dragging me with him. I kept struggling, trying to breathe and to stay calm and figure out what I was going to do about this. I'd had enough of this bullshit. I needed to end this, but I still didn't want to make a scene.

I had more than enough self-defense training to deal with assholes like this, though, and it was past time to use it. I leaned into the drunk suddenly, catching him off-guard, and I snaked my right leg around his ankle and yanked while using my upper body strength to push hard at his chest. The guy's arms went slack in surprise, allowing me to step back while he went down hard. He tried to catch himself, but on the way down, he bumped into two couples dancing close by. One of the guys he slammed into turned around. The guy was built like a tank, and he wasn't pleased with the interruption. It was also pretty obvious he wasn't above picking this bastard up off the floor himself in order to show him just how much he appreciated being shoved.

That was all the distraction I needed to weave my way through the crowd and away from the entire situation.

Fuming and tense, I searched the place for Sara. I was totally done with this stupid club. It made me even angrier that it had taken me so long to deal with the jerk. After all, I was tough. I'd had to be, growing up the way I had, but that didn't mean that shit like that didn't bother me. And if that asshole had known who my father was, he would have pissed his pants.

Still, I didn't like thinking thoughts like that, about using my father's name to save me. There were going to be so many more times in life when I needed to be able to save myself.

I wandered around in the darkened corners of the club, passing booths and drunks until I finally found Sara in one, her tongue shoved down the throat of the guy she'd been dancing with earlier. He was kneading her ass and she was practically crawling up him. *Fucking hell.* Sara was drunk, and I didn't want her to get taken advantage of or do something she would regret. She might be enthusiastically kissing him now, but who knew how she'd feel about it later?

I sighed as I approached and tapped her on the shoulder. "Sara." She swatted my hand away without even breaking the kiss, so I leaned in beside them as best I could, until I was able to get right next to her ear. "I need to get out of here!" I yelled loudly above the music.

She finally turned, and it was probably pretty obvious from my face that something was wrong.

"Okay, just let me say goodbye." She gave me a wink.

I sighed in irritation. There was obviously no rushing her, and I had to get out of this club *now*.

"Fine. I'll just head over to that little store we saw across the street and get us some snacks. I'll call Marco when I get outside and have him bring the car around back in fifteen minutes…" I trailed off as Sara nodded and turned back to the guy.

She gave me a thumbs-up behind her back, indicating that she'd heard me, and I knew she'd meet me outside soon. She wasn't too drunk to make that promise and then not keep it, so I made my way to the back door, mentally shaking off the feeling of that jerk's hands on my body. *My* body.

*How dare he fucking touch me like that?*

The cold air that washed over me when I finally exited the building was a relief. It doused some of my anger, too, but the stifling heat of the club still clung to me, making me feel itchy and uncomfortable. I wanted out of this dress, which reeked of alcohol and sweat. I walked around to the side of the club, heading toward the store I'd noticed earlier, which still had a neon sign flashing in its barred window. But once I got to the front of the alley, I stopped and sagged against the wall. A few deep breaths, and maybe I'd be able to wash away the rest of my anger.

The situation was over. I'd handled it. My training had come in handy. I could defend myself. I could *take care* of myself. And I wasn't going to allow that asshole to ruin the rest of my night.

I knew I had to focus on Sara, because I knew what stage of the break-up aftermath we were entering into. Sara was going to want to eat a ridiculous amount of sweet-and-salty crap, and drink an equally ridiculous amount of tequila, all while she sobbed on my shoulder about her ex. I'd been through this with her before, and the pattern was just about always the same.

I fired off a text to Marco to let him know when and where to meet us, but I didn't wait for a reply before tucking my phone back into my tiny black wristlet. Marco had been my driver for years. He'd been handpicked by my father to take me wherever I needed to go, and I knew he'd be where I needed him to be.

I took a few steps down the dimly lit sidewalk toward the grocery store. I could cross the street in fifteen feet and be right there. It didn't matter that the street was eerily quiet or that it was barely lit up by the few working streetlights. I would be fine.

The grocery store looked shady as hell, but junk food was junk food. The people who owned the place were probably nice. They'd likely just been trying to make a living by buying real estate in a shit neighborhood because it was the only thing they could afford. And they likely stayed open late because the bar crowd's money made it worth putting up with drunken behavior.

I was imagining what the store owner looked like—probably a big, burly man who didn't take any shit from anyone—when a shadow stepped into my path. I was just a few feet down the sidewalk, and I froze, terror crawling up my throat once again. The guy who stepped into my path didn't look anything like the asshole back in the bar, and I let out a temporary sigh of relief because of that fact alone. How stupid could I have been, exiting into the alley? Talk about a mistake. That guy could have followed me outside. Attacked me or accosted me.

I wasn't using my head. I wasn't being careful.

But I also wasn't going to let my guard down again. I eyed up the stranger in my path, appraising him carefully. This guy was older. Probably in his late twenties. He was tall, but not the same kind of tall as the other guy. This man wasn't lanky. This man was dressed in an expensive black suit that he filled out well, and his jet black hair was combed back neatly. I would have guessed he was Italian or had Italian roots, from his bronzed skin and his dark eyes.

"Kind of late to be walking out alone at night," he said, but his voice wasn't greasy or creepy like the voice of the asshole from the club. Adding to the friendliness factor, this man smiled at me, and it was a charming kind of smile that would probably have melted the panties right off any other woman.

Yet, icy tendrils of fear slithered down my spine, and I couldn't say why. This guy was being nice. He was *dressed* nice. Maybe… too nice? What was a guy wearing a three-thousand-dollar suit doing in a neighborhood like this?

I tensed and silently went through a list of self-defense maneuvers in my mind. My hand instinctively reached for my clutch, but from the way the guy's dark eyes tracked my every movement, I knew I wouldn't reach it in time—not if he didn't want me to.

This guy looked kind, but he exuded danger. In fact, the little hairs on the back of my neck stood on end, but I forced myself to breathe. Showing fear could only entice an enemy to violence. How many times had my father told me that?

"I-I was just going across to the grocery store," I stammered. I was well aware that I was shadowed in almost near darkness, since the nearest working streetlight was quite a ways away. The street around us was filled with parked cars, but no one was actually in them.

"A little bit late, though, isn't it?" the guy repeated. His dark eyes seemed to be devouring me, and I shivered again.

I thought about making a run for it, but in heels, I knew I was no match for this guy. If I'd been wearing the most expensive pair of runners on the planet, I probably never would have been able to make it to the store before him. That knowledge didn't stop me from checking the street again for any signs of escape.

All of a sudden, heavy footfalls sounded behind me.

I whirled around to see a second guy in a suit approaching. He was dressed all in black, like the guy in front of me, but though they bore a vague resemblance to each other, this guy's aura was nothing like that of the first. For one, he didn't smile at either of us as he closed in. His face was hard, his glacier blue eyes flinty. His skin was bronzed and his hair was jet black, making him resemble the guy who went right on grinning at me like he couldn't help himself.

*He's toying with me.* The realization made me feel sick, like he knew a secret that I didn't.

The second guy walked up from behind me and stood beside the first. They shared a heated look which was loaded with meaning that I couldn't understand.

"What are you doing?" the second suit asked the first one. His voice was rich, deep, and commanding. It made the hairs on the back of my arms stand to attention, but for an entirely different reason.

And then those eyes landed on me, but they weren't cold like I'd expected. They were *hot*, and set in a hard face that somehow intimidated me at the same time that it intrigued me. The man's face was chiseled into sharp angles—hard, high cheekbones. A hard jawline, too, and lips drawn into a tight slash. His nose and forehead were high and strangely at odds with the rest of his hardened features. Features that, I thought, could be considered beautiful. Just like his eyes. His face was one of those faces that could be transformed with a single expression, and I knew that much just from a glance.

I had the oddest impression that he could control those expressions at will, too, and that was terribly unnerving. Those eyes swept down my body, appraising me. The only mercy I had was that I could step back into almost total shadow.

The stranger tore his gaze away and stared down the first suit. "I think it's time we get back."

"I just wanted to say hi. Make sure the lady's all right. It's a little late," he said again, in an annoying tone that grated on my nerves.

Apparently, it grated on the other guy's, too. His massive shoulders bunched up in that suit, speaking to some sort of anger that definitely went beyond this moment alone. And while the first guy was well-built, this guy towered over me. His physical power was obvious, but there was something else behind it, too. Something latent and far more deadly.

If the first guy exuded danger, this guy lived and breathed it.

*"Hey!"*

The shout in the night came from behind me and made me turn for a second time. I let out a massive sigh of relief when I spotted Sara running toward me. She was actually sprinting, despite her towering heels. Out of breath when she reached me, she took in the two suits standing in front of me on the sidewalk and let out a low whistle.

"Wow." She looked sidelong at me. "You've been busy."

*Jesus, fuck.* Did she really think that these guys were ours to take home for the night? Like I could just dial them up or produce them out of thin air? Didn't she see the same thing I did when I looked at them?

The first suit took a hard look at my cousin that I didn't like, his eyes scraping over her breasts and landing at her hips. He raked them upward next, not at all ashamed of his brazen appraisal, and treated Sara to the same glistening smile he'd given me.

Except that, on Sara, it worked. She giggled.

I grabbed her arm so tightly that she squeaked. "Come on. We're going to get some groceries. From the grocery store. Right over there." I said that very obviously, hoping that the two suits would get out of our path.

The first one nodded at Sara and never lost his cocky grin. The second one said nothing. He only stepped aside and let us pass, but even after we were down the sidewalk and across the street, I could feel his glacial gaze burning into my back.

I glanced back as soon as I felt that it wouldn't be obvious I was looking. Both men were gone. Either they'd stepped into the shadows or they'd disappeared as quickly as they'd appeared. Like specters.

I shivered violently again.

"Why couldn't we stay and talk to them?" Sara whined.

"Because we need cookies and ice cream, some chips, some… some… I don't know. What I do know is that we *didn't need* some of *that*."

Sara bit her bottom lip petulantly, but followed me into the store without protest. We armed ourselves with junk food and, when we came back out, I was relieved to see Marco parked by the alley.

We hustled over to the car and climbed inside.

"Can you take us to my condo?" I asked Marco pleasantly. "Please? Sara's going to be staying over with me tonight."

"Sure thing." Marco turned back around in the driver's seat and the sedan crawled away from the club, slinking into the darkened street.

"Oh my god, that guy was *hot*!" Sara exclaimed. "They were *both* hot! I was hoping you were going to bring them home with us. What a way to end the night! All that dark hair, those nice-shaped eyes, I don't know what color…"

"Sara!" I cut her off. I glanced at Marco pointedly, but she didn't get the point. God knew which one of the two strangers she was talking about. Maybe both. She didn't even realize their eyes had been different colors. The first suit had had dark brown eyes. The second, that frozen-over blue.

I settled back in the leather seat, but my thoughts were just as tangled as Sara's. I couldn't stop thinking about those eyes. Eyes that were so blue and pale they could have been gray. Eyes that were flinty and cold, but burning with intelligence. It had been as if all of the emotion that handsome face wouldn't betray had been bottled up and trying to escape from those unearthly eyes. I hated that I couldn't stop thinking about them… about him.

And his hair was so dark that I was sure it would be jet black, even in the daylight. His face, as strong and hard as the rest of him. He was definitely drool-worthy, and I was sure he knew it, too. He was the kind of guy girls fought over, and he probably encouraged that, getting a cheap thrill out of knowing he had that kind of power over women.

Guys like that especially pissed me off. Pride is one thing. I didn't mind a guy who took pride in himself and his accomplishments. Hell, I was damn proud of who I was. But it was a real turn-off when a gorgeous guy was over-the-top arrogant.

Not that this guy had seemed all that arrogant. I didn't know that he was, certainly… but I imagined that he would be. Dressed in an expensive suit that looked hand-tailored. Gorgeous as sin. Yeah. He'd be arrogant. Or at least, I wanted to think he would be, and then I could let my imagination play without having any regrets for not getting to know him better.

31

If I was able to forget about the arrogance, the danger of him, then I could imagine… well, other things. I could imagine his sensuous mouth doing deliciously wicked things to my aroused body. The sort of things that could make a woman writhe in ecstasy. Ecstasy induced just by the touch of his mouth and the flick of his tongue. I thought about how his wet, rough tongue and hot mouth would feel on my nipple, his tongue lightly flicking at my skin before gently biting the hard peak, and then licking again to soothe the sting. I imagined those powerful hands stroking my naked body, grabbing my ass, and pulling me roughly against his hard cock. What would he do then? Would he lay me down? On a bed? On the floor? Would he rub his cock over my slit, coating it with the moisture that his touch elicited? Would he bury himself inside me?

Would he use long, deep strokes? Or would he pound into me at a frantic pace?

I felt my clit throb and dimly realized that my panties had become damp. I unconsciously wriggled a bit, trying to ease the dull ache that was forming.

"Elisa!" Sara barked, snapping her fingers in front of my face and jerking me from my sinful thoughts.

What the hell was I doing? Fantasizing about a guy who I knew nothing about and would never see again? Maybe I needed to put more thought into dating again. It had obviously been too long since anything other than my pink vibrator had touched me if I was turned on by a brief encounter on the sidewalk.

"Are you even listening to me, Elisa? Why is your face all flushed right now? Are you too hot? Wait… *oh my god*, you were thinking about *him*, weren't you? You were thinking about getting nasty with that guy! I can't believe you! You're lusting over him right now! I knew we should have gotten their numbers…"

She would have continued on, her voice getting higher in pitch and volume until the entire car rang with it, if I hadn't leaned over and slapped a hand over her mouth.

I cast a look at the front seat, but thank god Marco was oblivious to us, as usual. He was paying attention to driving. Total attention, I hoped.

Or, at least, he had the grace to pretend that was the case. In reality, he was likely listening to everything that was going on, and the thought of that made my face heat up until I felt sure it was scarlet.

"Stop," I begged Sara. "Just stop?" I crossed my legs, trying to swallow down my longing. I didn't want Sara to see just how affected I was. I didn't want *me* to notice how affected I was.

"Well, I would have settled for the other guy. The one you clearly didn't have eyes for," Sara huffed.

I closed my eyes in embarrassment and searched for something to say to take Sara's mind off the topic. "Your birthday!" I blurted out a moment later.

"What?" She looked at me, clearly wondering what the heck I was on about.

Sara loved birthdays. I could seriously work with this. "Your twenty-fourth is coming up so fast. I was going to surprise you, but I know you hate surprises."

"It's not a surprise now," Sara said dryly. "Whatever you're thinking."

"Well, I was thinking that we could plan it together. That would be fun, wouldn't it?"

"You hate parties."

"Not your birthday party."

Sara looked skeptical, so I was about to try to fish another idea out of my ass, but then she smiled, obviously warming up to the idea. "Really? You'd throw a party just for me?"

I snorted. "You're like a sister to me. So, yeah, of course! You deserve to be celebrated."

"You're not just trying to get me off track from talking about those two random, drop-dead-gorgeous guys in the middle of the sidewalk? *God.* A night with them would be something that a person could only dream about."

"Sara!" I begged. "Stop?"

"Right. You don't want to talk about that. Well, if I can get a party out of the deal, then I'll take a party."

33

I hugged her shoulder against me gratefully. Even if she knew I had ulterior motives, she was going to go along with this to spare my exploding in humiliation in front of Marco.

But that was who we were to each other. Sara might have been my cousin as far as the world was concerned, but she was also my best friend. My mom died in a car accident when I was five. Her dad ended up in prison a few years later, serving a sentence for racketeering. Ever since, Sara and her mom had been like the mother and sister I'd never had. They'd been there through all of the tough times in my life. Through the times when I'd really wished that I had a mom to guide me.

Sara was my biggest champion all through my years of studying nursing. It wasn't easy, and there were so many times when I wanted to just give up. It wasn't what my father would have wanted me to be doing anyway. It would have been easier, sometimes, to think about just doing what he'd always wanted me to do. Being who he'd always wanted me to be.

But Sara kept me going—toward being the me that *I* wanted to be.

"Themes," Sara said, rising to the occasion. "Let's start talking about themes! And guests. And where we're going to have the party."

I let out a long sigh of relief. Not only was Sara done talking about the two mysterious, black-clad strangers, but maybe I could be done with thinking about them. No, not them. *Him.*

And with Sara off and rolling, we spent the rest of the ride home shouting out party themes, trying to top each other with outlandish and totally impractical ideas. I knew I would have to ensure that we threw Sara the biggest, *best* party ever. She deserved to be showered with love, and I planned to do exactly that.

For Sara. Not because I needed to keep my mind from drifting back to a haunting set of blue eyes.

# Chapter 3

## John

Saturday breakfast at Uncle Leone's was a time-honored tradition.

Leone owned one of the most desirable properties in a neighborhood that was exclusively home to rich, powerful men and their families. His own massive brick structure rose four stories high.

I had to admit that I barely even noticed the house when I pulled up to it and parked my car in the underground garage. Punching in the code for the security system, I let myself in through two sets of steel doors before I emerged on the ground floor. The fact that I could walk straight in was a privilege not extended to many.

The house was all old money. It was an ancient building, over a century old, but had been meticulously maintained and updated. The artwork and statues could have enriched any art gallery, and heavy drapes hung at all of the windows.

I stood at one for a few minutes, until I saw a black car drive by. Our men. They did the rounds of my uncle's house a few times per hour, serving as a surveillance system that went beyond anything any security company could install, and Leone had it all.

I called out Leone's name as I walked through the luxurious living room with the heavy antique pieces, moving on into the kitchen. My uncle's chef, a round man in his forties, was already in the process of scurrying around the space, which was so modern that it would have been the envy of most five-star establishments in New York. The chef, Walter, was heavyset. He was a quiet man who never said a word unless it was about cooking or food, and that was how my uncle preferred things.

Leone stood off to the side, a stately gargoyle. He was sixty-five, but so in shape that he looked like he'd outlive every single one of us. He was fit, dressed tastefully in a hand-tailored suit like those I wore, and sporting a shock of white hair. His dark brown eyes missed nothing.

"Hello, Uncle." I leaned down and kissed his knuckles, honoring tradition even if I secretly thought it was archaic.

"Hmph," he replied as I straightened. It was his usual response, but there was an edge to the sound that wasn't usually there. It put me immediately on alert.

"What's going on?" When Leone didn't answer, I turned to Walter, pasting on a smile. "Something smells delicious." That was obvious, but I needed conversation to fill the gap until we sat down in the dining room.

Walter turned to me, beaming from ear to ear. "A traditional English fry-up breakfast. I thought it'd be nice to have a change."

I had no real notion of what that entailed other than sizzling eggs and sausage, so I glanced around Walter and noticed a pot of beans.

My uncle continued to stand there leering at both of us, his demeanor making me fidget. His dark mood clouded the room like a violent storm about to break.

"Should we sit down?" I indicated the dining room. The house was so old that it was far from an open-concept design. The dining room was just off the kitchen, separated by thick walls.

Leone nodded and we stepped into the other room, which was filled with antique furniture, gilded artwork, and rich drapery—just like the rest of the place. The table had ten chairs around it. Leone took the head, and I sat to his right.

He said nothing, even after Walter brought in our breakfast. Leone ate in silence, and I joined him in doing the same.

I ran over possible scenarios in my mind. Maybe one of our men had been idiotic enough to have been caught by the cops. There could be trouble with the Gambinos. Granted, there hadn't been trouble with that rival crime family in quite a while, but when you had two different and powerful families running territories right next to one another, trouble often happened. The Gambinos had been our only real rivals for years. and would always need to be watched carefully.

I was anxious for Leone to speak, but he finally did so only when we were nearly done eating. He pushed away his plate and fixed me with a hard gaze. "Where were you last night?" he demanded, and I heard an accusation in his tone. "I heard you went out on a run."

*Fuck. So, that's what this is about. Dario's damn exchange by the nightclub.*

I'd known that it could cause me all kinds of shit, and I'd been right. I took my time chewing before I answered. I wanted to work out how to play this.

"I went out with Dario for a quick exchange," I told him simply, making sure I looked my uncle in the eye as I did.

"On a money exchange, yes, I heard all about it. But I don't understand why you went out on such a minor run like that in the first place. You're the underboss, John, and that means something. At least, it's supposed to," he added, setting down his coffee cup a touch too roughly. "You can't be seen on silly, petty runs. It hurts your reputation as the heir to the Colombo dynasty! Plus, it puts you in a dangerous position. Anything could have gone wrong. We can't afford to have you picked up by the cops for something like that, and we can't afford to have a two-bit rival rat decide to try to gain status by taking out the underboss of this family. You should know that."

I couldn't tell my uncle that I'd felt the need to check up on my brother. Dario might have fucked up quite a few times in the past, but he was my younger brother. I'd always be the one looking out for him.

"Dario is *quite* capable of doing a money exchange alone," Leone said flatly, seeming to read my mind. "He doesn't need *you* there with him for that," he added with force, when I'd remained silent for what must have been a beat too long.

The dark cloud which had only been covering my uncle before now settled over me, as well. That unsettled feeling, the itch beneath my skin, was back. There was no way in hell Leone knew what I'd been up to last night without someone having ratted me out. He had eyes and ears everywhere, all over New York City, but they weren't supposed to be reporting on my activity.

I was above that, and everyone knew it.

Someone was going to get a not-so-pleasant "pleasant" visit from me when I figured out who'd whispered in my uncle's ear. How fucking dare they? An underboss should be allowed to go where he fucking pleased without having to explain himself to his soldiers.

"My apologies," I bit out, wiping any expression from my face. "It was a mistake on my part, and one that I will not repeat." I was totally sincere. Leone had no respect for a man who couldn't acknowledge his mistakes. Neither did I, for that matter.

"You better not. I don't want to have to bail you out of jail or fish you out of the river."

That was the end of it as far as my uncle was concerned.

The tension in the expensively furnished room remained thick. The more I thought about the bullshit, the thicker my anger became.

Apparently, my uncle sensed it. "It doesn't matter who spoke to me, John. What matters is that you maintain your status and stay away from trouble."

I hated that he spoke to me like I was still nine, but my uncle was the one person in the world who could see past my perfectly perfected blank expression.

"You want to teach the snitch a lesson," he continued. "But that is beneath you, too. Do not let those under you think they have hurt you in any way. Do not show weakness. I will not stand for infighting amongst our family when what we need is unity."

I nodded my agreement, though my anger still simmered.

There was no reason to argue the point with my uncle. I could find out who the rat was on my own, and when I did, I would deal with them in my own way, no matter what my uncle thought about it.

Unfortunately, thoughts of rats somehow summoned Nevio Storace, the seventy-five-year-old consigliere to the Colombo family. He slinked into the room like a grease stain.

While my uncle seemed somehow youthful, even in his older years, Nevio had always been older than dust. He was stooped—bent like a snake, perfectly poised to whisper insidious words in my uncle's ear. While my uncle trusted Nevio, I never had. The man reminded me of something wretched. Something fetid, like old meat left out to rot. He was no real rat, but he reminded me of one with the way he scuttled around.

He seemed to have come out of nowhere, as he often did. I imagined that a chill swept through the room, like a window had been left open. My uncle might respect Nevio, but I hated having him around. He was too attached to the old ways, and that just didn't fit with how business was done. He was giving Leone advice based on traditions that could hurt the family down the road. But what did I know, so far as they were concerned? My uncle never would have listened to such concerns. He considered them nonsense, and would have snarled another warning at me if I'd ever chosen to voice my doubts about the old man.

Nevio ignored me and headed straight for Leone, though I narrowed my eyes at the obvious slight. Nevio leaned in and said something to my uncle, speaking too low for me to hear. He was being unbelievably rude, and I was surprised my uncle allowed it. Maybe I needed to address my concerns regarding Nevio, after all.

When Nevio finished speaking, my uncle shoved his chair back. "I'm afraid I need to cut our time together short. Please forgive me, but something has come up."

I sat stunned, waiting to see if there was some joke—much as that wouldn't have been like my uncle. Saturday breakfast usually lasted into early afternoon. Not the meal itself, but the business and visit associated with the meal. The tradition had begun soon after my parents had been killed. Leone's way of showing me that I still had family and would reign over the business when my time came. The formality of it had worked, too. It had helped me heal and taught me what was important in life.

Saturday breakfasts weren't ever cut short because something "came up." That feeling of unease slammed back into me forcefully.

"I don't understand. Is there something I can help you with?" I asked before my uncle could leave the room.

"I'm sorry, Johnny," he said kindly. He came back around the table and put his hand on my shoulder, leaning in. "This is something I need to take care of myself. I will speak with you later."

With that, he and Nevio walked out of the room. I was left to gape at the empty space.

I was confused and concerned, but I was also enraged.

I didn't gape. I didn't get left to wonder what the fuck was going on around me. Why were they keeping something that was clearly so momentous from me? I was the underboss, poised to take over as boss one day.

I sat there at the table, my anger as real and palpable as the thick drapery hanging at the window. I had no idea what was happening, but I meant to find out, and find out fucking fast.

But, everything in time—I had to calm down first, and not go off half-cocked in a way that might suggest my uncle could ever be right to keep something from me. With that in mind, I resolved to continue my day as I'd planned... albeit earlier.

\*\*\*

Even the gym hadn't helped to rid me of the disquiet that had plagued me all weekend.

I couldn't even blame it all on the breakfast with Leone, though that hadn't helped matters. On that note, I still couldn't work out what the fuck was going on—why he'd cut our morning short and vanished with Nevio. It seemed like utter bullshit, and I hadn't gotten the promised call of explanation yet.

But this fucking feeling I had... well, it had been there before that breakfast. It was the whole reason I'd gone out with Dario on that fucking run. It was why I'd ended up in the middle of a sidewalk, staring down that blonde.

She was yet another question mark fucking up the weekend.

When I'd asked Dario about his strange behavior, he'd shrugged it off and said he was just having some fun. He'd seen a beautiful woman and wanted to make conversation. Repeatedly, he'd told me he'd just wanted to make sure she got wherever she was going without a problem, but that hadn't been what it looked like from the car.

I'd seen her on the sidewalk, coming from the club. I hadn't been able to see her face since it had been in the shadows most of the time, but her body had been outlined by the streetlights. No man would forget curves so lush and sensual as that. And her blonde hair had spilled down her back, lit up like gold.

I knew I'd tipped my hand the second I got out of the car. I couldn't help it. I wanted to get the fuck out of there and Dario needed a dressing down. One did not mix pleasure with business. One did not conduct business the way he was conducting it. I'd laid into him after the woman and her friend had walked past us and we'd gotten back in the car.

Even after the girls had left us behind, though, it had annoyed me that I hadn't been able to catch a good look at her face. For some reason, it had pissed me off that we were the ones standing in the light. We were the ones who stood as if we were naked before her, for her inspection. I'd been able to feel those eyes on me the entire time. Eyes that I couldn't see.

All because my brother couldn't keep his dick where it belonged and stop fucking up the smallest jobs. Dario was the reason that my uncle was disappointed in me.

Was that what had been wrong at the breakfast? Was Leone losing trust in me? Losing faith in my ability to do my job and control my men?

Thinking about that made me think about the snitch. I'd made a few discreet inquiries, but no one was giving the person up. I needed to be in the know about all the shit going on underneath me, yet those fuckers were protecting one of their own. From me of all people. I understood when they needed to keep things on the down low from others, but *me*? That didn't sit right.

And if I took it any further, my uncle would hear I was defying his order to leave things alone.

"Assholes," I growled to myself as I headed to the bathroom. The workout in the room I'd dedicated to gym equipment had done nothing at all to take the edge off. Maybe a cold shower would ease the burning anger I still felt.

I slammed into the huge bathroom, flung open the glass door, and wrenched the taps on. Outside the glass enclosure, letting the water stay cold, I peeled my sweat-soaked clothing off. The second I stepped under the freezing spray, though, I changed my mind. I flicked the taps the other way, and soon warm water spouted over my aching muscles. I closed my eyes as the water sluiced over my body, willing myself to get a fucking grip.

I did not fuck up. That's not who I fucking was.

With that thought paramount over every other, I grabbed a bar of soap and began to wash off. When it felt like my blood pressure had eased, I let my mind wander, and it ended up going over the events of Friday night. Not the debacle with Raquel, and not the exchange with Dario. No, my mind went back down that dark sidewalk and landed straight on *her*. The fiery little blonde with the hidden face. She'd stood up to Dario all on her own. She hadn't backed down. Hadn't trembled, even though she was much smaller than him, and had been alone on a dark night with a stranger who could have meant her harm. Dario would never have meant anything of the sort, of course, but she'd had no way of knowing that.

I imagined her as a force to be reckoned with, like lightning waiting to strike. I loved a woman with a strong spirit, who didn't lie down and take whatever life threw at her passively. She'd be hard to handle. A challenge in every way. A challenge wearing gold stilettos and a tight little dress.

A challenge with dark, velvet eyes.

I thought about her body, recalling every sizzling detail. That black, sequined dress with its plunging neckline and tight fit had showed off her hourglass curves to perfection. I imagined that she had plump, glossy lips, which I just knew would look like fucking perfection wrapped around my cock. That woman exuded sex without even trying.

I imagined what would have happened if I had met her alone on the sidewalk. If she had been waiting for me, ready to meet with me in the dark, in secret.

I would have dragged her into that alley by the club and pressed her up against the wall.

Her lips would have been wet, her breaths coming in short bursts as my hand traveled up her waist to those killer breasts.... I could almost feel myself grinding against her as she moaned. I wondered what kind of panties I'd have found upon snaking my hand down her body, to her slightly parted legs. Would her panties underneath a dress like that be silky and black, or lacy and white? A thong? It didn't matter. I would have ripped off whatever was there so that I could stroke my finger along her folds and feel that wetness signaling how much she wanted me.

"Fuck me," she'd have whispered in my ear while she pulled my face to hers for a searing kiss. "Please, I need you inside me."

She would beg me. Breathlessly. And I would refuse. I would throw her legs wide and drape them over my shoulders. I'd settle my face right in her pussy, but I wouldn't touch her. I'd make her look down her body and watch as I ran my tongue slowly up her slit, circling around that tight bud before making my way back down to her opening. She would try to lift her hips, but I'd anchor them with my hands, and I'd taste her. Lick her until she was begging for me again.

Or maybe she would drop to her knees in front of me and keep her eyes fixed on mine. She'd pull out my throbbing cock, and she wouldn't break eye contact as she grasped me and began to slowly stroke down the length of my shaft, cupping my balls before her hand made its way up to the head. She'd give me a sly little smile, then cast her eyes downward only as her tongue flicked out to taste the little bead of moisture at the tip of my dick.

As I thought about how swollen her lips would look as I plunged my cock into her mouth, my hand slid down my soapy body and I grasped my rock-hard shaft. I started stroking myself, the friction of my hand and the soapy lather I'd built up sending pulses of pleasure through me. But it wasn't my hand I wanted wrapped around my cock—it was hers, or her lips, or her...

"Mr. John?" Mary's sharp voice outside the bathroom door knocked me from my fantasy instantly. "You have visitors, Mr. John! Mr. Leone and Mr. Nevio are here to see you." The nervous edge to her voice was unmistakable.

Well, that certainly killed my erection fast.

*Fuck, what's this about?*

My uncle rarely surprised me like this, which only had me further convinced that some serious shit was happening. I hoped Leone was ready to finally fill me in.

"All right!" I shouted as I stepped out of the shower and quickly dried myself off. I slipped from the bathroom into my room and hastily threw on a shirt and pants.

My uncle was fastidious about appearances, so I took as much time as I could to make sure I was prepared, knowing that Mary would have told him I was in the shower and would need a minute.

When I finally entered the living room, I found my uncle and Nevio standing at the windows, staring at the city below. It wasn't dark yet, but the view was incredible whatever the hour.

"Ah, so nice of you to join us, John," Leone said dryly. "Please, take a seat."

Maybe I'd made him wait a little longer than he thought acceptable, despite his having found me in the shower. But he was usually more respectful of me and my home when he visited.

Nevio hung around in the background like the inky shadow he was, but my uncle and I moved to the seating area. Once I was settled into one of the high-backed leather chairs, Leone in the other, he started. "We're here to talk to you about the Profaci family."

*The Profacis?*

They were a small-town crime family, and I couldn't imagine how anything related to them would warrant a surprise visit to my home. Annoyed, I wondered if he was about to try to pawn off some unimportant shit on me, just to teach me a lesson for going on a run with my brother. He'd been annoyed enough, I supposed I wouldn't put it past him.

"What about them?" I asked guardedly.

"We have always believed them to be harmless, which may be why we haven't given them the right amount of attention." Leone paused, frowning. "That lapse has allowed them the chance to secretly expand their business into our territory. Not just ours, but that of the Gambinos, as well. They've been quietly moving in on both territories, and are now poised to make trouble."

I was stunned silent for a moment before I managed to speak again. How could some unknown family have made a move into territory owned by two of the biggest, most influential families, and without anyone noticing?

"The same Profacis that have Flavio as their underboss?" I asked. I knew that had to be right, but I just couldn't believe it. Flavio wasn't a threat. On the rare occasions when I had bothered to give him the time of day, he'd been unimpressive. He had no business sense and no presence. I shrugged at the very thought of it. "I can't see it."

"It doesn't matter if you can see it or not!" Leone snapped icily. "We have intelligence that suggests otherwise. While we haven't been watching them, they've been growing in strength and numbers. The Gambinos picked up on their activity a few days ago. Now is the time to act. Before it's an issue."

"You got your intelligence from the Gambinos?" I struggled to keep the incredulity out of my voice. The Gambinos were our enemy. Why would they give us information? The only reason they'd do something like that would be to lure us into a trap that would benefit them.

"The Gambinos haven't been an issue for us for years, John, and you know it. They stick to their territories and we stay in ours. I might not have a lot of love for that family, but there've been no instances of them infringing on our business—not in recent years. The Profacis don't seem to understand this unwritten rule, so we're going to have to sort them out. Sooner rather than later," Uncle Leone added emphatically.

"Understood. But what are you suggesting? We can deal with this swiftly once we have the go-ahead, but this is the first I'm hearing of there even being an issue."

Leone sat back, his gaze remaining on mine. "I don't want you to do anything yet."

Silent, I just sat there, trying to figure out what was happening. I didn't often get shaken or put off-guard, but this visit had done it. My uncle had just talked about action. Why was he at my home if he didn't want me to deal with the problem?

"I'm keeping you informed of developments so that, when things change, you are aware that it's coming. Understood?"

Leone was looking at me intently now, but something wasn't fucking right about this. All the disquiet I had felt over the past couple of days crept back up. My entire body felt cold, like I'd been trapped in ice.

I allowed myself to screw up my face in confusion. "What do you mean by *change*? Uncle, you aren't planning to cede any territory to the Profacis, are you?" I didn't even pause to give him time to answer me, the thought was so ludicrous. "That will make us look weak, especially to the Gambinos. And if that happens, the truce you seem to think exists will be worth nothing. On top of that, any small-time player will leap on the chance to push us out," I reminded him.

Leone just smiled, but it was a little patronizing, which surprised the fuck out of me. Leone had always treated me with the respect I deserved as the heir apparent to the Colombo family. *Always.*

"Don't worry about us losing territory or looking weak, John. You *know* I would never let that happen." He stood then, and Nevio moved from his place next to the far wall of my living room. I'd pretty much forgotten he was even there. He was preternaturally quiet. "I'm working on ideas at the moment that will lead us to the best possible outcome for all of us. A war between crime families must be avoided if at all possible. No one wins when our men have to be sacrificed."

"I can work on ideas with you, Uncle," I said, standing up. "Let me help resolve this. I can be diplomatic when it's called for."

"You'll get a chance to do your part, John," Leone said, taking my hand in his as I walked him and Nevio to the door. "For now, just carry on as you are. I'll be in touch soon."

They left as suddenly as they'd come, and my house rang with a deafening silence.

What the hell had just happened? My uncle had been dealing with the Gambinos without me knowing it? The low-rank Profacis thought they could leave their little backwater and swim with the sharks? That had to be all Flavio's idea. It was something that dimwit would come up with. But whether or not that was the case, why was such an insignificant family making my uncle nervous?

I just kept from slamming my fist into the wall, my emotions were running so hot again. I hated that I was being left out of whatever my uncle was planning, even for a short time. How would I take over the family one day if my uncle didn't even trust me with something so trifling as whatever this was? I again considered whether the way he was acting might be punishment for Friday night, but my uncle wasn't petty.

He'd warned me today because he cared about me and our family, and I knew that.

I hated waiting, though. I hated feeling useless. I hated that the empire I'd helped to so carefully construct felt like it was on the verge of falling, and there was not one fucking thing I could do to stop it from happening.

# Chapter 4

## Elisa

Wine made everything better, didn't it? That was just a fact of life. Wine made even the hardest of tasks seem just that little bit easier, which was why I knew I was probably going to need a glass—or three—that evening when I sat down and really started planning out Sara's party with her.

Organizing a world-class birthday party for my fantastic cousin had actually sounded like a fun idea when I'd thought of it. And it had been a good distraction, both to get me out of a tight spot and to take Sara's mind off of her recent break-up.

I'd overlooked the small fact that I had zero experience in planning a party. And that I didn't even *enjoy* parties.

Deciding on a theme, guest list, invitations, venue, menu, signature drinks, entertainment, decorations, table settings, favors, cake and dessert options, photographers, and a kick-ass gift for the birthday girl was a lot of damn work. I wanted everything to be perfect for Sara, but I hadn't bargained for quite such a to-do list.

"What have I done already?" I wondered out loud as I scanned my seemingly never-ending list. "And what needs doing first?"

I had graduated from college in winter since I'd taken some summer classes to speed things up along the way. Since then, I'd been dragging my heels on sending out resumes. I knew that I wanted to, no question. I wanted to be a nurse more than anything. I was proud of graduating, too… but part of me also needed a break after four straight years of really tough school.

Party-planning just wasn't the break I'd envisioned.

That's why I was currently sitting in my condo, flopped out on my comfortable leather couch, considering a second glass of wine. Given that it was after dinner, I felt like it was an appropriate hour.

I *still* needed to get a list of guests from Sara, though. And she was taking her sweet time agonizing over who to invite from among the friends she and her ex had shared; she'd be snubbing some, she felt sure, but couldn't decide exactly who. I thought she was making this guest list more of an issue than it needed to be, but Sara cared, and because of that, I had to care with her. So, the guest list *had* to be perfect. It was utterly essential that it was perfect.

"This is too much," I groaned as I let my head flop back against the soft couch cushion. Hopelessness washed over me. I could apparently graduate from nursing, but ask me to plan anything and I was as good as useless.

I tried to focus on what it would feel like in the end—the pride of a job well done, and Sara's reaction when she arrived at a stunning party. I imagined us having the time of our lives celebrating her birthday, our champagne glasses full and us looking fine as hell. The last thing she would be thinking about was her break-up. The last thing I would be thinking about was the guy from the sidewalk on that night when we'd gone out to the club….

Thankfully, my phone went off at just that moment, banishing thoughts about icy blue eyes that I shouldn't even have been thinking about. Assuming it was someone calling me back about something for Sara's party, I picked it up and was surprised to see my dad's number. I knew he'd be at the office at this time of night, so I couldn't work out why he'd be calling me. His work hours were precious to him—and it wasn't like him to call me for the heck of it. My dad never did things like that.

I stared at the number through another ring, wondering what he wanted. An icy feeling of dread had already begun washing over me by the time I answered and squeaked out a weak hello.

"Elisa!" My dad didn't sound like he was about to deliver bad news, at least. "I have plans for a lunch tomorrow afternoon. I'd very much like for you to be there."

Ugh, well, that might not have been bad news as far as my father was concerned, but for me, it was bad enough. My dad saying he'd "very much like" me to be there pretty much meant that I had zero say in it. And, honestly, I'd rather be party planning—which said a lot. I had a feeling that the only reason my father ever wanted to have lunch with me was to express his displeasure at my career choice. Now that I was a recent graduate from nursing school, he could no longer tell himself that my education was just about becoming an educated, well-rounded woman. He had to admit that I'd soon be venturing into the working world, not just going through a phase.

I'd told him multiple times that I was working on my resume and would be sending it out soon. No doubt, this was a last-ditch effort to try intervening.

But I couldn't help that we looked at the world differently. My father hated that I didn't share his traditional views. He wanted me to be looking for a husband, not a job. He figured my role in life, now that I was all of twenty-two years old and a college graduate, was to look after a household and kids, socialize with the right people, and attend the right charity functions. But that wasn't what I'd worked so hard for.

That lifestyle created an illusion of philanthropy in an attempt to hide my family's underworld connections, so that we could appear like any other rich family, but that had never been my goal in life. And I personally didn't think that any amount of charity would ever hide the fact that we were one of the top crime families in New York City. Not that I didn't believe in charity—because I absolutely did, I believed in helping people—but I thought it was a poor shield for the real facts.

Essentially, that's why I'd gone into nursing. To separate myself from the illusion of life my father wanted for me, and do something to *actually* help people. By doing more than throwing money at problems, which was certainly what he'd envisioned for me.

51

I might have grown up in an underworld family, but that didn't mean I supported even a small portion of what went on. I respected my father, in a way, for what he'd built, but I simply didn't want anything to do with the unsavory side of it. Instead, I wanted to distance myself from the family in whatever small way I could, and follow my own calling. I yearned to help people, to be a balm to their pain and a beacon of hope in their darkest times. I could do that as a nurse. I could *not* do it as a wife married to someone my dad chose for me. And whatever he had to say about it, I was going to continue on my course, even if it caused tension between us. At the end of the day, I was the one in control of my destiny. Not the Gambino family. And I knew that, in the end, my family would still love me.

Thinking about all this, I saw no reason to have another long, painful discussion about it. "Actually, I'm sorry, Dad. I just don't think I can. I'm pretty busy. How about I make your favorite this weekend, and we can have a nice home-cooked meal together?"

"No, sweetheart." His voice was firm, and while not unkind, his tone was commanding. "We're meeting with friends and I need you there."

I tried one last time to get him to change his mind, not liking the idea of meeting with "friends." "You know that Sara's birthday is coming up and I'm planning a large party for her, and—"

"Sara's birthday can wait." He sounded a little annoyed, which surprised me...he usually cajoled and nagged me when he wanted something. He rarely got mad. "This is more urgent. You know that I wouldn't ask you if it wasn't something important, don't you?"

I opened and closed my mouth a few times, wishing words would come, but I found myself without anything to say. Finally, I just reached out to the nearby wine bottle and poured myself the second glass I'd been contemplating. At this point, I understood my father. This wasn't just a family lunch, but a business meeting, and I needed to be there. I knew that now. This wasn't about my career choice, and I wouldn't have to participate in any way beyond playing the role of a dutiful daughter supporting her adoring papa.

Except… Dad had needed me to do this many times before, but this time felt different somehow. I didn't like the way my stomach was roiling at the thought.

My father wasn't going to be denied, though, and since I was already disappointing him with my "questionable" career, I could suck it up and attend this lunch in order to keep the peace. Maybe it wouldn't be so bad. I loved spending time with my father, and there was sure to be good food. Hopefully. I sighed quietly.

"Okay, Dad, I'll be there. Send me the details. Who else is going?"

"Sara, of course, and Maria, as well."

That made it a little bit easier to bear. Sara and my aunt Maria were two of my favorite people in the world.

"And Uncle Carlo will be there, too," my dad added, as if it were an afterthought.

"Okay. I guess I'll see you tomorrow, then."

"I'll send you the details in a moment. I love you."

People could say what they would about my father, but I knew he loved me and he had never been afraid to say so. "I love you, too," I told him, as I ended the call.

Afterwards, I sat holding my phone in my hand. I found myself glancing around the room until my eyes fixed on a picture of my mom. It was framed, hanging up on the wall with other family photos.

A familiar stab of sadness hit me right between the ribs. I tried not to spend too much time dwelling on us losing Mom because it broke my heart all over again. This time, for some reason, it seemed like an extra gut-punch on top of the uneasy feeling I had about this luncheon. I bent forward, tears welling in my eyes, because it hurt that much. It *really* hurt that she wasn't here anymore.

Dinners or lunches with dad always brought on thoughts of my mom. I had vague memories of watching her style her long golden hair while getting ready for the dinners she attended with my dad. I'd tried over the years to produce the exact shade of gold that my mom had, but no dye seemed right. I'd given up in college, but left my hair blonde because, by then, I'd gotten used to it. It was better than the mousy brown that was my natural color, even if I'd never match my mom's shade.

I remembered the scent of her perfume sometimes, too. *Jasmine.* God, I loved that scent.

I knew that if my mom had still been alive, she'd have been at my father's side tonight, and if the topic of my nursing career had come up, I knew she would have supported me. She'd been kind and gentle, always doing something for someone else, regardless of who they were. She'd even been the inspiration for my job choice, as it felt like a way I could honor what she'd taught me.

I really couldn't get lost in these thoughts. Not if I needed to face Dad and the rest of the family, plus whoever else was going to be there.

I set my phone on the coffee table near the notepad where I was doing my party planning. It was funny how, just a few minutes ago, I'd been so worried about this party, and now it seemed like the last thing I needed to stress over.

I knew that my role for tomorrow would be purely ornamental. I was to smile and look pretty, as if I didn't have a thought in my head. But that just bugged me. My mom hadn't been that kind of woman. She'd been stunning, yes, but she would have had a lot to contribute to the business if anyone had let her. Not that I wanted to be a part of the business, but the fact that my gender made the rest of them think a bit less of me just made me so damn angry.

A text message from Dad came through, confirming all the details and letting me know when Marco would arrive with the car.

I would be nice to see Maria and Uncle Carlo, at least. Along with Dad and Sara, my aunt and uncle were my favorite people in the world. I didn't get to see them enough anymore.

I chose to focus on that instead of my other reluctant doubts.

No matter what happened, my family would always come first.

# Chapter 5

## John

*What the fuck are we doing here?*

I shot Leone a look as walked toward an unfamiliar restaurant. I could tell by the way he held his lips that this wasn't the time for me to question him. Yet, I could barely contain my rage at being dragged from my condo after my uncle and Nevio had shown up unannounced again. I'd simply been told we were going to lunch. Just like that.

They'd snapped their fucking fingers and I had to jump. Blindly.

My uncle drove. Nevio sat in the front, and I took the back. I felt like I was being heralded to my own demise and there was not a single thing I could do about it. I'd even been told to leave my Glocks at home. None of it made any sense. This wasn't how we did things in our family. This wasn't how my uncle conducted business. This wasn't how I ran my operations. All of it was flat-out wrong.

When my uncle parked, I realized that not only were we at a restaurant I didn't recognize, but it wasn't even in our territory. I nearly leapt from the car.

And when two more black cars pulled up and parked off to the side, and Piero and Dario joined us, I was confused as well as put on high alert. That was even before I spotted some of our soldiers down the block. Two of our men joined us next—big beefy guys who'd been trained as bodyguards. My uncle didn't take any chances, but normally,

I knew what his plans were so that I didn't have to stand at his back and fucking guess.

I might have appeared composed, walking beside my uncle, but alarms screamed inside my head. I kept my breathing even while scanning the area for threats.

This outing might be the one time in my entire life when I was happy to have Nevio at my back. At the very least, he'd be good for taking a bullet that had been meant for me.

We remained silent as we walked inside the restaurant. It was an expensive place, likely five-star, and I let out a small sigh of relief when I saw that all of the tables were full. It hadn't been rented out in an effort to trap us inside and lure us to a bloody demise.

There would be no butchery in here—not right now, at least.

The host, clad in an immaculate tux with a white collar, led us straight to one of the private, back rooms. My hackles rose. As I'd suspected, this wasn't about the fancy fucking food. It was business. I felt stripped naked without my Glocks for protection, even if the packed restaurant assured me that nothing was going to go down. That's not how we, nor any other family, did business. The gory, public blood baths were a thing of the past. Now, business was conducted quietly, to draw as little unwanted attention as possible.

When a line of waiters crossing in front of us made for an opportune moment, I halted where I was and stared my uncle down. I should have been given time to prepare for this. I should have been let in on what was happening. I should *not* have been going into this blind.

"What is this?" I demanded in a hiss, leaning closer to my uncle. I didn't want to draw any attention, but this need-to-know shit was ridiculous. "Why are we here?"

Leone glanced back at me. "We are meeting with the Gambinos."

It had been said so simply that I was astounded, as if it was normal to cozy up and meet with our biggest rivals every day of the week.

*What the fuck? Why are we meeting with them, and why the hell wasn't I told ahead of time about it?*

This was absolutely something I should have known prior to walking into this place. And it was something that my uncle would never have kept from me before. My stomach tightened and my hand itched to palm my Glock. Was this some kind of trap? Not for my uncle or Nevio, but for me?

I looked sidelong at Dario, but he wore the same blank expression I probably did. Piero paid no attention to me as we all began moving forward again. It was his job to remain sharp, and he and the other guards were busy looking around and appearing threatening.

I forced myself to keep calm and make my voice neutral—when I finally found my voice, that was. "Why?"

"The matter we are here to discuss affects both the Colombos and the Gambinos," Leone stated. "There are things that need to be worked out. Changes."

Suddenly, it was clear. We were there to talk about the damn Profaci family. It made no sense that my uncle wouldn't have informed me about this meeting ahead of time, but that had to be it. What he'd told me a few nights ago at my condo hadn't been near a proper briefing.

"Changes? Changes involving the Gambinos?" I asked in a low voice.

Leone looked me in the eyes. "There is a proposition on the table that could benefit both families. One that I believe would make things easier for us with the Profacis, and in the future of our business in the long term. This is important, Johnny, and I need you to have an open mind."

Flashing lights swarmed my brain. This was not going to be good—not if he was telling me I needed to "have an open mind" of all things. And I didn't know what this proposition was, but if the Gambinos were involved, it couldn't be good.

Still, I realized there was nothing I could do until I heard what was said. Leone obviously wouldn't be going into detail in the middle of a restaurant floor, and it was too late for anything other than to simply bide my time. Afterwards, I could try to find a way to change my uncle's mind about whatever this was. I would not question my uncle further here, though, not in front of the enemy. We needed to appear united and strong.

We rounded the corner and entered a dimly lit room. We were the first ones there, but the unease that was settled at the base of my neck only increased. My hair stood on end. My teeth clenched. I couldn't shake the feeling that I was walking straight toward my own demise.

My uncle walked around to the other side of a huge table. It was made up of many other smaller tables pushed together. There had to be at least fifteen seats.

"Sit here," Leone said, pointing to a chair next to the one he was settling into. "Relax, Johnny, everything will be fine."

I did as he asked and sat down, but I did *not* relax. Leone and Nevio flanked me, while Dario took the seat by Nevio. Piero and our guards took the corners of the room. They tried to blend in with the shadows, but big men were impossible to hide.

My eyes roamed the room, looking for possible exits and blind spots, counting the servers standing to the side, and looking for any bulges in their uniforms that could signal they were armed. I would not let my guard down, no matter how blasé Leone appeared, and I didn't think he'd want me to. He would expect me to be vigilant around the Gambinos, even if this was supposed to be an amicable meeting.

But seriously, how the fuck were the issues with the Profacis so bad that we needed to go outside the family for help? To our enemies, no less. And the Gambinos *were* our enemies. They were our enemies for a reason.

Shortly after completing my third scan of the room, I felt my uncle tense beside me. The Gambinos had arrived. They were strutting in confidently, like they owned the fucking world. Clearly, they were more prepared for this meeting than I was. I kept my hands on the table in front of me—always a good move when trying to keep things civil—showing that I wasn't reaching for a weapon. Even if I did wish I had one pointed straight at Gastone Gambino, head of the Gambino family.

Gastone was followed in by his brother, Carlo, and their ancient consigliere, Luigi Abis. The man was over eighty, but no less sinister than Nevio. I knew for certain that he had been a huge crime boss in Italy before he'd come here to evade arrest.

Gastone and Carlo were close to one another in age. They looked similar, as well, both of them being regal men. Dignified. Well-dressed in crisp suits, they had full heads of salt and pepper hair, and the same olive undertone to their skin that my family shared. That was about the only thing we shared, however. Gastone and Carlo were far more aristocratic looking than any of us. They were shorter, not nearly as powerfully built, and nowhere near as rugged.

Still, there was no mistaking the aura of power that Gastone wore like a mantle. He was head of his family, and he walked with the weight and privilege of it.

Beside me, my uncle stiffened further.

I was about to look at him, but something else drew my attention.

At the tail end of the Gambino group was a gorgeous older woman with dark hair and dark eyes. She had her hand on a younger woman's shoulder—obviously her daughter, since the resemblance was uncanny. She looked so damn familiar that my head spun. Where had I seen her before?

I could have sworn that Dario made a noise low in his throat, but I was obviously mistaken because there was silence from that end of the table; I only knew him well enough to know that, in another setting, that sound would have been there. I didn't tear my eyes away to look at him, but if I had, I knew that, for once in his life, I'd have seen his face perfectly composed and ready to do business.

But then another woman entered the room, and as soon as her elegant heels cleared the doorway, my entire world titled crazily.

I barely even registered any of the Gambino goons taking up their positions around the room. All I could see was *her*.

I hadn't seen her face. It had been too dark, and she'd been hidden in shadow. I hadn't seen it, but I had *imagined* it a thousand times since that night.

There was no mistaking her body. Her sensual curves and those full breasts. She was wearing a more dignified, simple black dress. It covered her completely, and she'd paired it with an elegant black cardigan, but I

59

knew it was her. The cascades of blonde hair that I'd caught sight of that night were twisted into a tight swirl at the back of her head.

I let myself stare at her openly. Appraising her. Drinking in her face.

She was even more beautiful than anything I could have created in my mind. Her face was a work of art. Her cheekbones were high, her nose straight and tiny. In contrast, her lips were full—the most perfect shade of soft pink. Her skin was flawless, and a lighter shade than the other members of her family. She met my eyes, and I knew the minute she recognized me. Her whole body tensed. Her hands fluttered nervously on the back of the chair she was about to sit down in. She tore her eyes away—eyes that were shockingly green—and sank down in her seat. Right beside Gastone Gambino.

Seated there, she could only be one person.

His daughter.

I might not have known what she looked like, but I had known that Gastone had a daughter. I made a point of knowing my enemies, and that often meant residual information about their wives and daughters.

I hadn't known who she was that night because I hadn't been able to see her face. I really hadn't gotten a good look at the other girl with her, either. Now, I knew. I had no doubt that my brother had known the *entire* time.

It was why he'd stopped her. Why he'd been having his fun.

Because he'd seen.

He'd *known*.

I wanted to look at him now, in silent accusation, and do it menacingly, but I kept my gaze trained straight ahead and betrayed nothing.

The woman who I had been fantasizing about for days, unable to banish from my mind, was the daughter of my enemy. A mafia princess.

Well, wasn't that just fucking fabulous.

As soon as *Elisa Gambino* was seated, she glanced around the table in open astonishment.

It appeared that she hadn't been expecting to see any of the Colombos at a family meeting, and she very clearly hadn't been expecting to see me. Her eyes first flew down the table to land on Dario, and then danced over my face like a soft, fleeting caress. They were rich and deep with shock. Her cheeks turned scarlet in another instant, and she tore eyes away like there had been no recognition on her part.

She'd taken the chair beside her father, and Gastone Gambino took her arm and whispered something into her ear. Elisa nodded her head slightly as she visibly tried to regain her composure.

I tried to drag my eyes away and focus on something else. My uncle was extending a welcome to Gastone and his family. I should have been concentrating. Someone would order wine and fucking breadsticks soon, and then we'd get down to business. I should have been focused on that. Instead, I was fixated on *her*.

*Elisa Gambino.* Her hair was up, exposing her slim neck. The delicate column was accentuated with a beautiful sapphire pendant that rested just above the cleft of her cleavage. She looked like a damn goddess. She'd been sexy the night I'd seen her, but today? Today, she was stunning.

I couldn't help but notice how intensely Elisa watched me, even though she tried not to make it obvious. I could tell she didn't know who I was. She was waiting to hear my name. Her gorgeous green eyes were wary, but tinged with interest.

*Green.* I had imagined that her eyes would be dark, but they weren't.

I pasted on a bland look of boredom that I had a feeling would piss her off. I needed to keep the upper hand here, but in my head, I was rolling her name along my tongue over and over again, liking the way it felt. "Elisa" definitely suited her. The name was sweet and classy.

The air seemed to thicken as we continued to look at each other. There was something deep and magnetic in my chest that made no sense, and I was sure the rest of the room had to feel it, it was so fucking intense. I knew *Elisa* sure as hell did. Her breasts were rising and falling at a more rapid rate, indicating she was struggling to keep her breathing under control.

*Good.* That meant I wasn't the only one affected.

The conversation had been progressing around us. Food had been placed on the table, but neither of us made a move to eat. Neither of us realized any of it until it was there, as far as I could tell.

I startled when I felt my uncle lightly touch my arm.

"Now is the time," Leone declared, his deep, slightly raspy voice commanding everyone's attention, "to tell you why we're all here and reveal our plans of how we intend to stop the invasion of the Profaci family. Don Gastone and I have been discussing this issue, and have decided that it is time our families came together."

*Together?* That certainly got my attention. The Colombos and the Gambinos never did anything together. Until now, apparently.

"Uncle Leone…" I turned to him and spoke quietly, just for him to hear. "If the Profaci family really is that much of an issue, we can take care of them alone. We don't need them."

I caught Elisa's eyes as I glanced across the table once more. She was definitely concerned about this development, as well.

"We have decided on a course of action that will make the Profacis think twice about interfering with either of our interests," Gastone spoke up. "One that we know will cement our truce." He paused for longer than I liked. "Marriage," he ended emphatically.

*Marriage?* I would have been less surprised if Gastone Gambino had suggested a goddamned blood oath. Marriage? Between us and *them?* No, this had to be a joke. No way was my uncle thinking of uniting our families in such a way. Marriage was *sacred.* It was not something to be taken lightly. We believed that marriage vows were binding. *For life.* There had never been a divorce in our family—never. So, how could we think of forever tying one of our own to a family who had caused so much damage to ours? Granted, we had caused just as much damage to theirs, but that only meant they should feel the same.

I shook my head and bit down on my bottom lip so that I didn't let fly the string of curses that were forming on my tongue.

"Yes, marriage," Leone said, nodding in agreement. "I know that Gastone and his family take the sanctity of marriage as seriously as we do. And, since we agree on the power of marriage, we have decided that a union between our families is the best way to bring us all together. *Permanently.* We all want what's best for family, and uniting our interests will send a strong message. One that the Profaci family can't help but understand."

Elisa studied the dishes that had been set out on the table. Though, as far as I knew, no one had ordered a damn thing. It looked like she was uninterested, but I could tell from the tension in her shoulders and the set of her jaw that she was paying very close attention to what was happening.

"Who are we going to sacrifice?" I asked flippantly. I knew I was being disrespectful to both my uncle and Gastone, but I couldn't keep the bitterness from my voice. This was not a good idea. Not for anyone.

Leone looked at me. Then Nevio looked at me expectantly. Both their looks said that I should know the answer, even though I hadn't known a damn thing about this meeting.

And then it clicked. *No. Oh no. Absolutely not.* A wash of heat overwhelmed me. *Me.* I was the sacrifice. I was the one they expected to sleep with the fucking enemy. Actually *sleep* with the enemy.

*Holy fuck.* How the hell could my uncle do this to me? Without a word of warning. Without consulting me about my own fucking life. *My future.*

"W-with who?" I stammered awkwardly. I *never* stammered. I sat back a bit in my chair, stunned. My uncle's eyes moved across the table, and I followed them, slowly.

*Damn.* This was… this was just…. I didn't know *what* to think. My uncle's eyes had landed right on the furious blonde sitting across from me.

On Gastone Gambino's daughter.

The gorgeous goddess sitting with the enemy.

The mafia princess who I couldn't banish from my mind.

*Elisa Gambino.*

# Chapter 6

## Elisa

*I've felt this before.*

This sensation. Numbness. Disbelief. Horror. Grief.

I'd been five years old the last time my entire world had ground to a halt.

My dad was the one who told me. Told me that my mom was dead. At first, I couldn't believe him. I couldn't understand the words he was saying. Words meant to console me. Words meant to explain to a five-year-old why her mom was never going to hold her again. Never going to tuck her in and read her stories at night. Never going to take her to the park; never going to bake with her. Never going to do any other *firsts* with her again. She was gone. Just like that. Just... just snuffed out.

I clearly remembered how that sensation felt. Like prickles. Like a hundred thousand tiny pinpricks—bursts of pain that bloomed over every inch of my skin in a wave that encased my whole body. It burned. It set my lungs on fire and made my throat hoarse like I had just spent hours screaming.

That sensation was back now.

Pain. Disbelief. Grief.

My heart pumped horror through my blood with every single beat.

*Not me. Not this. This is my life. My. Life. My life, to choose who I'll love. My life, to choose who I'll marry.*

A moment of stunned silence pervaded the room. It wasn't just in my head. All around the table, there were people gaping at me. I turned my head slowly, like it weighed a thousand pounds. Light trails seemed to follow every single movement I made, and I blinked hard and thought about pinching myself to make sure that this was real.

*No. I already know it's real. We wouldn't all be here otherwise.*

I darted my gaze quickly toward Sara, a few seats down from me. She looked just as wretchedly horrified as I felt.

I raked my fingers anxiously through my hair as desperation coursed violently through my body. I wanted to run. I *needed* to get the hell out of this place… but I was frozen in place in my stupid chair with all of the stupid dishes of food steaming in the middle of the stupid table.

No one touched them. No one said anything.

Maybe only a second had passed. Maybe a minute. Or an hour? A year? My whole life?

It was impossible to tell.

Finally, I found my voice. "Dad?" I asked plaintively, turning my heavy, weighted head in his direction. My brain felt like it was throbbing. And my dad wouldn't look at me. Why wasn't he looking at me?

I needed him to reassure me that he would never let anything happen to me. Certainly not give me away in some marriage to a complete stranger. To the *enemy*, at that.

A marriage like this would tie me to a life that I wanted to distance myself from—and he knew that. I didn't want to be part of any criminal activity. I'd trained so hard to be a nurse. I could see my dreams, dreams which were so close, yawning far off in the distance.

"Elisa," Dad said sharply in warning, "there is much to be discussed here."

"There is… there is *nothing* to be discussed." I knew better than to embarrass my dad in front of anyone, least of all the enemy, but I couldn't stand back and do nothing. I had to fight for myself. *For my future.*

I stood abruptly. My chest was heaving, my lungs screaming for air. "I don't want any part of this!" I hissed. I studied my dad, hoping that he could see the apology on my face. But I had no choice.

I was only staring at him, but I could feel the eyes of every other person in the room on me. The back of my neck prickled with the sensation. I felt hollowed out, but I wasn't going to fall. I wasn't going to back down.

And, there were his eyes. *His eyes.*

I knew they were on me. John Colombo, son of my father's enemy. The man from the sidewalk that night. A man who I couldn't erase from my memory. With ice blue eyes, granite features, and a powerful presence that haunted my dreams and waking hours. Had he known who I was that night? Who was the other man who'd been with him? A brother? A cousin?

What did it even matter? I hated that I thought about him at all. My illogical, primal desire for him made me sick.

My dad's voice was firm when he answered, "Sit back down."

God, how I wanted to be strong. How I wanted to disobey.

I hated that my legs gave out like they'd just turned to water.

I didn't just sit. I collapsed into the chair I'd just pushed back.

I dared another look at Sara. Her fearful expression was echoed deep in the pit of my stomach.

I sat there waiting. Unbidden, my gaze was drawn to *him*. To the last person in the world I wanted to look at. Yet, I couldn't stop myself, and that in itself turned my icy cold fear to rage that burned swift and deep.

His eyes were just as cold and blue as I'd remembered. His face was drawn into hard lines which were impossible to read.

*This was him. This was his idea, and the protests are all for show. He saw me that night. Had he already planned this? He somehow found out where I was, and wanted to eye up the goods in person before he was certain?*

The man stared me down without blinking. I hated that it felt like he could see right through me.

When I tore my eyes away, I dropped them down to my clenched hands. They twisted in my lap, my knuckles so white that there was no color in them at all.

The meeting continued on. People were speaking, and I could hear the sounds of voices, but they came at me like I was in a room with thick concrete walls and they were on the other side. I was alone.

No one could get to me. Not even the words that they were saying.

This couldn't be happening to me, I assured myself. I deserved a life away from crime, away from the Colombos. I deserved to be the only one guiding my life.

Thinking that, I wanted to run over and grab Sara and scream and cry with her. I wanted to rail at the sky that this made no sense. That it was absurd. I wanted her to reassure me that everything would be fine, that she would always be there and that she wouldn't let anything happen to me, even if the rest of the world had gone to straight-up shit and was totally against us. I wanted to....

Through that thick layer of concrete—or fuzz, or cotton, or padding, or whatever was blocking out the sounds in the room—something penetrated. A noise. A noise like popcorn. *Microwave popcorn.*

Two quick pops, one after the other. *Loud* pops.

*Popcorn? We're in a restaurant, aren't we? Why would they be making popcorn?*

I tore myself out of my stupor as even louder, more terrifying noises ricocheted through the restaurant.

Chaos erupted in the room. Sara screamed from a few chairs away. Our bodyguards—or should I say, my father's goons—rushed up from their position at the back of the room. Chairs scraped back, almost as loud as those strange sounds. People yelled, but I was still in a fog. A flurry of black suits and rapid motion flooded my vision.

And then it finally came to me, and when it did, I wanted to laugh hysterically and scream until my lungs gave out.

*Gunshots. Those sounds were gunshots. Not popcorn.*

The sound came again—popping, loudly. Not from within the restaurant, but from outside.

My whole body turned to one icy block, frozen in time and space. I couldn't move. I couldn't make a sound. Everything felt like it was happening in slow motion as people came together in chaos around me. We were all here. The heads of the Colombo and Gambino families. I'd thought that no one would dare move against us, but how easy would it be to pick us all off when we were all in the same place, at the same time?

I had one more absurd thought. One horrible thought.

*At least if I die here today, they can't force me to marry John Colombo in the future.*

*"Elisa!"* My name rang out, but it wasn't my dad's voice, or one of his goons.

Strong arms—arms like steel, and even stronger hands—wrapped around my arms from behind. I was yanked out of my chair so forcefully that my head snapped forward and I bit down on the tip of my tongue. I was dragged backward before I could slam breath back into my smarting lungs, and slammed against something hard. Something cold was at my back.

Something even harder shielded me from the front.

I finally tore my heavy eyes open and blinked. I blinked again when I realized that it wasn't an object covering me. It wasn't even one of my dad's goons. The solid warmth pressed up against me belonged to John Colombo.

My enemy had instinctively used his body as a shield to guard mine from the shots. And as awareness flooded me, I realized that it wasn't over. Those shots were still sounding, loudly, coming from every direction. I squeezed my eyes shut against the horror, and when I opened them again, all I could see was black. The black of John's suit.

The fine cloth pressed against my chin because I was so much smaller than he was. He was massive, a granite wall there to protect me. A shiver raced up my spine. Fear, but with an aftershock that I couldn't define. I felt ridiculously safe. Like nothing terrible could happen to me. Like I was protected.

It must have been the shock, because I knew that none of those things were true.

John's heavy breathing matched mine.

"Are you all right?" he asked me thickly. His voice held no fear. Just concern.

I was about to answer when the whole room was plunged into darkness. This was more than just the lights flickering off. That blackness filled me with terror because it felt like the entire world was coming to an end.

I whimpered without meaning to and John pressed himself harder against me. Somehow, his solid presence stamped down my rising panic.

"I-I…" I stammered, trying to get words to come, but they wouldn't.

John didn't wait. He grabbed my wrist and angled his body—moving away, but tugging me with him. He dragged me, moving with so much force that I was propelled forward.

"Where are we going?" I couldn't imagine that he could see any better than I could. But he kept dragging me along, and I kept stumbling along through the thick blackness.

There were voices ringing out in the room, calling out words that I couldn't define. What was wrong with my ears? I wanted to weep when I thought of Sara, my aunt, my uncle, my dad…. Were they okay? I couldn't hear any screams. I couldn't hear their voices. Something terrible could have happened to them.

"Where are we going?" I asked again, my voice little more than a hiss of air.

"Out of here. There has to be a back entrance."

That didn't seem safe. The gunshots had come from outside, hadn't they? But even if they had, would the ones doing the shooting make their way inside? A lump rose in my throat as terror sank its talons deep into my chest. I felt shredded. I wanted to collapse again. I wanted to curl into a corner and sob, but I couldn't. John's hand was like an iron manacle at my wrist, propelling me forward.

"I can't leave them," I rasped. Adrenaline sang through my veins, keeping my tears at bay. "I can't leave my dad. My family."

"Their bodyguards got to them. I was the one who got to you. It's not safe in there. They're probably moving, too. Your dad, my uncle, the rest of them—their guards are armed. They have phones. They're making calls now, to our men."

He sounded so calm. Like this shit happened every single day. And maybe it did. To him. But *not* to me. Or maybe it didn't happen to him, either, and he had some sixth sense or some supernatural ability to remain calm under even the worst of circumstances.

*Trained. He's been trained for this. For the worst.*

70

I'd never wanted to be a part of this life. I'd never wanted to be a part of the violence or the fear. But maybe it had been inevitable. How long had it been since my family had been at war? I almost couldn't remember a time when I'd had to worry that my dad wouldn't be coming home. Almost.

With another few twists and turns, by some miracle, John flung a door open ahead of us and bright daylight spilled into the darkened entrance. Still, I hesitated. Thinking again of my family, left behind in that darkness, I ground my heels into the floor and tried to resist John's strength.

"No! My family is back there. You can't know that they got out! Or that they're going to get out. What about all those other people in the restaurant? Did they make it out?"

John's face hardened, exasperation clear as he spoke. "Whoever is doing the shooting came for us. They'd let everyone else go. The last thing they want is a bloodbath of innocent people on their hands. That would bring down the law like they've never seen it before. Us, though? Don't think that we don't have a far reach, but who's going to mourn the death of a big player in the underworld? No one. If multiple members of our families are killed, the rest of the wider world will have something to celebrate."

I swallowed, letting that statement sink in. It sickened me. I couldn't imagine other people, people who didn't even know my dad, Sara, or my aunt and uncle, or me… other people celebrating our deaths.

I had nothing to say to that, and John tugged me the rest of the way into the bright light. I stumbled forward and blinked away the moisture that had sprung to my eyes. The sunlight burned for a second before I could angle away from it.

I realized that we were wedged between two tall buildings. Thank god the alley had an opening on either end. We wouldn't be trapped. There was some sort of overhang from the restaurant's roof shading us, and three large dumpsters just ahead. It smelled like old cooking oil and sour garbage. The day hadn't been overly warm, but I wasn't sure if it was the chill wind blowing through the alley or the cold terror that made me tremble.

A sound at my back made me whirl around. I prepared for the worst, expecting to see a crazed gunman, but John relaxed at my side and some of the tension drained out of my muscles. It was his brother, the other man from the sidewalk that night.

"Dario," John breathed out.

Dario pulled out a gun from the back of his pants and tossed it to John. He produced a second one from his suit coat for himself. John didn't ask where he'd gotten them. Probably from the goons in the room. Everyone sitting at the table had been unarmed, I knew instinctively—that was how a meeting like that worked.

Dario looked frantically down the alley, then back at us.

"Don't," John cautioned him. "It would be suicide to go out there."

"They're probably gone. Pulling away. If I hurry, maybe I can catch sight of them. Put a bullet through a window or a tire for good measure."

"Are you insane?" John hissed. "You'll get yourself killed."

Dario grinned, John's words of warning clearly rolling straight off his suit-clad back. He obviously felt himself impervious to the danger. "You need to get her out of here. Go. I'll cover the front."

"Cover? Wait for the men—"

"You can't stay here. It isn't safe." Dario glanced at me again. His eyes were deep and brown, unlike his brother's. "Get her out of here."

I didn't know what to say or how to process all of this, but I watched as John hesitated. It was clear he wanted to protest, and for good reason. I wouldn't have sent a member of my family out into the middle of the street for anything. I was surprised when his big hand curled around mine. "Come on. We can't stay here."

"That's the spirit." Dario grinned, though nothing was funny. He shrugged at John, did something to his gun, and then ran through the alley at full speed and rounded the corner of the building.

Even through the shock and the terror, I noticed how strong John's fingers were wrapped around mine, and I couldn't help looking down. *Is it ridiculous to be fixated on a hand?* The nails were well-manicured. They were square, and looked just as strong as the blunt fingers that grasped mine. I even noticed the little white moons at the bases.

*Those hands are steeped in blood.*

Still, I left my hand in his and let him pull me through the alley, heading in the direction opposite of his brother. We ran blindly, so fast that my lungs heaved, my legs burned, and my hair came loose and whipped around my face, blinding me further. I barely had time to take anything in. I was concentrating too hard on the physical pain.

I trusted John to get us out of there safely.

*Trusted my enemy.*

But what choice did I have?

"Stop." John pulled me in to a tight, confined space between two new buildings.

"Here?" I whispered, but John pressed his finger to my lips before glancing in both directions to ensure we were alone.

His massive body angled in again, shielding me. He didn't press against me with anything more than his index finger on my lips, but that finger, combined with the intensity of the adrenaline careening through my system, sent my heart rate into overdrive. I was acutely aware of the warmth of his body, his distinctly masculine scent, the hard planes of his chest....

My heart pounded so violently that I was afraid it might explode out of my chest and drop onto the dirty pavement below. Something else ate at my stomach, too. It felt like a swarm of bees, and I blamed that on the adrenaline still pumping through my body.

I couldn't blame the throbbing between my legs on adrenaline, though. I hated that I ached there. That my body responded to John's proximity so instantly and with just as much violence as what had happened back at the restaurant.

It must have been the shock messing with my brain signals.

John slowly bent his head toward mine, and when those icy blues met my gaze, I saw that liquid desire swam in them. I was so shocked that my knees turned to jelly. The hard brick at my back was the only thing that made it possible to remain vertical.

73

But there wasn't time for desire, whether it made sense or not.

"We have to go back," I insisted. "We have to find out what happened to our families. We just left them there. That wasn't right."

"No. We stay here until I say it's safe."

"This was your idea, wasn't it? The families coming together?" I'd changed tracks fast, my mind whirling back to the news I'd been given at the restaurant—before the shots.

John's expression darkened and his eyes clouded. "I had *nothing* to do with it. I had no idea what my uncle was going to say. I was as shocked as you were." His eyes appraised me coldly, but I still felt a wave of heat wash over me. "I want this marriage about as much as you do." His sinful lips quirked up at one side, in a smug smile. "Now, how about a thank-you for saving your life?"

"How about a kick in the nuts instead?" I retorted.

John eyed my impractical heels with amusement. "I'd like to see how much damage you could do with those."

"I made it here in them, didn't I?" I crossed my arms over my chest, putting a little more space between us. I knew I sounded like a broken record, but maybe one of us needed to. "We need to go back. I need to make sure my dad is okay. And the rest of my family." When John's icy demeanor never wavered, I studied him imploringly, my courage faltering. "They're all I have," I finally said. I hated that I'd dropped my guard, sounding so weak in that moment, so I gave him a look cold enough to match his own. "I would have thought that you'd be just as frantic to ensure that your family is okay, too."

I'd thought his eyes had been cold before, but I'd had no idea. Now, they stared daggers into me. I wanted to take a step back, away from that horrible look, but the wall behind me kept where I was.

"I don't know who the fuck ever thought a match between us could work."

Irrational pain stabbed at my insides with his insult. "What's that supposed to mean?" I whisper-screamed at him before I realized how irrational that question was. *God, brain, you can start working again anytime now.* But I wasn't just scared now. I was pissed off, and that made no sense.

My thoughts were all twisted up in knots because of the adrenaline. The shock. The worry about my family. I wasn't making sense even to myself.

"If you don't let me go back, I'll fucking scream," I hissed at him.

"You will not."

"You can't stop me."

I opened my mouth to make good on my word, but John's mouth slammed over mine, cutting off the rising panic, the concerns for my family, and even the scream that would have given us away to anyone within blocks. His warm lips banished the fear and the ice from my stomach, flooding it with white hot heat.

*I don't want this. I don't want him.*

Even though my mind was in denial, fire ripped through my limbs and I melted against him. John's strong arms came around my shoulders while his lips moved hotly against mine.

"N-no!" I muttered, pulling my lips to the side in order to get the protest out. I finally found my strength and, through sheer force of will, tore myself away from John and stumbled away a step. *What the hell did I just do?* My lips tingled violently with the force of his kiss. And I knew I had to say something, but I had nothing. My mind was a mess, and my body was in total disarray.

I needed to put him in his place, but my brain was a mushy mess… and nothing was coming.

John drew in a noisy breath and his nostrils flared.

Before either of us could say anything, though, I heard my name called. Softly. In the distance. The voice was insistent. Worried.

"That's one of my father's men," I whispered. I recognized the voice, even though I couldn't immediately place the face.

"Are you sure?"

I listened again. The voice was coming closer, my name getting louder.

"Yes. I'm certain."

"Good." John's mocking smile was back. He put a hand on the brick wall, leaning into it so casually that, for some reason, it made me want to grind my teeth.

There were a thousand things I wanted to say to him. Above all, I wanted to tell him that he needed to figure out a way to undo this. He needed to change his uncle's mind in the same way I needed to change my father's. But I couldn't now. Worry had already taken over. What if my dad was injured, or worse? Why was I even standing there wasting time over a stupid marriage that would never take place, if I had anything to say about it, and not rushing back to find my family?

"I have to go," I told him.

John said nothing. He just stood there, silently appraising me in nearly the same way he had in the restaurant when I'd walked in. It made my blood boil, but I couldn't even begin to pretend that all of what I felt was rage.

Even as I walked away, I could still feel John's eyes burning into my back.

# Chapter 7

## John

I couldn't pretend that I wasn't both relieved and totally pissed when I arrived at Leone's house that evening for a meeting.

As soon as Elisa had left the alley earlier, I'd whipped out my phone and dialed my uncle's number. With her, I might have downplayed how worried I was about my family's safety, both so she wouldn't panic and because she was still the enemy—my saving her life and our questionably impending nuptials aside—and so I'd refused to allow myself to show any sort of weakness. I'd been so relieved when my uncle answered that phone, my legs had nearly given out right there in that narrow, dusty alley.

Everyone was unscathed. None of the Gambino family or my own family had been injured.

Since the shots had been fired from outside, my uncle figured it was a warning. Whoever—and we all suspected it had been the Profacis—had fired those shots had known about our meeting. They'd known that both our families would be in the same spot at the same time, which only meant one thing. Someone in our ranks, or the ranks of the Gambinos, was a rat.

When I arrived, my uncle's living room was already filled with men wearing black. Whether they were clad in suits or in the black combat boots, pants, and long-sleeved black shirts that served as the uniform of our soldiers, it looked like a damned funeral was well underway.

The room already buzzed with conversation, and it sure as fuck didn't stop just because I'd walked into the room. I heard the name "Profaci" being tossed around, but there were other names, as well—speculation about business deals that had soured in the past, and men who wanted to make a name for themselves, to be fucking heroes.

I had no doubt that if the gunmen had been anyone but the Profacis, they'd soon be on the wrong side of the turf. They wouldn't live another day to take another shot at us. The situation was considered worse because we'd been in the middle of a meeting, with women present. As a rule, women and children were left the fuck out of just about everything that ever went down between the families.

I sat down roughly in a vacant, high-backed chair that didn't belong to this side of the century. My uncle loved nice things, but those things were never new. He hated modern design—architecture, furniture, all of it.

I couldn't help but think about Elisa's flashing eyes, and how they'd looked at me in that alley. When she'd dared me, with those rich jade orbs, to find something wrong with her. I'd been caught completely off-guard. Not only had she not thanked me for saving her life, but she'd told me that she didn't want the marriage, and then asked me why the hell I wouldn't want her. Just like every other woman, she was a mass of confusing contradictions.

*Except, she's not like any other woman.*

If Elisa had been hurt—whether she was my enemy or not, no matter that I didn't want to marry her—there was no telling what I would have done. Even thinking about those bright, intelligent eyes being shut forever made me want to leap out of my fucking chair and put my fist through the wall. If I couldn't reach a wall because of the crowd, I'd settle for hurling some expensive piece of art out the nearest fucking window.

"John." My uncle had finally acknowledged me. Nevio glanced up from the chair nearest to him. My skin didn't crawl, as per usual. It must have been the latent adrenaline still plunging through my veins.

"Uncle." I nodded and bowed my head in greeting.

Leone didn't ask me for my thoughts on the matter. He didn't ask for advice. It was clear that he already had our men out there, trying to figure out who the shooters had been. We couldn't act until it was clear. If we attacked the Profacis without provocation, it would just incite undue violence.

We needed proof.

But I could tell by the look on my uncle's face that the only business he wanted to discuss with me was the proposition he'd put forward in the restaurant. He stood and walked over to me, and I remained seated in deference. When he put his hand on my shoulder, I stared up at him with a blank expression even though I wanted to wince.

"You know that, through marriage, you will be helping your family in ways that the rest of us never could. You would be uniting two ancient enemies as one. Together, we could rule this city."

"We already rule the city," I retorted.

Leone snorted. "Through the truce, yes. But, united, the Gambino territory would be ours, as well. Their men would be at our disposal."

"But so would ours for them. We already have enough men. We have enough money."

"But do we have enough power?" my uncle replied. "The truce was never stable. It might have lasted all this time, but it could have been broken at any time. It was only by some miracle that it held. You know that we need to unite as a common force against our enemy, against the Profacis. Especially now."

I shook my head. "We don't know for certain it was them."

"No. But we all *know* that it was."

I wanted to speak my thoughts about the rat in our midst, but when my eyes swept the room, I knew this wasn't the right time. Dario and Piero were out with their men, and I didn't want to upset my uncle by mentioning talk of a rat who he probably already suspected. Nothing escaped Leone's sharp attention. If he wanted to speak to me about it tonight, he would. If he didn't, then as soon as I got out of there, I'd be on the phone with Piero, even if I had to go behind my uncle's back to do it.

Even if I had to do it with my brother.

I thought of Dario in the alley earlier, running into the thick of danger. Urging me to get Elisa to safety. No matter our differences, he'd been willing to put himself in danger to keep me safe. To keep the women at the meeting safe. I'd called him right after my uncle, feeling relieved beyond words to know that he was fine. By the time he'd rounded the corner of the building, whoever had fired those shots had been gone.

*Dario.* If I asked Dario to find out who the rat was, he would bring him to me and I could punish him myself before Piero got his hands on the bastard. Once Piero had at an enemy, there wasn't much left to go around. That was, if Dario could find the culprit. He wasn't exactly circumspect, but at least I knew that I could trust my brother.

"I don't think it's the right move," I said with as much respect as possible. "I don't think it's the right move for any of us."

"It's the only move we have left." Uncle Leone swallowed hard. "It's already done. Gastone Gambino has agreed. We never found common ground before. No business deal could bring our families together like this."

I glared at him. "Marriage isn't a business arrangement."

Leone's brow jacked up. He stared me down like he'd used to do when I'd been a child who wasn't capable of grasping what he was trying to tell me. "Marriage has always been used as a business arrangement. Do you know nothing about history, boy?"

I hated that he used that word. *Boy.* That tone. Patronizing me. And what made it worse was that he knew that, in the end, he would get what he wanted. I would capitulate, because I wasn't the one in charge. Leone was. As the head of our family, he gave the orders, and orders were meant to be fucking obeyed without question.

"It will be a 'name only' type of deal," Leone said, softening his earlier tone.

"What do you mean?" I asked cautiously.

"Like a business merger, it's just to cement bonds. I'm not saying you need to fall in love with Gambino's daughter. Hell, you don't even need to sleep with her. The pair of you can lead your own separate lives with only family arrangements keeping you together. You'll have to live

80

in the same place, but that doesn't mean that you aren't free to live your own life."

An insidious thought wormed through my brain.

How the fuck would I ever live with Elisa Gambino and not take her to bed? She was sensual. Beautiful. Fiery. I'd already fantasized about fucking her before I'd known who she was. Now that I'd seen her face, stared into those mesmerizing eyes, and even memorized each and every one of her features, how the hell was I *not* supposed to want her? She was made to bring a man to his knees. She was the kind of woman a man would worship.

She was a goddess. A princess.

It jarred me to realize how much I wanted her. *Physically.* My body ached with pent up desire. Whenever I thought about her, I couldn't concentrate on anything else.

No, Elisa Gambino was dangerous. She was too spirited, and she would never make a good wife. Living with her would be impossible. She already made me feel out of control in a way I'd never before experienced, and that made me furious with myself.

"I can see you're reluctant, John, but sometimes these things have to be done. We all take our duty seriously…"

"I take my duty *very* seriously," I argued, stung. "I always have and I always will."

Leone shifted position. He angled away from me and turned his gaze to Nevio.

Nevio stared back blandly, like he was bored with all of this. But then he commented, "*Someone* needs to marry the Gambino girl. But I don't suppose it has to be you… we always have Dario," he suggested in his usual wheedling tone.

I couldn't hide my reaction. I stiffened and sucked in a sharp breath. I would have loved to remain stoic so that I gave nothing away, but my body betrayed me. Uncle Leone hadn't known before that I had a sort of fucked-up attraction to Elisa, despite her being the enemy, but it was out there now.

Worse, Nevio knew it, as well.

The mere mention of Dario marrying Elisa had flooded me with horror. All I could see was him taking his marriage duties very seriously. Kissing her, touching her, fucking her, and making her writhe and moan underneath him.

Jealousy has always been called green, but I didn't see green. I saw red. I saw *black*. The world around me shifted and coalesced into something seething and dangerous. My hands fisted on my chair's armrests. I wanted to leap out of it and tear Nevio's throat out for the suggestion alone that he should give what was *mine* to my brother.

"So, you think Dario isn't a good match for Elisa?" Nevio asked in his gruesome voice. I loathed the man more than I ever had.

But I also realized suddenly that my rage and my desire had blinded me. Not only had I given myself away, but I was staring at Nevio like I wanted to kill him. A man my uncle put more faith and trust in than any of his own blood relations.

I ripped my gaze away.

"Who else, then?" Nevio continued. He was taking a perverse amount of pleasure in this. In knowing that I hated him and that he had the upper hand. That he had my uncle's confidence, his ear and his trust. I might have been my uncle's second, but Nevio would always be ahead of me. *Above me*. He would always be more powerful as long as my uncle was the head of this family.

This time, I was careful. I throttled my anger back and kept any other emotion out of my tone as I cut off further speculation. "I'll do it." I looked my uncle in the face when he turned. "It's my duty. It's already been stated publicly, and I will obey."

"Yes?" Leone wanted confirmation. When I nodded silently, he broke into a broad grin. "Your sacrifice for the greater good is noted. I am incredibly proud of you."

My uncle might have been smiling. He might have been stalking confidently across the room to place his hand on Nevio's shoulder like he wanted to congratulate him for a job well done. A plan carried out to fruition. He might have been barking orders to the men in the room so that all but his two bodyguards cleared out.

He *was* doing all of those things, but it barely registered.

This marriage was bound to be a mess. It would be filled with complications, and I didn't just mean where my unexpected weakness for Elisa Gambino was concerned. Even though I had agreed, Elisa didn't want to marry me. Maybe she could still convince her father to see reason. Gastone Gambino must have a weakness for his only child. He had a father's love. I had seen it in the way he'd looked at her in the restaurant. He was firm, but not unwavering. He'd put on a strong front because we were there watching. But what he said to her in private could be quite different.

That possibility should have filled me with elation. It should have, but I somehow felt anything but excited at the thought.

# Chapter 8

## Elisa

"I still can't get over it." Sara laughed giddily. We were holed up in my old bedroom at my dad's house, locked away from the horrors of the afternoon to speak in private. "I mean, that was an actual near-death experience, wasn't it? I've never seen anything like that happen before! Not once. It was *wild*."

I shot her a dirty look. "What's wrong with you? It's not fun to *nearly die*. It's not fun to worry about losing a member of our family. Someone could have been hurt! What happened this afternoon was *serious*." My tone was only harsh because the danger was still very real to me. Unfortunately, so were the adrenaline rush and the strange excitement I'd felt with my enemy's body pressed so close to mine.

The ridiculous smile left Sara's face. She dropped her eyes to my white bedspread and started to pick at the lace that had been tucked over the pillows. "Sorry. You're right. It wasn't fun. I didn't mean it that way."

"I know." I sighed. "I'm sorry, too. I'm just on edge."

"Well, yeah. It was fucked up," Sara agreed. "What happened before the shots. I mean, the shots, too, but—you know what I mean."

I did. "I never wanted to go to that meeting," I muttered, squeezing my eyes shut with the thought of all of it, but the only images that played out in my mind were things I didn't want to think about, so I popped my eyes open again and stared at Sara's sympathetic expression. "I didn't know they were going to do something like that. That… that my own dad would… would…"

"Offer you up as bait?"

"Yes. Exactly! It was like getting my leg cut off and getting thrust into shark-infested waters."

"Jesus," Sara groaned, "that's pretty graphic."

"That's how I felt."

"We were there." Sara reached out and grasped my hand. Her palm was cool and clammy, but I welcomed the touch. "We're always here for you, no matter what happens."

"I have to change his mind." It was obvious who the *who* was in that sentence. It sure as shit wasn't my intended groom. He wanted this marriage even less than I did. *Or, so he says.* He could say anything. That didn't mean that I had to believe it.

"Your dad?"

"Yeah." I sighed loudly. "I should have been warned. No one should have an arranged marriage sprung on them like that."

"No one should have any marriage sprung on them, period."

I nodded, struggling for words.

"Hey." Sara's hand squeezed mine. "I know it's a bit fucked up, a *good bit* fucked up, but it could be worse, couldn't it?"

"I have no idea how!" I wrenched my hand from hers as gently as possible and reached behind me to grab one of the pillows away from the tufted, black velvet headboard. I'd loved it when I'd been younger, but right now, it struck me as totally gauche. I hugged the pillow to my chest and leaned back against the headboard anyway.

"Well, he could be gross. He could have two heads. Or a small penis."

"Sara!" I shoved the pillow into my face. "We are not talking about his bits. That has nothing to do with it."

"No? You're telling me you haven't thought about him that way? And his bits?"

I groaned out loud and shook my head into the pillow. "Only before I knew who he was!" I blurted out. I groaned again and plunged my face further into the plush, feathery surface. "Don't start with that," I begged her from inside those smothering depths. "I can't listen to that right now. Or ever."

"So, a marriage with no bits involved would suit you just fine, then? Or if they changed their mind and arranged it with some old dude? The head of the family, perhaps?"

"Sara!" I raised my head so sharply that my neck cramped painfully. I reached up and rubbed the spot. "What the heck is wrong with you? Of course I would mind! I don't want to get married to anyone! Not John. Not his horrible uncle. Not that vulture who was with them at the meeting!"

"My god, could you imagine being married to that nasty old turd bag?" Sara snorted. She laughed softly then, and despite my anger and fear over the whole situation, I couldn't help but join her.

The laughter dispelled some of the tension in my muscles, and I felt just a little bit better, even if it truly fixed nothing.

We were both silent for a few minutes after that, and then Sara brightened with one of those *I have an idea* looks that could only mean trouble.

"We could just run away," she whispered.

That transported me back to when we'd been kids. We'd used to talk about running away a lot. I didn't know why, since we hadn't had it that bad as kids. I'd felt loved whenever I'd been with Sara and her mom. Even when I'd been with my uncle. Certainly with my dad. The pain of losing my mom was always with me, but that wasn't the reason that I'd used to dream about it. I guess maybe I'd just wondered what it would have been like to start my life somewhere else. To be someone else.

To be free.

"We can't," I said softly. It was fun to fantasize about, but we both knew it wouldn't ever really happen. It couldn't. We had too many ties there in New York. "We can't leave our family."

Sara's eyes fell. "I know. It would break my heart."

"Mine, too." And the worst part was, I knew that I would do anything for my family. My love for them could be my greatest strength, but it could also be my greatest weakness. "I'll just have to talk to Dad again. I have to make him understand that not only do I *not want* this marriage, I don't want to be part of this life. What I *want* is to hand out my resumes and get a job. I want to be a nurse, not some asshole's arranged bride."

"But if you don't," Sara said cautiously, unusually serious, "what would happen? The Colombos already know about the marriage plans. If you refuse, what would they do?"

"I don't know," I whispered. It made my breath hitch in my lungs to think about there being a war between our families. About the people I loved getting hurt. Even the men I didn't know—they had families, too. People waiting at home for them. Wives. Children. Moms, dads, brothers, and sisters.

A noise from downstairs broke through the heavy silence that had settled between us.

"What was that?" I leaned forward on the bed, listening.

"Probably just my mom talking to Uncle Carlo or your dad."

After the scene at the restaurant, I'd been rounded up by my dad's men and brought to his home. We'd all been brought there, to our family home. It was an ancient house, with thick stone walls on the lower floors and bricks above that. Even the basement was surrounded in stone. The house had always made me feel safe as a kid. I wondered, now, if that was just another illusion I'd suffered from.

"No." I paused and leaned forward harder, like that extra inch could improve my hearing. "It was something else."

Sara strained forward on the bed, too. "It kind of sounded like the front door opened."

"Yeah."

"It's probably nothing. Just the men coming and going."

Everything had been chaos after those shots. My dad had already been barking orders by the time I'd gotten to the house. He'd come and hugged me as soon as he saw me, as had my aunt and uncle, but then I'd grabbed Sara and pulled her up the narrow staircase to the second floor, and down the hall to my old room.

It still looked exactly the same. Frilly white curtains at the windows. The big, queen-sized bed that my dad had purchased for me as a teenager. An antique tallboy dresser and the matching longer one with its huge mirror. It was all antique, finished in rich wood tones. I didn't know about the wood. I didn't even know what period it had come from. I'd never thought about it when I was younger.

I stared at the patterns inlaid into the front of the tall dresser. It stood off to the right in the huge room, beyond the matching end tables. The house itself was over three thousand square feet. Large, and even though my dad could have had much larger, newer, and better, he didn't want it. He wanted this. The house that he had shared with my mom. The house where her presence seemed to linger still. A house filled with good memories.

Sara and I were so quiet that we were able to pick out a voice we didn't recognize.

Prickles of foreboding exploded along the back of my neck. "I have to see who that is," I said, and shifted off the bed.

"I don't think that's a good idea," Sara cautioned me.

"I have to. Are you coming?"

Sara hesitated, but then she grinned like a co-conspirator. As kids, we'd played in this house. The place might not have any secret passages, but I had the advantage of knowing just where to step so that I wouldn't make a sound. We'd used to make a game of it when we'd been little. I guessed we could make a game of it as adults, too, even though we hadn't done any sneaking around in years.

Sara followed me out the door and down the hall. She was careful to follow my steps. I was cautious, keeping to the thick, woven rug that ran the length of the hall. When I reached the railing, I stuck my hand out and Sara did the same. The wood was warm and smooth underneath my palm. I stepped lightly onto the first step, keeping toward the inside wall. The second step was harder, since I had to dodge straight to the outside. The third, fourth, and fifth steps were all taken straight down the middle. The wood creaked on the sixth step and I winced, but it was a tiny little sound and we continued picking our way down.

When we reached the landing, there was no one around. The room opened up into another hallway. Part of it faced the front door while the other part led back to three rooms. There was a bathroom back there, a room used just for storage, and another large room at the end, which served as my dad's study. He had a massive desk in there, as well as towering bookcases and rows and rows of cabinets. I also know that he kept most of his liquor in there—whiskey and bourbon, sometimes even scotch. He hardly ever drank, but sometimes I'd find him there, sitting behind his desk and staring out one of the massive windows, nursing a drink.

The study was his alone, and I kept away from that room as though my presence would somehow ruin something vital for him. It was his space, masculine and mysterious, and I respected that it was my father's world and not my own. My dad often conducted business there. There'd been so many nights, as a kid, when I can remember deep, masculine voices drifting up through the floorboards from that very room.

"There," I whispered to Sara.

She nodded, her eyes huge.

"He has to be meeting with someone. Not his men. He wouldn't take his men to the study right now unless they'd found out who let those shots off. If that's the case, I want to hear."

"Me, too," Sara whispered back.

We nodded at each other like we were kids again, and then I crept down the hall with her on my heels. The heavy wood door was open a crack. I slithered along the wall, my back to it, flattening myself out like I could make myself invisible that way. Sara did the same. We stayed like that, hardly daring to breathe.

I nearly let out a squeal when I recognized the deeper voice. It took me a second, but I was able to place it. *Leone Colombo.* I couldn't see the boss of the Colombo family, but I could see my dad sitting behind his massive desk. He had a drink in front of him, amber liquid in a crystal glass. I imagined that Leone Colombo was being treated to a drink, as well.

And I knew instinctively what they were talking about. *Me.*

"John has agreed to the marriage arrangement," Leone Colombo declared in a gruff, proud voice.

*Agreed?* Why would John have agreed? He'd told me he didn't want the marriage!

My stomach spun and I felt sick. I cast a desperate look at Sara, whose eyes were even wider than when I'd last looked at her. I put a finger to my lips and she nodded.

"I see," Dad said, and I stood on tenterhooks waiting for my father to shoot this shit down before it got out of control. "That's good news."

My jaw dropped, and I felt certain that all of the color bled from my face. Had my dad lost his mind? Didn't he care at all about what I wanted? What I felt? I was his only daughter! How could he think of just trading me away? My mind whirled, and I thought again about running away with Sara.

*"What are you doing?"*

I practically leapt out of my skin when Uncle Carlo whispered from behind us. I whirled around, Sara with me. My uncle shook his head and motioned for us to follow him.

I reluctantly did, my face burning at being caught listening in on my dad's conversation. The rest of me burned with anger, however, because how could he even be considering this? How could this be good news?

I'd held onto the desperate hope that I could change his mind. That hope was bleeding out like a gut wound now—surely, painfully, horribly.

As soon as we were in our living room, I turned to my uncle. "You have to help me, Uncle Carlo. *Please!*" He was maybe the one person in the world who could help me change my dad's mind. My father's brother could always get through to him.

"They're still talking about her marrying that guy!" Sara hissed. "She doesn't want to marry him. Can you imagine? She doesn't even know him!"

My uncle shook his head sadly. "I can't do anything about it. It's your father's order, Pumpkin...."

I did *not* want him calling me by his pet name for me if he wasn't about to give me what I wanted. What I needed from him. Tears stung

91

the corners of my eyes and I had to bite down on my bottom lip to keep it from wobbling.

"This marriage will be good for everyone," he continued. "I know it might not seem like it at the moment, but there could be a lot to be gained from this. This marriage would end a war that's been going on for a long time. The safety of everyone would be guaranteed."

"There hasn't been a war!" I whined. "There was a truce. And what happened today proves that it wouldn't guarantee anyone's safety."

My uncle shrugged helplessly. "I know that you don't believe me, but it truly is for the best."

"So, you're just going to send me into the lion's den like a fucking piece of meat!" I snapped. "I'm tired of hearing about the greater good." I knew that was a petulant thing to say, but I couldn't help it.

"I know you don't mean that," Carlo said softly. He set his hand on my shoulder, and it was nearly my undoing. When he looked at me, I thought again about him and the rest of the family. About my aunt. About Sara. About my dad. About all of our men whom I didn't even know.

A heavy sensation of doom settled over me. I had never felt so helpless in my life. And it was because I knew that I had no choice.

I had already lost my mom. I couldn't lose my dad, too.

Sara sensed my defeat. She rushed forward and wrapped her arms around me, and I collapsed against her, the tears flowing freely now.

We cried together, our bodies shaking. I sobbed unabashedly, slobbering and sniffing, hiccupping noisily. Sara just clung to me. She let me ride out the pain, the desperation... the sense of loss.

When I opened my swollen eyes, I realized that Carlo was gone.

I wiped at my eyes and sniffed, staring around the empty room. I knew that he hadn't betrayed me, even though I knew where he was. He'd gone and joined that meeting.

My eyes landed on one of the photos hanging on the wall. There was one in particular that I loved. Surrounded by a thick black frame, my parents looked so happy. I looked happy. I was standing in the middle of them. They had their arms wrapped around me, and they were both so young. My dad had never looked old until after my mom had died.

"Your dad loves you," Sara whispered in my ear. She caressed my back with slow, gentle motions. "If he wants you to marry John, then he has to think that it really is for the best."

I sniffed. "I-I know." My voice was weak and watery.

"Then I think you should go in there and tell them what you want. Not that you won't agree to the marriage, but that you have your own list of demands that have to be met. It's probably the only time you're going to get a chance to be heard."

That made sense. My spine practically cracked as I lifted my head up and brushed at my eyes again. I knew I looked like a snotty, red-eyed mess, but I really didn't care. Sara was right. This might be my one chance to stand up for myself.

I would not go down without a fight. That wasn't me.

I nodded, and we walked back down the hall together.

"I'll wait for you out here," Sara said softly.

We both knew she couldn't go in, so I simply nodded. Her support meant more to me than just about anything.

The door was closed, but when I tried the handle, it opened easily. I pushed on the heavy door, and three sets of eyes landed on me as I stepped inside. My dad. Uncle Carlo. Leone Colombo. And one more. Someone I hadn't known was in there.

John. Colombo.

*Of course he's here.*

My body heated up, but I tamped down the strange sensations gripping my chest. I was already trembling, but I would not shake. I would *not* waver. I would *not bow.*

I was a Gambino, and that meant everything to me. I could save my family. So, I *would* save my family. And I wouldn't just save them. I'd make them *proud.*

93

John's presence was not going to stop me.

"Since no one is ever going to ask me for my opinion, I'm just going to have to tell you what I think." My voice was loud, unwavering, and strong even though the heat of all those eyes burned though me.

"I'll agree to the marriage, but I have my own conditions."

My dad's jaw clenched, but after a moment, he swept his hand over the desk, indicating that his guests in the expensive, black leather chairs would listen.

Whether they would or wouldn't, I was going to have my say.

# Chapter 9

## John

It turned out that the mafia princess wasn't just beautiful. She had a steel backbone.

I couldn't quite tell how Elisa was truly feeling because her face was stony and hard—as hard as that of any one of our soldiers—and that alone was to be admired. Her shoulders were set back, and she still had on what she'd been wearing earlier that afternoon, but the dress might as well have been a suit of armor. No matter what she might feel on the inside, she was ready to go to battle on the outside.

And I couldn't deny it—my dick leapt to attention. Elisa Gambino wasn't just sexy. "Sexy" was a token word to be bandied about. Used to describe a beautiful woman. A desirable woman. A sensual woman, even. Elisa was so much more than all of that. She was intelligent, too. Brave.

And she loved her family enough that she was willing to sacrifice her own happiness for their well-being.

"I'll agree to the marriage," Elisa said again. She shifted almost imperceptibly closer to her father. Her hands clasped in front of her waist, she wouldn't look at me. She didn't look at my uncle or at her father's brother, either. She was looking at the man who loved her most in the world. A man whose primary job it was to keep her safe.

A man who was now, for all intents and purposes, giving her away.

It hit me that it had to be hard for Gastone Gambino to lose his daughter this way. Not even to just lose her, but to risk having her hate him for the rest of her life. For the rest of his life. He was doing this for a peace that was clearly more important to him than anything, even his only child, but it had to hurt.

It had been a long time since I'd lost my parents. My uncle might have cared for me the best way he knew how, but it wasn't like this. It wasn't with the kind of unspoken love that I saw being passed between Elisa and her father. When she brushed her fingertips over his shoulders and he reached up and clenched her hand, my chest ached.

If I had known that kind of love at one time, I didn't remember it now.

"This isn't what I want," Elisa told her father in a quiet voice, "but I also know that this is what I need to do. For all of us. I've worked hard to make a life for myself. I want to be a nurse," she added, looking around at all of us before setting her gaze back on her father. "I know that you don't approve, but it's important to me. I won't just give that up. I want to work, and I want to work *full-time*."

I held my breath. Traditionally, being married to the underboss would have been Elisa's full-time job. Working could too easily be seen as an insult, suggesting her man didn't earn enough to keep her in the lifestyle that her status demanded. It didn't matter that she didn't want that status, or even that life. And this was such a shock, I didn't even *know* how I felt about it.

"I wish you would stop with this nursing nonsense," Gastone declared wearily. "I've told you enough times—"

"It's not nonsense!" Elisa declared emphatically.

"I will not have John look like a fool!" Uncle Leone growled. "What will people think if she works?"

Elisa had the presence of mind not to scowl at being discussed like an object, in the third person. She didn't stomp her foot or state that she was no trophy, but she did look between the men evenly, her shoulders still straight and firm. "It's always been my dream. I won't agree to the marriage if I can't work," she said firmly.

"Your dreams are going to have to change now," Uncle Leone said as he shook his head. "You will be the wife of a Colombo. I can't have you making a fool out of my family."

Elisa inclined her head and stared my uncle down. Not many men, even our hardened soldiers, would have dared to do that. "That is my one and only condition," she said flatly. "If I can't work, then this marriage will not happen. I will not consent to it, even if you drag me up to an altar and demand it at gunpoint."

Elisa was adamant, but both her father and my uncle shared a look that said they considered her dreams to be nothing more than nonsense.

To my surprise, I found myself cutting in to defend her.

I cleared my throat, and addressed myself to my uncle when I spoke. "It wouldn't bother me if she worked. I value traditions, but I'm also a modern man, and part of that is being reasonable."

"Do you hear yourself?" Leone hissed. "Do you know what you're agreeing to?"

"Yes." I desperately wanted to know how she was reacting to this, but I kept my eyes on my uncle, my voice firm. "If that's the one condition standing between us and peace between our families, then I think it deserves to be met. She's already trained. Nursing is a respected position. I think that, in our current time, in the society we live in now, it would be more valuable for me to be seen to have a wife who cares, who gives back, who works hard to serve others, than a wife who wears a designer dress and absurd jewelry to charitable social functions."

Leone's jaw clenched. I could see Gastone Gambino's mind working behind his narrowed eyes. And I finally dared a glance at my future bride. Elisa's face was still hard, but I thought I could see something that bordered on gratefulness in her eyes.

"Well?" Gastone had directed that question at my uncle, so I remained silent.

Leone breathed in deeply. Then he leaned forward and grabbed the glass of amber liquid that he hadn't yet touched. He held it aloft. "To a long-lasting peace, then."

Gastone grabbed his glass and raised it. I reached for mine and joined the toast. We threw back the whiskey. If I hadn't been watching Elisa so closely, I would have missed how she relaxed just a fraction. But I *was* watching.

Afterward, Gastone studied me. His future son-in-law. His only child would soon carry the name of his long-time enemy. "I think you two should go outside and let us work out the issue of the wedding."

Leone nodded. Now that the one final hurdle to our nuptials had been removed, he looked happier than I had ever seen him. It gave me a bit of a start, in fact, to see his face bathed in true relief. This had meant more to him than I'd realized.

Elisa shot me a scathing glance that neither her father nor my uncle paid any attention to. We were dismissed. In another moment, she changed tactics and looked pleadingly at her uncle, who swept in to take my seat as soon as I stood. He shrugged at her and accepted the glass of whiskey that her father had stood to pour.

We were to be left out of the celebrations, apparently.

We left silently. Outside, Elisa glanced around like she was looking for someone, but the hallway was empty. She charged ahead and I followed, even though I knew she didn't want me there.

"I think I need some fresh air," Elisa said weakly after stalking through the house. Apparently, her voice was the first part of her to let go of the firm front she'd put up for me and our families. I wondered if she knew she'd let that part of her vulnerability show, or if she'd even intended it. Perhaps to get me to leave her alone?

But I wasn't about to let Elisa go outside alone. Not after the events of the afternoon.

Even if some of her father's goons were out there, I didn't trust any of them to keep her safe. And I wasn't entirely surprised by my primitive response. She was going to be my wife. It was now my job to keep her safe.

Elisa walked through the house deftly. I followed her, keeping a slow pace because my stride was so much longer than hers. She threw the back door open with more force than it warranted, and I shut it with an equal amount of care. She didn't notice, or I'm sure she would have been annoyed.

The Gambinos' backyard was huge. Sprawling, lush lawn glowed in the darkness. A large deck extended from the house, and to my relief, it was well lit. Flower gardens skirted a tall, stone fence. That fence had iron bars with spikes on the top, too. For décor, of course, though if they skewered an intruder like a piece of raw meat on a kabob stick, who would complain?

Elisa stalked across the deck, over to the side of the fence that had no flower garden. The lawn butted right up against the stone. To my annoyance, it was the darkest part of the expansive yard. I followed after her—not cornering her, but giving her space.

I did get to appreciate the tilt of Elisa's jaw. What little light reached us danced across her high cheekbones and her full, sensual lips.

"Thank you," I blurted out like an idiot. It was too late to stop myself. "For agreeing to the marriage. They'll probably want it to happen as soon as can humanly be arranged. With our families, I wouldn't put it past them to have everything ready in a week."

Elisa's lips parted in outright shock, and I could see that I had stunned her. Obviously, she'd thought that she'd have months to prepare, or possibly even time yet to change her father's mind. Dismay flashed through those jewel-toned eyes, but then she shut that door—hard. She schooled her face, sinking her top teeth into the lush pillow of her bottom lip to keep it from trembling, or to keep herself from saying something that she didn't want to speak aloud. She wasn't going to give me the satisfaction of letting me see her emotions, not any more than she already had.

I wanted to trace that spot on her lip with the pad of my thumb. I wanted to trace it with my tongue. And then to have those sweet lips wrapped around my dick.

*What the fuck?* I swallowed the thoughts. They'd come from nowhere. I should *not* want that from this woman in front of me. I should not be at all intrigued or enthralled by Elisa…. But there I was getting hard again. I angled away from her with a curse that I had to bite off.

I was about to ask her something token about the house or the yard to distract myself, when my phone buzzed in my back pocket.

Without thinking, I lifted it out and swiped viciously across the screen, half-relieved for the distraction. I barely processed it, though, my eyes still half-turned to the woman nearby. Until my phone had

99

rung, I'd been unable tear my eyes away from Elisa. She was so sensually captivating in the dark, with the shadows writhing over her face in the same way I wanted her writhing under me.

I realized, then, that I could blame my desire for Elisa solely on the fact that she was the one woman who would obviously never bow down to me. She was a spitfire, and while the thought of breaking her was appealing, that wasn't in my future. Neither was controlling her, or bending her to my will.

She'd be my wife.

Christ, I had never even considered what that would fully mean. I was so far away from wanting to be married, wanting a family, wanting any of that, that it was laughable.

Elisa's eyes flashed down to the bright light of my phone and she gasped, pulling me from the thoughts that I kept getting mired in.

I followed suit quickly, but not fast enough. I was shocked to see that I'd opened a text from Raquel, without even thinking about. It was a photo of her spread-eagle on her bed, completely nude. There was no message. It sure as shit didn't need a caption.

I swore and rammed my phone back into my pocket. "I'm sorry," I muttered. What else was I supposed to say?

I had never been an awkward person before, but I felt every bit of the mortification that clumsy people must feel. And I cursed myself for it. Why was I apologizing for something that wasn't any of Elisa's business?

Elisa was still staring at me, so I shrugged and added, "I told her a long time ago that I wouldn't see her again. She obviously hasn't gotten the hint."

Elisa narrowed her gorgeous eyes at me. "I won't marry a playboy." Her cheeks reddened and her hands clenched at her sides. Right. So, that was why I'd had to apologize. Defuse the bomb before it went off and destroyed all of my uncle's truce. I might not want to get married, but I was part of the Colombo family. A proud fucking part, and I'd do my fucking duty as I always had.

"You think you need to take your... your gross little wiener and stick it into whoever and whatever you please?" Elisa fumed. "To prove your manhood, or whatever? Like carrying a gun?"

100

"Tiny?" I knew I should be working away at the bomb that was her anger, but Christ. *Tiny?*

"That shit won't work with me!" Elisa's whole face was now scarlet. "I won't get married if those vows mean nothing to you! It would be so… so humiliating! I don't care what my father wants. I'm not going to waste my life being with a man who embarrasses me at every turn."

"Whoa, wait, what the fuck are you talking about?" I snapped. "We're not talking about vows or being faithful. That woman is from my *past*, and she didn't listen to me. I'm going to ensure that it doesn't happen again. I'll block her number. I was with this woman *in my past*, but I broke it off for good last week, and we were done before that. I'm sorry you had to see it, but I will tell you now, and you *will* listen, because I'm not going to repeat it. Marriage is sacred to me. I will take those vows seriously. There isn't anything else to discuss."

Elisa's eyes widened. "Oh, really? I don't see it the same way. I don't know you from a hole in the ground! A really gross, disgusting hole that I don't want to be in, but somehow fell into anyway. I'm not just going to take your word for it when other chicks are sending you naked photos."

That did it. Without warning, I advanced on her, backing her up and trapping her against the stone wall with a hand at either side of her face. I could see that there was only one way to get my point across. One way to force her to listen before all of this went to shit over something that I had no control over. This mattered. This marriage might be a sham. It might be an agreement between our families. But I wasn't going to fuck that up. And while there might have been something more, something I didn't understand bearing down on my chest, but I didn't want to think about that. And, right now, I didn't have to.

In the cage of my arms, Elisa's chest heaved wildly. She was trapped, her back literally to the wall. I realized that I was being a brute, and that what I'd just done was the last way to make sure that she'd ever listen to someone like me, but I had to try something. I bent my head to try to say something that Elisa would listen to, to try to find something fucking soft in all of the hard layers that I'd wrapped myself in over the years, but when I looked into Elisa's eyes and I realized that the fire there wasn't just rage, all I could get out was a groan.

101

My dick didn't just react. It nearly tore clean through my pants. I kept my body away from hers, so she couldn't feel how badly I wanted her, but I couldn't resist bending my head and drinking in her delicious scent.

Cinnamon and vanilla.

I couldn't stop. All of my careful control slipped and I inhaled sharply at the delicate crook of her neck. I could feel her pulse fluttering madly there, like a trapped bird. Her chest rose and fell unevenly. Her hot breaths pulsed out against my cheek, but she didn't demand that I release her. She didn't try to knee me in self-defense and sprint rapidly across the yard.

No, she wanted this, too.

That made me harder than anything else. My dick throbbed violently. My balls ached. I had to taste her. It was an instinct so furious and primal that nothing could have stopped me. I grabbed her by the waist and hefted her up against the stone wall so that our faces were even with each other. She reacted immediately, instinctively, her legs wrapping around my waist. My erection jammed straight into her stomach, and she gasped near my ear.

I brushed my nose along her throat, over her jaw. She gasped again and her sweet breath hit me in the chin. Her lips parted in clear invitation. Her pupils were huge and dark. The air between us thickened, with the heavy fog of desire filling up my lungs until they burned.

Elisa squirmed against me, rubbing against my erection. She purred and ground her hips in again. All of the stars from the night sky above us dropped down to descend straight behind my closed eyes. I could never remember wanting a woman this badly, even as a fucking teenager.

I was out of control, and I knew that, but I couldn't dial it back. A satisfied growl rumbled in my throat.

I couldn't keep my hands on the damn wall any longer. I tore one away and ran my fingers down the petal-soft skin of Elisa's arm. She whimpered and swiveled her hips again. I kept going, rounding the sweet crest of her shoulder. I splayed my hand and trailed my fingers over her delicate collarbone. This woman was made of fire, but she was also so small. So delicate. So *mine*.

But even as I thought it, Elisa slammed her legs back onto the ground and tore away from me. She whirled, clean and neat, breaking the hold so cleanly that she'd obviously been trained to get out of a grab before. She didn't have to kick me, jam me in the nuts with her knee, smack me under the chin, or jab for the eyes. She just separated herself, with hardly any effort at all.

I couldn't have been more shocked.

She gave me a scathing look of fury and triumph. She *knew* what she'd done to me. She'd felt my erection. Heard me pant at her throat like a fucking animal. She knew now that she had some strange power over me.

She was the one with the upper hand.

And she might be the woman who was going to be my wife, but I couldn't truly make her *mine* and she knew that. Looking back at me, she said nothing. Not a single word. She just let those eyes linger on me, those enflamed emeralds that were cold enough to burn. Then she turned sharply and strode back into the house. The silence in the yard closed in around me.

What the fuck was I thinking? Whatever I had done had been fueled only by my erection cutting off the fucking blood flow to my brain. That was the only way I could explain how I'd lost control and let Elisa see straight through me.

She might not have a weakness for me, but she'd definitely discovered that I had one of my own.

For her.

# Chapter 10

❧

# *Elisa*

*What the hell was that?*

What the hell had just happened? I'd been so good at standing my ground in front of the two dons, but with John... well, he just left me speechless. There were absolutely no words for what he had just done.

How could he?

And, more importantly... how could I have let him?

All over that stupid photo. Was that what it was? When I thought about John, my future husband, having sex with another woman, I'd just lost it. He was the one who'd trapped me, but the way I'd acted after that.... I should have kneed him in the balls. Clawed at his face. I knew enough self-defense that I could have gotten myself out of the situation.

But I'd done more than that.

I'd rubbed up against him. I'd whimpered with want. I'd ground my nails into the hard muscles straining at the back of his neck. I'd felt *him* though his pants.

No, he didn't have a tiny anything. I'd felt the thick, hard length of him, and he was anything but small.

Thank fucking god I'd recovered in time. And I'd made it seem like I'd been toying with him, even though I knew nothing about doing something like that. I thought he'd bought it, too, though I'd never played hard to get in my life, and I certainly didn't mess around with other people's emotions. *Coy* was a word that was not in my vocabulary, and if I'd had to flirt with someone to save my life, I knew that I'd be dead faster than I could blink.

But instead of letting John torture me, making a point, making me listen in a way that words would never be able to do, leaving me wanting, leaving me aching, I'd been the one who'd left him.

*Me.*

Afterward, I'd had nowhere to retreat to other than my old room. I'd shut myself in and flung myself onto the bed, unable to deny that I was breathing just as hard as John had in the yard. I'd had to lean against the headboard to keep myself upright.

My heart rate calming, I finally lifted my hand and brushed a trembling finger over my bottom lip. John's body was more dangerous than any weapon he could have pulled on me.

I had limited experience with men. Most guys figured out who my father was pretty damn fast, and that was it. The ones who I'd actually made it to the bedroom with had been fumbling and awkward. I'd just about always been left unsatisfied, wondering if that's all there was to it. I'd never really understood why people made such a big fuss about sex, in fact, about kissing or about any of it. In my opinion, it had never seemed that great.

My opinion had just changed, though. John had done more with one wicked touch than I'd experienced in the entirety of my life.

*It's just been too long. It's the adrenaline from earlier. It hasn't worn off. I'm just... off. That's all. It doesn't mean anything.*

Who was I kidding? I might have been celibate for the last year while concentrating on finishing school, but that had nothing to do with my body's reaction. John had awakened something in me. Something primal and all-consuming. I'd already thought about him. Thought about him in *that* way. About his hands on my naked skin. About him tasting me. Taking me. Laying claim to my body.

That was the problem.

That was why I'd reacted like I had before I'd managed to salvage the situation and let my anger give me the strength to pull away.

106

Now, considering it, I gave myself a literal shake. I was annoyed to realize that my panties were totally soaked, but I couldn't deny that they were, and what that meant. I shifted on the bed, uncomfortable with the new sensations heating my body.

But I saw that stupid photo when I closed my eyes. I'd never seen a text like that before. It made me so angry that I couldn't breathe. My blood boiled again just thinking about it.

Just because John could kiss me to distract me didn't mean that he'd keep his vows. I'd be stupid to believe otherwise. For one thing, our marriage was a sham. Even if it hadn't been set up that way, I knew nothing about John other than that he was rich and powerful. And that he was also sinfully attractive. That tended to go to a person's head. If he thought he could have any woman he wanted, what was stopping him from doing it? A few words?

I knew I was naïve, but not even I was inexperienced enough to believe that.

It didn't help that my body was still betraying me—even now, after the fact, now that I was alone. I felt drunk. I was still throbbing between my legs. Throbbing all over.

What would he have tasted like?

The dark tang of powerful masculinity, erotic promise, and the spice of whiskey?

*Stupid.*

Yes, it was stupid, but when I thought about having sex with him, I couldn't deny that I wanted it.

When he was my husband, he'd have a right to my body. I instinctively knew that he would never force me. He wasn't that kind of man. I also knew that he would never *have* to force me. I would have given myself willingly to him right up against that fucking fence, in the middle of my dad's backyard, before I'd regained control. I'd nearly been that gone.

Sex was a natural part of marriage. That's how I would excuse it. I wanted to have children one day. Unless I wanted to conceive them immaculately, I would have to have sex. And I knew that, even should we want to produce a child and nothing more, it would *always* be more for me.

What the hell was I going to do?

That was the question.

So, right in that moment, I made a decision.

Even if I couldn't keep my body out of the equation, I could keep my heart out of it. My body could betray me. It could be used. It could be physically and biologically made to feel things, but my heart was my own. It could never be manipulated. It could never be turned off and on. If I kept my heart to myself, I would never get hurt.

***

I didn't want to be here. I didn't want to be doing this.

I wasn't prepared to see John again—not this soon. It had only been thirty-some-odd hours since that embarrassing scene in the backyard, but here I was, jammed into a hotel room and trying to get a stupid fucking dress on. Alone.

After the unnerving scene in the backyard, I'd called Sara from my room. I'd forgiven her for not being there when I came out of that meeting in my dad's office. Maria had found her lurking in the hallway and escorted her out of there pretty fast. I'd told her what happened, but left out the part about the backyard.

After that, I'd forced myself to have a cold shower.

My dad had found me in my room after his guests had left. He'd explained to me that they were going to create a backstory for us. I was supposed to have been madly in love with John. We'd kept our love one big secret until deciding it was the right time to speak to our families. And now everyone was going to get a big, peachy, happy ending because our marriage would be bringing two warring factions to peace.

My dad seemed thrilled with the lie. It was key that we'd have a very public engagement and a big wedding, with all of the important people there. That meant fewer of my friends and more of my dad's underworld cronies. My entire family had already gone into overdrive, rushing to make plans. As John had guessed, they wanted it done as quickly as possible. Part of that public engagement was a photoshoot that someone—either my aunt or my uncle, or possibly someone from the Colombo family—had quickly thrown together.

Currently, that left me alone to get myself ready for photos that I most certainly did not want, for a marriage that I would never be happy in.

My dad wasn't going to be there for the photo session. Thank god Leone Colombo wasn't scheduled to show up, either. Sara was unavailable to help me out on such short notice, and I hadn't been willing to ask her to drop her plans for this. That left me, a male photographer, and John when it came to putting on this dumb dress that I couldn't get zipped up. There were also some of my father's men in the hallway outside the room, but it wasn't like I was going to ask them for help.

You'd have thought that a big-ass, luxury hotel would have someone come up and offer to help get me ready, and fiddle with my makeup or my hair, but I guessed my dad had overlooked that bit. I was on my own. I'd done everything so far to make myself presentable. It had taken just over an hour now, and I knew that there were two goons on the other side of the door, standing in the hall, waiting for me to make an appearance.

"Fucking, come on!" I hissed at the dress as I tried to reach around and tug the zipper up. That was a big fucking no-go. It refused to budge.

I thought about phoning down to the front desk and asking if any housekeeping staff were available, but that would be totally humiliating. Plus, I doubted my dad's guards would let anyone through that door—not even a little old lady.

I bent, contorting myself into a horrible shape, and grabbed for the zipper. Finally, the thing slid up.

I didn't want to be late, because that would mean that I'd cared to make myself look perfect, and I didn't care about this at all… at least, not about this stupid photoshoot or the actual wedding. I wasn't excited and I wasn't taking extra time to get myself ready—because that would mean something.

I gulped as I faced myself in the mirror. The difficult dress was gorgeous, I had to admit—black, elegant, and form-fitting in all the right spots. I rather wished it didn't fit so well, in fact. But I didn't want to stay in the room and brood, so I opened the door and stalked out, head as high as I could possibly lift it under the shit-pile of stress that I'd suddenly found myself under.

My dad's guards escorted me down to a massive room which was complete with rich red carpets and matching scarlet draperies on the huge windows. It looked like something out of a castle, and I didn't doubt that the hotel hosted tons of expensive weddings.

John was standing over by the window, staring out at the city, though from this floor, I couldn't imagine what there would be to look at.

He was wearing an immaculately tailored black suit. He always wore black suits. I bet that, when I moved into his stupid place—which my dad had also explained was the only reasonable option—all I would find was a closet full of black clothing.

I refused to let myself admire the cut of the suit or the way John filled it out.

And I got lucky because the photographer, a man a few inches shorter than I was, wearing a loud-patterned blue shirt, black pants, and bright blue shoes, came rushing over, eager to start. He had a camera with a massive lens poised in his hand.

"Hello, I'm Frederick! And you look beautiful," he said, sporting a big, reassuring smile.

I found myself relaxing right up until John came to stand behind me. He slipped his arm around my waist and tugged me to his side. I tried not to be wooden, although I guessed it didn't matter. The photographer would just assume it was nerves I felt.

"Tell us where you want us," John said, his voice filled with forced cheerfulness. It sounded real, but I knew it wasn't. Unless he enjoyed torturing me, which he very well might.

So, with our photographer directing us, we got down to the terrible business of trying to look happy and hopelessly in love. That involved me having to look into John's deep blue eyes. Study his lips. Touch his chest. Lean in against his broad shoulder or into his firm side. It involved his hands on my waist. His fingers burning through my elegant black dress in more than one spot. It was torture. Every. Single. Minute.

"Can you stand a little closer together?" Frederick asked after twenty minutes of walking around the room and smiling warily.

"I'm sorry, I'm really not comfortable in front of the camera," I responded lamely.

Frederick just laughed. "I know it can be uncomfortable, even for a goddess like you. You could be a model, sweetheart. Just relax. This is your engagement! You'll have these photos forever. They'll be seen by a ton of people. You want this to look totally authentic. You want your life to *shine* through."

What I wanted was to deck this guy, even though none of this was his fault, but I kept that to myself.

Frederick walked a few paces away, and John leaned in to me. "Will you just come closer and try to relax?" His voice, even as a whisper, seemed to dominate the room. "We should just get this over with." He couldn't hide the flicker of something in those pale blue eyes. Jealousy? Was John actually angry because the photographer had called me a goddess, even in passing? Could that possibly be what I saw? It sure looked like it.

I choked back the urge to laugh. Me? John was jealous over something so small? Over me? A rush of strange, heady power swam through my veins. It was a foreign sensation for me to realize that I had something over another person. Something that I didn't quite understand.

I knew that I needed to understand it, though—and fast. If I had this one thing, I needed to wield it. It needed to become a weapon that I learned to hone.

"Maybe it's hard for someone like me to actually fake feelings!" I snapped. Weapon or not, no matter how far I stood from him, I couldn't pretend that my body didn't turn into a gooey, sticky, hot mess around this man.

"As opposed to people like me?" John set his hand on my shoulder and yanked me to his side. I gritted my teeth tightly together while jolts of white hot heat ripped through me.

*I need to figure out how to hone my own fucking resistance to him, too.*

Frederick took one look at us, standing side by side, John with his hand on my shoulder like he was my dad or something, and sighed. "This isn't really working, is it? We need to shake this up a bit so the pair of you don't look like you hate one another." He was kidding, but god, he was so close to the truth.

"Don't worry, darling," John crooned sweetly, "the camera isn't so scary. He's right. You're beautiful. A *goddess*. Just relax." His hand left my shoulder and swept around my waist, and he turned me to face him before I could protest. My hands landed on his massive chest and I gripped the front of his suit to steady myself. More because my head was swimming than because the movement had thrown me off balance.

"Yes!" Frederick shouted eagerly. "That's it!"

John tilted my chin up, and I was so stunned that I let him. He brought his face a few inches from mine, and when he looked at me, his eyes were so dark with unspoken emotion that I nearly crumpled on the spot.

*He's just selling this. His entire life, he's been an actor. This isn't real. It's for the camera. Men like him don't have a depth of emotion just waiting to be discovered and tapped into. He isn't a fucking well.*

I wanted to be away from John as soon as possible. Correction… my brain told me to get away. My *body* wasn't in such a hurry, and that was a major problem. I could feel wetness pooling between my legs. My hands tingled from the warmth of his body leaching through his suit.

Now I really wanted these photos to be over as fast as possible, so I acted, too. I turned my face up and smiled at him like he was the love of my whole fucking life. I looked into his eyes like he was my savior, pretending he'd be taking me away from a world of violence. I looked at him like I wanted him more than anything in the world.

Frederick snapped away madly until, at last, he let out an excited cry. "I think I've got it! Yes! Yes, that was great!"

I let out a sigh of relief and spun away from John.

"So, we're free to go?" I asked thickly.

"Yes, yes, amazing job. Thank you. I'll have everything ready for you within a couple of days. You make a beautiful couple, if I'm allowed to say so. Good luck with your wedding and with everything after that. I'm sure you'll be very happy together."

Frederick was a nice man. I went up and shook his hand before I motioned to my dad's guards to come flank me so that I could go back up to my room. If our photographer wondered about that, he never said anything. Maybe he hadn't noticed the burly suits hovering on the periphery of the room.

I didn't turn around to see if John was going to leave the room or not. I told myself that I didn't care.

I let my dad's guards take me back up to my room. I'd packed a small suitcase with my dress, my makeup bag, my curling iron, and my hair products, and I was eager to get back into the jeans and blouse I'd worn to the hotel. I hated this dress. It was one of the most expensive ones I owned, a gift from my dad for my twentieth birthday, but it was structured and uptight, and I didn't like it. I'd felt like I couldn't breathe in it when I first tried it on, and that was especially the case today.

This was actually the first time I had ever worn it, though, so maybe that was it. I let out a sigh under my breath when I realized how stupid that was, to want to compare how I'd felt in it today to some other day. What was I going to compare it to? A time before, to see if it was John that made the dress feel too tight and impossible to breathe in? To see if it was him that had made it feel like it shrunk on my body?

I stood in front of the massive king bed and reached behind me, trying to dislodge the stupid zipper. It didn't budge.

"For the love of fuck!" I growled. I stalked over to the full-length mirror on the far side of the ritzy hotel room to see if I could get the damn thing undone. I couldn't see the top, since it was too high up, and I couldn't manage to angle myself that way.

I grabbed the zipper head so hard that my shoulder cracked with the movement. I let out a cry and rotated my arm back around, but it had just been a nasty sound. No damage had been done.

I stalked over to the bed and sat down hard. The comforter was so soft that it dipped under my weight, even if the mattress didn't. I put my face in my hands and scrubbed them over my eyes and forehead in exasperation.

The door opened just then, and, surprised, I leapt up from the bed.

When I saw who it was, I rolled my eyes and cursed under my breath. I couldn't believe my dad's guards had let him into the room. And without any warning—what if I'd been undressed already? "For the love of fuck. Come on!" John shut the door gently behind him. "Go away!" I snapped. "I seriously am not in the mood to see you."

He shrugged, like that was an appropriate response. His eyes traveled down the length of my body, consuming me. It unnerved me so badly that I spun around.

"Well, if you're here, undo this zipper. It's stuck. Just take it down an inch. Until it hits my hand." I cranked my arm behind my back and waited.

I didn't know what I was doing, and I couldn't believe I was doing it. Needing help with a zipper was a flimsy excuse, now that I thought about it. Talk about my brain giving in to my body. We were in my room. *Alone.* I couldn't trust my body's responses around this man, and I had just asked him to touch me!

No, *not me.* The *zipper.* The stupid zipper.

Maybe it was a test. To see if John was honorable, or at least half-decent.

A test of my own power, though I couldn't exactly figure out how to make that test work. It wasn't like I had the option of multiple choice.

John approached, his heavy steps sending flurries of shivers racing up my spine. All I could do was wait, my hand flung up behind my back as if that was enough to ward him off.

His fingers brushed my curled hair over my shoulder with such gentleness that I nearly gasped. I could feel him. I could feel him *everywhere*, even though it was only his hand on my shoulder. Those fingers trailed lower, grasping the zipper head and easily tugging it down. He didn't stop until his warm hand met mine.

I nearly cried out at the contact.

I ripped the zipper the rest of the way down and whirled. This was no stupid test. This was all of my frustration boiling over. John's hands closed around my shoulders. I reached up and tugged his face to mine, and he claimed my mouth eagerly, possessively, with enough heat to burn own the entire building around us.

I opened my mouth, parting his lips, and his tongue thrust into me. He kissed me stupid, and I was weak enough to lose myself. All of my anger and desire had simmered since that night at the fence. This was about that. This was about the ache that refused to be sated. The flames that had consumed my every waking moment since then.

John's hand tore my dress away. It had an off-the-shoulder neckline, and a bra built into it, so that meant I was bare once it went down.

"Fuck, Elisa," John groaned as my breasts spilled out of the dress. He kept ripping, tearing at the fabric until he'd dragged it down over my hips. I kicked out of my black heels, sending them flying, and stepped out of the fabric.

I needed to stop this. I need to fucking *stop*, but this was exactly what I wanted. This was what my weak body craved. Maybe it would be like every other time. John would fuck me. I'd learn that it wasn't great. He'd come and I'd be left wanting. Frustrated. Angry. He'd take what he wanted. I'd give it. I would take nothing for myself, and at the end of it, I would decide that it would be best if this never happened again.

I'd get it over with and then I'd move on with my life. With our life, together, since that was the way it had to be. I'd move on, and he'd lose his hold over me. I wouldn't be so weak in the future.

John claimed my mouth again while he backed me up, straight into the wall. My spine hit hard, but not hard enough to hurt. The rough contact sent white hot heat ripping through my limbs.

John's tongue swirled over mine like an erotic dance. This wasn't just a kiss. He was claiming me. Fucking my tongue like he'd stroke me down there. Thrusting in and out of my mouth like he'd thrust in and out of me. Somehow, I knew it, and I sensed that this wasn't something I'd be walking away from so easily as I was telling myself.

That thought was enough to make feel all of the helplessness and vulnerability the man brought out in me, and I let myself give in. I shut my brain away, and let my body direct me.

115

I whimpered and arched my chest into his. My sensitive nipples scraped along the fabric of his suit, and no matter how expensive and soft it was, it sent fire raging through me.

John brutalized my mouth while his hand snaked down. I thought he would cup my breast, but he trailed his hand lower. He brushed his fingers over my flat stomach, until he reached the lace of my black panties. He groaned, and I hissed into his mouth. I scraped my teeth over his bottom lip and he groaned again, nipping me in response.

I responded dizzily, instinctively, blindingly, by arching into his hand. His fingers slid under the lace, curling over my sensitive bud. I mewled into his mouth and my hips bucked into his hand. His fingers slid lower, through my slick wetness. He parted my slit, coated his finger in my wetness, and broke the kiss.

I panted, confused, until he brought that finger up and painted my bottom lip with my own arousal.

"Taste yourself," he commanded me.

I tentatively flicked my tongue out, and when the sharp musk of my own desire hit the tip, I gasped in surprise.

"Now, I'm going to taste you. I'm going to fuck that pretty cunt with my mouth. I'm going to fuck you until you're writhing against my face. I'm going to eat you out until you're dribbling down my chin. I'm going to make you come. Again. And again. You'll come with my tongue inside of you and then you'll come on my cock. Do you understand?"

I could only nod, mutely, because *holy fuck.* Any thoughts about putting the brakes on had disappeared hard and fast.

When John hit the floor before me, going to his knees, my legs nearly buckled. He took hold of my hips, steadying me. "Lean back," he commanded, and I did, hitting the wall hard again. He lifted me easily, settling my legs on his broad shoulders.

I should have been embarrassed. I'd never had anyone do this to me before, and it was broad daylight, the curtains open. The room was *bright.*

But all I could think about was my legs on his shoulder, my raging heartbeat, and his hands on me.

"Christ, you're beautiful." John grazed my thigh with his teeth before he kissed away the sting. "You're so fucking beautiful."

His powerful hands gripped my panties and, with a single hard yank, he tore them clean off my body. I cried out in shock more than protest. And then I curled my fingers into his thick, black hair, yanking his face into me.

His tongue was hot and insistent. He opened me up with his fingers and licked every droplet of moisture from me. I wanted to protest the intimate position, to protest something, put up some semblance of the resistance that I was supposed to hold onto, but his wicked tongue flicked over my clit, and I was done. I threw my head back against the wall and melted.

*I was supposed to have a weapon. What was it?*

I realized that I was wild. That a proper young woman wouldn't be banging her head against the wall, mewling out random noises and swiveling her hips into anyone's face, but I couldn't stop. It just felt so *good*.

John suckled my clit until I thought I was going to go crazy with longing. I bucked into his face, wanting more, begging, aching, but his tongue danced way. I cried out at the unfairness of it until he kissed me lower. He traced the seam of me again, lapping at my arousal until he came to my entrance. He entered me brutally, curling his tongue and spearing me, and my whole body shook. I grasped his hair tightly, hanging on as he plunged his tongue in and out of my entrance.

"Fuck!" I cried out. "John! God. Please!"

He shifted from beneath me and stood up so abruptly that I couldn't stop my gasp of outrage. He leaned back, looking at me where I'd slid down the wall to land on the floor, and then backed away so slowly that I wanted to scream. He stood, and since I was sitting, he towered over me. He wasn't smirking, but he might as well have been. His placid face destroyed what little control I had left.

"You… you…" I realized what he was doing. Paying me back for how I'd left him in the yard. He thought I'd teased him, and now he was teasing me. Taking back some of that power that I'd thought I had over him.

"Just a little teaser for the wedding night, *fiancée*," he said obnoxiously.

I could only watch in horror as the bastard waltzed, actually *waltzed*, out of the room. Just like that.

Leaving me alone.

I blinked into the space where John had just been standing. The room smelled dusky, like sex. Like *me*.

I collapsed back against the wall.

My body thrummed with frustration. I ached between my legs. I was soaking wet, swollen and glistening with need. I stalked to the bed and grabbed up the clothes I'd arrived in. Slamming my body into them angrily, I ignored the pulsing between my legs, the strange fullness in my breasts, and even the quivering in the pit of my belly.

I needed to get over this humiliation. Channel the rage I felt into something productive. Some form of resistance. Something to keep me safe from whatever it was that came over me every single time I was in the same room with John.

This wasn't breaking the deal I had with myself, no matter how bad it was. I could give over my body. John could make me come as many times as he fucking wanted. *Or not.* I fumed about how easily he'd manipulated me. Teased me. Turned me into mushy putty in his bastard hands. I wouldn't let that happen again. Next time, I'd be sure to return the favor. If he could do this to my body so easily, I could do it to him. I knew that I affected him, too. I'd learn to use that. Maybe we'd have each other, over and over, and get rid of the desire plaguing us, and then we'd be free to live our own lives, within the confines of marriage, but also separate. Other couples did it.

I might never be free of him, but I wouldn't lose myself.

I'd make sure of it.

# Chapter 11

## John

"We need to get out of here for the night," Dario declared as he slumped on my couch. "You've been working yourself ragged this week. You should let loose so we can have a good time. You're so fucking quiet, John," he added. And then, after another few seconds had passed: "Thinking about your upcoming marriage? You need to take your mind off that."

I rolled my eyes. I didn't want to participate in the one-sided conversation.

Dario knew that the wedding was a sham, as did the rest of the family, and our men. It was vital that they knew what was happening since the sudden peace with the Gambinos had created a lot of questions. I didn't need to worry about anyone's discretion. Anyone caught spreading information would be severely dealt with.

That thought reminded me that I hadn't found the rat who'd given away our restaurant meeting, but I had too much on my mind to worry about that. I'd had to let it go—for the moment, at least. Not forever. Just until after the wedding.

The Profacis had been blamed for the shots fired that afternoon. It felt like a thousand years ago, and I was still waiting for Leone to tell us how and when he wanted to act. To punish the Profaci family. The wedding took precedence, unfortunately. I'd have liked nothing better than to distract myself by getting my hands bloody.

*A distraction is exactly what I need.*

I hadn't been able to stop thinking about Elisa since our engagement photos. Since what had happened afterward. That shoot had been days ago, and I still hadn't slept properly. I hadn't been able to eat. All I could taste was her sweet cum on my tongue. All I could see was her perfect pussy. She was so fucking tight.

I should have fucked her harder. For longer. I should have thrown her on the bed, slammed her down on my dick, and taken her sweet cunt from behind. Again. Over and over again.

*Control. Don't lose control. Get a fucking grip.*

I snorted at myself, still ignoring Dario as he kept talking. He'd shown up an hour ago, and after consuming more of my bourbon than I would have liked, he'd sprawled out on the couch and refused to let me get back to burying myself in business. Or fantasizing about burying myself somewhere else.

I gripped my glass so hard that my fingers ached, but I didn't toss back any of the amber liquid swirling at the bottom. I wanted to enjoy the bourbon, stare out the window over the city, and force myself to think about business—not about Elisa.

I wouldn't think about the way her eyes flashed when she was angry, the quirk of her mouth when she smiled, or the warmth in her eyes when she looked at someone she loved. She was utterly beautiful. Completely intoxicating.

She was *mine*.

I glanced to my brother when he called my name again, repeating the same complaints. "I'm not quiet," I told him. "And I might be thinking, but that's something I need to be doing."

Dario snorted. "You don't need to think about anything. You're getting married in two days. You need to come out with me and have some fun. It's been forever."

"You know the rules."

"I know," Dario responded irritably. "No clubs," he said, mimicking my uncle's stern tone. Despite myself, I actually had to bite back a grin. "I wasn't talking about that."

120

"You've been planning this?" I didn't like the sound of that. "Why are you planning anything?"

"Because you never spend time with me anymore. It's like you've forgotten I'm your brother."

I rolled my eyes, knowing this was *not* going to end well. I wasn't going to finish the night peaceful and at home—not with the buttons my brother was pushing, and the look on his face.

I threw back the bourbon that I'd wanted to enjoy. Maybe this was what I needed to banish Elisa from my mind. Even just a few hours of peace would be worth the annoyance of whatever Dario had planned. Maybe a small part of me knew that he was right, too. He was my brother, and he was closer to me than anyone else in the world. "Fine," I ground out. Dario knew that I cared about him. He knew that he was probably the only person—aside from my uncle, possibly—that I truly did care for. I still had trouble admitting it, though. Getting kind words or emotion from me would have been like expecting to find water from inside a pulverized stone.

"Are you serious?" Dario jumped off the couch. He was far too excited, and I already regretted agreeing.

An hour later, I knew I should have listened to my instincts. I never should have come out. If I'd had any idea what Dario had been planning, I would have refused and given him yet another lecture about his lack of responsibility. But I hadn't known.

The venue our car sat outside of technically wasn't a club. It was exclusive, discreet, and high-end.

"You planned a bachelor party for me? Are you fucking kidding?"

"Everyone's already inside," Dario said, ignoring my sour mood. He tried to coax me into agreement with another plaintive look. His immaturity made me want to smash my fist against the dash. "Just come in and stay for ten minutes. That's all. Please?"

"Who the fuck is *everyone*?"

"You know. Everyone. Piero. Some of the guys."

"You brought your own men to a fucking party for me?" Now, I really wanted to punch something.

"Come on. Jesus, John, you seriously need this. I know you never used to be fun, but now you're all, '*I'm second in command, so I have a huge stick up my ass all the time.*'" Dario rolled his eyes and jammed his elbow into my side from across the car. I resisted the urge to smash my fist into his face instead of the dash. I would have, though, if he hadn't been my brother.

If I got out of the car and called one of our men, or even a cab, Dario would never let me forget it. He'd be petulant and whiny, like a spoiled kid who hadn't gotten his way. I ground my teeth and vowed to myself that this was the last time I'd give in to Dario. I hated that I had a weak spot for him, too. After this, it would be tough fucking love for my brother. He would learn if I had to nearly kill him to get it into his head that he was an adult with responsibilities.

He could start by finding me the piece of human excrement who'd ratted our meeting out to the Profacis. I knew I should talk to him about it, but instead I swallowed the conversation back. It wasn't the time, and sitting outside of a strip club was definitely *not* the place.

"Fine." I threw the car door open so violently that the hinges creaked. I stepped out into the cool, dark night. I wasn't about to let anyone see me out here, so I ducked my head and barreled toward the entrance.

The two brawny bouncers at the door obviously either knew who I was or had been briefed as to who to watch for. They let me pass, holding the door wide open. There was another burly fucker just inside. This one was wearing a pinstripe suit, of all fucking things. He led me—and Dario, who had caught up with me—down a dark hall and into a large, private room.

As soon as I got there, I wanted to turn around and walk back out. The room was dimly lit. There were private, discreet booths throughout the area, with a stage in the middle. Half-naked women walked around topless in little thongs and towering heels, carrying trays of shots and glasses of alcohol. Naked women writhed sensually on the stage, some grinding against poles and others doing routines on the floor.

The room was packed with guys I knew. Guys who looked to me for leadership.

*I shouldn't be here.*

Dario obviously didn't give a shit about how I felt about the place. He grabbed my arm and steered me straight into a booth, where he sat me down hard and took a seat across from me. He gestured madly to a blonde waitress with big, fake breasts. She came around and deposited a few drinks into his hands without asking what he wanted. Dario passed one over to me, grinning broadly.

"You need this," he insisted.

I could see the worry on his face. He truly thought that he was doing this for me. That it would help me relax. Yes, he was worried, and since we didn't use actual fucking words to communicate emotions to each other, this was the next best thing that he'd been able to come up with.

"It's your second to last night of freedom. Enjoy it," he urged me.

I wouldn't. I looked around the room, at the men leering at the naked women gyrating on stage, at the fake breasts, the fake bodies, the fake lips, and the fake hair. It was all fake. I tossed my drink a good ten feet from the booth out of anger, but the music was thumping so loudly that the shattering glass couldn't even be heard.

"Jesus Christ," Dario swore. "What the fuck is wrong with you?"

"What's wrong with me? I hate this shit. You know that."

"It's hardly the first time we've been here."

"The last time I was here was seven years ago."

Dario just shrugged. He turned his head, ignoring me to watch the girls undulating up on the stage.

I closed my eyes, but that made me picture Elisa, and I felt guilty for thinking about her in a place like this. She was so pure. So innocent. So *perfect*. I felt like bringing her here, even in my mind, was wrong.

And I should never have closed my eyes for another reason. That moment of weakness left an opening for Dario. I inhaled, and cheap perfume flooded my nostrils.

"Last hurrah, right?" There was a woman standing in front of Dario, talking to him in sugary tones.

Dario shook his head. "Not me. Him." He pointed at me, and the woman turned. She had the largest breasts I had ever seen, covered only by tiny, sparkly pasties. Her bright red G-string matched her nipple covers. She grinned at me in a way that she probably thought was sexy, and then, without any warning, gripped me by the shoulders and straddled me.

I tried to protest, but she was already grinding her hips against me, the skimpy G-string she had on barely covering anything. The lights from the club flashed around us. I could smell the alcohol on her breath as she leaned in with her sticky pink lips to whisper something sugary in my ear.

"Stop." I grasped her firmly by the shoulders.

She jerked away in surprise, her face twisted in confusion.

"I'm sorry. Thank you, but I'm good for tonight." I lifted her off of me and set her back down hard on the floor. It reminded me of the night when I'd tossed Raquel out of my condo. Another night of bad decisions involving my brother.

But that night hadn't been all bad.

That had been the night I'd first seen Elisa.

The woman gave me a forced smile. She'd tried to be nice. I grabbed my wallet and peeled out a few hundreds. "Here." I stuffed them into her hand. She looked down at the money and her eyes widened.

"Um, thanks," she said in her sugary tone.

"Goodnight," I added.

Point taken. She disappeared fast enough, probably to tuck that money in a safe place—which had to be somewhere in the back, given that she had no safe places in what she had on.

"What the fuck?" Dario asked as I stood.

"I'm leaving. Thanks for the party." I softened the blow by adding, "Seriously. I really just need to get home."

As I walked away, I watched my brother signal to another girl. He might not be happy about me leaving, but he could see that I was serious, and he wasn't going to try to drag me back. The scantily clad woman got down on her knees in front of him and he began unzipping his pants. I wanted to go back and drag him out of there, too. Him and every other guy in there who was supposed to be there for me, in fact. But I

124

just ground my teeth and kept walking. I caught Piero's eye. He'd been standing on the far side of the room. Not watching the girls on the stage. Not watching the girls working the floor. His eyes weren't even on the waitresses or on his men.

His eyes were on me.

I thought the expression in his gaze held a challenge, but when I blinked, it was gone. He nodded at me, and I nodded back.

Everyone else was too wrapped up in what they were doing. Some guys were doing a lot, if the women in front of them and the ones writhing on their laps were any indication. I felt centuries too old for this shit.

As I stalked down the darkened hall, I thought about Elisa on that night in her backyard. The photo she'd seen. The hurt and the accusation on her face. I'd promised her my vows would mean something. I'd meant it. I didn't understand this last night of freedom bullshit. If other guys wanted to partake in it, that was their business. Hell, most of those guys in the private room I'd just left had wives at home. It was their choice to make, but this wasn't for me.

I hated clubs. I always had. Even though this wasn't the sort of club that we were warned to stay away from, it was still a club of sorts, and I detested it.

Outside, free from the nightmarish party, I leaned against the wall and waited for my head to stop spinning. The beat from back in that room still pulsed through my brain, even in the silence of the night.

I swore and rammed my hand into my pocket. I palmed my phone and punched in a number for a cab. I didn't want one of our men to drive me home. A cab would be faster. I wanted to get out of here. To get the fuck back home. Drink my bourbon and stare out the window like I had planned on doing all along.

I wanted to think about *her*.

No... I'd come out here because I *didn't* want to think about her. Because I couldn't stop, but I *needed* to stop. I needed to get control of myself. I needed to get my head back into the game. The Profacis were still out there, and I couldn't afford to be caught off-guard.

My wedding was two days away.

I'd get through it. Get it done. Move Elisa in. Move her into my bed. I'd claim her. Fuck her. Make her truly mine. I'd make her scream. Make her writhe. Make her come again, this time on my dick. Over and fucking over. I'd fuck her on every surface of the house, and then I'd move on. Not on to someone else, but I'd move on in my head. I'd fuck her out of my brain, out of my mind, and then I'd be able to concentrate. I'd get back to business. I'd find the rat, and I'd make him suffer. I'd deal with the Profaci threat.

I'd go back to the normal, controlled, collected person I'd been before meeting Elisa.

I'd concentrate on being the underboss of the family, on patiently waiting for that day when the city would be mine.

The fact that those things seemed less important than ever was only proof that I needed to get my shit together as fast as possible.

# Chapter 12

## Elisa

"You look *amazing*," Sara gushed as the young hair stylist stepped away from me. "I love your hair in curls like that."

I glanced between her and Maria. I knew they were responsible for the small team of hair and makeup artists who'd arrived at my condo that morning. They were both still in their jeans, but we had a bit of time before we had to get into our dresses.

*My dress. God. Today is my wedding day.*

My makeup was already done, and my hair was just about finished.

I should have felt like a bride, but I didn't. I'd accused John of not taking his vows seriously, but how was I supposed to promise to cherish and obey a man who I didn't, and would never, love?

"Thanks." I managed a watery smile for my cousin.

She and Maria both looked gorgeous. Their makeup was perfect and each of them had their dark hair swept up into a beautiful up-do. Sara sported a fishtail braid at the front of hers. Maria's thick hair was twisted into ropey strands and piled on top of her head. Her hair was still as raven black as it had been when we'd been kids. I didn't think she dyed it, but my aunt had her own secrets. And I knew if she did dye it, she wouldn't tell us.

I thought again about my dress.

Sara and Maria had treated me to a shopping trip the day after the engagement photos. There'd been so much to do, so much to get ready for, so many details that I'd had to talk through with my aunt and Sara—and occasionally my dad—that I'd felt so overwhelmed I'd barely had time for thoughts about John.

During the day, at least. The nights were another matter. I couldn't keep him at bay then. He was alive in my dreams. He did sinful things to me in those hours of sleep. Every single morning—and several times a night—I woke up drenched in sweat, aching and throbbing between my legs.

Sara giggled happily. Over the past few days, because she was so involved with taking care of details, she'd obviously gotten far too used to the idea that I was happy about this wedding. I wasn't.

My body might tremble at the thought of sharing a home, and a bed, with John, but the rest of me remained in rebellion. I'd already given up hope that my body would be anything less than a traitor.

I couldn't control it, but I could control other things.

I'd sent out a stack of resumes to various hospitals and care homes yesterday. It made me feel more in control. More like I was doing something for myself. I hoped I'd receive a response back soon. If I got a job, then my days, and my nights, would no longer be my own. I'd bury myself in work. John would see to whatever it was that he did. We'd have our own separate lives.

"Don't you think we should get the dress on you?" Sara had been asking about it all morning.

I had to admit that it was beautiful. I'd found something I loved, and when I'd tried it on at the shop, Maria and Sara had both bawled their eyes out. Mine had remained perfectly dry. I thought it was ridiculous to splurge on a designer gown, but my father had insisted that no expense be spared. Forty thousand dollars was a mere trifle to him.

This wedding wasn't going to be a display of two people in love. It was a flexing of our two families' newly combined might.

The lady who'd fitted me had said that the dress could only be ordered. I wasn't sure who'd changed her mind, but when the dress had arrived at my house the next day—perfectly packaged, without a wrinkle, tailored exactly to my size—I knew that one of my family members had obviously reached out.

I wasn't a princess in a fairy tale, though. This wasn't my big day. This was a sacrifice for my family. It was never going to be anything more.

"Not yet," I whispered.

"Come on," Sara pleaded. "Let's just get it out. It will be fun. Plus, what if we can't get all those buttons done up in time?"

"It's a zipper! The buttons are just there for show."

Sara looked deflated. A storm of vengeful hornets returned to my stomach. Yet, I finally nodded, giving in to her enthusiasm, and the stylist sprayed the last bits of my hair into place. I reached for my purse to tip the stylist. We were in the kitchen, since it had seemed like the best place for the stylists and makeup artists to spread out all of their things over the big table and the island. Everyone had already been paid. Maria had taken care of those details ahead of time, but a tip would be nice. My cell was in my purse, too, and I reached for it just to check the time. I was sure it was way too early for any dresses yet. Much as I just generally didn't want to get into it, I also didn't want to wrinkle or spill anything on it.

I swiped the screen to check the time.

"What the—" There was a text on the screen. The tiny icon made my heart stop beating before I'd even swiped it open. My entire body went cold.

*Do you know what you're getting yourself into?* The words were written just above the photo. I tore my eyes away from the image just long enough to check the number. I didn't know it. I forced myself to click on the photo, enlarging it even though I could see all of the details full well despite the dark permeating the background.

It was clearly a club. A strip club. The man in the photo was also clearly John. Just as clear was the woman with massive breasts who was sitting on his lap.

The photo was a screenshot, and everything had been cropped out except for the date and time. *Two. Days. Ago.*

John had been at a strip club, letting random, barely clad women sit on his lap. That woman was just about naked. She did have something covering her nipples, and when I enlarged the image, I could see a string on her hip that probably meant she was wearing panties, but that was it.

And, still, I felt like a fucking idiot.

John had gone out after he'd been in the hotel with me. Not the same day, but that didn't matter. Before our wedding. Right before. Was this just proof of how little he cared about me? How he'd fuck around with women when and where he wanted because he felt that it was his right, even if we were married?

But then, why should I be surprised? John wasn't different from any other guy. This wedding wasn't his choice. He didn't love me. He didn't even *care* about me. I'd thought that he'd respect me enough to keep his dick in his pants, though. He'd *told* me that he would. He'd told me he'd respect his vows. Did he think this was okay just because we weren't married yet? One last night of fucking freedom?

And had he just been toying with me in that hotel room? Proving a point? Doing it because he could? Did he like what he could do to me with just a single glance and hardly a touch at all?

That disrespect was a hard pill to swallow. In fact, I couldn't swallow at all.

"Hey," Sara said, clearly sensing that something was wrong. "What's going on?"

Mutely, I turned the phone to her. She groaned when she studied the photo. "Well," she said after a moment, far too cheerfully, "I mean, lots of guys have bachelor parties. He's fully clothed, too. His friends probably dragged him out. Most guys do the last night of freedom crap."

"I know," I whispered, "but how do I know it ended there?"

"Who the heck even sent you that?" Sara looked around for her mom, like Maria could talk sense into me, but she was seeing the stylists out the door. They must have packed up while I'd been sitting there, and I'd been so consumed by the photo that I hadn't even noticed.

"I don't know."

Sara clicked her tongue. "Well, I think we should get your dress on. You're getting married and you don't want to be late."

"What does it even matter? Why go through with this sham ceremony? My husband clearly won't be faithful to me."

"You don't know that!" Sara insisted. "It looks pretty innocent, and whoever sent you that photo is probably just trying to cause trouble. We might be at peace with the Colombo family now, but we have tons more enemies, and so do they. It's probably from someone who doesn't want the wedding to go through." Sara paused. "You are going through with it, aren't you?"

"I—"

"You have to! You know that."

I finally cleared the photo off my phone by deleting the text. I couldn't look at it any longer. I did check the time, though, and realized that Sara was right. I had to get the stupid dress on. Somehow, the time had just evaporated. I'd thought we had hours yet, but my last moments of freedom were quickly vanishing.

"We shouldn't be late," Sara whispered when I didn't move. "You know this isn't exactly a normal crowd, and if anyone thinks you're not going to show up, shit could really go down."

I knew she was right, but I didn't *want* to get the dress on. I wanted to tell Sara everything. About the hotel room. About that night at the fence. She couldn't really understand anything if she didn't know what had gone on. She couldn't understand my hurt and embarrassment.

"Can you just give me a minute? Alone?"

I could see the hurt flicker on Sara's face, but I just needed a few minutes to think. She nodded, and I slipped from the kitchen to head upstairs to my bedroom. There, I shut the door and leaned hard against it.

*Can I really do this?*

I knew that I couldn't *not* do it.

There would be violence on a level that I had never seen before. Everyone I loved could get caught in the crossfire. I had given my word. And, unlike some people, I didn't break it.

My stomach churned. It was bad enough that I had to marry a total stranger. How could I marry a man who disrespected me? Who lied to me? Who let other women into his bed? I knew that I wasn't just hurt. I was jealous. Of course I was jealous. I was going to be his wife, sham marriage or not.

I was allowed to be upset. I was allowed to feel betrayed. I was allowed to feel *humiliated.*

I locked the door and walked over to the bed, where I threw myself across it and slammed my hands up over my face. If only I could stay this way forever. If only I could cut out the rest of the world.

If only I could run away, like Sara and I had always talked about.

I lost myself in that daydream. I lost myself in memories.

For a little while, I lost myself in anything and everything that didn't have to do with this wedding.

When a sharp knock sounded at the door, I sprang up from the bed frantically, realizing that I'd lost track of time. How long had I been lying there? I checked the mirror above my dresser quickly and realized that half of my hair was squashed and flat. My eyes were red-rimmed even though I hadn't been crying.

The knock sounded again, sharp and angry.

"Jesus, Sara, I'm coming!" Annoyance rose in my throat because I was already stressed. It would be a miracle if we could make it to the church even half an hour late now. I tried to breathe, but I couldn't breathe. There wasn't enough air in this room—it was too tight and constricted.

"You can't go in there!" Maria's high-pitched voice made me jump. "It's bad luck to see the bride before the wedding."

*What the fuck?*

"I *have* to know what's going on."

John's deep voice drifted through the door, shocking the hell out of me. I bolted for it, twisted the lock free, and threw it open. He stood there dressed in a black suit, and it looked like one of his regulars— he probably hadn't even thought this day warranted something new or special. He was irritatingly charming with his sensual lips and those clear blue eyes. Freshly shaved, and with his raven black hair swept back from his forehead. Worst of all, he smelled good. I hated that my stomach cramped just at the sight of him.

"What are you doing here?" I hissed.

"Your cousin called me. I know about the photo." He sighed. "Look. Dario, my brother, asked me to go out with him. I didn't realize where we were going. He can be, well, incredibly annoying."

"You didn't have to go in."

"I know."

"You didn't have to get humped by some random stranger."

"I know."

"By a stripper." I knew that I was going on and on about something that was likely nothing, but I was stung. Embarrassed. Did I really know what I was getting myself into? Part of me wanted to hear John's denial. Part of me secretly thrilled that he was there—that he'd cared enough to come after Sara's call. But the other parts of me, centered in my brain and intelligence, poisoned that small seed of hope. John was there because he had to be there. Neither of us could afford for this wedding not to go through.

"I told Dario that I'd spend ten minutes in there. Put in an appearance to satisfy everyone and leave. He ordered drinks for us. We were sitting in a back booth. I was trying to shut it out until I could get the hell out of there, and when I opened my eyes, he'd ordered up a girl, too. She sat down on my lap, and I pulled her off just as fast. That was all that happened."

"Oh, I'm sure you had your arm twisted real fucking hard to walk in there!" I replied from my doorway, shutting out the image of Maria stalking off down the stairs. "I'm sure those ten minutes were the worst of your fucking life. I'm sure you didn't enjoy that woman at all!"

"Actually, I didn't. I didn't want to go in there. I didn't want to have anything to do with it. I wanted to stay at home and drink bourbon. *Alone.* I regret going. I'm sorry. But nothing happened."

"How? How do I know that's the truth? You could have done anything after this photo was taken!"

133

"If I had, don't you think they would have taken those photos and sent them to you?"

That made me pause. John's cool logic was like water on my anger. I crossed my arms, trying to hold onto the anger on behalf of my self-respect if nothing else, but I was battling with my own reasoning. "You humiliated me," I pointed out quietly.

His jaw ticked, and a vein throbbed at his temple, but there was something soft in his eyes.

The lump in my throat was back now, and tears stung the backs of my eyes. I blinked hard. I would not cry. I would not cry because of John. I would not let him see it.

"That was never my intention. It was just a bachelor party that my brother planned. They had fun without me. I don't know who took that photo or who sent it, but it was someone just trying to make trouble. While you might not like the truth because it throws a wrench into any excuse for you to hate me, that's what happened. I said I would honor my vows, and I will." He stepped into the room, and I stepped back automatically.

I didn't want him close to me. I didn't want him to be able to sway me physically. "Would my father still want me to marry you if he knew that you did this?" I asked, wondering what he'd say. Wondering what the truth was.

"I didn't see the photo, and it probably looked bad, but you have my word. As my wife, you'll learn that I don't give that lightly, and once given, I never go back on it. I give you my word, too, that I'll do everything in my power to make you happy."

We were both surprised by that statement. I blinked at John. His lips thinned out like he wasn't happy with the admission, but he didn't take it back.

"Please don't change your mind." John had ground out the words, like it was hard for him. That *please* had been the worst bit. "There's more than us at stake."

"Don't you think I know that?" I hissed. My neck was so tight with the stress of all of it that I could barely turn my head left or right. My chest ached worse than anything. "That's all I can think about. That if I don't do this, people can and will get hurt."

John stepped closer. He reached out, and I froze. He ran his fingers over one of my curls, not touching my face or my neck. Just my hair. "I would never do anything to hurt you."

He'd said it with such sincerity that it made my stomach ache. I closed my eyes and saw my mom's face. Her blonde curls. Her laughing eyes. The easy love she'd had for me and my dad.

She'd left everything behind to marry my dad. Born in Finland, she'd taken a job as a model at just sixteen and traveled through Europe for years, advancing her career. She'd met my dad while he was traveling. He'd started in Italy, but wanted to travel to France and eventually Spain. She'd met him while working on a job in Paris.

He saw her sitting outside a café, drinking coffee, just watching the people come and go in that beautiful, wonderful city, and fell instantly in love. I guess she fell pretty hard, too, because she gave up her career to marry him. She moved to New York.

She followed him. Trusted him. She put her faith in him.

She loved my dad—adored him. Still, it must have been scary. All those unknowns. Giving up her job. She had no education to fall back on if her marriage didn't work out. But she married my dad anyway, knowing full well that he was involved in the criminal underworld… but she loved him, and she didn't just see a member of the Mafia. She saw the man he truly was.

Could I do the same? Could I learn to trust John? To find some kind of middle ground with him? To have a peaceful marriage? Could I even give him one one-hundredth of what my mom had given to my dad?

God, I wished she was here with me. I could have used her advice now more than ever. Would she have told me to follow my gut and run before John could ruin me, or stay and do what was right for the family? Help to build this bridge between the Gambinos and Colombos for a better future, even if it meant sacrificing just about everything I held dear?

"All right," I whispered. I stepped away quickly and walked to the window. "All right. I believe that someone wants to come between us so that our families can't unite. It makes sense." That was as much as I was willing to give. "I'm going to get dressed. I'll be at the church just after you get there. We'll be late, so assure everyone that everything is well. Say I had a malfunction with my dress, and panicked and called you to ensure that violence didn't break out or something terrible. I *am* coming. I *am* going to do this." I didn't turn around. Instead, I studied the city street below me instead. There was a black car parked outside. John's car. As I looked out, a hand waved out the window at me, and then his brother opened the driver's side door and waved up like he'd been watching the window the entire time.

I flushed and backed away. At least the brother had a sense of humor, although I could definitely blame him for dragging John to that stupid club in the first place. That was certainly believable enough.

I kept my back to John and stared at the wall. I knew he would do as I'd asked. "You really should leave now," I added. "It probably truly isn't good to see the bride before the ceremony, and we could use all the luck we can get."

## Chapter 13

## John

*That photo. That fucking photo.*

I knew a photo wasn't what I should be thinking about while standing up at the altar waiting for my bride, hoping like hell that she'd follow through on her promise and actually show up. The worry of that was bad enough, but I'd had those worries before. Last night, I'd had a dream that I was standing at the head of the church, alone, with a whole room full of mystified guests waiting for a bride who'd never show herself. Most grooms probably dreamt about that shit the night before their wedding, but I wasn't "most grooms" and this wasn't a love match.

And, now, I had that photo to contend with.

*Who the fuck would have sent that? Who was there, watching me, waiting for an opportunity to try to cause trouble? Did they send that photo in hopes that Elisa would call the wedding off?*

Could it have been Nevio? I tried to remember if he'd been at the party. I wasn't sure. I knew he wasn't my biggest fan, but would he really stoop that low? Nevio had to know he'd be hurting more than just me. It had to be someone not in the family, right?

My skin crawled when I thought about an enemy getting so close to me. Unseen, watching, waiting. Had it been a member of the Profacis? Someone they'd paid to spy for them? Or was it yet another rat? The same rat from the restaurant, maybe?

Either the rats were adding up into a horde, or it was just one bastard that I had to find and deal with. After the wedding, assuming it went through. *No. After. After* the fucking wedding—because it would happen—I would find the bastard and I would make him pay for the harm that he'd caused. The trauma and pain he'd made my future wife go through. On her wedding day!

If it wasn't the same rat, I might make whichever one I caught first pay for both deeds.

My thoughts were interrupted by a movement at my back. I glanced behind me to find Dario standing there with a concerned look on his face. He didn't move from my side, which was a good thing for him. I wasn't in the mood to say anything to him at the moment. I had informed my uncle, when I'd arrived at the church, that Elisa might be slightly late—a problem with her dress—but that she was coming. It was obvious that he'd passed that information along, because the church, which was packed, hardly stirred even though Elisa was twenty minutes late.

Together, we looked out over the packed church. *Friends. Extended family.* Yet, I spotted very few familiar faces. That unnerved me, but then, standing up in front of them all, with no weapons and no men at my back for protection other than my unarmed brother, should indeed have been unnerving. I was glad that Dario was there, at least. Amidst the abundant white roses spilling from the ends of the pews, the massive vases at the front of the church filled with more of the same, and four hundred curious eyes, waiting for a bride who didn't want to show, I was indeed thankful for my brother.

I'd fought my uncle on the wedding party. He'd wanted a big show, but I'd insisted we do this part my way. I didn't have many men who I considered friends. I did like the men I worked with, for the most part, but it wasn't the kind of relationship we had, to have them stand at my back.

The only man who deserved that honor was my brother.

In the end, I'd won out. Elisa only wanted her cousin and her aunt to stand up with her. She had friends who I knew were in attendance, specifically because my uncle had poured over the list and bemoaned the fact that there were many young people on Elisa's list of guests who weren't part of our life, and who might very well question the authenticity of her sudden decision to marry a man who she hadn't even mentioned to them once.

The white-robed priest stood off to the side, still as a statue. He clearly wasn't worried about a tardy bride, either. I'd hardly noticed the magnificence of the massive stone structure we stood within, but I set my eyes on one of the stained glass windows. I focused on the image—something religious—but fuck if I knew what scene it depicted, and I tried not to think about the thousand things I had to worry about at the start of tomorrow. I'd put them off for today, though that wouldn't last forever.

Suddenly, the heavy wood door at the back of the church cracked open and I saw Gastone stick his head out and give a signal. I stood a little straighter, resisting the urge to fiddle with my clothing, which felt tight and uncomfortable. The ancient lady at the organ off to the side started pounding away with a fervor reserved for rock stars. Those blaring pipes apparently declared the starting point of the ceremony, too, because the door was opened again and Sara emerged. She made her way up the richly carpeted aisle. Her mother, Maria, followed behind her. Both of them were stunning, sporting simple yellow dresses that flowed to the floor.

It was only another minute before the music changed, signaling the wedding song. I didn't know anything about church music, but I'd been to enough weddings in my life to recognize it. All of the guests, who must have numbered two hundred or more, stood in a great wave. I didn't notice a single one of them.

My attention was entirely transfixed on the back of the church, where Elisa stood with her father. Her arm was looped through his. She had a small bouquet of red roses in her hands. A long veil with lace on the edges was pulled over her face. Her dress, which fitted her perfectly, was beyond breathtaking. *No, not the dress.* The dress was beautiful, with a heart-shaped neckline, tight-fitting over the hips and with a flare at the bottom, but it wasn't what captured my attention. No, it was the woman wearing the dress who knocked the breath right out of my lungs.

"Steady there," Dario said, like an idiot, from beside me.

I didn't know if I looked like I was going to fall over, or maybe I actually had swayed upon seeing Elisa. She was a vision. She looked like an angel. Pure. Innocent. Lovely.

It was hard for me to remind myself that I'd seen her just a short time before. She hadn't been in her dress at the house, but I'd seen her hair and makeup. I'd too distracted by the thought of the wedding not happening because of that photo to actually realize how gorgeous she was.

I noticed now.

Gastone led Elisa slowly up the aisle. She granted smiles as she turned her head, and I could actually hear sighs come from some of those assembled. Maybe they, too, thought that there was an angel in their midst.

Gastone stopped at the head of the aisle. He lifted Elisa's veil, kissed her on both cheeks, and said something softly into her ear. She gave her father a watery smile and blinked rapidly. I could only imagine what she was thinking. I was quite sure that those were not tears of happiness.

The priest made a signal, and after that, everything became a blur.

I supposed I should have taken Dario's advice to get my ass steadied, because I barely heard a word of the vows. I did go through the motions flawlessly, promising to love and to cherish her—not being entirely certain that I was capable of either, but it was like I was on autopilot. I wondered if every groom felt this way. A cross between the shock of nerves and the sickening sensation of having to perform promises in front of an entire building full of important people, all the big players in a dangerous life.

My hands didn't shake when I reached for the rings. I slid the gold band onto Elisa's finger with confidence. "With this ring..." I repeated after the priest, "I thee wed."

"With this ring," Elisa repeated, pushing the cold gold wedding band past my first knuckle to settle it in place. Her voice was melodic and strong. "I thee wed."

When I was told to kiss her, I obliged with a chaste kiss on the mouth, as was fitting. I could feel the burning stares of all those sets of eyes incinerating me. Her lips were unyielding below mine.

After it was over, I held out my arm and Elisa placed her tiny hand there. I steered her down the aisle, past all of those eyes. I didn't stop walking, though my chest was compressed so tight that I could hardly drag in any oxygen, until we were clear of the doors. There, I finally took a breath, even as Elisa ripped her hand from my arm. Dario and Sara were right behind us. Elisa went to stand with her cousin. She refused to look at me, and Dario clapped a hand on my shoulder.

"How does it feel to be a married man?"

"The same as it did a few minutes ago when I wasn't." I looked at my bride's stony face.

"Don't worry," Dario whispered in my ear. "She'll come around." He winked at me, and I wanted to plant my fist in his face. As brothers, when we'd been younger, we'd had our fair share of wrestling matches. Back before our parents had died. Our uncle had never allowed us to do anything as stupid as fight each other when we'd lived with him. It didn't stop the jealousy from ripping through my veins now, over Dario even thinking about Elisa that way, even though I knew exactly what he was implying. If I seduced her, maybe she wouldn't be so sour.

We stood off to the side, together, and I went back onto autopilot while an endless stream of people congratulated us. This wedding wasn't actually for us. This wedding was for my uncle and Elisa's father. They were the ones who would shift the attention as soon as we left in the limo waiting outside to take us off for photos. More time would be spent business conducted at this wedding than had gone into an actual marriage.

The fog didn't really clear from me until well after the photographer, who god knew who had hired, had had his way with us and our families.

I went where I was told. I smiled. I complied. Beside me, Elisa did the same. Afterwards, I got into the limo. Somehow, we made our way to the massive hall where we were to have our reception.

The place was decorated to sophisticated perfection—probably as a result of Maria and Sara's inspiration. They'd likely been behind booking the expensive, modern venue, deciding on the dinner, the decorations, and whatever entertainment or music was to follow. Of course, no expense had been spared. Our families were wealthy, and this was a show of that wealth and that power.

As a result, I felt like an imposter at my own wedding.

Everything went on around me. I didn't have to have much input. I hardly tasted the four-course, gourmet meal or the champagne I drank to the men toasting us. I wasn't the one giving speeches or making connections. My uncle was covering that. I hardly had to say a thing. I even smiled on instinct.

Beside me, I could sense Elisa going through the same wooden gestures.

I knew that, as soon as the evening was over, I'd probably be able to breathe again. I could get back to my work and get back to a familiar world.

When a DJ moved in and began to set up, I knew that Elisa and I would have the first dance. I studied the guy, unsure where I had seen him before, and then I realized that he was semi-famous.

Christ. There was really no limit to what our families had booked for us. The DJ alone had probably charged more than what the entire venue cost.

I glanced over at Elisa. She was standing with Sara and Maria, sipping a glass of champagne.

Through the radiance of her beauty, though she hid it well, I could tell she was miserable. Neither of us liked being the center of attention, or the reason for it. Part of me liked that about her. That she was as out of her element in this as I was, even though she was absolutely stunning in her designer gown.

I could have used a few shots myself, just to steady my nerves, but I hadn't touched a drop of liquor all night. Dario, on the other hand, was a few drinks away from ending up on the floor. I really hoped that he'd keep his shit together, especially in front of our uncle. Leone would be pissed if Dario embarrassed our family while everyone was watching.

Dario slammed back another shot at the bar, then ambled over to stand beside Sara. He leaned in and probably said something obnoxious. She was good enough to simply roll her eyes at him, even though her lips pursed in annoyance.

She didn't like our family any more than Elisa did. I did find it mildly amusing that Dario's charms were entirely lost on Sara. I imagined he'd keep trying all night, and whenever they were together by virtue of knowing the two of us, and she'd keep shooting him down.

I stood watching them, Dario like a sad puppy and Sara clearly walking circles around him, until the lights dimmed. There was a massive chandelier over the dance floor, and it flickered to life. The first warning notes of some sappy, slow song filtered through the hall. A song that I didn't even know. I told myself that it was just the fact that I had zero control over any of this that annoyed me, but I couldn't quite make myself believe it.

I did wonder what it would have been like to marry Elisa properly. Marry her when both of us wanted the marriage. Something small. Intimate. *Ours.*

I shook that daydream off, however, because thoughts like that had zero place anywhere in my life. I was having an increasingly alarming number of idiotic musings lately. They needed to be stopped.

I focused instead on Elisa, who walked dutifully over to me. She looked like a princess, and I was almost surprised that a trail of damn glitter didn't glisten in her wake.

She set her hand in mine and smiled up at me. She'd removed her veil earlier, and the curl was falling out of her lush blonde hair. Overhead lighting highlighted the gold in the gently cascading waves. Her makeup was still flawless, and she blinked at me through her heavy, dark lashes.

My hand tightened over hers instinctually. I had the sudden urge to wrap my arms around her and hold her. Promise her that, one day, I would mean those vows. I thought that maybe I possibly could. That one day I might grow to actually care for her. I already craved her. I'd thought about her body since long before I'd tasted her in that hotel room after our engagement photos. I'd craved the taste of her mouth, the soft heat of her, her alluring curves, and her tight wet channel wrapped around my—

"I know what you're thinking," Elisa whispered as I slid my arm around her waist. She set her hand at my shoulder and kept her other palm wrapped in mine. We stepped onto the wooden dance floor and started to move slowly in time with the soft strains of the music. "You're thinking about tonight. About taking this dress off of me."

My breath jammed up in my lungs. I felt like I'd been kicked in the balls as I studied her angelic face. I thought it was probably for the best that I said nothing, as she was obviously winding up to something, so I remained silent. After the way I'd left her the last time, I doubted it could be anything good.

I didn't want to admit to wanting her. It gave her power over me that I thought it best she wasn't aware of.

"I can tell. You have that look on your face. If I brushed against you right now, I bet you'd be hard."

I had no idea where the sensual side of Elisa came from, or where these words were coming from. Was this the minx from the night in her backyard, where she'd pressed up against me sensually before throwing my own desire in my face? She leaned into me now, and she wasn't wrong. My dick jumped at the gentle contact of her dress floating against me, her soft skin just inches away beneath that fabric. I had to remind myself that she'd wanted me badly enough in the hotel room. Her desire had blazed hot there, nearly matching my own.

Her breath tickled my ear as she shifted her hand up higher on my shoulder and leaned in. To anyone else, this was an intimate position. Just a happy bride and a love-struck groom sharing a special moment on their special day. To me, my new bride might as well have been carrying a grenade, getting ready to pull the pin.

This wasn't natural. This wasn't Elisa. Especially not after she'd seen that photo.

"Let me tell you that, until you prove to me, beyond any doubt, that you are going to take those vows seriously, you will never see me naked again. I won't let you set one hand on me. You won't be peeling this dress off of me tonight. You won't be sharing my bed."

Anger rose, ripping through my chest, but I swallowed back a harsh retort and steeled my voice to respond calmly. "I told you that the photo wasn't what it looked like. I already made it clear that I would adhere to my vows and take the marriage seriously."

"You've said so, but you haven't *proved* it. I married you because I had no choice. From here on out, the decision is yours. What happened in the hotel room won't happen again. I won't let you seduce me. I might be your wife, but I'm not *yours*, John. I'm still just... just *mine*. I belong to *myself* only."

I knew she was serious, but her words only heated my blood. She made me ache to prove to her that she was wrong. She was already *mine*. She'd been *mine* in the hotel room. She was now *mine* by law. She'd be *mine* every single day for the rest of our lives.

She had no idea what kind of a challenge she was putting out there.

The fantasy I'd had about our limo ride home quickly evaporated. I'd burned for her since the day in that hotel room, and for far longer. I'd thought that she might be as consumed as I was. She'd certainly seemed ready and willing enough last time. The look she'd given me when I'd stopped could have frozen even the devil's nuts clean off. I had planned on lifting that dress and pulling Elisa onto my lap, spreading her legs, having her sweet cunt wrapped around my cock as she rode me wildly the entire way home.

The song ended abruptly, and as other couples moved onto the dance floor, I spotted Gastone. I was happy to hand off his daughter to him. His hands replaced mine, his arms wrapping around her protectively. I stepped off to the side, blending into the background seamlessly for a man who was supposed to be the center of attention. I was more than content to observe every detail of what was going on around me while trying to calculate what my next move would be.

Apparently, it was not going to be having Elisa fuck me anytime soon.

I had a few drinks, sipping the whiskey slowly while I watched Elisa smile sweetly at everyone who wasn't me. She chatted openly with all of her father's friends. I figured they had to be Gambino acquaintances because I didn't know or recognize many of them.

Elisa shone. She radiated light like the beautiful bride she was. She put on a show when she needed to. I was willing to bet that this wasn't the first time she'd had to do it. Her father watched her closely, and it was clear he was pleased.

I caught my uncle's eye once, and he nodded at me before moving on to talk to a middle-aged man we did business with. Stolen luxury cars kind of business. I knew I should be putting on the same show as my wife. We were now standing on the same stage. So, I moved around the hall like she did, greeting my uncle's friends, speaking with the men we did business with, and even clasping hands with the men on the Gambino side.

It was exhausting. It was a relief for me—and likely Elisa, as well—when it got to be late enough for us to be heralded out of the sprawling, luxurious hall and into the limo. There was no hotel suite booked for us. I'd seen to that. The last thing I wanted was men standing guard at a hotel door all night and into the morning. I knew that I'd be much more comfortable in my own home, and it was the one other concession my uncle had made for me.

Sara hugged Elisa madly before passing her over to Maria to do the same. Her father hugged her, as well. He whispered something in her ear that I couldn't hear from where I stood by the open limo door. Dario, who was miraculously still standing, walked up behind me and gave me a hard enough slap on the back to rock me straight onto my toes.

"Good luck," Dario said pointedly. He might have thought he was kidding, but what had Elisa said in her room earlier? That we'd need all the luck we could get? She was probably right. My uncle nodded his approval from the throng who had rushed outside to see us off. Sara hugged Elisa one more time, and that was it.

We were off to start our new life together.

As the limo pulled away from the curb, my unhappy bride glaring daggers at me from the opposite side of the car, I tried not to think about that with any amount of bitterness. Elisa wanted proof that, from now on, she was it? I'd give her proof. I'd wage war on her so thoroughly that she'd beg me to take her. She had no idea what she'd started. In the end, she'd know.

She'd know, and she'd tell me that she was mine. Every. Single. Bit. Of. Her.

I thought on that while we wound our way through the city.

When we arrived at the condo, I swept Elisa out of the backseat like I was a love-sick groom. I carried her to the elevator, but even there, I didn't let her go. She remained still. She didn't make a sound. She was hardly even breathing, and I could tell that she was furious, but she was slowly learning that holding back was more powerful than railing at me and making demands that I had zero intention of complying with.

She kept her gaze steadfastly forward as we entered my home, even though she had to be curious. Her pride was greater than her need to ask me any questions or to voice her discomfort. If she was scared, there was no way my mafia princess was going to show it.

I carried her straight down the hall. Mary, wisely, was already locked in her room for the night. She'd obviously thought that this would be a real wedding night and probably had earplugs and cotton forced into her ears to keep out any sounds that might make their way through the thick walls.

I carried Elisa to the lavish guest room and dumped her unceremoniously onto the king bed there. Her expensive designer dress temporarily enveloped her, and she let out an indignant gasp. She didn't break, though, and refused to utter a word of complaint about the rude treatment.

I bent and grazed a chaste kiss over her forehead.

"Goodnight, wife."

She couldn't contain a hiss of rage as I left her there, shutting the door tightly behind me.

It wasn't lost on me that she'd have to find her own way out of a tightly laced wedding gown that there was no way she'd want to ruin. It was too expensive and too beautiful. She wouldn't be able to destroy it, no matter how much she hated me.

Not my wife, the very same wife who'd fought for the right to work. To be a nurse. A high calling that used up a whole heart and then some.

I'd planned on hitting the shower and going to bed, completely unaffected. I wanted to drive my *wife* wild with my steadfast composure. I wanted her to be the one who came to me. I thought I could wait until she cracked. Yet… thinking about her in that room with her dress on, her sensual body underneath it, just begging to be touched, tasted, and fucked thoroughly… that only drove me mad.

I stormed through the condo, grabbed my keys off the counter, and stormed straight back out.

I could feel my control slipping dangerously, so it was best not to be in the same building with Elisa until I could get it back where it belonged.

# Chapter 14

## Elisa

I had dreams, as a little girl, about my wedding. Later, I thought about how the wedding night would be. I thought that, when I found my perfect husband, we would spend the entirety of our wedding night showing each other, in a thousand different ways, just how much we loved each other.

*Yeah fucking right.*

In reality, my wedding night had been spent alone. I'd cried myself to sleep somewhere after three in the morning. That was the last time I remembered checking my phone, anyway.

Even after going to bed so late, I still woke up just after seven. I groaned when I saw the time, too—I couldn't even sleep in to get more of these shitty hours over with. But there was so much that was going to change soon, and I'd have to manage it somehow. My things would be brought here, first of all; probably today or tomorrow. I knew my father would have it seen to as soon as possible in an effort to make sure that I couldn't change my mind.

I picked up my phone from beside me on the rumpled bed and, without thinking, I dialed Sara's number.

With it being so early, I was actually surprised when she answered, even if her greeting was more of a whimper than actual language. "Holy god, what time is it?" she asked after the inhuman noises were out of her system.

I sighed. "Seven."

"Jesus. Shouldn't you still be asleep after the romp you had last night?"

"I'm not going into detail about what happened last night. Don't even try that."

"So, you didn't consummate the marriage?"

I face-palmed my own forehead so hard that the smack echoed through the room. "No. I'm still in my fucking wedding dress!"

"What? Why? What happened?"

"I don't know. I… I told John at the wedding that he wasn't getting in my pants anytime soon after that stupid photo I saw. He brought me up here and dropped me in the guest room, and then he left. I've got nothing to change into, and I'm not going to get naked in any bed here."

"Seriously? I would have cried! I would have cried all night if that was me!"

I felt like crying again after hearing the sympathy in Sara's voice. "I did," I admitted. "But that's over. Today, I'm going to be strong. I can't change this, but I meant what I said. My… my body might belong to John now, legally, but I won't give myself to him until he's proved he can be trusted. That he'll be honest with me. He has to earn that. And, as for my heart… that's never going to be his. It's the one piece of myself that he can never own. I swear that much, Sara," I sighed out. I hadn't meant to say all that, to admit all that, but it felt good to have said it all aloud. I could hold myself accountable to my best friend as well as myself now, no matter how John tried to get into my head.

"Shit," Sara sighed. "That's some heavy stuff for first thing in the morning."

"I'm serious!"

"Did you ever think that he might already be telling the truth? That that photo was nothing? Just some asshole trying to break you two up because it would be better if our families weren't one strong unit? Like I told you yesterday, sweetie, it looked pretty innocent. He was fully dressed, for crying out loud! Lots of guys go out for one last night. Lots

150

of guys go to *strippers*. I don't think he would have done anything, either, because I know for a fact that he wouldn't have jeopardized the marriage. You know that, too. His uncle would have chopped his balls off and made him consume them."

"Jesus, Sara!" I shook my head at the thought, trying not to imagine it. Part of me knew she was right, but there was that damned photo in the back of my mind... not to mention the way he'd dumped me in this guest room.

"I'm just saying. You might have made him pretty upset last night, marrying him and then telling him that you don't trust him. That's not how a marriage is supposed to go, Elisa, and we both know it."

"None of this is how a marriage is supposed to go! And whose side are you on anyway?"

"Yours. *Always yours.* That's why I'm trying to offer some helpful advice. Because you're probably not in the best frame of mind. He *is* your husband now—for better or worse and all that bullshit."

I didn't really want to consider Sara's words, but part of me felt just the smallest twinge of guilt. Sure, I was still sitting there in my wedding dress, muddle-headed and having not even had a chance to brush my teeth, but I wasn't the only one in this sham of a marriage. Sara was right about that much. And I'd been able to tell, despite John's stoic expression last night, that I'd hurt him with my words. If anything, that bit of pain had only been emphasized by the way he'd dumped me into the guest room and left.

He'd just been giving me what I'd wanted. No... giving me what I'd basically demanded. So, yeah, maybe I wasn't being fair. We were both pawns in this, and neither of us wanted to be married, but now we were.

Deep down, I knew Sara was probably right. John wouldn't have had sex with a stripper. He wouldn't have taken his clothes off. He wouldn't have followed anyone into a back room and things wouldn't have gotten out of control. If they had, wouldn't whoever had been taking illicit photos have taken one at that point?

I paused, taking a deep breath. That was an important point. And had Sara said that, or had that been John? Either way, it occurred to me now

151

that I should have listened the first time, and maybe last night would have been a lot more... pleasant.

"I guess maybe I made a mistake," I admitted quietly.

"That's the spirit!" Sara crowed, obviously much happier with my sensible change of heart. "You're chained to the guy for life, so you might as well make an effort, not wage war."

I plucked at the skirt of my dress, not even wanting to look myself in the eye at the moment. Thank goodness Sara wasn't in the room with me, though I nodded as if she was. "I know."

"Unless you want to run away? I'm still up for it."

I could feel tears threatening again. "I can't," I said, and somehow those words had some extra weight beyond anything else I'd been thinking yet. Because they were so true—I really couldn't run away at this point, could I?

"I also know that, sweetie. I was just putting it out there, trying to be funny. What's it called? Comic relief?"

I shook my head, smiling ruefully. "Thank you for answering your phone at an ungodly hour."

"You're welcome. You owe me, though. Breakfast at a decent hour at our favorite spot? Chocolate chip pancakes?"

"You're on. I'll text you later."

"Okay. Love you."

I'd needed the reminder. I'd needed to hear Sara say it. She was the one person who I knew I could always trust. I returned the sentiment and then hung up the phone.

After I gathered what dignity I had left back to myself and took a deep breath, I scuttled out of the bedroom. I flitted down the hall in my bare feet, finding the hardwood slightly cold against my toes. I pushed open the first door I came to, on the opposite end of the hall from where I'd slept. I expected that it would be the bathroom, but I stopped dead when the dark colors assaulted me. The bed. The two dark dressers. The black-and-white abstract artwork on the wall. The upholstered leather headboard. All of it was strong and masculine.

*John's room.*

I gasped and thought to turn, but I couldn't do it. Curiosity held me captive. I looked around, but upon seeing no one, I ventured in. The bed looked unslept in, the black covers unruffled. There was a big window at the far side of the wall, but heavy black drapes covered it. I flicked on the light and stepped inside. The room was unmistakably John's. Though it was neat enough to be a room that wasn't often used, I could smell him in the space—his spicy, masculine scent lingered everywhere here, as though the smell was a living entity.

It felt dangerous being in his room, but I still found myself walking over to the mirrored closet. The room was huge, and most of it was empty. The furnishings were modern and minimal. I spotted a closed door and assumed it was an en suite bathroom. The closet stopped right before it. It wasn't the cheap mirrored kind. It was the mirrored kind that opened up into a space so expansive that moving through the entry was like entering another room entirely.

There were racks and racks of suits hanging up. Pressed black dress shirts. An entire wall of black shoes.

Everything was black.

I shut the closet door partway, leaving it just like it had been when I'd entered, and turned. My dress rustled loudly, and for a minute, I froze. I felt the urge to laugh at myself, sneaking around my new husband's room, but I also told myself that I had every right to do it. This was my home now, right? Was it really exploring or snooping if John was married to me by law?

Trying to ignore the sound of my dress and how odd it felt to be wearing it now, I turned and stared at the neatly made bed. The sharp-edged, modern nightstand beside it had a book on it. I picked it up. *Shakespeare. No way.* I opened the cover just to be sure that it wasn't one of those fake books with a hidden compartment inside. But no, it really was a book. A whole collection of four Shakespeare plays.

*Does John like reading?*

My heart fluttered like it was full of winged creatures.

I loved reading. Maybe it was one thing that we had in common.

I replaced the book and found myself moving over to the larger dresser. I didn't care for the sharp angles and the dark, almost aggressive look of it, but I couldn't help wanting to investigate further after that Shakespeare surprise. Getting closer and running my hand along it, I noticed how very masculine it was… and I thought it suited John perfectly.

I pulled open the top drawer, hoping that I'd find a T-shirt or something that I could wear in place of the dress I still had on. It had worn out any semblance of comfort a long time ago.

The first drawer contained only neatly folded socks. Of course, they were all black. But who folded their socks, seriously?

I shut that drawer and opened the one below it. I immediately slapped a hand over my mouth to cover up the laughter that was bubbling up to the back of my throat. This was John's underwear drawer. Now, I decided that I was most definitely snooping unnecessarily, but I couldn't close the drawer. I feasted my eyes on the hilarious sight before me. I'd expected black, stately, uninspiring, proper mafia underwear for a proper, stately man, but what I'd found was the exact opposite. There were colorful boxer briefs in the drawer. Striped ones. Purple ones. Silky-looking ones. His underwear drawer was more colorful and vibrant than my own. Certainly more varied.

A noise down the hall stopped me from exploring further, and I shut the drawer guiltily and dashed out of the room. I glanced left and right, but there was no one there. But I'd heard something, for sure. I was certain of it.

I definitely didn't want to get caught in John's room, so I continued on down the hall, my dress trailing after me like a companion to my shadow. Finding a T-shirt or some other change of attire would just have to wait.

Luckily, I found the bathroom right away. It was practically larger than a house, with a massive stone and glass shower, a free-standing tub that most people could only dream about, a ton of abstract artwork, a towel warmer with fluffy towels—black, of course—and a sharp-edged, modern vanity with two sinks.

I stood in awe for a few seconds before I walked over to the vanity. I didn't dare look in the mirror and see what a wreck I was, so before anything else, I turned on the tap and washed my face with cold water. It felt incredible to wash all that makeup off. I never went to sleep with a dirty face, and at the moment, I felt grimy from head to toe. I did feel somewhat better after I walked over and dried my face on one of the black towels, though. And at least black towels meant I didn't have to worry about leaving mascara streaks—ever. The towel was softer than anything I'd ever touched in my life, too.

There was a robe hanging on the back of the door. It was obviously masculine. Black, duh, and made of some low pile terry that was surprisingly soft. I slid it off the metal hook, and then I spent a good forty-five minutes working the ties open at the back of my dress. Being free from the tight lacings felt like stepping out into a cool, cleansing rain after months of drought. Once I finally stepped out of the confining thing, I couldn't believe I'd slept in it. I must really have been exhausted. The robe was much more comfortable, even though it was approximately eighteen sizes too big.

Despite my resolve to be strong, I put my nose to the fabric and inhaled. It smelled like fresh laundry soap. Not like John. Not like John's cologne. Not like John's skin. Not like his body. I let out a sigh of what I classified as relief, though it might not have been only that. At least now I could leave the room without thinking about his naked skin having been in the same garment that was now rubbing up against my naked body.

Beneath the sink, I found a spare toothbrush and toothpaste, so that was my next chore, and it came closer to making me feel like a new woman than anything else had yet. I eyed the shower next, but I really felt like I needed to find out if anyone was waiting on me first. For all I knew, movers were sitting in the hall with my stuff.

I cracked the bathroom door again and nearly jumped a mile when I found a stoic, older woman standing just outside. She was probably in her sixties, with gray hair and kind eyes.

She smiled at me sweetly. "Hello. I'm Mary. The housekeeper."

"Oh." I let out a breath.

"Sorry, dear, I didn't mean to scare you. I heard you in the bathroom and thought I'd introduce myself."

"Hi." I stuck out a hand, feeling silly in the giant bathrobe. Mary took it anyway. Her fingers were strong for being so small and delicate. "Uh— do you... do you know where John is?" I asked. I didn't want to ask where his bedroom was, because that made me want to go scarlet all over. Plus, I knew he wasn't there, assuming I hadn't missed him returning while I'd been fighting with my stupid dress.

"I'm uncertain. I didn't hear you come in last night, but this morning, I was up early and his bedroom door was open. The bed was made. He's not here."

I was about to question Mary further, since I wasn't certain that I'd heard her right, but then the echo of a door slamming came from somewhere deeper in the condo. Mary gave me a sympathetic look, but only scuttled off down the hall rather than saying anything more.

*What in the ever living hell was that?*

But unlike the odd encounter I'd just had, that door opening could only have been John. My husband. That much was clear. And unless he slammed doors all the time, I could judge from the sound that he wasn't in a good mood.

I knew I couldn't just run back to the guest room to hide like Mary had. That wasn't who I was. Instead, I braced myself and tiptoed down the hall.

John was there, all right. His hair was mussed, his suit from the day before rumpled. His collar hung open, revealing a deep V of tanned skin, and his tie hung below it, so loose that it was an afterthought. His suit jacket was gone altogether.

He paused and stared at me through bleary eyes before he walked toward the kitchen.

The whole condo was dazzlingly modern and expensive-looking, but at the moment, I didn't give a shit about any of that. No, I wanted to know where John had been all fucking night.

I stormed over, ready to lay into him about leaving me alone on my wedding night, but John grabbed a glass out of the cupboard, turned, and set it down hard on the counter. Then he gave me an even harder look.

"Before you ask, *no*, I wasn't *with anyone*. I went for a drive to clear my mind. I ended up driving for a while. Endlessly. In circles. I couldn't come back here." His voice was thick, his words loaded like a gun. Before I could comment, he went on. "I've decided that we only have one way we can do this. You have to understand that I have no reason to lie to you. As far as my family is concerned, the wedding was what was expected of me. After that commitment, our ceremony, it's been made clear to me that if I discreetly want to pursue other interests, on the side, that's fine. However, Elisa, *my wife*, I told you that I wouldn't do that, and I meant it. I plan on keeping my wedding vows."

He took a breath while I was searching for my voice, and then continued as if this was a speech he'd been rehearsing all night. "We might not be a love match, but you're now my wife, and I'm your husband. A marriage should have trust and honor, and so I have no reason to lie to you. If you think that we should work it differently, then all you have to do is say so."

I swallowed, unable to believe that John could mean all that, all of what he'd just said. The ferocious glint in his eyes told me that if I wanted to have an open marriage, or whatever people called it—a marriage in name only where we both might see other people quietly—then he'd simply find whoever it was I was interested in and put him six feet below the turf. He was baiting me, I guessed. Making me intentionally jealous. Going too far just to prove a point, as if to suggest an open marriage was what he wanted, though it was clear I wouldn't be allowed one, just from the look in his eye.

The words I'd planned earlier—an apology of sorts—vanished from my mind. I wanted to think of something biting, a retort to put John in his place, to tell him that I was too smart for whatever game of manipulation he was playing. I wanted to inform him that, as far as trust went, I would *never* give mine just because he came home with a pretty speech prepared... but then those glacier eyes of his locked onto my face. And not just my face. Those eyes dropped to my lips. The hunger in them was unmistakable, and my thoughts crawled up and died a hard death.

I actually looked at John, then. At my husband. I felt guilty for his disheveled appearance. For the dark circles under his eyes and the lines bracketing the edges of his mouth. I had driven him from his own house. From his own bed.

On our wedding night.

*He spent the whole night driving aimlessly because he was frustrated. With me.*

Something terrible in my chest compressed. I was a nurse. Truly, I normally couldn't stand the thought of causing people pain, yet, by all accounts, that was exactly what I had done.

It was even more depressing to admit to myself how lonely the night had been for me. Now, more than anything, I wanted John to come into the bedroom with me. Even last night, I'd wanted to go to his room. I'd wanted to tell him that I'd changed my mind. I'd wanted to know that he was nearby, even if that meant sleeping on different sides of the bed and not touching. Yes, I'd been angry. I'd wanted to protect myself. But now I regretted the cold reality of what John had let me put into practice. I'd hated myself for my weakness already, but now I felt that hatred all the more.

The night had been miserable. *I* had been miserable.

What if that text and that photo really were just unfortunate situations? What if they were exactly what John said they were?

John's eyes were still focused on me, and I realized that my latest thoughts had been spurred on by the sudden warmth swirling through me like droplets of undulating dye. I could feel wetness pooling between my legs, slipping down the inside of my thighs. Pressing them together didn't stop the painful throbbing, either. I knew that my body longed for John.

"I...." I got as far as that word. The rest was just a hard exhale as John's eyes darkened.

"You what?" he growled. "You regret what you said last night? When you said that you wanted to be left alone, what you really wanted was for me to lay my claim on you? The proof you want is me, isn't it? Me touching you. Me teaching you what it means to come so hard that you can't even remember your own name? Is that what you spent the night thinking about, alone, in a cold bed?"

"I…." I couldn't speak. The words refused to come. I couldn't tell him that I didn't want him. It wouldn't be true, no matter how much I'd have liked it to be.

"Tell me that you want it. I won't touch you, otherwise."

"I want to tell you that… that I'm… *sorry*." It had been hard to croak that out, and I let out a heavy breath after I did.

John's expression blanked, but then his eyes glittered, and his lips twitched at the right side like he almost wanted to smile. "I asked what you wanted, not what you were or weren't." That could have come out meanly, but it hadn't. It had been more of a friendly tease, and my heart sped up in reaction.

And the almost wicked gleam in his eyes set my blood on fire.

"I… w-want you." The words had dropped from my lips like both an oath and a curse. I knew that I shouldn't want John, but he was the equivalent of rich, exotic chocolate. I couldn't stop craving him.

John closed the distance between us in an instant. He wrapped his strong arms around me and claimed my mouth. His lips were hot and insistent, brutal, and all I could do was whimper and let him in. His tongue thrust into my mouth, but he pulled away after a few long strokes that drove me mad.

As I gasped for air, John propelled me backwards, toward the kitchen counter. He tugged the tie from the robe and it fell open, exposing my nakedness below it. The cool air of the kitchen hit my heated skin and I gasped at the change in sensation.

"There's… someone… here," I gasped out as his lips found my neck, every breath and nibble he took making me madder for him.

"Mary? She won't be bothering us." John grasped my hips and lifted me roughly onto the counter.

I wanted to protest about the possibility of someone walking in and seeing me like this, naked in the kitchen, but I knew I was already too far gone to offer any protests at all. John's fingers hooked into the lace of my pretty, white panties and tore them down my legs.

"Spread your legs. I want to see all of you."

I flushed hotly at the command, but slowly opened my legs anyway. John's piercing blue eyes turned into a dark cobalt.

"So fucking perfect," he rasped, and then his hands were everywhere.

One tangled in my hair roughly, tugging until pain seared my scalp. The other splayed protectively over my belly, his rough fingertips tracing a delicious pattern over my sensitive skin. I had to bite down on the inside of my cheek to keep from pleading with him when his fingers didn't stop. When they explored lower. They skimmed over my clit next, and I couldn't help throwing back my head and rocking into his touch. His fingers spread me apart, smearing my slick arousal over my thighs, over my belly, and then up, over my breasts.

I bucked against the cold stone countertop, wanting his hand back on my clit… wanting those fingers inside of me.

The metallic sound of a zipper brought me back from the edge I'd already been hovering on, compliments of a single fucking touch. I could barely swallow past the thick desire in my throat when John's thick erection sprang free. The ache between my legs became a living thing—a thing intent on breaking me.

John's cock was swollen at the tip, beads of shiny moisture leaking down the length of him. He slowly stroked down the length of his cock with one hand, and my core literally ached for him.

John's other hand shot out and gripped the back of my neck, bringing my eyes up to meet his in a gaze that was so intimate, it took all of my breath away. His fingers, tangled in the remainder of my curls from the day before, bit into my skin, and an erotic shiver shot down my spine. With a groan, he brought his mouth to mine and brutalized my lips in a wicked kiss that made me dizzy. Still plundering my mouth, he grabbed my hips with both hands and pulled me hard toward the edge of the counter.

I spread my legs again, wrapping them around his muscular waist as he stepped into me. I pressed my heels into the hard muscle of his ass while I wriggled closer, and his cock jammed into my stomach. I nearly screamed in frustration.

John tore his mouth from mine and ground out dark, thrilling words in my ear. "I'm going to fuck you now. I'm going to fuck you so hard that, when you come, you *will* scream my name. You *will* be mine, Elisa. Mine, not because you're my wife by law, but because you want to belong to me. So I'm going to ask you now. Do you *want* me to fuck you harder than you've ever been fucked, Elisa? If you say yes, then you need to realize that your body will always be mine. Always."

*My body.* I shivered at the truth in his words. *You can own my body. You can take that, but nothing else.*

John stopped, frozen, and I realized that he was waiting for me to say something. To tell him yes or no. As if there was any doubt about how fucking badly I *needed* him.

"Yes." It was all I could grind out. Oddly, it didn't feel like a defeat for me.

John pulled back and then, with a single, brutal thrust, he buried himself inside of me. I bit down so hard on my bottom lip that I drew blood. The copper taste flooded my mouth while John's hips flexed, filling me. He thrust slowly, dragging his cock out and pushing back so languorously that I nearly blacked out from the pleasure and the torture of it.

I gripped his back, holding him as tight to me as I could. "Please," I begged. "More."

His powerful hips flexed and he thrust into me again. He was big and I was not, and the sensation of that wrenching pain mingled with a pleasure so hot that it gripped every bit of me. My thighs shook and my belly clenched as I rocked against the counter the best I could, swaying my hips in order to take John deeper, more desperate than I'd ever been.

He thrust harder, so hard that our skin slapped together. This shouldn't have been me. I shouldn't have been the woman getting fucked on a kitchen fucking counter and enjoying it. I shouldn't have craved

161

these sounds—these sucking, wet sounds echoing through the kitchen—let alone the friction, the burn, and the delicious fullness that wanted to draw me into madness. I shouldn't have been making these little whimpers, begging for more.

But every inhale filled my nose with the sharp scent of our desire. Of our bodies.

John plunged deeper, every stroke driving me further and further towards the brink, every stroke a move of pain and pleasure dancing a merry fucking jig with each other.

John's fingers bit into my hips as he lifted me clear off the counter and slammed into me with enough force to rattle my teeth. I threw my head back and moaned. He'd dragged me clean off the edge so he could hold me there, at his mercy and enjoying every fucking moment of it. I bent back, splaying my hands over the stone to keep myself from falling over. With the new position, my back arched and my hips up in the air, John hit deeper with every brutal thrust.

I couldn't hold back. The climax hit with a fury, rolling over me with an unexpected force and brutality that I never could have expected of myself. My whole body was drawn into it. I could feel myself trembling around John. Around his cock, buried deep inside of me.

While I was still coming, John lifted me right off the counter again. His hands supported my back as he pumped into me. He was wild, slamming into me over and over again while all I could do was cling to his shoulders. My nails bit into his flesh. He threw back his head and growled out something, and then I was set roughly down on the floor without warning. John spun me around and pressed down on my lower back so that I bent over, instinctively giving in to what he wanted. My hands barely grazed the floor before I felt the hot spurts jet over my back. John let out a roar then, and the warmth kept flowing. It dripped down my legs, down *our* legs, down to my feet.

Once I had stropped trembling, I slowly straightened and turned to face him. I knew my face was scarlet again.

John acted like it was nothing at all to him to fuck me in the middle of his kitchen, to paint me with his cum and have it drip down my legs while he watched. Not nothing, though, because I could see the flames burning in his eyes... but nothing in the way that it was perfectly normal and perfectly right, even when his bloody housekeeper was just down the hall.

"Why didn't you..." I stopped, realizing what I'd been about to say.

John knew. Of course he knew. "I'm not going to wrap up to be inside my own wife, and I don't think either of us is ready for a family."

"I... I'm on the pill."

John's face twisted with sheer rage for a minute, and I realized with a jolt that he must be thinking about me with another man. It was irrational, and filled me with anger, but there was a tiny bit of me that was also thrilled at his instant, jealous response. As quickly as the cloud stormed over his face, however, it cleared away.

I didn't have to confirm or deny anything, but there was part of me that didn't want to drive the knife in any deeper. The part of me that was clearly batshit crazy, obviously. Sex weakened a person's mind. There had to be medical science to back that up.

Still, I had to tell him.... "I haven't dated anyone in a long time, and even then, it was hardly dating. Everyone was scared of my father. Once they found out who he was, they were gone. I just stayed on it because, I guess... out of habit."

There was no mistaking the relief that flashed across John's face, but then his eyes darkened and he looked feral once again.

He adjusted his clothing, zipping up his pants. "You should shower," he said roughly. "While you still have a chance."

Those crazy parts of me went wild at the dark edge to his voice, but the saner parts of me overruled them. Before I could beg him for more, and perhaps for something I didn't want to think about at the moment, I darted past him, snatched up the robe, wrapped it around me, and scurried out of the kitchen toward the safety of the bathroom down the hall.

And yet, even though I told myself that I didn't want John to join me in there... I knew I was a liar. Nothing more than a blasted liar.

# Chapter 15

## John

I was forever losing control when it came to my wife.

The night had been pure fucking torture. I hadn't been able to stand being in my own house—unable to trust myself not to break down the guest bedroom's door like a wild animal. The drive was supposed to have cleared my head, but my head had refused to be cleared. I'd ended up driving aimlessly for hours. And then, eventually, I'd thought I had it under control. That I was going to be cold. Going to go about my business. Give Elisa what she said she wanted until she came to me, begging....

But one look at her as soon as I walked in that fucking door, and suddenly all of those cold hours during the night spent rationalizing and calming myself down had been for nothing.

As soon as I walked in, I could see the flames simmering under her skin. I could smell her desire. Obviously, the night had been long and empty for her, as well. She'd changed her mind. And I was like a wolf scenting blood. I lost my head completely.

If Elisa was the flame, that made me the fluttering, haphazard moth that incinerated himself into oblivion, but I didn't care. I might have feigned control, but I could barely hold it together.

I shook my head as I grabbed some cleaning products from under the sink, and then I went to work wiping down the counter and the floor.

Elisa was right. Mary was just down the hall. A little more discretion on my part would have been advisable. I sure as shit wasn't going to leave any evidence behind.

I at least had a fuck of a lot more tact than that.

I'd promised myself that, once the wedding was over, it would be back to business. There was a rat that I wasn't any closer to catching. Someone who could have destroyed everything. If the Profacis were responsible, I needed to find out. I *needed* to stamp out the threat. That meant finding out who'd been responsible for those shots on the day of our initial luncheon together, and finding out who had taken that photo. And once I found them, I would crush them, with or without my uncle's approval.

I threw the cleaning shit back under the sink and ripped my phone out of my pocket. I dialed Dario's number and slammed it to my ear.

My brother's voice was scratchy and thick, and I was reminded that it was the morning after my wedding; even if he'd gone to bed at some point, he probably wouldn't be sober for days.

"Are you seriously calling me this early in the morning when you should have better things to do?" Dario groaned.

"I'll call you at whatever fucking time I want. You're my capo, and that means that you have a job to do."

"John. For fuck sakes, it's three in the fucking morning."

Was he serious? *Jesus Christ.* "Dario! It's nearly nine! What the fuck kind of blinds do you have on your windows? It's been light out for hours. Drink some water, sober the fuck up, and get over here. We have business to discuss."

"Business? You have a new, hot wife. Why are you worried about business and not f—"

"If you want to see tomorrow's dawn, I would suggest that you forget whatever you were about to say about my wife and do as I've asked." The thought of blasting my fist into the counter in front of me was so tempting that I barely refrained. Before Elisa, I'd never been truly *jealous* before, but now? I didn't even want her name in another man's house— whether he was my brother or not.

"Jesus. When did you turn into such a—"

x

166

I hung up before Dario could continue.

I couldn't hear the shower running because the place was too well built, but I imagined Elisa down the hall, soapy and wet. I imagined climbing into the shower with her, tasting her skin, and then trapping her up against the glass while she moaned and begged me for more. I'd taste her tight cunt, thrusting my tongue up into her heat and tasting myself there inside of her. I'd bend her over and take her from behind again, but this time, I'd spill myself deep inside of her. I'd make her fully mine.

My dick roared its approval at the fantasy.

Temporarily, I abandoned my thoughts of the rat, knowing full well that Dario wouldn't be at the condo anytime soon. I knew I could head down the hall to make better use of my time, and I was well on my way when my phone buzzed in my pocket. I couldn't turn it off, not with my responsibilities, but I did consider the merit of stepping outside and hurling it into oblivion.

I let out a curse when I saw that it wasn't Dario phoning me back to whine about my orders. I answered quickly. My uncle, as usual, got right to the point.

"There's a new rumor this morning, put out by the Profacis, that the wedding was a sham. They're saying that it's a ploy by two families afraid of losing power. Two *weak* families who need the strength of a sham alliance to hold onto what they have."

"Is that not contradictory—"

"We *cannot* afford a war with the Profacis."

Even though it was nine in the morning, the option of pouring myself a drink and sitting down to ease the throbbing in my temples seemed like a good one. "I thought the wedding was supposed to avoid war," I pointed out. Was my uncle telling me that I'd just gone through with legal, binding vows for no reason at all? But even as I thought that and Leone grumbled an answer to disagree, I glanced at the counter where I'd fucked Elisa. *Nothing at all.* What I felt about her was *not* nothing at all. I didn't want to think about *that*, though, so I focused on finding a solution. "Maybe we need to flex our power. Together. With the Gambinos. Make sure that all of our associates know what crossing us means. We could find out who was responsible for leaking the information about our lunch to the Profacis and punish them. Make an example of them and whoever fired those shots."

"Now is not the time," Leone growled. "I have something else planned. Something far more public to silence any doubts."

My skin crawled as I waited for him to expand on that. Maybe my uncle was getting old. There'd been a time when he wouldn't have hesitated to follow through with what I'd suggested. There were laws in our world, and those laws had been shattered with those bullets. The Profacis *should* pay.

And then another voice commented on the line, "I've spoken with Carlo Gambino, and we are in agreement."

I nearly dropped the phone upon hearing Nevio's slimy voice. Had my uncle really just handed me off? "What agreement?" I demanded.

"You and Elisa will go on a very public honeymoon. Photographers will be staged to prove to the world that you are very much in love. Everything is planned. Pack your bags. You leave in two hours."

"Leave? Leave for where?"

"You'll find out soon enough. We don't need to waste time discussing the details when an itinerary will be sent to you shortly."

"How could—how could you book something so soon?"

"It was a gift. The honeymoon was already planned. You were to be notified of it this morning anyway, as a final surprise. The photographers are the extra addition as of this morning, but they're not hard to find, especially when large sums of money are offered as compensation for short notice."

"We can't just leave. I have work to do—"

"Your job is to serve your family. These are your uncle's orders. Should I tell him that you aren't in compliance?"

I'd never hated Nevio more than I did in this moment.

I wished I could wipe the smugness straight out of the bastard's voice. It drove me to insanity that my uncle trusted the man and often deferred to him. Did he always have to shove my face in fucking orders and family honor?

168

There wasn't any choice here for me now, however. "You know that I'll go if it's what my uncle needs me to do," I ground out.

"It is." Nevio's greasy smile was too easy to imagine, and the triumph in his tone was obvious. "You had better pack your bags. I imagine that most of your time will be spent convincing your wife to play along."

The line went dead with that.

I barely kept myself from hurling the phone at the far wall.

"Who was that?"

I whirled. Elisa stood behind me. She was wrapped up in my robe again. Her hair was dripping wet, her face perfectly devoid of makeup. She looked fresh and clean and astoundingly beautiful. Every muscle in my body yearned to take her again, but that opportunity had passed. Instead, I had to deliver news she certainly wasn't going to like. A honeymoon was one thing, but photographers? I knew she'd hate that. She'd barely tolerated our engagement photos. And she'd probably blame me for yet another forced disruption to her life.

"Apparently, our families booked us a honeymoon."

Elisa's mouth dropped open. "What? Where? When?"

I frowned, sighing. "I haven't been filled on the where, but as to the when, we leave in two hours. Or, more like one hour and fifty-five minutes."

"Fuck," Elisa swore. She didn't look amused at my dry tone. "They could have given us some warning! I don't even have any of my—"

Before Elisa could finish, my phone buzzed in my hand. I swiped it open and found an email with an itinerary attached and a single sentence. I looked back into my wife's shocked face. At least she wasn't angry or dismayed. *Yet.*

"Apparently, your cousin has packed your bag. It will be waiting for us when we get there. And according to this email, there's an outfit on its way—so you won't have to travel there in your wedding dress or that robe."

Unamused, she simply asked, "Where's *there?*"

I passed over my phone. "I just got the itinerary. You can read all about it. By the way. Surprise?"

# Chapter 16

# Elisa

I couldn't exactly complain about a surprise honeymoon. Apparently, my uncle Carlo had planned it, and he'd spared absolutely zero expense. From the first-class flight to the private boat ride over to the island itself, our trip itinerary virtually screamed money. I'd learned, from a quick search on my cell before we'd gotten on the plane, that Bora Bora was known not only as a beautiful scuba diving attraction, but also as a place that housed luxury resorts.

And that certainly seemed true of where we were staying. Our villa was huge, and it overlooked a stretch of the clearest blue-green water I'd ever seen. It came complete with a private pool, our own chef, a fitness instructor, a diving instructor, and a concierge who we could phone on a whim.

I might actually have been excited... except that, everywhere I looked, there were little reminders that the honeymoon, like our engagement photos and our wedding, was meant to be public. I didn't need to have my father explain to me that I was an exhibit, and in the end, this honeymoon had very little to do with John or myself. I'd understood that much right from the airport, when we'd gotten out of the taxi and I'd spotted a photographer with a massive telephoto lens pointed at us.

It had been the same in the airport while we'd waited to depart, and then when we'd landed. As we'd been stepping off the plane, John had taken my hand almost immediately, and while at first the gesture had surprised and warmed me, I'd then seen the camera pointed in our direction and understood.

It was all for show.

Now, in our villa, as I rummaged through my suitcase in search of a bikini, I couldn't help thinking of the photographers again. Had they followed us to the island? I shuddered at the thought. Bora Bora felt anything but private and romantic—as a honeymoon was supposed to be, I'd certainly thought—if there were going to be cameras stalking our every move.

Had my father sent his men along, or some of the Colombo men, to keep an eye on us? At the airport before we'd left, I had spotted a man dressed in black, off in the shadows outside the main doors. I hadn't pointed him out to John, assuming him to be one of John's men watching us, but it had still made me feel wary.

Was this what the rest of our life was going to be like?

*People will lose interest. They'll stop watching soon enough.*

I couldn't wait until I could have my privacy back.

On top of the wedding and the stress leading up to it, I was exhausted from the insanely long flight and travel time from New York to our destination. We'd been in the air for over eighteen hours, and then had to wait for the boat ride over. I'd slept as best I could on the plane, but I hardly felt rested. We'd lost five hours or so, too, to the time difference, which meant that it was a beautiful afternoon outside.

As soon as we'd been shown to our villa, a luxurious building with a massive bathroom, a California king bed, and champagne waiting on ice, John had changed into shorts and a T-shirt, and declared he was heading outside.

I wasn't sure if that had been to give me privacy—though, when had that ever mattered to him?—or because he'd wanted time alone to think. He'd made it pretty clear that he needed some space. *And... did he?*

I actually had no idea. I was married to a man I knew nothing about.

I did know that he'd slept on the plane. He'd fallen asleep immediately and hadn't cracked an eye until we'd touched down. Now, I tried not to recall how peaceful he'd looked resting, or to think about spending night after night with him in bed, waking each morning next to him. Eventually, John would cease to be a stranger in body, but would he ever let me in?

*Jesus. Do I want him to let me in? Wouldn't that mean doing the same?*

I finally located a red bikini. There was only one. Sara apparently hadn't foreseen the need for more than one swimsuit over a five-day period. *Maybe she imagined I wouldn't need to wear anything at all.*

I grabbed the bathing suit and stomped to the bathroom to put it on. The space was easily one of the largest, most overdone bathrooms I'd ever seen. The glass shower, free-standing tub, and triple vanity reminded me of the massive bathroom at John's. It seemed like overkill. At least the one back home only had two sinks.

I stripped out of my travel clothes. The jeans and blouse were wrinkled and old-feeling by this point, and I was glad to peel them off. When I slid my underwear and bra off, I stood naked in the bathroom. I looked at myself in the mirror for a second before I grabbed my swimsuit. It was one of my least favorites. I'd purchased it on a whim, but the bottoms felt too small and exposed too much. The top had complicated ties that I could never get right, either. Of course, Sara would have picked this one.

I pulled on the bottoms and, after fifteen minutes, managed to wrangle the top into compliance. I had to admit it looked pretty good on me. With nothing more to do but overcome jet lag, I stepped outside into the room and stared out the patio door. The villa opened straight out onto a section of private beach. Beyond that, the tropical waters stretched into infinity, blending with the flawless blue skyline.

I decided that I wasn't going to pooh-pooh all over this trip. This was my *honeymoon*. So what if I wasn't in love? It was still a five-day vacation to one of the most beautiful destinations that I could imagine. I wasn't going to let the little details ruin it for me.

I pulled open the glass sliding door and stepped outside. It was only late spring in New York, and the heat of the day here in Bora Bora weighed down on me. It was wet and fragrant, and I enjoyed breathing the salty air into my lungs. The sun was absolutely scorching, so I figured the sand would be blazing hot when I stepped off the shaded wooden deck. I had flip-flops, though, and the water was probably refreshing.

The first thing I saw was the black-clad figure lying down on the white sand beach, right by the water's blue-green edge. John didn't own any other colors, it seemed, but for that random drawer of underwear I'd sighted. Even his casual clothing, consisting of military-issue-looking shorts and cotton T-shirts that outlined every muscle in his glorious body, were industrial and functional.

I nearly giggled again when I thought about that underwear drawer of his. He didn't know I'd seen them, of course. I wondered if he had a different drawer with just regular black underwear, and that was his spontaneous, special occasion drawer.

John didn't turn when I approached. I had a towel from the room, and I dropped it onto the sand beside him. I kicked off my shoes, biting back a curse as the sand burned my tender insoles. I ran straight for the water. It was warm and inviting, and I plunged in without giving it a second thought, diving under the surface. I swarm hard, my eyes shut tight. I was about to find the bottom and push up for air when I ran straight into something hard.

I panicked, thinking it was a rock or a shark or some other horrible ocean-dwelling creature that a person wouldn't want to butt heads with—literally—but then I felt hands grasping my arms, pulling me up. I surfaced with an undignified gasp for air, clawing at the water that streamed down from my hair.

And I stared straight up into my husband's face.

"Good god!" I spat out salt water. "How the heck did you get out here before I did?"

"When you rushed past me, I dove in, too. You're not a strong swimmer. I wanted to make sure you were okay."

I found the bottom and stood, ignoring the truth of his remark. I knew I wasn't a great swimmer, but I did well enough, and where we stood, the water was only up to my neck. I only stared at John accusingly. "Really? Now you have to watch me, too?"

"They're watching me, as well."

"Right now?"

John shrugged. "They might give us a break now and then." The warm waves only reached halfway up his chest. He hadn't bothered to shed his T-shirt before diving in, and the wet fabric pressed against his muscles like a second skin. His dark hair was flattened against his head and his eyelashes were starred with droplets. The scenery around us was beautiful, but he was another level of hard, ethereal beauty himself.

"I don't know for sure," he added, "I didn't see anyone. But if they are, we should give them what they want."

I wanted to tell him that we would most definitely *not* give anyone what they did or did not want… but then John cupped my face and tilted it up to meet his.

At first, I resisted—I truly didn't want to give anyone a show. This should be private. *For us.* John, as usual, was insistent. His lips moved firmly against mine until he felt me give in. He suckled my bottom lip into his mouth and I felt my body turn to liquid, even in the water. I felt weightless, like time and space didn't exist for us, and I couldn't stop myself from setting my hands on John's chest and leaning into him.

I half-expected him to slide his hands under the water, to private places, but he surprised me again. Nothing about John was ever expected, it seemed. He did reach down, but he swept me into his arms and carried me through the warm water, back toward land. He didn't set me down until we were back on the beach. The grainy white sand stuck to my feet, but it didn't burn my skin like it had before.

"I'd like to take you back to the room and…."

He'd trailed off, but my body burned at the thought of what he wanted to do to me there. I couldn't tell if he wanted me to beg him, to show he was wearing me down, or if he was doing it for show because there was someone within hearing distance hidden in the fucking bushes, or because he truly wanted to do dirty things to me as badly as I wanted them. Or possibly it was all three.

"Yes," I heard myself whisper as I glanced around. I couldn't see anyone, but that didn't mean there wasn't someone out there to see us.

The room was private, at least. We could shut the heavy curtains at the sliding door and be locked in a world all our own. I nodded slightly, just thinking of that.

I knew I should hold out. That I shouldn't make it so easy for John to invade my territory, to wear down my walls, but I ached for his touch. I craved it like an addict, and I had only even had it a few times. That worried me, but I stopped thinking about it the instant John scooped me up.

I stopped worrying about whoever was out there, wrapped my arms around my husband's muscular neck, and let him carry me over the burning sand. His muscles flexed below me with every step. I could feel the tendons straining in his neck, the thick veins standing out in his arms, and his chest hard and warm against my side. He was built to absolute perfection, so it was no wonder that my body wanted him. This was a battle I was going to lose to biology and hormones every single time.

John threw open the glass door and set me inside. My feet hit the cool tile and I stepped back, watching his muscles bunch and flex as he shut the door. He locked it and wrenched the heavy cream-colored drapes into place.

And then he gave me a look that was so smolderingly hot it could have fried the water right out of my bathing suit. I felt myself go instantly damp between my legs, and it wasn't the salt water that was to blame.

With a growl, John stalked across the room and lifted me clean off the floor. I wrapped my arms around his neck and my legs around his waist, and I clung to him. His skin was so hot, it felt like I'd just been thrust straight into the middle of flames. His touch incinerated me, and his sure, steady hands gripped my waist as he claimed my lips so fiercely and passionately that I lost the ability to breathe. He swirled his tongue over mine, and then the world tilted crazily as we hit he bed. Our limbs were tangled, our hands frantically trying to tear away clothing.

My top came first, the strings giving way when John deftly reached behind my neck and pulled. He peppered scalding, open-mouthed kisses along my collarbone, working downward before he claimed my breast.

There, he sucked my nipple into his mouth and bit down so that I threw back my head and cried out. He scraped his teeth over the tight bud again and painful heat flashed through me. My belly quivered and my back arched, thrusting the peak further into his mouth.

Of course, because that was what I wanted, John tore his mouth away. I grunted in frustration until his hot lips raked over my belly. His tongue swirled over my naval. He tore away my bikini bottoms, wrenching them down my legs and tossing them aside.

When he pushed my legs open, he sighed as he stared at me. I blushed instantly, but the look on his face was so intense that I didn't even dream of slamming my legs shut.

He placed another hot, open-mouthed kiss right on my core, and then his tongue swirled over me, licking me from my entrance right to my tight, throbbing clit. My back jacked off the bed and my hands fisted in the covers. His tongue teased at my clit and I thrust my hips into his face, unable to resist him.

"Come for me. Come for me, sweetheart," he uttered darkly.

I swallowed down something about his being slightly overconfident in his abilities, but then he sucked my clit into his mouth, his tongue pressing down hard on the bud as he thrust two fingers inside of me.

I ripped apart at all of my seams. The climax was hard and fast. My muscles clenched while waves of hot pleasure swept over me. I trembled with it, my belly heaving, my thighs shaking, and my inner walls clenching around John's fingers. My hips arched up, my body curling into John's face over and over. I rode him, thrashing against him while his fingers plunged in and out of me, over and over again, sending me to a dizzying new reality. When the lights, the waves, and the hot, tight heat finally subsided, I glanced down. John's chin was soaking wet. He rubbed his hand over the moisture and, slowly, while I watched, licked every droplet off.

"You're fucking delicious," he said thickly. "The sweetest thing I've ever tasted. There is no comparison."

I was still limp and weak, but John grasped my waist and turned me over, onto my hands and knees.

My muscles still trembled, and I felt little better than a limp doll, but John arranged me so hard and fast that I didn't need to worry about actually getting myself into position. He spread my legs with his hand, opening me for him again. I was slightly mortified at the intimate position, but John's hand swept down over the curve of my ass, and then down lower, until he brushed my sensitive folds from behind. I forgot all about how I might look and gripped the sheets hard.

I gasped out my pleasure as his fingers smeared my arousal over me. His warm breath curled over my thigh next, and my head swam. He'd already tasted me. I'd already come. Surely, there wasn't more? "Elisa…" John groaned. His hands gripped my hips while his tongue swept through my swollen folds. He lapped at me, eating me noisily.

My face grew flushed at the sound, but he made a few more passes with his tongue, and then there was a brush of his fingers over my clit, and I forgot about that, too. He ate me like he was starved, sucking at my pussy, plunging his tongue into me over and over again. I was sensitive, and every single movement hit me like a jolt of lightning. I swayed on the bed, helpless, bucking back into John's face.

"Yes," I whimpered. "Oh my god, that feels so good."

John laughed darkly behind me. "Sweetheart, I'm still just warming up." His fingers echoed that sentiment, circling my entrance before he plunged them deep inside of me again. I bit down on my lip to keep a scream in. He felt so thick, just with those fingers inside of me. He suckled my clit while he fucked me with his fingers, and suddenly I could feel the heat gathering again. John knew what he was doing. He was a master at pleasure. God, he was a master at torture. As soon as the heat started building in my core again, he tore his mouth away from my clit.

"John, please," I begged.

"Please what, sweetheart?"

"Taste me," I panted. I couldn't believe that I was the one saying these things. Such filthy things. But while I couldn't believe it, it excited me as well. I could feel that, too, and I knew he could see it in me—that it excited me to be so out of control. To be taken like this. From behind. Exposed. Vulnerable.

"Like this?" John's tongue danced over my clit.

"Yes!" I moaned.

"Like this?" He licked me further back and I curled my fingers into the bed's soft surface.

"Yes. God. Like that."

"How about like this?"

I froze when his tongue swept up higher. No one had ever touched me there. Why would someone want to... to do *that*? I was about to tell him no, to guide him back to my aching core, when he did. He tasted me *there*. His tongue circled that secret spot. My entire body quivered. I felt like I'd just received a jolt of electricity. I was even more sensitive there, apparently, at that tight bundle of nerves.

I was too shocked to tell him to continue or to stop, but he didn't stop. He fucked me hard with his fingers, filling me over and over again while his tongue drove me wild at my other entrance. The heat gathering this time was entirely different than what I'd felt before. It was sharper. More intense. My stomach hurt with trying to contain it. My legs trembled so hard that I wondered how they still held me up.

"Let go," John commanded me. "Let go, Elisa." His fingers curled inside of me, hitting a spot that I hadn't even known existed. The room narrowed until it turned into a pinprick of light, and then there was nothing but darkness. The climax burst over me—not an explosion of light, but an explosion of black. There was nothing but darkness. A sea of inky, purple night that I swam through. A sea of fire and pain and exquisite pleasure. I drowned in that sea, struggling for air. Struggling to maintain my existence.

I struggled not to lose myself completely.

I screamed, I let myself go, and I came. I came until I thought I would die if the waves didn't release me from their grip. I came over and over again, until I could no longer hold myself up. I came until I was just a whimpering mass—panting, aching, and so fucking sated.

I finally peeled my eyes open to find John kneeling behind me. One hand was at my waist, keeping me upright. "Oh my god," I whispered, awe in every word.

John grinned at me, and right then, I knew he was the devil himself. He stood up, letting me enjoy every second of the show. He peeled away his clothing, revealing his powerful, beautiful body below. My mouth went totally dry as I watched him palm his massive erection. He was so thick that I doubted I'd be able to wrap a hand around him, but he didn't ask me to touch him. Instead, he smoothed his hand over the thick, angry red tip, smearing the beads of liquid down the length of his shaft.

He watched me carefully while he touched himself, and it sent tendrils of fire curling through my belly. Frozen there before him, I waited for John to claim me fully. To take what was his, because there was no doubt in my mind that my body had surrendered completely. He'd made my flesh and bone a traitor to the delicious pleasure that he could awaken in me.

He gripped my ankle and tugged me toward the edge of the bed. I let out a strangled cry of surprise, and the sheets that were still gathered in my fists tore free and came with me. I balled my hands into them as John's massive cock rammed up against my entrance, the thick head spreading me open. I mewled, but my legs opened wider and I wriggled my hips to take him. He didn't slide in fast, only going inch by inch, teasing me.

And then, without warning, he filled me with one wicked thrust.

I screamed. I threw my head back and chanted his name as he pulled out and filled me again. His second thrust was harder, stretching me painfully, but the third one was faster, and this time I was ready, my body already accommodating his thickness. My inner walls clenched around him and each hot drag of his thick cock sent me spiraling down into an abyss of pleasure.

I clawed at the bed while he thrust harder, his hips pumping into me. Our skin slapped together, the bed fucking moved an inch, and I cried out something incoherent, but I didn't care. I wanted this. I *needed* this. Wild, hot lust ripped through me as John pumped into me, over and over and over again. My inner walls clenched around him and my legs trembled so violently that I wasn't sure how I wasn't a heap on the bed, but he just kept going.

The fire that burned through me built to a blinding point, and suddenly I was coming again. The pleasure assaulted me, mingling with the beautiful pain radiating through my sore muscles. I nearly blacked out as wave after wave crashed over me.

John pumped harder, and I could feel my body clenching around him again with every wicked thrust. He went wild, and it was all I could do to hang on to my sanity. I wasn't prepared for the roar next to my ear. I was totally unprepared for the seductive wave of heat that overwhelmed me at feeling John lose control.

He came hard, deep inside of me. The hot jets filled me, and then overflowed me and trickled down my thighs.

*He'd claimed me.* Marked me as his. And I was stunned, because nothing this… this *dirty* should have been this *hot*. I shouldn't have wanted to be claimed. I shouldn't have wanted to be marked. I shouldn't have wanted to be his.

I managed to shift myself away from the edge of the bed before I collapsed. I crawled up to the pillows and gripped one with what little energy I had left. I had zero bones left in my body. I couldn't even be bothered to fight John or pull away when he slid onto the bed behind me. He didn't tug me into his arms, but he did drape one over my hip. His hand splayed out over the curve of my side, his fingers flat against my belly.

Lying there, I realized how badly I'd needed the release that he'd given me. And I'd need more, too. I'd always need more.

It had never been like that before. Not with anyone. Ever.

My eyes were heavy, and when they drifted shut, I didn't bother to fight the blackness closing in. I was too comfortable. I realized that, too. Too *content*. It was just the aftermath of what we'd done, I told myself as I gave into the feeling. It wasn't a real emotion. I couldn't trust the safe feeling I felt when John's arm was wrapped around me.

I couldn't trust that at all.

No. It was just the afterglow I was feeling, that's all.

181

# Chapter 17

## John

I never planned on falling asleep beside Elisa, but I woke with a start to find the room dark. I shifted off the bed carefully so that I wouldn't disturb her—my wife. She was sleeping soundly, her shoulders rising and falling evenly. I threw on a fresh set of shorts and walked over to the patio door. There, I pulled back the thick drape and stared outside. It had probably been dark for hours. Beyond the stretch of white sand, the ocean beckoned.

"Thinking about going for a swim?"

I turned to find Elisa studying me. Her hair was mussed wildly on one side. Her cheeks were flushed from sleep, and a sheet crease ran from her chin all the way to her right eye. She was entirely too adorable.

My hand tightened on the drapery before I let it fall back into place. One didn't find their wife adorable. One found their wife alluring. Enticing. Sexy. Beautiful. *Adorable* was a new word for me. It might not have been a big one for anyone else, but for me, it was so much more than just eight letters.

"I was."

Elisa threw back the sheet and, for a moment, my blood surged. She walked over to her suitcase and grabbed out some kind of a gauzy-looking cover-up and slipped it on. The green matched her jade eyes, and the sheer fabric wasn't doing anything to calm the raging erection I had going.

"I think the night is the best time for a swim. The sun isn't so brutal. The water is probably calmer. The sand won't burn the crap out of my feet." She smiled shyly. "I don't know. Do you think it's more romantic?" When I looked at her blankly, she smiled back. "I think it is."

She walked past me and pushed back the drapery, and then she slid open the door. I was just about to ask her about a bathing suit when she took off running, her hair flying out behind her as she laughed her way happily down to the beach.

She looked like a nymph, and all I could do was stare. Beneath the bright moon and ethereal stars, she could only be described as a vision.

Sand puffed out behind her with every light step. She flew over the beach, casting aside the gauzy cover-up when she neared the tide. She didn't stop when she reached the water's edge, but kept going and then dove in. She swam hard, and like it had during the afternoon, my heart rate increased.

What if she ran into an undercurrent? A tide she wasn't expecting?

I slipped out the door without bothering to close it fully behind me. I was running across the sand, my bare feet churning it up, before I even knew what I was doing. With my long stride, it only took a few seconds before I reached the water. I plunged in, the coolness being a sudden reprieve from the warm night and the sticky humidity that had hit me full blast upon our door's opening.

I spotted Elisa at least fifty feet away. She was treading water. When she saw me, she threw back her head and laughed. "It's nice, isn't it?" she called out.

I swam for her. I was a good swimmer, and my powerful strokes took me closer in moments. I kicked hard. The water was calm, but as I'd suspected, there was some sort of undertow that tugged against me. Elisa bobbed up and down in the water. She appeared to be getting further away, even though I was swimming as fast as I could. She clearly had no idea of the danger.

I wanted to call out for her to stay where she was. And I opened my mouth to do it, but all that came out was a cry of pain. The cramp in my leg had struck without warning. It was vicious, attacking my thigh and spreading lower, down my knee and into my calf muscle. I grabbed for it on instinct and went under.

I broke the surface gasping for air, spitting water out of my mouth. The salt stung my eyes, and the pain in my leg didn't let up. Instead, it burned stronger, like someone had opened me up and stuck in hot coals and sharp knives. I felt like my entire leg had been split open, all the skin flayed off and the muscles exposed to the stinging salt.

I tried to make a sound, to keep myself floating, to use my arms to stay on top of the surface, but the cramp was too strong. I couldn't move my leg, and when I couldn't kick, I floundered. My head went under, the water rushing up to meet me. It spilled into my mouth and rushed down my throat in an acrid burst. I tried to kick, but with only one leg, it was useless. I used my arms alone to propel myself back up to the surface, where I gasped out a breath before the water closed in on me again.

The darkness came fast, the black of the sky above and the dark water below. The bottom was too far away for me to even think of touching it or pushing off, let alone with my leg feeling as it was. My arms burned with the effort of trying to find the surface alone, and the undercurrent sucked at me from below, pulling me down. *Sucking. Tugging.* My lungs screamed for air. Every cell in my body cried out for that life-giving substance. Elisa was out of my mind now—I could only focus on survival, my lungs were so desperate. I had one last burst of energy, and even with one leg, I used it to try to fight my way to the surface.

I connected with something solid, my fingers brushing against it. At first, I thought it might be a rock, but rocks didn't float and I hadn't come up on a shallow stretch. My leg still hung uselessly down below me, suspended in water. I flung my arms about madly, trying to connect with it again, but there was nothing but water.

I felt like my head was going to explode now. Bright lights bloomed like colorful flowers behind my eyes.

Something soft brushed at my shoulders. A shark? I panicked, trying to turn and spin around. Suddenly, that softness turned into something hard and firm. *Firm hands.* They closed around my shoulders, and I was propelled upward. Up, toward the surface. When it gave way and I broke through, I gasped and choked, eager to get at the oxygen that I'd so desperately needed.

I gagged and spluttered, rasped in and out, my lungs like rusty bellows. Vaguely, I was aware of those hands still helping to support me as my leg screamed with pain. My throat stung, and my leg was worse than useless as those hot coals burned from the inside out. My eyes could barely focus on anything.

*"It's all right."* Elisa's gentle voice came to me like a siren's song, except that instead of luring me to my death, she'd just saved me. "Just relax. We'll make our way back to shore together. You can float if you don't struggle. Are you okay? I've got you."

I wanted to laugh at the absurdity of that statement. Elisa was half my size—delicate, gentle, and kind, but she was also calm and certain. And, somehow, she was helping me remain afloat.

I remembered, somewhere through the slog of water in my brain, that she was a nurse, and so she'd been trained to deal with a crisis. Thank god.

"It's not that far." Her hands stayed under my shoulders. Now that I was on the surface and the panic had passed, with Elisa's help, I did float far more readily. She guided me, half-swimming, and half dragging my useless ass along in her wake.

It might have been humiliating, but I was so damned thankful for the air I was pulling into my traumatized lungs that I said nothing.

Elisa had *saved* me. With her hands still on me, I realized how easily I could have drowned.

"Cramps are a bitch," Elisa said as we got closer and closer to the beach. "They can take down anyone. I wouldn't feel bad. You could be the best swimmer and still run into trouble. It happens more often than you think."

"I know you're a nurse, but I didn't realize you were a lifeguard," I rasped. My throat felt horrible, parched and painful. She really hadn't looked like all that strong of a swimmer earlier that day.

"I'm not. But I have been swimming since I was a kid—I'm a sloppy swimmer, but I do fine. Sara got a cramp once in our pool. She just went straight under. I had to save her, too. Luckily, she didn't need mouth to mouth."

"And me?"

"I think you're going to be fine," Elisa said dryly. She turned, though, and I could see she was actually smiling. She knew the danger was over.

As soon as my feet dragged the bottom, Elisa released me and I hobbled out with her help. I threw myself down on the beach. Elisa, who wasn't wearing any clothes, retreated to the water. I could tell she was touching the bottom, but all that was visible above the inky surface was her neck. Her hair floated around her on the surface of the water. She looked like a sea sprite. I didn't think she was too deep, though, she seemed so close—I suspected she was crouching down, to keep herself covered by the tide and still keep an eye on me.

I massaged the cramp from my leg, feeling the muscles like stone under my hands. I'd never felt anything like it.

Apparently, shit like this was why people said you should always swim with a buddy.

After most of the pain was gone and my muscles were sore but soft again, I got slowly to my feet. I walked up the beach and got Elisa's cover-up. I held it out toward her and watched as she walked out of the water, a living vision if I'd ever seen one. I watched as she tugged on the thin garment and then lifted her wet hair. The garment clung to her wet skin, soaked instantly, outlining her lush curves.

"I was going to suggest stripping down right here on the beach actually, but getting sand up the butt crack would suck."

My lungs emptied out in sudden laughter and I felt an entirely brand new burn start—also from lack of oxygen. She only grinned at me as I caught my breath.

"Speaking of mouth to mouth, I was thinking that I might try giving it to you anyway. You disappointed me by not completely drowning out there, so I didn't have to do it." She reached up and gripped my shoulders. One hand found the wet hair at my neck and twisted a strand coyly.

"That's very funny," I said dryly. I knew she wasn't going to let me live this down anytime soon, but I found that I actually didn't mind the teasing. "I bet if I had died out there, your life would have been a lot easier," I told her quietly.

A shadow darkened Elisa's eyes—so much so that I could see even in the darkness around us, just by the light of the moon and stars. "Don't say things like that. We might be kidding around, but that's not funny."

"Because you might care just a little, or because you're a nurse and that's not in good taste?"

Her forehead wrinkled. "Just the latter, I guess." I could see that wasn't entirely true, and it hit me hard.

If she cared and I cared that she cared, what did that say about me? My own emotions? What I was starting to feel whenever she was around? And, god, even when she wasn't. And we'd only known each other for days, yet.

"I think a warm shower would be nice," Elisa said, changing the subject. She broke away and started up the beach, but just before she reached the door to our villa, she turned and glanced over her shoulder.

My jaw nearly hit the sand when I realized that she actually wanted me to join her.

I wasn't going to wait around for her to change her mind, though. Whatever had come over her, whatever our differences, whatever problems we still had to work out, the physical stuff clearly wasn't one of them.

At least we had something.

And the fact that my wife might be half my size and not a brute like I was, but she could still save my life in a pinch… we had that, too. It wasn't something that I'd forget anytime soon, that sensation of drowning, the lights that had burst behind my eyes, and the way my whole body had screamed in agonizing pain.

I brushed off the feeling of terror that had begun to close up my throat and hurried up the beach.

A shower sounded like the perfect way to wash the incident away, especially if my beautiful, willing wife was in it waiting for me.

# Chapter 18

## Elisa

The swim had scared us both, but I couldn't complain about the aftermath. Despite nearly drowning, my husband had definitely held up in the shower. And afterward, in the bed. And again on the desk. I wasn't starting a new trend with furniture or anything, but I wouldn't forget that. We'd finally fallen asleep only when we'd both been too exhausted not to.

The next morning, after sleeping in, and then enjoying food that had been prepared and brought to our room by an exclusive chef just for us, we decided on another swim. I'd thought John might be afraid to go back out into the water, but I quickly realized that there was nothing my husband feared. He didn't mind that the water had given him one hell of a fuck-you the night before. He plunged right in—swimming after me and then beside me, still watching to make sure that I was fine even though it had been me who'd saved him the night before.

I might have acted calm during all that, I knew, but I'd been terrified. Thinking of it today, I was just relieved that I hadn't had to try to breathe life back into him right there in the middle of the water. Dragging an unconscious form back to the beach and performing frantic CPR would have been much worse.

I didn't think my heart had stopped knocking at my ribs for hours after it had happened.

So far, my honeymoon had definitely been eventful. And it was a beautiful day out now—the sun hot and bright overhead, the scene before us something that I could only ever have imagined from watching movies or seeing travel ads.

When we headed in to shore, tired from swimming, John glanced off to the right. It was clear that he wanted to stay out on the beach, and I wasn't going to protest.

It both alarmed and amused me that we seemed to be on the same wavelength, for once.

There were umbrellas and chairs off to the side that I hadn't particularly noticed before. John dragged a couple over, moving the huge umbrella last. He looked ridiculous doing it... ridiculously sexy in those wet clothes that were glued to his body, that is, but also sort of funny. It made me feel strangely shivery inside, in that he didn't just call for some attendant. They were undoubtedly waiting in the wings, probably not far off, ready to do absolutely anything for us.

I sprawled out on the hard wicker chair. It was quite ornate for something that had to live its life on a beach. It was shaped like any other patio lounger that a person would find poolside. Comfortable, I glanced up at the sun overhead and thought of how bronzed I would be after five days underneath it.

John stretched out beside me. He folded his arms behind his head and I wondered what a stranger would think if they were watching. Did we look like a relaxed couple, stretched out and staring at the gorgeous scenery? Did we look like we were happy? Did we look like we could be in love? I lay back thinking about that, closing my eyes.

"I'll be right back," John said after a bit of time had passed. I turned in my chair, but he was already up and walking away.

It gave me butterflies to stare after him. He was truly built like a god. No wonder my body betrayed me with him, over and over again. A nun would have betrayed her vows for a man who looked like John.

My skin started to buzz, and I felt heavy and achy between my legs, so I turned my attention back to watching the placid ocean. There was hardly any breeze, and it was so flat, I thought that if I threw a rock out there, the ripples would just have to carry on forever.

John was back soon, carrying a plate of cut-up fruit and two bottles of pale amber beer. I wondered if he'd gone to the room and called for it, or if he'd run to one of the buildings behind our villa. The bottles were so cold that they were already soaked in droplets of condensation.

I had to laugh. "You're quite dexterous," I told him as John passed over the plate. There wasn't much that I recognized besides pineapple and strawberries. I accepted a beer and took a long pull of that first. The ice-cold bubbles felt like heaven tracking down my dry throat. When I licked my lips, I tasted salt from the ocean.

John surprised me again when he sat down and held out his bottle. He clinked it against mine. "Cheers," he said, predictably—like a normal person.

"Cheers," I echoed. I wasn't sure if this was just for show or not, but I pushed the thought from my mind.

I tried a yellow piece of fruit. I didn't know what it was, but it tasted pleasant. It might have been a mango, but it was so fresh that it was actually hard to tell. Everyone said that fresh, tropical fruit would ruin grocery store produce forever. I could see why.

The strawberries were just as delicious.

"I know you might disagree, and I won't push you, but I think we should talk."

I nearly dropped the plate of fruit onto my lap. My bottle of beer was tucked between my legs, cold and wet. I rested my hand on it and looked back at John. My *husband*. "Talk?"

"Talk. Get to know each other."

I wanted to laugh. The idea seemed so absurd. We'd had sex quite a few times now, in the most intimate of ways. None of those times had shown us to be anything close to shy or any shade of vanilla with each other. We'd said vows, too, giving ourselves to one another legally. *Now* he wanted us to get to know each other?

John grinned at me. "I know what you're thinking."

"You always seem to know."

"You have a very expressive face."

I huffed.

"That's not a bad thing."

"For you, it would be. In your line of work."

"Are you accusing me of being stoic?" Just to be an ironic bastard, he looked anything but at the moment.

"Yes. You're absolutely unreadable," I insisted. "I know you've spent a lifetime perfecting it, too, so don't pretend otherwise."

My comment hadn't been intended to draw blood. It was simply a fact, and my father was the same way, but despite that, a shadow crossed John's face. He sat silently for a moment, and then he turned to me looking so serious that he could have *redefined* stoic with his stony complexion.

"Can I ask you something? If we're talking?" I asked.

John nodded. Still, I really didn't know how to tell him what had been bothering me. I'd wanted to talk to my dad about it, but with the wedding and everything happening so suddenly, I hadn't had a chance. I didn't know what to say to my dad, though, either—or how to say it in a way that my dad would understand. "Do you promise you won't make fun of me?" I asked, more quietly.

John gave me a strange look. "I won't make fun of you."

I sighed. "At the lunch that day—you know. *The lunch*...."

"Yes. I know."

Of course he knew. I'd have laughed at myself for doubting that if what I wanted to talk about hadn't been so serious. "I... there was a man. One of *your men*. Or, well, one of your family's men, I mean. Um, he was standing at the back wall in the room, with the other guards. I know that those men are supposed to be big and look scary. My dad has plenty of creepy-looking guys, but I always knew they wouldn't hurt me. That they've been around to help protect me. This guy, though... I don't know. I caught him looking at me and he was... it was *strange*. I don't think it was in a kind sort of way, is what I'm saying. Trying to say, anyway. He wasn't leering at me, but there was... something in his eyes, I guess. They were horrible. It made me feel afraid."

John didn't laugh. Far from it. His expression had turned grim, like he considered my fear a great affront. "You remember what he looked like?" he asked.

I frowned, trying to recall. "I do know he was older. Not a young guy at all. Also—there was something about his face. I don't know, not disfigured really, but something... I'm sorry, he was standing too far away for me to see him clearly."

"That's fine," John said. "I'm pretty sure I know who you're talking about."

"Oh?"

John nodded. "He is a creepy bastard, but I promise that he would never hurt you or any of your family. He's intense, but it's because he takes his job seriously. He's been with us for a long time. Ever since I was a kid."

I processed what John had said. He seemed so sure of himself. And I appreciated that he hadn't laughed, but I still wanted nothing more to do with that man—ever. "He's scary. My dad doesn't have any men who look like that," I added belatedly, feeling silly for pointing it out even as I said it. Was it really just that weird face that had bothered me so much? I didn't think so, but it was so hard to put my impression into words.

"I'm sorry if you were afraid, but I promise you my uncle's men are here to ensure your safety now, as well as my own."

I thought about telling John about the man I'd seen in the shadows at the airport, but that would probably sound a little too much like I was complaining, and I didn't want to be annoying. I didn't want him to think that I was trying to pick apart his family or find fault with his men. I hardly knew about even my father's men, really, other than the drivers and the guards he sometimes sent for me. John was far more immersed in the life than I was.

"If it makes you feel better," John went on, "I did tell my brother that I'd stay in contact while I'm here. I can tell him to keep an eye on the guy. Possibly put a tracker on his phone or his car."

I didn't know what to say to that, but I was surprised. I really hadn't thought that John would take me seriously. And here he was doing just that. He wasn't dismissing my fears at all, and that made me feel something much warmer than the hot sun glaring down at us from above.

"Would you really?" I asked.

"I can talk to Dario."

"Your brother. He was on the sidewalk that night."

"I didn't know who you were."

"Really?" I paused. "But he did."

"He did, but he didn't tell me."

The plate of fruit and the beer were both cool against my leg. I picked up a piece of pineapple, but I didn't eat it. I stared at the sweet yellow fruit as I thought about how strange it was that our fates had somehow twisted together like this, and now we were here. That night felt like it had been centuries ago.

"Thank you," I found myself saying. "For what you did that day. At lunch. I never did thank you. I yelled at you, if I remember correctly."

He smiled. "It was more of a scathing retort."

"Hmm. You literally covered my body with yours so that I wouldn't have to take a bullet. You did it without even thinking. You got to me before my dad's guards even had a chance. I really am sorry that I was nowhere near grateful."

"You were worried about your family. Scared. Stressed. It was excusable."

I raised an eyebrow at him, amused that he'd be willing to make so many excuses for me. "I think I offered to kick you in the nuts," I pointed out.

"But you didn't."

"No. But I wasn't nice, either. That's not me."

John's eyes narrowed, but it might have been because the sun was extra bright overhead. "You saved me last night. I think that might make us even. Except that I was about two seconds away from really being dead. I don't think there was any real danger at the lunch, so you might still have the upper hand."

I laughed, and finally popped the pineapple into my mouth. The sugary, tangy juices rushed over my tongue. God, the food here was amazing. "I won't tell anyone, if that's what you're worried about. It can be a secret."

"Good. I wouldn't want anyone knowing that a leg cramp could take down the heir to the Colombo family."

194

I grew serious, thinking about that. John was in line after his uncle. I was my father's daughter, of course, but I'd always tried to separate myself from that part of his life. I'd never been expected to take up the business and keep things going after he was gone. He'd never actually talked to me about any of that before—even the possibility of it.

But I didn't want to think about those things at the moment. We were actually doing all right so far. Away from New York, away from our families, away from our regular life, we were both out of our comfort zones.

We were two strangers, just regular people.

Out here, I didn't feel like I had to worry about protecting myself, about the power struggle, or even about my desperation to cling to my independence. I did still have my guard up when it came to the deeper, more meaningful things, but my body was willing enough. And it helped that John seemed different here. Lighter. Or maybe it was me who was entirely different. Who wasn't looking for a fight at every turn. Who wasn't trying to be this tough, unfeeling person that I wasn't because I had to do that in order to hang on to the pieces of me that were still me.

"I've decided that I'm going to tell you something," John said softly, breaking into my thoughts. I turned from the gentle waves and stared at him, curious now. "Something about me. About what happened when I was younger. That way, maybe you'll see that you can trust me. Not just to keep my vows, but as a husband. Maybe we can start to actually make this marriage work."

My mind spun. Was that actually what John wanted? To make this work? Or was this just another trick? It seemed real, but was that possible? Was this John that I was seeing on my honeymoon the real John? The John who also didn't have to be so tough and impenetrable? Or was this softer, more understanding man going to disappear as soon as we left?

I didn't know what to think or whether I was supposed to reciprocate with something deep and meaningful. Silence was often the best tactic, though, so I stayed quiet, nibbled another strawberry, and waited.

# Chapter 19

## John

*Would talk of death put a damper on the beautiful, sunny day?*

The question was moot, as I knew that it would, but I'd already decided that I'd tell Elisa about my parents. If I opened up and told her something deeply personal, maybe she could finally put to rest her suspicions about me, and perhaps even some of her fears. It was worth the attempt.

"My parents used to take vacations sometimes," I began. "I don't know if vacation is the right word exactly, but they'd spend time away together. They were deeply in love. We were young, Dario and me. It was hard for my dad, I'm sure, being so involved with the business and having a young family."

Elisa nodded solemnly. I was sure she could relate to that much. She'd grown up in the same life I had. That alone made me feel more connected to her than I ever had to another woman. No other woman I'd ever been with had been connected to what we did. Elisa might not have wanted to be part of the life, but she had an intrinsic understanding of what it meant.

"They'd usually rent a yacht. They enjoyed getting away and seeing new places. We'd do family getaways together, as well, but those trips were for me and my brother. My mom was a planner. She liked to include special things that kids would enjoy. We never went on a yacht or a sailboat with them, though—my parents thought of that as their special time."

Elisa picked up another strawberry and chewed thoughtfully. "I'm sure it must have been nice to get away like that."

"It was. Even as a kid, I understood that."

Elisa braced herself—visibly so. It was pretty apparent that this story wasn't going to end well. She must have known that my parents were dead. I'd already started, however, and I couldn't stop, so I kept going.

"No one knows what happened... not exactly. They were on a yacht together in the Caribbean. The boat caught fire during the night. There was only one survivor. A deck hand. When he was found, he'd been in a lifeboat, floating aimlessly for five days. He was delirious. It was days after that before anyone could put together what had happened, before he could tell anyone what he'd seen that night. He said that he'd dozed off in the engine room, and was awakened by what sounded like gunshots. There was smoke everywhere. He thought he heard the sound of another boat speeding away, but the smoke was so thick that he couldn't see a thing. The yacht was already engulfed in flames, but he managed to make it to a lifeboat. He called out to the other crew, my father's men, anyone, but he never got a response. He freed the lifeboat, but he had no way to make a distress call. I guess no one did. On top of that, the captain hadn't filed his route with the authorities, and it took an additional six days after that deck hand was found to locate the spot where the yacht had sunk."

The silence between us was heavy and uncomfortable. I'd never told anyone, in such detail, about what I knew of that night. The facts still haunted me. I'd just been a kid when my uncle had sat me down and given me those details. I could still hear Leone's voice. I could still see the tears shining in my uncle's dark eyes, and the heavy creases of sorrow already adding years to his face.

Now, I found that, unexpectedly, there was a heavy, burning sensation at the bridge of my nose. It took me a minute to figure out what the sensation was. I hadn't cried since I'd been eleven or twelve years old, and even then, it had been because Dario was an asshole, and while play fighting, he'd punched me straight in the face. He'd nearly broken my nose and my eyes had burned with tears that I'd barely been able to hold back.

But there'd been no room for emotion in my life before Elisa. I'd thought about my parents' death often over the years, but all I'd felt had been confusion mingled with rage. A sense of injustice. A burning desire to find out what had happened and take my revenge. I'd lost the normal emotions that accompanied grief a long time ago, so I was astounded and ashamed now, to find all that returning.

Elisa reached out, but when I froze, she let her hand fall to the arm of the chair. She reached for her beer instead and sipped it. I realized that I'd told her my story in order to build up her trust, but by denying her connection and sympathy, I might have just ruined what tenderness she could have felt for me.

I stared off at water lapping the beach until my eyes and nose stopped burning.

"I'm sorry," Elisa sighed. "About your parents. I didn't know what happened. My… my mom was killed in a car accident when I was young, as well. Growing up without her was so hard. I missed her all the time. My father loved her very much. He was never the same after that, but I know I'm lucky to still have him. I also had my aunt and Sara. We're very close."

I said nothing, though I could hear the truth of her words in her voice. There was just nothing more to contribute to a family discussion. My uncle had not been like a father figure. He'd raised Dario and me, made sure we had our needs met, but his wife had passed long before we'd been in the picture, and he'd had no notion of how to be nurturing. Still, we'd survived. Grown. Taken our places in the business. That was enough.

"I missed her most on our wedding day." Elisa's voice cracked.

*This was a terrible idea.* Instead of getting to know each other, we were trading griefs that couldn't be changed. What had I been thinking? This wasn't going to help her trust me more. This was going to make her see me as *weak*. A man who got choked up when thinking about his long-dead parents. It was pathetic, really. In my world, men might be warm toward their wives and children—loving, even, if it came to it— but emotional? Men did not get emotional.

199

Elisa reached out again, and this time her fingers fluttered over my arm. "I do understand, John. Really." Her eyes brimmed with pity. "You don't have to be so strong when you're with me. It's perfectly all right to—"

I couldn't help it. I pulled my arm away. The hard reality of my position in life was chasing away whatever irrational softness had permeated the moment, and I had to let it.

"They were murdered by a rival family, Elisa. I'm sure of it," I said, my voice flat. "It was too convenient, otherwise."

I glanced over to her, wanting to judge her reaction, and saw that Elisa looked like she'd just been hit with a vat of scalding oil. The pity had vanished from her eyes, and she stared at me, apparently trying not to comprehend the meaning behind my words. "What do you mean?"

"It had to be a rival family." Seeing her face, though, I realized that I had jumped way the fuck over lines that should never have been crossed. The only rival family with enough power to take down my parents, at that time, had been the Gambinos. In other words, Elisa's father.

Her cheeks turned scarlet as my words broke down the walls of her incredulity and shattered the peace between us. "You're saying that… that you really think that my…. that my dad could have…."

I felt my mind stutter in reaction, trying to figure out why I'd ever thought to bring all this up, and do it so clearly. Now that the damage was done, I couldn't work some force of magic and undo it. And Elisa had no qualms about showing *her* emotion. Her face crumpled and her dark eyes swam with unshed tears. I wanted to put a bullet in my own head or bust up my own knees for hurting her. For covering for my own inability to process the shit I had gone through by throwing out something so toxic as this. Even if it might have been the truth.

"There was *speculation* that it was a hit. I'm not saying that out of hindsight." I tried, and failed, to defend myself and what I'd suggested. I knew I was doing irreparable damage, though, and so I tried to offer some sort of doubt by way of apology. I forced myself to shrug. "Just forget what I said. I didn't mean it."

"Didn't mean it, John? What the fuck? How can you not mean something like that? *Oops, sorry, I just accidentally accused your dad of indirectly killing my parents. It just slipped out.* That's what you're saying?"

"No!" I raked a hand through my nearly dry hair. The residual salt felt sticky between my fingers. "Just… I shouldn't have said that. It's the past. It happened a long time ago. We're living *now*, and that's all that matters."

"There was never any proof!" Elisa went on. She was working it out for herself, ignoring what I'd just said. "There couldn't have been, or your family would have moved against mine. There would have been a bloody war!"

"There was enough bloodshed without proof, until the truce."

Elisa glared at me, eyes flashing. "Don't give me a history lesson on my own family! I know what my father is and isn't capable of, and he would *never* do something like that!"

Elisa grabbed the plate of fruit and punctuated her statement by hurling it at me. She missed, but a strawberry smacked me on the forehead in passing. Then she stood sharply, reaching for her bottle of beer, but I exploded out of the chair and deftly plucked it from her hand. Her face twisted up and her nostrils flared, but god help me, she was still beautiful.

"I could forgive you for a lot of shit, John Colombo, but I will *never* forgive you for this."

"Yeah, well, your last name is Colombo now, too, sweetheart."

"It might be," she hissed, "but at heart, I'll always be a Gambino, and you'll always be a monster."

"A monster. How classically old-fashioned of you." I forced myself to sneer back at her.

"A… a… monster shithead, then!" She kicked sand in my direction before she turned and stormed off toward our villa.

I watched her go, knowing that I'd just executed a masterful fuck-up. I hurled Elisa's beer into the sand, peeled off my shirt, and strode purposefully back toward the ocean. This honeymoon wasn't exactly going to be filled up with marital bliss. If I exhausted myself with a swim, maybe Elisa would sense that I didn't have the energy to fight with her whenever I finally made it back to the room.

# Chapter 20

## Elisa

My honeymoon might have gone down as the worst in history. Certainly, it had been the most silent. After that last conversation on the beach, I'd stayed in the room most of the time, or gone out on the beach alone. When John hadn't been brooding silently in the vicinity, I'd had no idea where he was. We'd shared the bed at night, but with it being so massive, we hadn't had to sleep anywhere close to each other.

I thought I'd set a record for the least words I'd ever said in a week's time. The last thing I'd said to John had been that he was a monster shithead. I'd been satisfied to let that juvenile description linger.

At least he had no doubt what I thought about him and his ridiculous notion of the past.

It had been a relief to get home, even though I did feel totally jetlagged. The second after John dumped his bag in the doorway of the condo, he disappeared without a word. That suited me just fine. I spent the first day back sorting out the boxes of my things that had arrived while we'd been gone. I'd packed up a lot before the wedding, Sara and Maria had packed up everything else, and then it had all been sent on over. My furniture had gone into storage.

After the trip, it was nice to get a good sleep in my own bed, even if it wasn't technically my own. I claimed the guest bedroom fully now, refusing to share a bed with my turd of a husband.

Tuesday morning, I woke up feeling refreshed. I purposely put thoughts of John from my mind as I showered and dressed. If I'd been talking to him, I would have told him that I was going for lunch with my father that day, and that I had an interview that afternoon. The hospital had called me on the third day of our honeymoon, asking me if I'd like to come in for one. I'd scheduled it for the day after arriving home to give myself enough leeway to recover from jetlag, but also to avoid delaying any longer than I had to.

I was brimming with nerves as I sat in the backseat and was driven to one of my father's favorite restaurants. I wasn't sure how much longer I'd actually have a driver sent by my father, but at least for the moment, he still answered my calls. I supposed it was something that John and I would have to work out.

*Just another thing in an unending line of things to be worked out.*

I was excited for the lunch, though, since it wasn't the kind where I'd be used as an object. This would just be my dad and me. I was itching to see him again, even though I knew it would mean lying to him about the honeymoon. I did have a set of questions that I needed to ask him, too. What John had said had been bouncing around in my skull for almost a week. I knew it wasn't true, but I had to hear it from my father.

I arrived at the restaurant right after my dad. He was just sitting down when I walked in and spotted him. The place wasn't fancy. It was nice enough, with all tables and no booths, and with white-and-black-clad servers and tasteful music, but not the type of place where a person needed to make reservations months in advance. It wasn't family fare or comfort food, but I guessed I probably wouldn't taste the food anyway.

I was so nervous that when my dad ordered a blue rare steak with mashed potatoes and asparagus, I said that I'd have the same, even though I really wasn't a fan of undercooked meat and I hated that particular vegetable.

Once our server was gone, I gave my dad what I hoped was a cheerful smile. He smiled back, which indicated he believed that I was doing all right. So far, I hadn't even had to tell a single lie.

"Elisa, it's so good to see you back. You look beautiful."

"Thank you. It's good to see you, too." I brushed my fingers over my father's hand. He looked well. I wouldn't use the word happy, but then, I didn't think I could ever truly use that word to describe him.

"The Profacis have had no choice but to accept the marriage. They've backed down for the moment, and made no moves into either of our territories. None of our associates have been approached by any member of the Profacis, either."

"That's good news." I was pleased to hear that my dad's business was going well. I didn't ever want anyone to get hurt—and, in truth, the threat of aggression frightened me.

My dad frowned at me then, and suddenly my nerves were back. "That said, I know that you didn't really have a choice in the match," he acknowledged. "I wanted to find a good husband for you. Someone who would treat you well. Someone who could protect you and give you the life you deserved. Now that it's done, please tell an old man that you're happy. That you *will* be happy. I couldn't stand to think that I've made a mistake in this."

"No." The lie had already been fully formed, ready on my tongue. "No, you didn't make a mistake." I took my dad's hand again. "And you're certainly not old! I'm going to be fine, I promise."

His smile was so relieved, it made me want to cry as he gripped my hand harder. "Good. Good," he said, in a way that made me realize just how concerned he'd been. I only wished I could tell him the truth, but I wouldn't do that to him.

"There is something, though, that I… that I wanted to ask you."

My dad nodded. "Yes. Go ahead."

"I… I mean, it's about business." I lowered my voice and leaned in, aware that we were in a very public place. "I… if someone ever wanted to have the don of a, well, a family… um, removed… they couldn't just order it, could they? I… I mean, something like that would have long-lasting consequences. It would endanger everyone. Certainly, one don would have more respect than that for another. It couldn't be done, could it?"

I wasn't sure if my dad's shock kept him silent or if he was considering how to lie to me in a convincing way. He did look at me, strangely and sharply, but when he shook his head, I let out a sigh of relief. I'd known he wasn't going to lie, simply because he didn't have to.

"No. Something like that would not be done. It *could* be ordered, but it would *not* be ordered. Do you understand? Even the worst enemies have respect for each other."

I'd been right. Thank god. My father never could have done something like that. Not only would he never have ordered the hit of a don's *wife*, but he would never, ever have put his entire family and his men in jeopardy like that. My father was a firm believer in leaving women and children out of things. *Always*. And even if I could have believed that he'd get beyond that particular sentiment, I knew that he had far too much respect for the old ways of doing things. My dad dealt with his enemies in other ways—just for instance, by declaring a truce and, later, through securing the marriage of his only daughter in an alliance. That was how my father did business. He didn't hire thugs to kill a young man and his wife in the prime of their lives. He would never leave two children orphaned.

I collapsed back against my chair. I'd known that my dad couldn't have had any part in such a horrible thing, but the reassurance he'd just given me still turned my bones to liquid. I was so relieved that I had to brush tears from the corners of my eyes.

"Elisa? Are you all right?"

"Yes, yes," I stuttered hurriedly. "I'm just really glad to see you again. I know it's only been a week, but while Bora Bora was beautiful, I missed home. I missed you and Sara, Maria, Uncle Carlo...."

"Family is the most important thing." My dad's face was softer than I'd seen it in a very long time. "Always remember that."

"I will," I said solemnly. "I promise."

"I'm not just talking about us now."

The realization sank in that my dad was talking about John and maybe even the other members of his family. I did nod to signify that I understood, but then I grabbed my water and sipped it, pushing myself to move the conversation on by gushing about all of the wonderful things I hadn't actually seen and hadn't actually done on my honeymoon.

*** 

After the lunch with my dad, while I was chauffeured to my interview, I programmed the hospital's address into my phone. I then did some quick configuring to calculate how far it was from John's condo. It was quite a distance, and that made me even happier. If I added time in to commute every single day, that would mean a few less hours I had to spend with John. I'd never think of his condo as my home. He might be my husband, but I'd meant what I'd said. I'd never forgive him for thinking that my father was capable of murdering his parents. Why had he even brought that up? How long had he been thinking about it? Since he'd first met me? How could he have kissed me and… *and had sex with me*, while that was in the back of his mind? Was he really so detached? Had he done it out of duty? Had he only been pretending to enjoy our time together?

Even I couldn't think it was possible that he'd brought up the conversation to hurt me, but I also couldn't really make sense of what he might have been thinking.

I arrived at the hospital twenty minutes early for my interview. I was taken to a small office and given a seat for the wait. It wasn't modern. The desk ahead of me was straight out of a bad eighties movie, and the seats were uncomfortable, but I was too excited to care.

Eventually, a petite older woman—probably in her mid-fifties, with salt and pepper hair cut short, big glasses, and a warm smile—entered the room. She shut the door behind her and offered her hand. I stood and shook it.

"I'm Dorothy. Thank you for coming in today."

"Thank you for calling me back!" I was embarrassed at my own enthusiasm, but Dorothy didn't seem to mind. She sat behind her desk and opened up a file that I assumed held my resume.

207

"So, you just graduated? This would be your first real nursing job?"

"Yes, that's right."

"You included your transcript. You had excellent grades."

"Thank you."

"Did you work hard or are you just naturally smart?"

I shifted nervously. "A bit of both?"

Dorothy grinned. "Well, we like to see new, enthusiastic faces. This place only gets better with more positive energy flooding through that door. You seem like a compassionate person."

"How can you tell?"

"You have that sort of face. Anyway, even if you're faking it, if you can get your patients to believe you're compassionate, that's all that counts." I obviously did have a very open face, because Dorothy laughed. "I'm kidding. Sort of. There are a lot of days where you just have to smile and push through, no matter how tough it gets. Believe me, it can get real tough."

"I imagine it can."

"Are you prepared for that?"

I nodded. "I hope so. I guess I'll learn along the way. I don't know if anyone can ever be prepared to see terrible things—hard things, people in pain. But I know I would do my best, anything that I could, to help, and I've worked hard to get the opportunity. I can promise you all of that, at least."

"Good. I like that you're not afraid to be honest." Dorothy picked up a long piece of paper from beside her computer. "Now, I guess we can get into the real interview questions."

An hour later, I emerged from the hospital buzzing with elation at how well the interview had gone. Dorothy was genuinely nice, and I'd felt relaxed enough to tackle even the toughest questions she'd thrown at me. After the questions had been done with, Dorothy had informed me that the hospital had a state of the art pediatric ward. I knew all about it already, of course. It was one of the reasons that I'd applied. I would love to specialize in that area of nursing. I enjoyed children, and would love to devote my life to helping them, even if it would be, at times, heartbreaking and hard.

I took out my phone right there on the sidewalk in front of the hospital. A middle-aged couple had to dodge around me and shot me a dirty look. I gave them an apologetic one back.

I thought about texting Sara or Maria, or even Carlo or my dad, but instead I found my finger hovering over John's name.

*Why would I want to tell him that I had an interview?* I didn't understand the urge to text him and not my family. Especially not him first. Not before anyone else. I was angry with him. If I was going to speak to him again, ever, the first thing he was going to hear was that my father had most definitely had nothing to do with his parents' deaths. I'd drive that fact home if I had to use a fucking hammer to do it. I might just need one, I knew. Like any wife, I supposed, I was learning that my husband had a very thick skull. I would *make* him listen to me.

The first step toward some kind of reconciliation would be to actually say something, though. Anything. To get the communication flowing again after I'd shut it down for so long. I had no idea where John even was right now, after all, and he was my own husband. I'd barely even seen him since we'd arrived home from the disastrous honeymoon.

I fired off a quick text, stating that I'd had a callback and gone for an interview, and that I was excited about it. I did copy the text afterward, and send it through to Sara and Maria. To avoid getting another lecture from my dad prematurely, I decided I'd only tell him about it if I got the job.

I tucked my phone back into my purse and stood in the middle of the sidewalk. My chest felt like it was about to burst with happiness. It was gorgeous out. There was no breeze, spring was giving way to summer, and the sun was doing its best to green up the entire city.

I knew I should call for my driver, but I was so elated that I decided to take a short walk to calm my racing heart before I had to cram myself into the backseat of a car. So I started walking, familiarizing myself with the hospital's area as if I already had the job. I cautioned myself against getting too excited, but Dorothy had seemed so positive that I couldn't do a very stern job of it.

I walked away from the hospital, down the block lined with parked cars. Despite my excitement, when I crossed the crosswalk to the adjoining

209

street, I felt a prickle of unease slither down my spine. I glanced around, half-expecting to see a car hurtling toward me while I crossed, but there was nothing. Just a row of parked cars on either side, and some traffic stopped at the light. I wasn't about to become a human pancake.

*Still.*

The strange feeling lingered with me, and I couldn't help stealing a glance over my shoulder once I'd safely crossed the street. I did spot an ominous black car with tinted windows, but it was parked at a curb and there didn't appear to be anyone inside. There were lots of black cars in the world. Lots with tinted windows. It was parked, too, I reminded myself, so it was hardly suspicious.

Nevertheless, I shivered when I thought about someone watching me. I was sure that the car didn't belong to any of my dad's men, but maybe it was one of the Colombos'. Maybe they were watching me, to keep me safe. Or maybe they were spying on me for John's sake. I stared the car down and finally decided just to walk over and check in. If it was our men or John's men, then they'd see me coming and unroll the window or something. If it was someone else, or if the car was empty, I'd look like an idiot, but I couldn't go without checking.

I crossed the street again, when the walk light came on, and headed down the block toward the car. My chest tightened with fear, but I refused to let it show on my face. When I got closer, strangely enough, the car roared to life and quickly pulled out of its parking spot.

It sped down the block away from me.

I stood there puzzled. Maybe it had just been someone in their car, waiting for a break in traffic to pull out. Maybe they'd been finishing up a call or something. Or maybe it was just a black car with someone going on about their business, whatever that was, and I was being incredibly paranoid.

Still, it didn't seem so warm and nice outside any longer.

I looked around and noticed that there was a fast food restaurant across the street. It would be safe because it was public. Even though I'd just eaten, I'd order a drink or something so that I could sit inside. Without another thought, I snatched my phone out, called for my driver, and told him that I'd be waiting there for him to pick me up.

# Chapter 21

## John

I was in the middle of a meeting with Dario at one of our warehouses, talking about cars and other bullshit that I didn't care about, and trying to keep myself from thinking about my unhappy marriage and all the ways I had fucked it up, when my phone went off. I glanced at it, thinking the text might be some actual instructions from my uncle, and was stunned to see Elisa's name on the screen.

Dario went on talking while I read the text about a job interview. Elisa seemed genuinely excited. I remembered how she'd fought for the opportunity to work, and how I'd supported her that night.

If I supported her in her job search, maybe then she'd actually be open to saying a few words to me here and there. She *had* texted *me*, so that had to mean something. She wouldn't have done it out of obligation, right? So... did she actually want me to share this with her? To be excited with her?

Did she want me to know, or had someone put her up to filling me in on what was going on in her life because I was her husband and it was the right thing to do? I pulled my thoughts away from Elisa. I'd been too distracted lately. Not that I'd had time to think about anything other than the storm of my uncle's plans for an alliance, a marriage, and a surprise honeymoon. This wasn't the time for me to be second-guessing a fucking text message.

"Can I talk to you about something?" I asked Dario suddenly.

"Of course." Dario glanced around at the men milling about the warehouse, loading and checking crates of supply, before walking away into a private corner that would be out of earshot of anyone but us. He lifted a brow. "What's going on?"

I made sure my voice was low enough that even Dario had to strain to hear. "I should have talked to you about it before, but I couldn't find a good time. When I was on my honeymoon, I talked to you about keeping an eye on things, but there was only so much I could say over the phone. I wanted you here, keeping watch. You know that."

"Yes. That was clear."

"I want to talk to you about something else. The shooting that day at the restaurant."

Dario nodded. His eyes grew shadowed, indicating that the day hadn't sat easy with him, either. "You think someone tipped off the Profacis that we were there?"

"How would they have known, otherwise?"

"It could have been a staff member at the restaurant. Someone there who recognized us. Someone having lunch, even."

"Someone with mafia connections who knew just who to call?" I asked.

Dario sighed. "You're right. That would be odd."

"It was neutral territory. That in itself should have made it an act of war. We know it was the Profacis."

"We don't know for sure, which is why our uncle hasn't moved against them."

"He's hoping the alliance will do the job," I reminded him. "So far, they think it's working. I have my doubts."

"An alliance won't fix everything. It won't stop a violent family with huge fucking aspirations from growing more violent. They're obviously big dreamers," Dario said with derision.

I agreed with the sentiment. The Profacis thinking they could take on both our families? That was a serious fucking dream, alright. Shooting shots into the air was one thing. Moving against us was another. *Still.* "I don't like it. Someone tipped them off. I've been so wrapped up with all

212

this other, uh, wedding and family stuff, that I've been too distracted to deal with it. Leone wants me to leave it alone, but I can't do that."

"You're talking about a rat?" Dario asked.

It made me realize just how distracted I'd been—that the word had been in my thoughts constantly, but this was the first time I was actually talking to Dario about it. "Yes. Keep your eyes and ears open, all right? It could have been anyone. Any of our soldiers. One of the Gambinos' men. I want you to try to find out who it was. Yes, to keep us all safe, but I know it's also probably an impossibility for it to be as simple as that until someone else does something or slips. Just keep watch. If there's someone who looks disgruntled about something. Someone who just looks off. Someone who voices complaints or has aspirations of their own, let me know."

"Of course." Dario eyed me seriously. "You really think it was someone in our ranks?"

I shrugged, trying to ignore the pit in my stomach at the very possibility of that. "I don't know. I fucking hope not, but a chunk of cash or a promise can make men do stupid things."

"I'll figure it out."

I clapped a hand on Dario's shoulder. That pride I'd felt outside the restaurant that day, over the changes in my brother, flooded back. I didn't want to see Dario lose the best parts of himself. He was, at heart, a joker. He used his humor and wit as weapons all on their own. I didn't have that skill. I did think he was too carefree sometimes, yeah, but I could also tell he was doing his best—not just as a capo, but as my brother. If I'd had any doubts that he could be serious when it counted, what he'd done at the restaurant that day had banished them from my mind.

"One other thing." Lowering my voice even though we were already talking in hushed tones, I told him about what Elisa said about feeling uncomfortable about one of our men. "He scared her."

"He could scare anyone!" Dario scoffed. "He's not exactly someone to bring home to meet the parents or someone you'd trust your baby with."

"No, but still. Would it hurt to put a tracker on him? I doubt you can get at his phone. He keeps shit pretty tight. But his car?"

213

"I could get to both."

"How?"

Dario shrugged.

I frowned at him, hoping he understood the gravity of what I was asking him to do. "This is serious. We both know all of our guys are loyal. *We do.* This guy's been with the family for decades. Leone trusts him. I told Elisa that I would, though, and she's… well, let's just say she doesn't need another reason to be pissed off at me. Will you do it? Just to ease her mind?"

"Of course."

"Discreetly?" I added. "If he found out, he'd think that we doubted him. After so many years of loyalty, it would be like us spitting straight into his face."

Dario nodded, for once looking entirely serious. "I realize that. I'll be discreet. I can get the car, for sure. If I have doubts about the phone, I'll leave it."

I clapped Dario on the shoulder again. "Thank you."

I left the rest unsaid, and hoped that touch would convey what my words couldn't. In our family, we didn't talk about pride. We didn't talk about love.

Dario nodded, and I knew that he understood. He turned, walking away with a purposeful stride and leaving me alone in the shadows.

There was a car in the background—some expensive import that was being stripped down. That was his business, though, and he was already annoyed that I'd stopped by. He always thought I was checking up on him, even when I was just doing my job.

I walked out of the warehouse and climbed into my car, feeling slightly better at having done something, though it hadn't been much of anything at all. Out of habit, I turned and scanned the backseat, though I kept the car locked no matter where I was, even if it wouldn't be leaving my sight. Now, again, I gave it a visual once-over, checking for anything out of place. I'd learned to be paranoid a long time ago. Just a small dose went a long way in keeping a person on the right side of the ground.

Everything appeared normal, so I sat there for a minute and thought. I wanted to do something for Elisa. Something to show her that, even if she had sent that text out of obligation, I'd still back her.

I had Sara's number from the wedding day, from when she'd frantically called to explain about the photograph. I shot off a text since Sara knew Elisa best. A minute later, a response came in, followed by a fuck-ton of emojis. Happy faces, suns, flowers, clapping hands. Apparently, Sara approved of my choice. I hesitated, and then, after five minutes of trying to figure out how to insert the damn thing, I sent her a thumbs-up. It was the first time I'd ever used an emoji in my life.

After hitting the flower shop, I drove straight home. When I opened the door, it was obvious that Elisa had just gotten back. She was still wearing a set of black heels, a black pencil skirt, and a pale pink blouse. Her blonde hair was swept back into a low bun. She looked professional, but she was also breathtaking. Then again, when was she not stunning?

Suddenly nervous and embarrassed, I thrust out the massive bouquet of peonies that I'd picked up. Elisa's mouth dropped open as her eyes swept from the pink and white flowers up to my face.

"How did you know that those are my favorite?"

There might have been an accusation in there somewhere, but I couldn't be sure.

"I asked Sara," I told her simply.

"You asked my cousin?"

"I texted her. I wanted to get you something to offer my congratulations."

"I… I didn't get the job yet."

My hand grew sweaty on the glass vase. I walked over and set it down on the counter before it got the chance to slip and fall to the floor. "I'm sure that you will."

Elisa's face lit up with a huge smile at my confidence in her. For just a second, she dropped her guard, and I was struck by how beautiful she was when she was genuinely happy. I realized that I'd do anything to have her smile more. To be the reason for it. I just needed to figure out a way to apologize for what I'd said on our honeymoon. And prove that I meant the apology, for that matter.

Elisa's smile faded a bit, like she'd just remembered she was supposed to be angry with me. She studied me. "I have something I need to talk to you about. Will you sit down?"

My stomach clenched into a tight knot, but I accepted her invitation. No matter what she had to say, if she was finally ready to say *something*, I'd listen.

Elisa sat down on the couch. I took the opposite side. She faced me, sawing at her bottom lip until she finally spoke. "I had lunch with my dad today, before my interview. I... I needed to ask him. Before you think that I betrayed your confidence, I didn't. I promise. I just asked my dad, in very random terms, if it was possible... what you told me. He didn't just deny it, John; he told me that it was *impossible*. That there would be far-reaching ramifications for an act like that. My dad has this code of honor," she rushed on, even before I could think of what to say. Shock had practically frozen my heart

"I knew that he would never even consider something like that," she went on, her eyes wide against mine, "but I needed to hear it from him. He told me that it wasn't *possible*. I also know my dad well enough to know when he's saying something to placate me versus telling me the truth. He wasn't placating. He was absolutely being honest."

Her eyes implored me to understand, and I sat there silent, simply amazed at her openness and directness. Most of my men wouldn't dare to look me in the eye the way she did.

"Elisa, I—"

"I'm sorry," she said, cutting me off. "I'm sorry that I got angry and said that I'd never forgive you. I didn't want to discuss it with you until I talked to my father about it. It would have made for a disastrous honeymoon anyway, but I could have tried to be more understanding. We could have reasoned it out."

*Is she actually apologizing to me? Holy shit.* That made me feel like a first-class asshole.

I swallowed my shock, and then I leaned in toward her and took both of her hands in mine, keeping my gaze solidly on hers. "I never should have said what I did. I didn't mean to put it out there like that.

I do still think that it was a hit, and I know our families were enemies at the time, but I didn't mean to directly put the blame at your father's doorstep. I promise you that. It didn't even occur to me you'd take it that way until I'd said what I'd said, and then I couldn't figure out how to make it right—how to take back what I'd said. Yes, I think it was a hit, but it could have been anyone. My father had many enemies, I'm sure. Some who thought they could probably make a name for themselves by taking down a powerful family. It could even have been a friend of his. Friends are often more dangerous than enemies," I added, perhaps more to myself than to her.

"Why did... you? I thought... did I just assume you were talking about my family, then? Or did you say that? It's stupid now, that I can't even remember correctly!"

"I was at a loss and... I was getting emotional, and I've made myself believe that emotions are a danger. Unguarded, they can be. I've lived my life thinking that the only safe things to feel are bitterness, rage, and ambition. Possibly grief, since it could be used to spur those other feelings. That's what drives a person forward. I've always used the absence of feeling to save me from losing control. I'm not sure exactly what I said, to be honest with you. Probably that it was another family. But I promise you I never meant to imply your father or family had anything to do with it. I just wasn't thinking. The emotions got to me—one reason I keep them at bay."

Elisa's face softened in understanding. And, yet again, I was shocked—that she'd been the one to apologize, first of all, and now the way she was looking at me.... She was so naturally compassionate that I knew she'd make an exceptional nurse. If she could sit here and fathom what I was telling her after everything that had happened, then she could face just about anything her career could ever throw at her. She was delicate and beautiful, but she had an iron strength to her that most men lacked.

"I'm sorry that you were once a little boy, John, finding out that your parents were gone," she said quietly. "I know how hard it was to lose my mom. I have no way back to that time I had with her, but I still relive that moment, sometimes over and over again. I remember exactly what that

217

pain felt like. It's something that stays with you forever. I'm sorry for my unkindness when I should have understood that grief makes a person do and think things that aren't always rational, even if it's old grief."

I was astounded. "You weren't unkind, Elisa! And you're right. I was living it all over again. I don't talk about it. *Ever.* I could see the pity in your eyes and… I couldn't take it, if you want to know the truth. I was taught to be strong. Not just strong. *Impenetrable.* That's how our family works. That's how a man in my position is expected to act."

Her eyes hardened just a bit, and she shook her head as if trying to negate the facts of what I'd just said. "Jesus, John!" Elisa cursed. "I see the same thing in my dad, and I've watched it change him and destroy a lot of the goodness that used to be there. Please don't become that."

There was something in my chest, something that ached. It was an unfamiliar sensation. "You put so much tangible good into the world. I'm so used to bringing the exact opposite that I barely notice it anymore. I know how to survive, not how to be kind. I'm like a demon, and you're pure and good, and now you're trapped at my side."

Elisa laughed.

I just watched her, struck mute. Hearing that happy sound was one of the greatest joys I had ever known. It was right up there with her smile. I couldn't think of a single thing that could top either of those, even if I was confused by Elisa's reaction.

"That's quite dramatic," she explained. "Aren't demons just fallen angels or something?"

I smiled. "I wouldn't know anything about otherworldly beings. I shouldn't have stated that metaphor."

"Well, I make my own light. You can't make it go out."

God, to have her faith in that. I was still afraid that I'd dim it, at least. Break her. Destroy her, even. "That's exactly what I'm afraid I'll do."

"Don't be. You won't. I think you're vastly overestimating your power."

"I don't think so."

"You seem to forget that I grew up in this world, too, and I'm still the way I am. Yes, I might have been fairly sheltered by my father, and yes, I might have distanced myself from it, but there are things I still know!

218

*Hear. See.* I'm not as naïve as you think. Plus, even if I don't get the job today, I'll get one soon enough. I'm going to be helping people. Putting goodness into the world. Making a *difference*. It's what I've always wanted. I think that should balance out any bad karma you put out there."

I just stared at her, realizing she was serious. "Christ."

She grinned at me. "I'm kidding—mostly. You're not a demon, John. I know what you're saying, but I refuse to accept it. You're not a demon, and you're not dark. That's not how a person is measured. I'm a nurse. I know lots about the mind and the body, and I know that people aren't made that way. Your argument is flawed, so I refuse to accept it as valid."

Now, I was the one gaping at her.

As if she sensed that I needed it, she stood up, came right up beside me, and set her hand on my shoulder. Willingly. Elisa might have been the first person who'd touched me with any kind of real tenderness since my parents had died, period. And her light touch made me realize that there was a void inside of me that no amount of power, money, or violence was ever going to fill.

Elisa's phone rang, shattering the tender moment. She removed her hand, giving me a sheepish look after glancing at the screen. "It's Sara," she said. "Sorry. I was hoping it might have been the hospital. I didn't want to miss it."

"You should answer."

She danced away to stand at the window. "Hey. Yes, I missed you. Yes, I'm fine. Everything's fine…. Shit! No, I totally forgot. Yes, I know I've had a lot going on, but that's no excuse…. What do you mean you don't want a party? Yes…. We could do that…."

I listened to her side of the conversation while I observed her freely, given that she was facing away from me. She was so beautiful that it nearly burned my eyes.

I realized that I didn't want her to be wrong. I didn't think that her light could or should make up for the man I was, but I certainly wanted it to.

# Chapter 22

## Elisa

How exactly did one person let another person know that they might be ready to resume a physical connection?

It was the question that haunted me. It had been five days since we'd sort of made up for our fight on the honeymoon, and I still couldn't figure it out.

We'd fallen into a sort of pattern. It started with the fact that I tried to find things to do to fill up my days. I'd hung out with Sara, done some shopping, and sent out a few more resumes just in case I didn't get the job I'd already interviewed for. I'd actually gone grocery shopping as a response to the fact that I'd looked up a few good recipes to try out, too. I wasn't a great cook, but learning to get better seemed like something worthwhile to do with all of my empty hours. I had unpacked all of the boxes with my clothes and personal things into the guest room. Some things, I'd even set out around the condo here and there. I didn't make any drastic changes because it still didn't really feel like my space. I attempted to chat Mary up, but she remained shy, and very clearly didn't want to participate.

The hours during the day felt long, like they weren't my own. And I didn't like feeling like a stranger in my own life.

John often came home late. He obviously took his work and his position seriously. While his absence should have made me happy, though, it didn't. I felt lonely. That contradicted everything I knew about myself, too, which made me feel even more lost.

After the apology, I'd been determined to make an effort. I never had been a quitter, and I realized that this was my life now. Maybe I was just going stir crazy, or maybe I really had undergone a change of heart. Either way, I found myself thinking about John—a lot.

I thought about him until my skin felt like it wouldn't stretch to hold in the frustration that was slowly building inside me. Sometimes, I felt like I'd go insane from it.

John hadn't touched me since our honeymoon. We were now speaking again, though, which left other questions. Was there something wrong with me? Before, he'd touched me at every opportunity. Why hadn't he made a move to continue that? Was he just... done with me? Had that just been an act for the honeymoon?

He'd said that he'd be faithful to his vows, and I believed him now. But faithfulness didn't necessarily mean sexual interest, I'd come to realize.

Or, was he just too busy with work?

Should I have given him some kind of signal? Just the thought of that seemed absurd, though. Was I really considering seducing my own husband? Me? Me, who had steadfastly rejected the idea at every turn?

Once a traitor, always a traitor, maybe. I guessed that was true of my body, at any rate.

I knew the solution to most of my problems was to keep busy and keep my mind from spinning in unproductive circles. There was always something going on in New York, after all—even on a Tuesday night. But I didn't feel like going out, even though I'd pretty much run out of things to do around the house. It was after dinnertime and John still wasn't home, so I'd given up on any plans to make something for us.

My stomach growled with hunger, but after flipping through some of the take-out options nearby, I abandoned that idea, too.

I felt restless. John didn't have any wine in the house. What he drank was mostly the hard stuff, but Sara had been over on the weekend and brought a bottle of white. There was still a little bit left in the fridge.

I poured that into a glass and set the empty bottle on the counter. To curb my hunger, I cut a few pieces of cheese off the block I'd bought and plucked a few olives out of the jar. I nibbled at that while I sipped the wine. Either I was super-hungry or it was a good combination, because it all tasted divine.

I'd hooked my phone up to the sound system in the house before, so all I had to do was open up a playlist and soon my favorite retro tunes—interspersed with a few newer, guilty favorites—were pumping through the condo.

I sat down on the couch and tucked my legs up under me. I still had some wine to sip as I browsed my phone. Sara had declined having a birthday party after everything that had happened, but I'd promised to do something special for her now belated twenty-fourth birthday. She'd had it on the weekend, and had come over here to hang out with me, but insisted that she didn't even want a family dinner.

That wasn't like Sara, though. She was always up for a celebration. I privately thought she was still upset about her ex. I'd mostly forgotten all about her terrible break-up, honestly, but over the weekend, she'd said something about the asshole who'd broken her heart. The comment had reminded me that the world was still turning, going on as it had before, even if so much had changed for me.

In short, I'd been a shitty cousin and a worse friend lately, and it was time that I step it up a notch.

I was in the middle of looking at a website for a place where you could go and throw real axes when John walked in.

My fingers instantly turned to butter and I nearly dropped my phone as I observed him. He was dressed in a black suit, as per usual. His hair was swept back off his forehead. He looked handsome as sin, even if he did look tired, and my heart started pounding. My head swam, too, but that might have been the wine I'd had on a virtually empty stomach.

"Hey," I said, trying to be warm. What I really wanted to ask was if he'd take that two-thousand-dollar suit off so that I could enjoy an even more fabulous view. No, that wasn't quite right. I wanted to ask him if he'd take off *my* clothes so that *he* could enjoy the view. Did he not enjoy the view anymore? Did he not even want to look out the window? Was the view already old and boring?

223

*Fuck. This window metaphor is a new form of pathetic right here.*

John wasn't a "hey" or a "hi" person. He nodded at me, gave me a tight smile, and walked over to pour himself a drink. He splashed in a dash of amber-hued whisky or bourbon, I couldn't be sure which. I'd already learned that he wasn't the kind of person who tossed back his liquor and filled up for another round. He'd just pour a single glass and take his time enjoying that one, when he had it. He stood by the window after pouring, his handsome profile silhouetted by the dusky lights, and sipped his drink.

"How… how was your day?" I realized that it was the trivial thing to ask, the kind of thing that any and every wife would ask her husband, but it was still hard. The words felt strange on my tongue. I felt flat-out *awkward*. I gripped the wine glass harder.

"Long. Uneventful, but in our world, that's a good thing. Productive."

I knew it was best that I didn't know the details. John probably thought I didn't *want* to know them. He was right, for the most part.

The song playing in the background switched over to an incredibly sappy love song. It was one of my mom's favorites. "My parents used to dance to this in the house when I was little," I blurted out. When John turned, I continued—it would have been weird not to. "My mom had a cassette. She'd put it in the stereo in the living room. She always had it wound to the exact right spot. She'd just put it on and hit *play*. My dad would ask her to dance. Like, actually *ask her*. I'd be sitting on the couch and they'd start right up, swaying together. It used to make me laugh. It's probably one of my favorite memories of them. I had to add it to my playlist."

John's smile was soft, but not indulgent. "It's nice."

"No, it's not," I said, and laughed. "It's straight-up power ballad cheese."

"Nothing wrong with that."

I couldn't believe that *John Colombo* had just said those words. I stared at him in awe. He set down his drink on one of the side tables and walked over to where I was sitting. He offered me his hand.

"Restart it," he said softly. "It's so good, I need to hear it a second time."

I giggled like I was freaking twelve years old. "What? Are you serious?"

"I am."

My phone was still in my hand. I'd forgotten all about it. Without letting myself think about what I was doing, I restarted the song as he'd asked.

But John kept his hand extended, and I realized that he wanted me to take it. Was he seriously asking me to dance with him?

I set my phone down and slid my palm against his. Liquid lightning flowed from his arm into mine. I inhaled sharply before I set my wine down on the coffee table, and then I let John lead me over to the big open space on the floor in front of the windows. His hand swept around to my lower back and he pulled me in close. My hands wrapped around his strong neck. I could feel the soft hairs there, and the stiff collar of his suit jacket. I stared straight into his chest because I was suddenly too nervous to look up at his face.

We swayed slowly, dancing in front of those huge windows with the city looking on. It would have ruined the moment to say something, so I remained silent. I just enjoyed the song that had so much meaning for me.

I knew I'd remember this moment forever, just like I remembered my parents dancing.

I finally did dare to look up, somewhere near the end of the song. My bones had turned to butter, so much so that I couldn't believe I was still standing. John's hand burned against the back of my shirt.

John stared down at me. His eyes were so blue and soft that they reminded me of that beautiful, tropical ocean which I hadn't taken enough time to enjoy on our honeymoon.

My lips parted, and John bent his head. I expected the kiss to be burning and demanding like all of the others we'd shared had been. I expected an onslaught, a powerful tsunami... but what I got was the gentlest of waves. John's lips lapped at mine, tasting me like the ocean lapped at a beach. Gently. He explored my lower lip with his tongue before groaning at the taste. I shyly tasted him back, gently but eagerly. I could taste the bourbon he'd drunk, rich and spicy, and for some reason, that excited me so badly that I began to tremble.

How could he make me want him so violently with such a soft, tender kiss?

I melted against him, my legs nearly giving out. His hands circled my waist. One slipped under my shirt, caressing the patch of skin above my jeans. His fingers were warm and rough, and I throbbed between my legs. I knew that if I checked, I'd find myself slick there, ready for his touch.

He claimed my lips again, a little more desperately this time. I parted them, and his tongue swept in to mingle with mine, so that I imagined we both tasted wine and bourbon, sweet and spicy.

I kissed him hungrily, like I'd been waiting to do for a week. His hand swept up higher and massaged my breast over the lace of my bra. My nipple pebbled under his touch and I moaned, arching my back to thrust the tight bud against his marvelous fingers.

"Christ," John groaned against my lips. "Can I take you to the bedroom? *Our* bedroom?"

I didn't miss the use of that word. *Our.* Not his. Not mine. *Our bedroom.*

"Yes," I panted. I wanted him to take me there. *Somewhere. Anywhere.* I would have given in and let him take me right there where we were standing, but I sensed that it would be different this time. Intimate. Tender. That it would be more than just our bodies attacking each other, taking from each other. That, this time, I'd give and I'd give willingly. And I'd take, as well, and he'd give, and we'd have a shared pleasure that was created, not *demanded.* I had no delusions that it wouldn't still be just as hot and wild… but in a brand new way.

I was so fucking excited to figure that out that I could barely whimper something which sounded like a hoarse yes. The word sounded like it had been wrung from a freaking goose, but John got the message.

He hoisted me up and I wrapped my legs around his hips. He started walking while I started trying to shed clothing. His and mine. My hands were frantic and ineffective, and John laughed before plundering my mouth.

"I thought you'd lost interest," I panted, breaking the kiss.

"Lost interest?" John asked in what sounded and looked like amazement.

"You didn't…?"

"I wanted to give you time."

My hand threaded through his hair at the base of his neck. *"Time?"*

"I wanted to do things the right way."

That simple explanation touched something deep and raw inside me.

We got down the hall eventually, leaving a trail of clothing behind us. My back bumped a door, and John pushed it open. He carried me over to his huge bed and set me down gently to tug the rest of my clothing off. He stripped his away, and *holy shit*, I knew that I'd never get tired of looking at my husband. He was so wondrously built.

Smooth skin, corded veins, rock hard abs, and chiseled muscle everywhere else.

I guessed that, sometime between getting married and now, I had become more used to my own nakedness, too… because I didn't have a single urge to cover myself.

John stood at the edge of the bed, and when I sat up and shifted off to land on my knees, he groaned. His cock was so hard that it stood upright, along his abs. I took him into my hand, running my fingers over the velvet sheath, smearing a finger over the tip where beads of moisture bloomed.

"What are you doing?" John asked thickly.

"I want to taste you. You've done it for me so many times. Not that I think I have an obligation or anything. It's because I want to."

The room was dark since John hadn't flipped on the lights. There was just the slightest amount of light filtering in from the window, but I could see him clearly. He looked just as amazing in shadow as he did in the light.

I kept my hand wrapped around John's cock and stroked him slowly. We both sighed in pleasure. I loved the silk of his skin, so soft even though he was rock hard. Saliva flooded the back of my mouth, and more than anything, I wanted to taste him. When I slid my hand down to the base of his cock, I leaned forward and swirled my tongue over his engorged head. The salt of his arousal coated my tongue, and I groaned against him. I gathered up all that moisture, swallowing as I took him deeper into my mouth.

227

"Jesus Christ." John's hand twined through the strands of my hair. He didn't force me to allow him to set the pace, though, ramming in and out of my mouth like some other man might have. Instead, he stood stoically, clinging to me.

I used my hand, running it up and down his shaft while I worked the tip of him with my mouth. He was so huge that I knew I couldn't even get more than half of him to the back of my mouth. I did take as much as I could, all the way to the back of my throat. I nearly gagged myself, but then I pulled back and tried it again, swallowing when I felt him there.

"Holy Jesus Christ," John amended above me.

I really didn't know what I was doing. I was fairly inexperienced with things like this, but John seemed to like it. His fingers tugged at my hair again as I used my tongue to torture him, swirling, licking, sucking him back. The sounds of it were loud, but that just made my whole body ache. I felt empty between my legs, empty and soaking wet. I hadn't realized that doing this would make *me* feel so much pleasure.

John's hips finally moved. He pressed into my mouth just slightly, and I took him deeper. I had to angle my face to the side to take more of him. I didn't move, and he got the signal. He pushed in and pulled out, his hips pumping into me, fucking my mouth gently while I struggled to take more of him, and I fucking loved it.

I'd always kind of thought this was degrading. Now, I had no idea why. I didn't feel anything less than ridiculously fucking sexy down there on my knees before him, giving my husband pleasure. I could see why he liked to taste me. It was to give, but it was also to take. If John was doing that to me now, I thought it was likely he wouldn't even felt as wild as I did right now. I could feel the buzzing between my legs, and I knew that if I even brushed my clit with my finger, I'd come.

John's hips flexed as he thrust into my mouth. I held my breath and worked him as he thrust, taking him eagerly. I thought about what it would be like for him to lose control and finish in my mouth. And I was surprised at the thought of it, because I never would have considered it before. And now I wasn't just considering it…. When I thought about swallowing those hot jets, a rush of wetness trickled down my thighs.

John's hand left my hair and both his hands cupped my face. His hips stopped flexing, and he gently guided me up to stand in front of him.

He kissed me hard, his tongue sweeping through the seam of my lips and into my mouth before I could ask him why he wanted me to stop.

"Was going to come," he rasped as he broke the kiss.

"I wanted you to."

John's cock twitched between us. "Soon. But right now, I want to be inside of you. I want your tight heat wrapped around me. I want to *feel you come* on my dick. I want to bury myself inside of you and fill you up with my cum, Elisa."

*Holy. Shit.*

My body vibrated, and my inner muscles clenched down at the words, finding nothing but emptiness. A fresh wave of moisture trickled down my thighs.

Before I could choke out some kind of response, John backed me up to the bed. He lowered me down, spread my legs, and settled between them. I wriggled beneath him, clawing at his shoulders and opening myself up for him. I wrapped one leg around his waist and kept my other foot on the bed.

John's thick cock brushed against my clit, and just that mere brush sent me arching off the bed.

"God, John…" I moaned.

He didn't tease me or take his time. His cock was at my entrance, slick with my own arousal, and he simply pressed forward, filing me with just the crown. I bucked up against him, my hips moving all on their own, trying to take him deeper. He gripped my hips and lifted me clean off the bed, and then he pushed in all the way. Every time we did this, I was amazed at how huge he was, how thick and long. He filled me full, and my body had to struggle to take him.

He thrust hard, pulling out and pushing in again. He waited then, pulsing inside of me, letting me feel how desperately he wanted me. My fingers clenched over his straining shoulder muscles. I was caged in by John's one arm while his other hand held me up so that I could take him, take him deeper and harder, and I loved it.

I bucked wildly against him, my hips rising and falling with every thrust. I could feel myself clenching around him. I could feel myself throbbing in time with those thrusts. The heat built inside of me with every thrust, and my legs trembled as waves of heat washed over me. I could feel that knot in my belly, that coil of pleasure, getting closer and closer to snapping.

With a few more brutal thrusts, something inside me burst and I came apart. The climax swept over me. Blinding heat and pleasure crashed through me. I screamed John's name, my whole body curling and clenching and throbbing in time. I mewled and bucked and was wild underneath him.

I clung to him, and he guided me through it.

He flexed his hips hard and thrust one more time, filling me so full that I went over the edge into a second wave of pleasure. I felt the hot jets burst deep inside of me as John strained above me. I clung to him, and afterward, he lowered his forehead to mine. He kissed me tenderly before he eased himself down beside me.

We were both panting still, our skin flushed and sticky.

"Holy shit," I breathed. I had never felt so... so... *connected* to another person before.

This had never been easy for me. Never, with anyone but John. With him, I felt like we fit. I knew that every single time we did this, it would be perfect. It had been perfect every single time so far. This time had just been different—not frantic and hurried like before. This time had been far more tender. And it had just felt so... so... *right*.

John bent his head and suckled my nipple into his mouth. He scraped his teeth over the bud, but more gently than he ever had before.

I whimpered and responded by threading my hands through his hair, tugging his face into me.

A soft knock at the bedroom door made me freeze. John's head jerked up sharply. I must have looked worried, because he grinned. "It's just Mary."

I let out a squeak. "She knows that we... that we're in here..."

"This is our bedroom. You're my wife. Yes, she knows that we're in it."

230

I didn't know what to do with myself. I didn't know why I wanted to hide, but for some reason, I felt like I had just done something entirely naughty and now I'd been found out.

It wasn't necessarily a bad feeling.

"I'm sorry, Mr. Colombo, but there's a woman at the door asking to speak with Mrs. Colombo. She looks quite upset!" Mary called through the door.

"It's probably Sara," I whispered. "I don't know what she's doing here, though. She didn't text me or call me...."

"You've been indisposed for a while. She might have tried."

John was good enough to let me go. I scampered from the bed, but then I realized that half of my clothing had gotten stripped away out in the hallway. John walked calmly over to the dresser and produced a black T-shirt and a pair of workout shorts with a drawstring.

"Here. To get you down the hall to the guest room."

"Thanks."

My brain was working in overdrive as I flung open the door and ran down the hall. I darted into the room I'd been staying in and threw on some clothes.

I found Mary hovering anxiously in the living room. Sara was seated on the couch.

She was sobbing so hard that I could barely understand a word. All I could do was run toward her and wrap her up in a tight hug. She only clung to me, sniffling noisily and wetting my shirt with her tears.

"That... b-b-bastard! He-he-he's freaking... he knocked up his new girlfriend! Except... she's... she's four months pregnant! *Four months!* I just found out. He... he w-w-was obviously...." Sobs broke into whatever she might have said next, and I held her tighter.

She didn't have to say it. Sara and her scumbag boyfriend had broken up just shortly before we'd gone to the club that night. The first night I'd seen John and hadn't known it was him. Sara had found out her guy had been cheating on her, yeah, but this was a hard blow to take, I knew. Obviously, it had been going on for months, and she hadn't suspected a thing. His piece on the side had been fucking pregnant with his child before they'd even broken up.

231

"Christ," I muttered. *The sick fuck.* I glanced over Sara's head at John, who'd just come into the room. He was dressed in his usual work attire, and that made me want to laugh since we'd just been in the bedroom completely freaking naked, skin to skin, so connected, and then we'd been slightly interrupted, and now he was immaculate again, like it had never happened. Except that I knew it had, and that made me feel weirdly glowy and warm inside. I offered him an apology with my eyes.

He was too nice to look upset about being interrupted. *Sort of* interrupted. I wasn't entirely sure if John was the cuddling type. I would have said no, but he'd surprised me in other ways.

"I'll order pizza." John took out his phone. "Unless you have something else in mind?"

"A hit on the bastard would be nice!" Sara sobbed.

John nodded, pushing buttons. "Okay. One pepperoni with extra cheese and dipping sauce coming right up."

My heart fluttered. It was a stupid time for it to jolt like this, but it did. It should have given that crazy little skip when we'd been dancing. When John had offered me his hand. When he'd kissed me afterward, all soft and tender.

It hadn't.

It was doing it now.

Over pizza of all things. And an incredibly dry sense of humor.

I knew then, for the first time, that there was a possibility that in the future—some way far off, *distant* future—that I might be able to feel something for John. Something soft. Something tender. Something real.

Something worth making my heart flutter again.

# Chapter 23

## John

Having ordered comfort food that was obviously very much needed, I did what any man would do after being wound to the point of teeth-grinding sexual frustration. I ran myself to the point of puking before I stopped. My lungs screamed, my muscles ached, and my chest puffed in and out like a dusty accordion protesting getting played for the first time in a decade or two. Sweat dripped down my forehead and stung my eyes. My clothes clung to me like a second, sweat-sodden skin.

Running was all I could do.

After all, I wished I were still in bed with Elisa. Just being next to her was an entirely new experience for me. I had never done the aftermath bits with anyone else. We'd been having a moment that I would have liked to see extended well into the night.

I thought about Elisa pressed up against me, her warm, sticky skin next to mine, her vanilla and cinnamon scent swirling around me. I thought about wrapping her in my arms, caressing her silky hair, and even simply watching her as she fell asleep. Watching her afterward, too—wrapping my body around her and keeping her safe.

My body reacted to the tender images just as viscerally as it would have if I'd thought of fucking Elisa in a hundred different positions on every surface of the house. It shocked me, and I didn't know how to work that out except to run, and run, and run. And after that, I thought the best thing to do was to take my ass straight down to the gym. That often helped me to work out my frustrations and clear my mind.

I wasn't upset that Elisa was there for her cousin when she needed her. No, I was glad that my wife had people in her corner, family who she was close to. And I wasn't angry with Sara. She was genuinely upset. Hell, I owed her a debt for the call she'd made on the day of our wedding, when Elisa had been freaking out over the photo, and then, more recently, for texting me back about the peonies I'd bought.

I wasn't angry at anything.

Unless my dick counted.

In that case, yes, I was angry at the bastard, because even after an hour of pushing myself to my limit, the fucker refused to calm down.

My brain refused to stop processing images that involved Elisa spread out upon my bed, her honey blonde hair fanned out behind her like a damn halo, her legs spread in invitation and her pussy wet, glistening, and ready for me.

Every time Elisa and I had sex, it had been rushed—until tonight. Tonight had been different. It had been slower. Tender. Sensual. Intimate. All the things I hadn't known that I was capable of. I'd thought that any emotion I expended was a liability and a weakness, but it didn't feel like that with Elisa.

That amazed me.

It also amazed me that I wanted more.

She was like a drug. No matter whether or not I took my time with her, if we were rushed, if the sex between us was brutal and hot, or if it was tender and unhurried… the experience was just as potent, no matter how we did it.

I wished I was still in bed with her, memorizing every curve, every detail, every bit of her skin. I wanted to inhale the sweet scent of her hair, and kiss her at the juncture of her neck, at the base of her throat. I would have brought her to the brink again just by teasing one of her beautiful nipples before I'd ever touched her anywhere else.

*Fuck, this is not helping.*

I was distracted. My body refused to obey my commands.

234

I didn't know when things had changed. When *I* had changed. I no longer spent my days scaling a mountain of revenge, intent on getting to the top. I no longer felt the same burning desire to avenge every wrong perpetrated against me and my family. Vengeance wasn't my only companion. I knew I should back the fuck off whatever precipice I was standing on and head straight back into territory I knew was safe. Thinking about Elisa every minute of the day wasn't just a distraction. It was *dangerous*. And now, I doubted that whatever power she had over me would lessen—I'd thought that once, but if anything, her pull over me was only getting stronger.

I'd thought it would wear off eventually, but now I was seriously starting to doubt it.

But I was still making the right calls at work. Still getting shit done. I wasn't slipping up. I just wasn't myself.

Not that anyone could tell. On the outside, I was still the same John Colombo, underboss of our family. On the inside?

*Why the fuck am I even thinking about what I'm feeling and terming it "the inside"? Christ.*

That just proved my point. The old me hadn't had a goddamned *inside* to consider. My so-called inside had recently been as black and hard as my outside. Now, I found myself feeling like a motherfucking melted popsicle or something. Like my ice was slowly getting chipped away to reveal a richer, softer, sweeter center.

*Fuck that nonsense.*

Maybe the workout had short-circuited something in my brain. I might have actually overdone it, overheating to the point of melting something vital inside. I blamed my exhaustion for my ridiculous thoughts.

I stormed out of the gym, deaf and blind to anything other than getting back to my condo and hitting the shower. A cold shower.

Inside, I hurried back to my room, passing by the guest room where I imagined Elisa and Sara had to be ensconced. When I stepped into the spacious bathroom, I threw the glass door open hard enough to nearly shatter the fucking thing, cranked the tap, and hurried under the cold spray.

I remembered doing this before, though. That first night when I'd seen Elisa.

As with that night, I relented. Shivering violently, I switched the shower to a temperature that a sane man could tolerate. The warm water soothed away the gooseflesh coating my body. Unfortunately, when I wasn't thinking of my own discomfort, my thoughts drifted back to Elisa.

I would have made her beg tonight, had Sara not shown up. I would have tortured her, denying her an orgasm until she begged me. Begged me to fill her with my thick cock.

Or begged to taste me.

I groaned as I thought of her on her knees, her hair flowing around her shoulders and her pretty, full lips wrapped around my dick, taking me deep to the back of her throat.

Elisa was the first woman I'd ever not wrapped up with. She'd assured me she was on the pill, and I trusted her.

The thought of a child filled me with terror. I knew Elisa wouldn't lie to me about being on the pill, however, and I did trust her. Plus, she wanted to work. She wanted a career. It was important to her. She obviously didn't want a child yet, either… but what about in the future?

I'd never given much thought to having a family. I'd known that I might have one eventually, but now that Elisa was my wife, the possibility wasn't so abstract anymore.

I thought about me and my brother, learning that our parents were dead. At the mercy of our extended family to care for us. I was living the same life that my father had. Elisa didn't want any part of the darkness that came with it. She'd been born into it, though, so she could never escape it—not with her family embroiled in it, too. Maybe that would mean she wouldn't want to bring a child into the same life she'd been unable to escape. Either way, it was nearly impossible to think of having children now, knowing that one day I could leave them in the same way my parents had left me.

I didn't want to think about anything happening to me. I wasn't afraid of death. I wasn't even afraid of pain. What I was afraid of was leaving Elisa alone.

236

*Stop. Thoughts like that are a weakness. Weaknesses can be exploited.*

I shut off the taps with too much force, threw open the door, and wrapped a towel around my hips. My dick was still rock fucking hard. I thought about using my hand to take care of the problem, but I doubted that getting myself off would do the fucking job.

I dressed in silence and then sat on the edge of the bed. I needed to stop thinking. Feeling. Over-thinking. Over-processing. I needed some action. Something to take my mind off the strange thoughts and foreign emotions.

*Thinking of myself as a fucking ice cream treat just proves that I need to get my shit together.*

I knew I should move, but my body was exhausted and I stayed right there on the edge of the bed. My mind was as alert as ever, though, and apparently my dick was, too.

I stayed there for what felt like hours before I finally realized that the condo was silent. I couldn't hear Elisa and Sara talking. I got up and walked down the hall. There was an empty pizza box sitting on the coffee table, but no Elisa and no Sara.

My stomach rumbled, but I ignored my hunger. It was easy to deny myself some of my physical needs, at least, if not so easy with others.

I ended up walking back to the guest bedroom that was now Elisa's room. I listened at the door, but didn't hear them. Still... finally, I cracked open the door and peeked inside.

I could make out Elisa's form, sprawled out on the bed in the darkness.

It was late, but not that late. I must have been in the gym and the shower longer than I'd thought. Sara had obviously gone home—maybe an hour ago or more.

I thought about waking Elisa to pick up where we'd left off. She might be pissed at first, but gradually, I thought her body would warm up to the idea. I'd make the lost sleep worth her while. My dick roared at the idea and my pulse kicked up like I'd just tried to run myself into the ground again, almost literally, but instead I just stood there and stared at her.

She was so peaceful in sleep. So innocent. Her lashes were heavy on her cheeks. Her flawless skin glowed golden from the small amount of light seeping into the room around me. Her hair was strewn about the pillow, and a few golden strands lay across her cheek and the bridge of her nose.

I knew I should let her sleep. She was obviously exhausted if she was already in bed. And I could wait. I very obviously needed an exercise in control.

I couldn't just leave her there alone, though. Every instinct I had screamed at me to stay.

I slipped quietly into the room. She was fully clothed on top of the covers. I pulled back the comforter, easing it out from beneath her, and still she didn't wake up. I smoothed it over her, then walked around the bed and slipped in behind her. I gathered her into my arms, pulling her tight against me. And then I inhaled the sweet fragrance at the crown of her head before I placed a kiss there.

Her warmth flooded through my clothing. Our bodies tucked together in a perfect fit even though Elisa hadn't arranged herself into the position just for me. Or had she? It was like she'd known that I'd come find her. Like she'd known that I'd need her, even though I could barely admit it to myself. It was like she'd left herself vulnerable just so that I could be at her back, curled around her protectively with my body warmed by hers, warming her in return.

I let her sweet scent envelop me as I closed my eyes.

This wasn't something I did. I never fell asleep with another person. I never held them so tight to me that my heartbeat echoed into their backbone. I never listened to each and every deep breath and treasured it.

This wasn't something I did.

But I did it with Elisa.

And I cherished every single second like a tangible treasure until I drifted off to the sound of her gentle breaths.

# Chapter 24

## Elisa

Mary was no easy cookie to crack. That was what people said, wasn't it? Maybe it was actually that she was a tough nut to crack. Either way, when I woke up early and found John gone, I made a decision.

Last night had been the first night when there'd been any tenderness in his touch, and I was sorry that we'd been interrupted—no matter how necessary it had been, since Mary had absolutely been right to do it. I only vaguely remembered stirring in the night. I'd woken up disoriented and realized I was in the guest room, but that John was there, in the bed with me. Both of us fully clothed, and I'd been half-asleep still. I'd fallen almost instantly back asleep, lulled by the warmth and safety of his massive body wrapped around me.

Thinking of that, I wanted to do something nice for John. Just something small, but something that showed him I appreciated his thoughtfulness last night. Something that showed him I wanted us to keep moving in this new, surprising direction together.

I hadn't forgotten about how John had ordered that pizza for me and Sara. He didn't even know about Sara and her penchant for junk food when she was upset. He'd just instinctively understood what we'd needed. I'd been so surprised and touched. It had been the smallest thing, but it meant something to me.

I hadn't meant to fall asleep so early, though, that was for sure. After Sara had left, I'd been exhausted by her emotions. I'd just sprawled out on the bed in my room for a second when I'd gone in there to get a pair of pajamas and a book, and the next thing I'd known, I'd woken in the middle of the night to find John there.

That was a wonderful, touching surprise.

And as soon as I'd woken up, I'd had my idea to do something for John, so I'd decided I needed to convince Mary to take the evening off. I knew she lived in the condo. She had yet to befriend me or say more than obligatory words to me throughout the day, but I thought buying her tickets to a play and treating her to a fancy dinner beforehand would help. Of course, that wasn't my only motivation.

She was so shocked when I presented her with two printed tickets and the instructions that a driver would pick her up at five-thirty, drive to pick up any friend of hers who she wished to take along, and take them to a five-star restaurant as my treat! The driver would deliver her and her plus-one to the play and pick them up when it was done around ten or ten-thirty. She protested wildly, but in the end, she accepted the gift.

That left the hours during the day to kill, but I filled them like I always did. Looking at recipes, browsing job postings, puttering around my room, and going out for groceries.

When Mary emerged from her bedroom at the end of the hall at just after five, wearing a black dress complete with high heels and dangly earrings, with her graying hair swept up, I actually stood there and gaped at her.

She looked back at me shyly.

"Wow," I said breathlessly. "You look amazing."

"Thank you." Mary actually blushed. "Thank you for the gift. It was most kind." If she had any idea that I wanted her out of the house because I was planning a romantic evening for my husband and didn't want to be interrupted by anything, she didn't show it. She also didn't seem to mind that I was basically bribing her into liking me.

"I hope you enjoy it. Have a good time!"

"I will. Thank you again." Mary smiled broadly at me before letting herself out the front door.

I realized that she'd never been so relaxed with me before. She'd never smiled at me. Did I make her nervous? I was John's wife, and she'd run his household for a long time. Maybe not *run* it, I supposed, but she'd definitely been used to John living as a bachelor. And then I'd come onto the scene and she'd probably had no idea what to expect. I imagined that some wives could be nagging, nitpicky, catty, and mean. No wonder she basically walked on broken glass around me. No, wait. Eggshells.

I couldn't seem to get my mind focused on anything other than the night I was planning. I'd found a recipe for dinner and one for dessert, and spent half the morning researching the methods of preparation since I knew almost nothing about cooking. I could do the basics, enough to feed myself properly, but I'd never prepared gourmet meals when I'd been living alone. I hadn't had the time, and there'd never seemed to be any point.

The minute Mary walked out, I got to work in the kitchen. I used my phone for a reference while seasoning the chicken and potatoes. Next, I prepped a salad and started in on the dessert. I went with something easy. Pumpkin pie. Or, so I'd thought. It seemed straightforward enough— put in the canned pumpkin, season, and mix up the crust according to the recipe.

Apparently pies were not for beginners. The crust turned out to be a nightmare, but after a few more videos, I figured it out.

After the chicken was in the oven and the pie was waiting on the counter for its turn, I mixed up the whipped cream. I knew I had to be careful with it. I hadn't thought John would have a hand beater, so I'd gotten one when I'd been out. I was careful not to add too much sugar or mix for too long. If I ended up with butter, that would be the end of that since I'd only bought one container of whipping cream and I'd poured it all into the bowl.

I imagined John getting home. I figured he'd be back around seven or seven-thirty, since that was when he walked in most nights. The chicken and potatoes would be done. The pie would be in the oven, giving off a delicious aroma. Everything would be perfect. I'd gotten a bottle of wine for the night, too. I imagined us sitting down at the table that we had yet to use for a meal. I imagined John's surprise at seeing the homemade meal prepared.

I imagined what would happen afterward, too. His hands on my body. His lips on mine. Tender. Passionate. Slow. And then rushed. I actually didn't care how it started… I just cared that it happened. I was slightly ashamed at the way my body craved John, but I'd given up trying to keep it from happening. I couldn't control it. I didn't understand how it was possible to want someone so badly. How it was possible to fit him like my body had been made for his. I also didn't understand how I could have gone from disliking him with a passion to, well, just having passion.

I'd been so steadfastly against caring about John, but maybe my dad was right. If it slowly happened, it wasn't a bad thing. John and the Colombos were my family now. I didn't think I could trust John completely—not yet anyway—but he'd made promises me that I now believed he'd keep. That made it easier in the moments when I felt strange tingles in my chest that had nothing to do with sexual chemistry. I knew I was letting my guard down, and that that was a dangerous thing to do, but I couldn't find it in me to build those walls back up as thick as they'd been before.

It was still easier to concentrate on anything but my own feelings, so I kept busy watching the chicken, finishing the salad, and putting the pie in the oven. John still wasn't home. I opened the fridge to set the bowl of salad back inside and saw the whipped cream.

John didn't strike me as someone who ate dessert, but the thought of using that whipped cream for another purpose other than pie struck me. My body tingled with heat and electric tingles shivered up the inside of my thighs. Instead of imagining myself smeared with the sweet, airy cream, I imagined it on John. I imagined licking it off of his skin. I'd never let myself properly touch him before. His skin would be soft. Soft, blazing hot, and hard underneath. I'd like to trace the pattern his veins took. Trace them right to his beating heart. I'd spread the whipped cream out lower, and lick and trace that, too. I imagined getting on my knees for him, taking him into my mouth. Tasting his cock again for the first time. The salt of his arousal would mingle with the sweetness of the whipped cream….

*Holy shit.*

I slapped my hand out on the counter to support myself. I felt like I could fall over. My whole body was hotter than the damn pie baking in the oven.

John would likely be home any minute, but it suddenly occurred to me that I could make the night even more memorable. I rushed to the bedroom and dug in the dresser which I'd filled up with the clothes that I hadn't hung in the closet. I didn't have any naughty lingerie. I'd never worn any of that in my life. I did have a delicate, sexy lace bra and a matching thong. They were soft and light as air. I felt dangerous even handling them. Dangerous in a naughty way, and dangerous in that they were so delicately made that it felt like the beautiful lace could tear apart in my hands.

I undressed and carefully put on the set that I'd never worn before. The set had been an impulse buy. I'd see them when walking downtown, displayed on a mannequin in a lingerie shop. I loved the floral patterns in the lace, and so I'd bought it without having a reason to wear it.

I picked out a flowy black dress from the closet. Something that would be easy to slip off. Once I'd checked on the pie again, I texted John to tell him I had a surprise waiting for him. If he wasn't on his way home already, that would probably hurry things up.

I set the oven to *warm* and put the chicken back in. The pie cooled on top. I went ahead and set the table next, placing the bottle of wine in the middle. When I realized that John hadn't texted me back, I took a picture of bottle of wine and sent it. Fifteen minutes later, I took a sneak-peek photo of the set table and sent that, too.

Another twenty minutes after that, I poured myself a glass of wine and sat down on the couch to wait. I sipped at it while I sent off another couple of texts to John.

When I'd finished the glass of wine, I called. The texts were all going unread. I didn't think that John was avoiding me, though; instead, I couldn't help worrying that maybe something had happened. There was no answer. I waited ten minutes and called again. The phone went straight to voicemail, so I left a second message. The first one had promised a surprise. This one was worried, asking if everything was all right.

I had another glass of wine. I tried calling again. This time, the phone went straight to voicemail without even ringing.

He had to have it turned off.

People only turned off their phones if they were doing something they shouldn't, right? That could mean illegal, but it could also mean….

*No.* I wasn't going to think about that. John had made me a promise. He wouldn't be with anyone else. He just… he *wouldn't* be.

I hadn't eaten all afternoon since I'd spent most of it shopping and preparing food, but now the scent of chicken and pie made me feel sick. I shut off the oven, but left the chicken inside. The pie was fine on top of the stove. I poured myself another glass of wine. My head swam with it, and my body felt overwarm. I called John one more time, left yet another clearly frustrated message, and hung up.

I sat down on the couch again, but this time I faced the windows. I was staring out at the towering buildings across from me when my phone went off right beside me. I jumped and snatched it up, expecting to see John's number, but it was Sara's.

"Hey," I answered, trying to keep my worry and disappointment out of my voice.

"Hey, yourself." Sara sounded much better than she had the night before. "We're going out! Are you coming!"

"It's Wednesday night." I didn't mention that I was currently sitting on the couch, drinking wine alone, waiting for a husband who wouldn't answer my calls while the meal I'd spent so much time on went to waste.

"I know. We're not *going out*, going out. We're just going to play some pool. Darts. Have some drinks and some wings or something. Just me and some girlfriends. Are you in?"

"Pool and darts? You don't like either of those things!"

"Yeah, I know, but I'm trying to *not* think about other things."

I didn't want to instigate another crying fit like the one she'd had last night. I did know what Sara was trying not to think about. It was good for her to get out of the house and get her mind off her piece of shit ex. God, that guy was pure scum.

"I'll probably pass."

"No! You can't! What are you doing right now that's more important than me? If you say John, then I'll give you a pass, but that's the only way you're getting out of coming."

I sighed. I shouldn't have done it, but I couldn't help it. It was the frustration coupled with three glasses of wine on an empty stomach.

"I knew it! You're home alone and you're getting mopey and bored. You have to come. Please! I can pick you up in a half hour. Well, Leanne can. She's the one driving."

"I don't know. I should probably stay here."

"You sound sad, Elisa, and you shouldn't be sad! No one is allowed to be sad when they have the opportunity to go out and have a blast with their favorite cousin!"

I thought about calling John again, but I knew he wouldn't answer. Maybe Sara was right. Instead of moping and worrying, I could just go out and have a few hours of fun with her. I was feeling pretty shitty about the ruined dinner, and sitting in the condo alone would only put me in a worse mood.

"Fine. All right. I'll come."

"Really? Oh my god, yes! Okay. We'll be there in half an hour. Be ready!"

"Okay, okay."

"Don't ditch on me, even if John walks in the door! You deserve some fun girls' time!"

"I did promise you that I'd take you out for the birthday that I missed."

"This doesn't count. You have to do tonight *and* another night. Something better than wings and darts. I don't even like darts!"

I laughed. Sara could always pull me out of a bad mood. Just like she'd come over last night when she'd been upset so that I could comfort her, we knew we could count on each other.

At least the evening wouldn't be a total loss.

I hung up the phone and got changed into a set of jeans and a blouse more suitable for a pub, put on a pair of ankle boots, and finger-combed my long hair into a ponytail. Finally, I rammed the chicken and pie into the fridge more forcefully than I had to, and then I sat down to wait for Sara's call.

# Chapter 25

## John

There were some days where I wished I had a regular office job. Nine-to-five hours would be nice. Not having to deal with thugs trafficking arms for days on end, for instance, especially when it came to working out the finer details of moving a massive shipment. That was something that I could have done without. Not that I minded the cargo. It was the assholes moving it that ground down my nerves. They wasted more time and were more inefficient than any group I had ever seen. I couldn't exactly chew out my uncle for his choice, however, so I had to suck it up and deal with it.

That meant working long hours. In fact, I was so wrapped up with ensuring the business deal went smoothly that, when I stumbled outside of one of our warehouses and found that it was dark out, I blinked. Where the fuck had the afternoon gone?

I pulled out my phone to check the time, but the fucking thing was dead. I'd spent most of the morning and afternoon using it, and had thrown it in my pocket when I'd gotten distracted in the warehouse. I hadn't even thought to pull it out again until now.

I slid into my car and rammed my phone onto the wireless charge pad with more force than was necessary. Then I peeled out of the parking lot, blacking the street with tire marks and listening to the scream of the engine before I cautioned myself to calm down and drive normally. The last thing I needed was some overeager cop to pull me over.

It was nearly nine. Elisa had likely been at home by herself all day. I made a spur of the moment decision to take her out somewhere nice. I had no idea what she liked, but I needed to learn. Food, a show, the fucking ballet? I'd endure anything if it made her happy. Honestly, I just wanted to spend time with her.

The thought had me squealing the tires on the next right turn as I pressed down on the gas too hard.

*What the fuck is happening to me?*

I couldn't say that I fully hated the transformation, either. The truth was, I *did* want to make Elisa happy. That much was just in the interest of self-preservation. Most husbands would have said the same thing, but it went deeper than that for me now. It wasn't just about taking her out so that she'd be more willing to let me enjoy her at home afterwards. At least, that wasn't the sole motivation.

Even when I thought about her sensual body and all of her beauty, it wasn't just about a need. I'd never been selfish as a lover in the past, but with Elisa, that was different, too. I felt a strange burn in my chest when I thought about her, and that had never been there before.

I was so eager to get home, I found myself speeding again. The car was built for it, and I had to check my excitement.

I didn't get excited. Not like this.

Not at the prospect of a date in and of itself, and Elisa's excitement and enjoyment.

That wasn't me.

Me or not, though, when I made it home and walked into the condo, I was already formulating an idea for tomorrow night. I'd take Elisa to one of the most expensive places in New York. I'd make sure I could secure a reservation, no matter how much it cost. Afterwards, I'd take her out somewhere. To a show or something. Whatever she wanted. I'd let her choose.

But even as I pushed open the door, I could sense that the place was empty.

248

"Hello?" I stepped in, but complete silence enveloped me. The first thing I spotted was the table. It was made up with two settings, featuring an unlit candle in the middle and an opened bottle of wine. I was surprised when I cracked the fridge to see a pan sitting on the top shelf—complete with a roasted chicken, vegetables, and potatoes. A bowl of salad sat below that, and wrapped up nearby was a pumpkin pie. All of it clearly homemade.

Elisa had cooked this for me. She'd prepared dinner, and I hadn't come home.

Guilt stabbed at me, and I had *never* felt guilty about doing my job before.

This was what I had always avoided. Having an attachment outside of work. It just made things messy.

"Elisa?" I walked through the condo to what had become her room. I knew that I had better formulate one hell of an apology. Her door was open, though, and she wasn't there. A rumpled black dress lay on the bed.

"Mary?" I waited. There was nothing.

Finally, I knocked on Mary's door. That wasn't something I did. I *never* went into her personal area. But it was clear she wasn't home, either.

I couldn't remember the last time Mary had gone out anywhere, especially in the evening. And I didn't think it was possible that Elisa and Mary would have gone somewhere together.

I finally remembered my phone. I'd had it on silent all day, and it had remained on silent when I'd pulled it out. I'd been so distracted driving home that I hadn't even looked at it. I stared at the screen now, shocked to see four texts from Elisa, and even more voicemail notifications. I went through them, listening to every single one. The sweet, promising texts. And then, in the voice messages, I could hear the hope, then the worry, and finally the frustration and anger in her voice with each new message.

*Fuck.*

I was angry with myself for making her worry. For coming home late when she'd wanted to surprise me with dinner. She'd done this for me. *For us.* And I'd managed, in classic fashion, to fuck it up, even though I hadn't tried to sabotage anything.

I tried calling, but of course her phone went straight to voicemail. I didn't think there was any point in sending a text. She was probably with Sara, or maybe she'd gone over to her father's house.

Elisa would have chopped my balls off if she'd known that I'd programmed her phone to track her. I would never have used the tracker because I didn't trust her, however. I just wanted her to be safe. If I'd been a normal person with a normal job and a normal marriage, I would never have done it. But I wasn't normal, and I didn't have a regular job. There were people who would have liked nothing better, if they could have gotten away with it, to serve my head up on a platter and feel pride in a job well done. And I would stop at nothing to keep Elisa safe, so, yes, sometimes that meant intruding on her privacy. She wouldn't have let me put the tracker on her phone if I had asked her, and I knew that. She wouldn't have seen the sense in it, and we probably would have fought, so I'd done it when she'd been sleeping one night on our honeymoon. Her phone had been in her bag, untouched.

She didn't even have a password on it. That just proved to me how naïve she was and how I had to make sure she remained safe.

I'd hoped that I wouldn't ever have to use it, and despite the fact that I figured she was fine, just pissed off, I opened up the app on my phone. I found her right away. She did have her phone on. She'd clearly just dumped my call when it had come through.

She was at a pub, quite far from the condo. She'd probably gone out with Sara. I hoped.

But I also wasn't going to take any chances. If Elisa was angry with me, if she didn't trust me, who knew if she'd gone out alone, or if she was even safe?

Every protective instinct I had went on high alert. Never mind Elisa castrating me—her father would put a bullet between my eyes if something happened to his daughter.

It only took me three minutes to get back to my car. This time, I didn't give a fuck about speeding.

I headed straight for the pub. There was no parking available nearby, so I stopped the car in the middle of the fucking street and left it there.

I turned and flipped off the first guy who honked at me. If he'd realized that I had two Glocks strapped to my chest, he would have been far less quick to lay on that fucking horn.

I spotted Elisa right away. The pub was mostly empty and there was no immediate threat lurking in the shadows that I could see. Thank fucking Christ for that.

I felt my lungs deflate when I saw Sara just a few feet away, throwing darts at a board with a few other women who looked to be their age.

I relaxed slightly. Elisa was fine. She'd just gone out with her cousin and some friends, like I'd figured. She wasn't alone.

It wasn't clear whether leaving or making myself known would be the better option, but when Elisa stood up from the table and swayed violently on her way toward Sara, I made a decision. It was pretty clear that she was drunk already, and there was no way I was leaving her alone now.

I walked over casually, aware that the guy behind the bar and a few other people were watching me. Right. I was dressed fully in black, and though I knew my guns couldn't be seen, people were still taking note that I wasn't following the place's dress code of jeans and a T-shirt.

Elisa started when I set my hand on her arm. She swayed when she turned, and I set my hand at her waist to support her. She immediately dropped her hand to mine and brushed it off forcefully.

"Go. Away."

She'd made the commanded icily, turning the words into a full sentence all on their own, and I couldn't blame her after all the trouble she'd gone to.

"This is my night out now. With the girls. You don't have a vagina, and you're not wanted here." Her eyes refused to focus on my face.

I wrapped an arm around her waist and, despite the way she clawed at me, I wouldn't remove it.

Sara looked at me nervously. "She's just had a couple beers. That's it."

"Are you sure it was just a couple?"

Sara rolled her eyes. "She's a notorious lightweight. I do think she was pretty buzzed before she came out, though. Don't worry. I was watching her. We were going to go soon anyway. Nothing was going to happen. I had plans to walk her right into the condo to make sure she got home okay."

I shook my head. "She can come home with me. Now. Thank you for looking out for her."

"You don't have to thank me. I was doing that long before you showed up."

I ignored the sugary-sweet barb and turned as Elisa elbowed me.

"I'm standing right here. You don't have to talk about me like I'm in another room," she slurred. "I'm not going anywhere with you. I'm having a good time with *my* friends. You don't get to tell me when to go." She spun away, grabbed my shoulder, and actually tried to bring her knee straight up into my crotch.

She might have had the element of surprise, but lucky for me, she was also severely hampered by how much she'd had to drink, and so she just about fell over when she tried to lift her leg.

I'd definitely seen enough. I shouldn't have done it, but I scooped her up in my arms. Admittedly, maybe I was also slightly pissed at my own wife trying to knee me in the nuts. She might be angry with me for being late after she'd gone to considerable work to surprise me, but she had to understand there were things in our life that I couldn't control—and work, unfortunately, always came above what I wanted to have happening in my own damned life.

I was going to carry her out, despite the fact that she'd be completely humiliated, but she fought me. Her palm connected solidly with my jaw and a loud smack echoed through the half-empty pub.

I let her have that one for free, but that was the only one she was getting.

I shifted Elisa in my arms, hauling her over my shoulder. She beat at my back, but I ignored her. I nodded goodnight to Sara and the other stunned women standing beside her.

"She's going to make you regret that!" Sara promised, but she said it to my retreating back.

I had no doubt of the validity of that statement.

252

My car was still in the middle of the road. There was more than one lane, and traffic was going around it. They must have given up on the horns since it was silent outside. As silent as the city could ever be. There were still sirens in the distance—the roar of traffic that never ceased, the buzz of humanity always on the go.

I wrenched open the passenger door and deposited Elisa inside. She glowered at me and said nothing. It was more disconcerting than if she'd hurled insult after insult at me. I slid her seatbelt over her, clicked it into place, slammed the lock down, and shut the door. I slid in beside her a few seconds later and started driving.

Elisa stared straight ahead. She refused to look at me. I didn't know what to say, so I gripped the wheel, ground my teeth, and said nothing back at her. My jaw stung where she'd smacked me, but I could guess that her palm was probably still smarting. No doubt, she considered it worth it.

"You're a controlling asshole, you smug, thoughtless Neanderthal," Elisa muttered when we were just a few blocks from home.

"I have no doubt," I responded dryly.

I didn't rise to the fight, and Elisa didn't put any other words of wisdom out there for my consideration.

I wanted to pick her up and carry her up to the condo, but she refused. She did waver slightly, but she kept her head up and I followed behind her, ready in case she tripped over her own feet. At least she was wearing flat boots and not heels.

In the condo, I let Elisa walk to her room. She slammed the door behind her. I stalked to mine and sat down hard on the edge of the bed, frustrated beyond anything I'd ever felt before.

I just wished that one thing could go right for us. I seemed to be fucking it up constantly, too, and that made me feel guiltier than before, which I didn't like. What I'd said on the honeymoon had been my fault. But last night? Tonight? There was nothing I could have done differently.

I waited an hour, going over work shit in my head to keep myself distracted, before I checked on Elisa. I wanted to make sure she wasn't passed out on the floor on lying in a weird position. I didn't think she'd been drunk enough for that, but I wasn't exactly sure. It reminded me that Elisa was still virtually a stranger to me. One who I'd like to get to know, but I kept botching every opportunity.

I pushed open the door again, just like I had the night before. Elisa was asleep, curled up on her side. She was breathing evenly and there was a half-empty glass of water on the nightstand.

I shut the door softly and walked back to my own room.

I was totally at a loss as to how to make this marriage work. I'd never had to worry about making a relationship work before. I had been with many women, but nothing that could be defined as a *relationship*. This was different. Elisa was *different*. If I hadn't felt anything for her, I would have been content to let her be miserable. I wouldn't even have noticed or cared.

But I did care. That was the ultimate problem, and I had no idea what to do about it.

Once again, I wasn't in control.

# Chapter 26

## Elisa

I woke up to blinding sunshine. I struggled to open my eyes, but it was hard when it felt like they were getting a straight dose of acid dumped into them. They felt grainy, and burned at the brightness spilling through the open curtains. My mouth felt even worse. Sour and dry.

I struggled to sit up as my head pounded, protesting the movement. I groaned and dropped it back down to the pillows.

"Shit," I muttered, recalling how last night had gone so off the rails. First it had been the dinner, then John not answering his phone, and then going out with Sara. I'd had way more than what I usually had to drink, which was generally nothing at all. Three glasses of wine and a couple beers were apparently more than I could handle.

I hoped Mary's night out had been better than mine.

Not that it had all been bad. I'd been having a good time with Sara and her friends. That part of the evening hadn't gotten bad until John had showed up. He'd acted like a controlling, overbearing, boorish asshole. He had not needed to toss me over his shoulder or pick me up in front of everyone. It had been embarrassing. I could have walked just fine.

I hadn't been that drunk. Just a little bit dizzy.

Still, I knew that I had been out of line, too. Shame assaulted me so hard at the thought of it all that I threw my hands over my eyes to block out the sunlight.

I should have just gone with John and said goodnight to everyone. He wouldn't have had to take me off like some little kid throwing a tantrum. I'd hit him, too. I'd actually *struck* him. My own husband.

If my dad could have seen me last night, he would have been ashamed of me.

It wasn't easy living with a shit ton of self-recrimination.

I needed a glass of water.

There was one on the nightstand from last night, still half-full. I struggled to sit up and I poured the remaining liquid down my dry throat. I swallowed hard past the slight nausea in my stomach. *God.* I needed to get up, get a shower, and get some food into my stomach. That would probably help my throbbing head. Even if it didn't, I still had to get my ass moving.

One glance at my phone, and I groaned again. It was past noon. How could I have slept past noon? I'd been dreading facing John, but he would have left a long time ago. I knew that I should call him and apologize for last night, too, but I needed a shower first. Then coffee. Probably some toast, too. After that, I might feel human enough to call.

I hit the shower. The warm water soothed the stiffness out of my limbs, especially in my neck. It eased my pounding head just a little, and I was toweling off when my phone rang from down the hall.

I yelped, wrapped the towel around myself, and ran for it.

It wasn't John. I did recognize the number, though, and my heart started beating wildly.

"Hello?" I was completely out of breath, but hoped that they couldn't tell on the other end.

"Hi, Elisa?"

"Yes."

"It's Dorothy."

"Yes! Dorothy, hi!"

"I'm sorry that things move so slowly, but I was wondering if you'd be free to come in for another interview. It's just part of the process. This time, it would be with myself and a few other people. I was really

256

impressed with you and you basically have the job. It's more of a formality than anything."

"Yes!" My head spun. I just about fell over. "Yes, I can come in as soon as you'd like!"

"Would this afternoon work? Around three?"

"Oh. Yes, for sure. Thank you! I'll see you then."

I hung up, still dazed. I didn't have a car, and wasn't sure if I should call for a cab or my dad's driver. I decided the driver would be a better choice. When I dialed the number, though, I got no answer. That was strange. He always answered.

I set my phone down, slightly confused. Maybe he'd call back. I could always take a cab. This was something that I should really work out with John, too. I couldn't not have my own car. He either needed to provide one of his men to drive me or he'd have to get me something. I had my own money, but I had a suspicion that he wouldn't approve of me simply going out to buy one. Plus, I didn't know about parking and such around the condo. If I bought a car and he told me it was useless, and insisted I drive one of his or get driven around, it would just be another thing for us to disagree on. At the moment, I was pretty done with that.

I picked up my phone, went to the recent calls, and selected John's number. All of the calls there just reminded me that he hadn't picked up his phone last night. I'd been so worried for so many reasons. Maybe I'd gone out with Sara for a lot of reasons, and not just because I'd been angry with John. I hadn't wanted to worry, and do it alone, but I'd also been angry with myself for immediately going to a place of mistrust and suspicion instead of being logical.

I was just sad that the whole evening had turned out the way it had, and that had turned into anger. Wild emotions and booze were a bad mix. Obviously. I wouldn't be trying that one again anytime soon.

John's phone went to voicemail again.

I wasn't sure if that was because he was pissed at me for last night or because he was busy. Either way, I was exhausted from trying to figure it out. From trying to do the right thing, only to have it blow up in my face. God, people always said marriage was hard, but I'd had *no* idea.

I decided that a walk might clear my head. There was a coffee shop down the block. I could pop in there and get something. I'd sit and I'd think and I'd figure things out. That was my promise to myself. I'd work on an apology and some sort of explanation that made sense without giving it away that I was starting to feel something for my husband which went beyond the physical.

That scared the heck out of me for so many reasons.

Because, really, should I tell him? Would he use that information against me? Would he laugh at me because he probably didn't feel the same?

But the feelings were just *starting*. There was a grain there, a tiny seed of something new and undeniable. I should have stamped it out to protect myself already, perhaps, but I just couldn't do it. Would John see that as a weakness? It felt sometimes like he was softening. When he'd kissed me a few nights ago, I'd thought that maybe he had a seed growing inside him, as well.

What if I was just imagining that, though? I didn't want to look like a naïve child, especially after my behavior last night had signaled me out to be just that.

I threw my towel onto the bed with a sigh and got dressed in jeans and a casual shirt. I'd change and worry about my hair and makeup later, before my interview. First, I needed coffee, and I wasn't ashamed to wander down the block with wet hair and a bare face.

I grabbed my purse, threw my phone in, and walked to the front door. But when I pulled it open, I stopped dead when two hulking giants closed in on me.

"What the—"

Giant One cut me off. "Sorry, Mrs. Colombo, we're going to have to ask you to stay inside for right now. Boss's orders."

"What boss?" I demanded sharply.

"John's orders," Giant Two said. He was just as big and thick and scary as the first one.

Both men were dressed in black. Both of them were obviously armed underneath their black suit jackets. They looked like a set of thugs who would be better off fighting with brass knuckles or their bare knuckles than with guns. Guns were too classy for them. The first had a scar that ran the length of his jawline. The second had a babyface which was totally at odds with the rest of him and which actually made him even scarier.

"Why?" I squeaked, embarrassing myself.

Both men's faces went totally blank, and it was clear that I'd get more answers from an inanimate object.

"Has something happened?" I asked anyway, stupidly.

They both just stood there, staring at me without blinking.

"I was just going to get a coffee."

"Sorry," Giant One repeated. "We can't let you leave."

"So I'm a prisoner in my own home?"

"We have orders," Giant Two echoed. Apparently, those were the only lines they knew. *Orders* and *sorry*. Oh, and *boss*.

*For fuck sakes.*

I turned and went back inside, slamming the door even though I knew I should just shut it gently. I whipped out my phone and tried calling John. Seven times. If he was going to act like a psycho and not let me out of my own home, then I'd act like a psycho and demand answers.

He never picked up. I left so many messages that, after the fifth time I called, the phone system itself hung up on me after the electronic voice stated that his mailbox was full.

I barely suppressed a scream. Irrationally, I opened the door and gave the two thugs a scathing look. "My name is still Gambino," I hissed, and I slammed the door again.

This was fucking bullshit. It was nonsense. What the fuck did they mean, they weren't going to let me leave? I had a job interview in a few hours! I couldn't just sit around waiting for John to decide to call me back. Was this his way of punishing me for going out and having a couple of drinks with Sara and her friends? If that was the reason he had me on lockdown, he could forget about ever having a nice, peaceable life again. I wouldn't be held in his condo like a fucking prisoner. I wouldn't fucking let him get away with treating me like this.

I thought about calling my dad, but then decided against it. If John was punishing me, my dad would be furious. Not with John, but with me.

I tried calling Sara, but she didn't pick up the phone. I wondered if she was still sleeping off a hangover, as well. I thought about Maria or my uncle Carlo next, but what was I supposed to say? That I was locked in my own freaking house and wondered if they knew why?

It would be too embarrassing.

I did worry that maybe something had happened. That thought, when it slithered into my brain, permeated deep and refused to leave. I stopped thinking about John as some asshole who'd put bodyguards at the door to teach me a lesson, and started thinking about whether or not he was okay. I knew that I hadn't wanted the marriage, but if something happened to him....

*Jesus.* I had no idea what I would do.

I stumbled over to the couch and sat down heavily. There, I set my throbbing head in my hands, closed my eyes, and wished with every fiber of my being that John would call me back.

# Chapter 27

## John

There'd been a time when we wouldn't have failed to see an attack coming. Apparently, that time was in the past.

I stood in the far corner of one of our warehouses. It was currently empty, our latest shipment of arms from this warehouse having gone out a few days ago. I stared at the wooden wall before dropping my eyes down to the dust on my black shoes.

Rage filtered through my blood, raw and scalding. I'd been awakened in the middle of the night by a call from my uncle. Last night, the Profacis had struck, injuring two of our men and three of the Gambinos' soldiers. I'd been awake since two in the morning, running on a few hours of sleep, but the desire for revenge pumping through me combined with adrenaline to keep me awake.

One man had died from his injuries in the early hours of the morning. The Profacis had struck out just like they'd hit us at the restaurant. As cowards. They'd driven by in two black SUVs at two of our warehouses, one of ours and one of the Gambinos'. They'd hit at the same time— opening fire and then driving away, leaving injured men in their wake.

The attacks might have happened at the same time, but they also seemed weirdly uncoordinated. A drive-by shooting was something that disgruntled gang members, drug dealers, and fearful men did. It wasn't an attack meant to instill fear, though it still created one clusterfuck of a morning for everyone involved.

After calling a private doctor to patch up our men, my uncle had needed to accompany Gastone Gambino to the house of the man who'd died in order to inform his wife. The man had had three children.

I'd expected a fast meeting to regroup, to decide on a course of action, but because we now had another family allied with ours, things were moving slow, and it was driving me out of my mind.

No one had seen this coming. My uncle and Gastone Gambino had thought the Profaci threat was low. It had turned out their silence only meant they were anything but pacified. This latest shooting might have been minor in the scale of how they could have chosen to move against us, but we knew for a fact it had been them. One of our men had managed to get the plate number, and we'd run it first thing that morning. Only an idiot would use an actual registered plate that someone would recognize. Or someone who wanted to send a clear declaration of war.

It was up to both of our families now to decide together how we'd respond.

The men around me were on high alert. Everyone had their guns out. Everyone's skin was crawling. Every single time a honk or a sudden noise came from outside, the hair on the back of my neck rose. It was far more likely that one of my men, unnerved by one such noise, would fire off their weapon inside the warehouse than it was likely that the Profacis would strike again in broad daylight.

I paced back and forth, growling under my breath. I couldn't shake the feeling that this was somehow my fault. It was one thing for my uncle to miss this. It was another thing for me, who had direct contact with our men every single day, not to see it coming.

Had I been so wrapped up in my marriage, distracted by Elisa, that I'd missed the signs completely? Had there been some warning that I'd failed to heed?

*Elisa.*

Thoughts of something happening to her stabbed into me so hard that I nearly doubled over. I'd posted two of our men at the door to keep watch before I'd left. There was no way I was leaving my home, or Elisa, unguarded. I'd known the minute she'd realized that she wasn't going to be let out. She'd called and called, but I hadn't answered. I had no idea what I was going to tell her. I didn't want to talk to her yet, when I still didn't know what was happening. My uncle and Gastone Gambino hadn't called a meeting yet, and I didn't want to worry Elisa before I knew all of the details. If I told her the reason that there were men at the door, she'd probably freak out. Maybe do something rash. I couldn't afford to be distracted by her and worried for her safety.

Just hearing her voice would throw me off, and I needed to focus. I regretted not picking up when she'd called, but I promised myself I'd call her as soon as I could.

*"John?"*

I whirled at the sound of my name. Dario stood a few paces behind me. He held up a hand and I realized that I must have a murderous look on my face. I didn't bother to wipe it away. Dario knew me better than anyone. I knew he could deal with my mood, and it wasn't as if he'd be confused over where it had come from.

Dario looked unsettled himself. The attack had rattled everyone because we'd been so unprepared for it.

"What?" I growled impatiently. But I didn't want to be short with Dario, for no reason other than it had been a shitty fucking night, so I tried to soften my tone along with my expression. "Sorry. Just... on edge."

Dario nodded in understanding. "One of Gambino's men just woke up. The one shot in the gut and chest."

I winced when I thought about the guy being operated on. We paid private doctors obscene amounts of money to keep their mouths shut and do their work in situations like this. If the Gambino soldier had been hurt badly, he might not have been moved. He might have been operated on while spread out on a table in a fucking warehouse. And if he had been moved, it had likely been to a discreet location—a clinic, at best. He wouldn't have had the advantage of an operating room, even though he would have had an excellent and skilled surgeon. But our men knew the risks of working for us, and we made sure that they damn well got the best treatment possible if something happened.

"Did he say anything?"

Dario lowered his voice. "He had a message from the Profacis."

My blood turned to ice. "What the fuck did he say?" My brother blinked at me. He actually took a step back, as well, and I realized that I needed to dial it down yet again and get myself the hell under control. Acting like this wasn't helping anyone. "Sorry," I said again, aware that I hardly ever apologized. "Did he say anything coherent?"

"He said that he was the message."

I let out a hard sigh. "Obviously."

"He's pretty out of it. What he said was unclear. I think he was just telling us what we already knew, unfortunately."

"That there's going to be a war."

Dario nodded. "I can't see how it could be prevented now."

I lowered my voice. "Anything on the tracker?" I knew Dario had been successful in putting the tracker on his car, but not on his phone.

Dario frowned and shook his head. "No. Nothing. He's out with the rest of the men."

I changed the subject back to the Profacis since they were our immediate concern. "Our uncle and Gastone Gambino won't bow down to the Profacis. There isn't any way they can advocate for peace now," I said, talking it out as I spoke and trying to find their motives. "No one thought that they'd strike like this—it's suicide on their part. They're outnumbered in every sense. We have allies beyond this city and this country. Power that they don't have. Even here, our contacts and our soldiers could wipe them out without lifting a finger."

"Maybe that's what they want us to think. Maybe they want us to move against them. Maybe it's some kind of a trap."

I considered that. The idea was worth *serious* consideration, actually. However we acted, though, we had to do it carefully. Reacting in anger, sending our men out to eliminate a threat… they could be walking into an extremely dangerous situation. What the Profacis had done and how they'd done it was suspicious. It wasn't how an enemy in our world acted. They'd broken just about every code there was. It said either they had zero honor and they were ready for us when we came, or that we'd vastly underestimated them and they were desperate, hungry for power, and willing to do what it took to expand their empire—rules or not, honor be damned.

"We can't endanger our men," Dario said again. "I won't be at the meeting, but please, if our uncle wants war, you should caution him against it. Not against flexing his power, but how he chooses to do it. Don't let his anger at what happened cloud his judgment."

Dario was right, but I knew he needn't worry about that. "Leone is rational, above everything."

"What about Gastone Gambino?" Dario asked. "It was his solider who died. The Gambinos were once our enemy. We don't exactly know how they operate in a situation like this. Don't let our uncle be swayed if Gastone loses his head."

"I agree." Dario was right about that, too. I had no idea how Gastone Gambino acted under crisis. "My guess is that he'll be as calm as Leone generally is. They're old. They've faced threats like this countless times before. They let their head rule ahead of their emotions, or they wouldn't have a family to run. They don't make careless mistakes."

"Just be sure."

"I will."

Dario paused, but then he spoke his mind. "Something about this doesn't feel right. They could have done so much more damage. We didn't see it coming. They could have torched the warehouses. Fucked up a shipment. Targeted one of us and taken *us* out."

I nodded slowly. Dario was right again, and I'd been thinking the same thing at the same time—and thinking the last bit, about one of us being taken out, terrified me. I wasn't afraid to die, but thinking about the Profacis hitting our families.... They'd already proven that they weren't willing to follow rules or codes. I was only glad that Elisa was trapped in our condo.

"Do you think it's a distraction?"

Dario had surprised me again, as I definitely hadn't thought about that. Dario might be carefree most of the time. He might be intent on breaking, or at least bending, as many rules as he could, but in times of crisis, this was just a reminder that he'd always have my back. "It could be," I admitted. "They could be planning something bigger. If we're diverted, trying to figure out how to act…. Have the men on high alert."

"That's already done."

"Then… just use your head. Keep in front of the situation. If it's a diversion, think about where the Profacis would strike next. Our shipments. The warehouses need to be more carefully guarded. Leave the empty ones. They don't matter. Put extra men on the ones with product."

"Should we notify our contacts?"

I hedged. Those men weren't a part of our world. They skirted around it, danced with us when willing, and sometimes even when they were unwilling partners, but they didn't understand even a fraction of what went on behind the scenes on our end and I wanted to keep it that way. The less people knew, the less they could talk.

"No. Not right now. If you think someone's vulnerable, assign men to keep watch. *Discreetly*. We don't want the whole city on high alert. Above all, we don't want anyone to think that we can't take care of what's ours."

"Of course. No weakness. Isn't that what our uncle is always harping about?"

"For good reason."

Dario hesitated, clearly about to say something, and then he finally did. "We might not have a weakness, but there are cracks in every bit of armor. The Profacis will find one." With that, Dario stalked off, leaving me with that sage piece of advice.

Overnight, my brother seemed to have been replaced with a different man. Despite the shit storm that had descended on us during the night, burying us knee-fucking-deep, my chest swelled with pride. It was quickly replaced by the serious reality of our situation, though. I felt the blackness descend again, settling heavily on my shoulders.

I wanted to slam my fist into the wall. Partly because I realized that, at the moment, I was completely powerless to do anything to protect the people I loved—any of our men, our empire… all of it. I hated sitting and waiting, but that's what I had to do until my uncle and Gastone Gambino were ready to meet.

What they decided would change the course of all of our lives.

266

# Chapter 28

## Elisa

I *hated* that I was going to miss out on the interview for the job of my dreams because there were two cave men standing guard at my door, inexplicably not allowing me to leave.

I hated being a prisoner in my own home.

And I hated that John wouldn't pick up his fucking phone so that I could get some answers.

Most of all, I hated feeling like I was powerless to do anything about the situation.

But I also realized, after I sat and really thought about it, that something must have happened. Something at John's work that had caused him to be on high alert. No one had called me, though. Not Sara. Not my dad. Not my aunt or uncle, so I wasn't worried that it was something which had to do with any of them. Probably some problem with one of John's contacts. An issue with their underground betting or gambling, stealing cars, running drugs, or whatever it was that John did… and I didn't doubt that he did it all. I wasn't naïve enough to think that the Colombo family wasn't involved in all of the above. I knew for a fact that my own father had his fingers in all of those things, though it would have killed him to know that I knew.

The numbness that crawled through me like slithering shadows when I thought about those things was probably just a coping mechanism that I'd put in place a long time ago, when I'd first been old enough to understand that my dad, and the rest of my family, did criminal things. I guessed I'd learned to deal with it because I knew my dad was a good man underneath all of that, or despite it.

Maybe my relationship to him made it easier for me to accept what John did. I'd known right from the start that he was in the same business as my father was, and I had years of practice making my peace with that.

What I did have a problem with was my own husband forcing me to stay in a house that wasn't even entirely mine, with guards at the door, and not telling me why. Would it be so hard for him to call and let me know what was going on? For him to send me a text? Just... just *something*?

Maybe he didn't respect me enough to do it. Maybe he didn't think he had to explain himself to me. If that was true, he had another thing coming.

I checked my phone again, alarmed at the time. If I didn't do something fast, I wasn't just going to miss my interview—it would be too late to even call and ask if I could reschedule. That would look extremely irresponsible, and who knew if they'd even consider me seriously after that?

No, I wanted the job too badly. I wasn't going to give up on the interview.

I sat for a few more minutes, and slowly, a plan started to form in my mind.

I had always been resourceful. I was, after all, my father's daughter.

It only took me a few minutes to run to my bedroom and throw a few things into a backpack. I changed my shirt, putting on a bright pink blouse. I knew that Mary must be in the condo. She was probably a prisoner, just like I was, even if she didn't know it yet.

I walked down the hall and knocked on her closed door. She pulled it open with a ready smile for me. That was a new one. She probably didn't know about the goons at the door, and she'd likely had a good night out at the play. I was momentarily distracted by the warmth her smile caused. It died away when she took in the seriousness of my face.

"What's happened?" she asked, like she expected me to tell her that someone had just died.

"I have to get out of here," I whispered. "I don't have time to go into the details. I don't even know what the details are. There are two guards at the door, though. Big goons of John's. They're telling me I have to stay in here."

Mary's eyes got huge. I'd been right. She hadn't known about the guards. "Why?"

"I don't know, and they won't tell me. John isn't answering his phone. I have an interview that I can't miss. I'm going to distract them, and I'm going to run down the block and ditch them. I'll catch a cab to my interview. Don't worry. I promise that when I get to the hospital where the interview is, I'll text John and let him know that I'm safe, and I'll wait for a driver before I leave. I'll be fine. I just wanted to let you know that I'm going to get out. And, uh, there's going to be some smoke."

"Smoke?"

"Yes. Smoke." I grinned deviously. "I'm going to light something on fire. A *contained* fire—it won't be dangerous, I promise. I'm just going to set off all the smoke detectors and sprinklers, if there are any. I'll yell for the goons and they'll come in to see what the heck is going on. I'll get past them somehow. For whatever trouble it causes you, I promise I'll make it up to you later, but I wanted to give you a heads-up."

Mary shook her head. "I don't like it. Mr. Colombo wouldn't like it."

"I don't care what John likes, Mary. I *have* to get to this interview. It's the job I've always wanted! I've spent four years working my butt off to become a nurse. I'll never get to be one if I can't even show up to the interviews. This matters to me. *A lot.*"

Mary's dark eyes roamed over me, taking in my clothing, the backpack on my shoulder, and the earnest expression on my face. Those eyes softened, and I knew that somehow I'd made a friend. She nodded, getting that same determined expression that she often wore. "I'll help you."

This was more than I could have hoped for, but I didn't have time to thank her properly. I thought I would have embarrassed her if I did, anyway. Mary followed close behind me as I stalked down the hall. She watched me as I moved to the kitchen and threw open the cabinets until I found a full tin of coffee grounds. I was in luck since it was one of those industrial ones. I emptied the grounds into the garbage can as fast as I could. Then I threw my backpack to the ground and fished out the book I'd thrown in.

*Sorry, trashy romance, you'll be of much more use to me like this.*

I tore out pages, scrunching them up and placing them in the can.

*"Here."*

I looked up to find Mary offering me pieces of cardboard. Boxes, toilet paper rolls, things that would burn slower because they were thicker. She'd obviously raided the recycling bin.

"Thank you!" I crammed all of it into the can and kept adding paper. I added more cardboard and more pages, layering it like a cake.

When it was done, I slid open the top drawer on the island, which I knew housed the barbeque lighter. I'd seen it in there when preparing dinner the day before.

I zipped up my backpack and threw it on my back. I was just about to light the can when Mary shook her head.

"Go stand by the door. Where you won't be seen. I'll light it. That'll give you time to slip out when they rush in. I'll scream that there's a fire when the smoke starts."

"Okay. You aren't going to wait for the sprinklers?"

"I'll let it get going. That should do the job pretty quick—alarms, sprinklers, or no."

My eyes brimmed with grateful tears that I barely kept back. I couldn't believe that we were doing this. I wasn't even sure what made me happier—the fact that I might get the heck out of the condo on time for my interview or Mary's newfound friendship.

She nodded at me once more, and I moved to the door before she set the paper on fire. We both waited, but Mary had been right. It only took a few seconds before the can was shooting out massive flames. The smoke detector came on instantly, its shrill blare blasting through the house, but the sprinklers were more reticent. I figured that only helped our cause.

*"Fire!"* Mary screamed dramatically. In another lifetime, she could have had a career as an actress. *"Fire! Help! Please!"*

The doors burst open so fast that I actually jumped in surprise. Goon One and Goon Two stormed in. Mary ran around in the kitchen in circles, as though she was hysterical over the coffee can that had spontaneously decided to combust. The hall was clear, and as soon as the goons had their backs to me, their attention focused squarely on Mary's theatrics and the flames, I rushed out.

I ran down the hall as fast as I could. I didn't dare wait for the elevator, but dodged left and threw open the door to take the stairs. I blasted down them so fast that I nearly stumbled a few times, and had to grasp the rail tighter as I told myself to calm down. I wouldn't be making it to any interview if I fell and cracked my head open.

I'd worn a bright pink blouse because I'd thought the guards would have seen me first before I could get past them. Even if they'd only seen a flash of pink, though, I was prepared now. I stopped and took out a long black rain jacket from my backpack. It had a huge hood. I threw it on over my clothing, zipped it up, and made sure the hood hid any of my hair and most of my face. If they were looking for a pink shirt, they'd be out of luck.

I abandoned the backpack in the stairwell, and when I reached the bottom, I forced myself to take slow, measured steps. I didn't turn and smile at the security guy in the lobby. I just walked straight past him, out onto the sidewalk.

When I was out of view of the lobby windows, I broke into a run, and I didn't stop until I reached an alley. I darted inside, waited for a cab to approach the curb or for one to go by slowly enough that I could possibly flag it down.

After just a few minutes, I realized it was a bad plan. No one would see me in the alley. I was too well hidden by the towering buildings around me. I stepped out, back onto the sidewalk, and resumed walking at a normal pace. I had to remind myself that the hood hid most of my face because I had it pulled so tight. I barely recognized myself when I glanced at one of the big glass windows of a building I passed.

I kept walking as I watched for a cab, but none of them were pulling over. I'd have to find a busy intersection where I could get lost in a throng of people while also having a chance of flagging a ride.

The sidewalk was busy enough. It was New York. When were the sidewalks not teeming with life? It gave me a modicum of comfort to realize that I was surrounded by people, and that I'd be hard to find as it was.

I was ready to stop, pull back my hood, and try to flag down a cab when my phone buzzed in my pocket. I pulled it out and sighed when I saw John's number. I knew I should answer. The goons had probably figured out that I was missing and reported it to John. I didn't really want to get anyone in trouble, either, and I could imagine that John's wrath would be swift and real.

I hesitated, though. I'd rather not get chewed out about the stunt I'd just pulled. I could easily just get in a cab and text John that I was fine, and let him know—as I'd promised Mary I would—that I was on my way to a second interview.

I tucked my phone back into my pocket, pulled back my hood, and stepped toward the curb. Before I could raise my arm to try to get the attention of one of the passing cabs, a black car pulled up to the curb a few feet back. I stared at the car, and a weird sense of familiarity hit me. Where had I seen it before?

I pulled out my phone again, a strange shiver chasing its way up every single bone in my back. I glanced at the car's tinted windows one more time before I turned away. I found John's missed call and ran my finger over it. The phone rang. It echoed through my ear. Something wasn't right. Maybe it was the adrenaline of making my escape, but the hair suddenly stood up on the backs of my arms. I waited as the phone rang again.

"Elisa?" John's voice—strong, alert, sure, and definitely worried—rang through the other end.

I sighed in relief, and I'd just opened my mouth to say his name when a rough hand clamped over my mouth, shutting off everything but a garbled scream of surprise. The phone dropped from my hand and

I was picked clean off my feet with a violent jerk that caused my back to crack and spasm in protest. My neck snapped back into a hard brick wall of a solid human chest. I smelled smoke, leather, and something sour. I was tugged backwards so fast that I didn't even have time to try to fight back. Instead, I was bent forward roughly and shoved through an open car door.

*That car. The black car.*

But I realized it was too late. I was already inside.

I scrambled over to the other side of the car and clawed at the door, tugging wildly at the handle. Of course, it didn't give. It was locked, and there was no lever in sight. I had no way to disengage it.

The man who'd grabbed me—clad all in black, he was a huge beast who put the goons outside of our condo to shame—got in beside me with more agility and speed than a person his size should ever have been able to move with.

The car shot forward, racing through traffic at a terrifying pace.

The bastard beside me clamped one meaty fist on my arm and tugged me against him. His hot breath spilled into my ear. "Don't struggle now, sweetheart. It will all be over soon."

I had no idea who he was, but he had to be a member of the Profaci family. It was the only thing that made sense, even though my father had said they were no longer a threat. This bastard wanted me to know who he was. He *wanted* me to be terrified.

I struggled wildly, trying to bring my free hand around to land a punch in my captor's face. He was too quick. He caught my wrist and held it in a death grip.

And then I got a good look at his face. He had big, blocky features that matched the rest of him. Chiseled cheekbones, a jaw with grizzled, black stubble, and dark, menacing eyes. Cruelty lived in those depths. They turned my blood to ice water.

I'd seen this car at the hospital that day, and he'd been watching me, I realized now. But I'd said nothing to John.

How stupid could I have been?

I tried to tear free of my captor, but he was too strong and too fast. He wrapped one big hand around both of mine, holding them in front of me like a set of steel cuffs. With the other, he produced something—a thick cloth. I smelled the chemical before he was able to get it close.

*No!*

I knew I had to fight. I couldn't let them get me unconscious. They could do anything with me if that happened. *To* me. They could take me anywhere.

Why hadn't I just stayed in the condo? Why hadn't I answered the phone when John had first called?

"Sweet dreams," the insidious, dark voice rasped thickly against my ear.

The rag was shoved across my nose and mouth, and even though I tried not to breathe in, attempting to thrash my face from side to side, it was useless. I felt the black closing in around the edges of my mind, and then my entire world went dark.

# Chapter 29

## John

Elisa's scream seemed to echo through my blood, permeating my veins and ringing through my skull. When her phone went dead, I hung up and tried calling her. Over and over again.

There was no one there, but I didn't want to believe what I already knew.

I tracked her phone, my fingers jamming at my screen frantically, even though I tried to tell myself to stay calm. The tracker still worked. Her phone was giving off a signal just a few blocks from the condo.

*Fuck!*

I'd called Elisa the second my men had called to tell me that she'd gotten past them somehow. She'd diverted them with the help of Mary, of all people. Started a fucking coffee can on fire and screamed for help. She'd obviously rushed the door as soon as my men had turned their backs to deal with the immediate threat.

Dread washed over me like I was getting drenched by a rogue wave. All I saw was red. My vision was coated in it, sticky and dark. I had to blink several times to clear it before I realized that I was back in the warehouse. I was still waiting on word from my uncle and Gastone Gambino. And I'd just sent Dario off twenty minutes ago with instructions.

This couldn't be a coincidence. Dario had warned me about a diversion, but could this have been the Profacis' real aim? I was chilled all

275

over again when I recalled Dario saying that he was surprised they hadn't tried to take one of us out.

I'd never thought that they'd hit our families.

Take one of our women.

*My wife.*

But they had.

She *had* been taken. She'd screamed into the phone and then I'd heard it hit the ground. If it wasn't the Profacis who'd taken her, then who? No, it could only be them.

Cutting back the rising need to do something violent to expel the animalistic rage rising inside of me, I punched Dario's number into my phone.

"John?" he answered immediately, his voice cutting through the haze of red starting to creep up again, bringing back some small semblance of calm.

"Dario. You were right. They've taken her."

"Who?"

"Elisa. They have Elisa."

"*What?*"

"She got outside. Got past the guards I had at the door. Whoever it was, they were obviously watching the condo. They got her. She tried to call me and I heard her scream and then… then, nothing."

"Fuck," Dario swore. He moderated his voice, though, probably just to keep me from rushing outside, jumping into my car, and driving straight out to find Elisa. "You need to keep calm. Don't do something stupid, John. You have to wait for us. Call our uncle. Call Gastone Gambino. We're stronger as a united force. *You're stronger* with our men beside you. We all want to get her back. We *will* get her back. Don't go out there alone, John, do you hear me?"

I'd never wanted to disregard good advice like I did at that moment. It took all of my strength to remain standing where I was. I wanted to find the Profaci scum who had taken my wife and put a bullet between his eyes. I wanted to make him suffer before I did it. Slowly.

I'd carve out his own entrails and make him eat them.

"Where the fuck is our guy?" I muttered more to myself then to Dario, but he heard me.

"I haven't seen him all morning," Dario responded. "Thought he was out with the rest of the men, securing our territory and looking for any more potential threats. That's where his tracker said he was."

Instead of relief, yet another surge of dread washed over me. I had to slam a hand out to the wall to steady myself.

I thought about Elisa and her worries back at the restaurant. That night out before the wedding, I'd caught the same guy watching me intently at the club. The photos that had been sent to Elisa could have come from him. Then there was the way he'd fallen off my radar that very morning without my even noticing it. The way he'd looked at her at the luncheon that very first day.

But it couldn't be him. That had to be my paranoia talking.

All our guys were loyal, would never betray our family. And this man been a loyal soldier, and more, for a long time. He was one of the men who'd trained Dario. I didn't consider the man a friend, but I had no reason or cause not to trust him. On top of all of that, the tracker Dario had put on him proved that he was doing his job, out with our other men, scouting to see if he could find anything.

"Can you get back here?" I asked Dario, realizing that I'd gone off the fucking radar for a few minutes while I'd been lost in thought.

"Yes."

"Good. I need a ride. I can't fucking drive when I can't concentrate."

"I was just going to say as much."

"How long?"

"Fifteen, twenty minutes at most."

"Good." I closed my eyes and thought for a moment. "I'll call our uncle. He's probably still with Gastone. I'll let him know."

"Fuck, this is going to get ugly."

"It will," I agreed, and I tried to keep the mirth out of my tone. The thing I wanted more than anything in the world was to paint the city with Profaci blood. I wanted to coat myself in it. *Drench myself.* Bathe in it to satisfy my need for vengeance.

"Stay where you are," Dario repeated. "Make the calls."

I shook myself out of my rage-induced thoughts. "Yeah." With nothing else to say, I hung up and clenched my phone tightly while I ground my teeth.

It wasn't just rage I felt, though. It was fear.

I, John Colombo, was afraid. Afraid that something would happen to my wife. Afraid that I'd never see her again. Afraid that I'd missed more fucking signs. She should never have been taken. *Never.*

I forced myself to dial my uncle's number and put the phone to my ear.

*** 

Gastone Gambino paced back and forth across my uncle's living room. We'd mobilized there within the hour, after my call to Leone. Our combined men were out scouring the city for Elisa.

So far, nothing had turned up.

I forced myself to sit, but I wished I was pacing like Gastone. At least I'd been doing something then, which would have been a hell of a lot more than I'd done to ensure my own wife's safety. Elisa being taken could have been my fault. No, it *was* my fault. I'd put my best men at the door, but she'd still gotten away. I should have put an army there. I should have fucking bolted the doors shut.

Tied her to a fucking chair with a guard watching her at all times.

On some level, I knew the thoughts were irrational. I couldn't have done any of that. I could have put more men at the doors, but we really hadn't been able to spare them. And I'd had no reason to think she'd try to effect some kind of escape, let alone with Mary's help.

I could have done more to find the rat. That much, I knew, and I blamed myself for it. I'd let my family down. I could have been indirectly, or directly, responsible for Elisa being taken. And still, *still*, I was no fucking closer to figuring out if someone had betrayed us.

A sharp sniffle drew my attention to the far side of the room. Sara and Maria were there. I'd protested against them being allowed in, but they'd come with Carlo Gambino, and it was clear that Gastone approved of them being there since they were so close to Elisa. He obviously didn't want to leave them at home unguarded, without himself or Carlo there to keep watch.

I couldn't say I blamed him. We didn't need anyone else going missing.

But Sara crying quietly in her mother's arms only further wrenched my already aching heart and tortured mind.

Dario was at my back. He set a hand on my shoulder like he sensed I needed it. He said nothing. Offered no more reassurances. He just stood there beside me after he dropped his hand away, and watched Gastone Gambino pace and my uncle brood quietly in his chair in a corner, next to Nevio.

We were all waiting for news that might come too late. I wanted to be out there looking, searching, doing something, but my uncle had forbidden it. His sentiment was closely aligned with Dario's. No one thought it was wise for a member of this family to make themselves an easy target. When Dario had driven me to Leone's, he'd told me that he preferred to see me without my gray matter leaking out all over the fucking pavement after catching a bullet.

The sharp, shrill sound of Leone's phone ringing shattered the heavy silence weighing down the room. Even Sara went silent, mid-sob. The entire world seemed to freeze in place as Leone slowly lifted his phone to his ear.

"Speak!" he commanded sharply.

There was a pause. He nodded. I couldn't miss how his hand trembled at his side. He balled it into a tight fist to hide the weakness, but he couldn't hide the fact that his normally robust coloring faded into a dull gray. Even Nevio frowned while he watched my uncle.

"Thank you. Stay where you are. You'll have your instructions shortly."

Leone hung up. He turned to Gastone first, which was bad news. Gastone had stopped pacing the instant the phone had rung. Leone's eyes tracked to me next. I could tell just from the look on his face that whatever he was about to say was bad.

"That was Piero." He faced Gastone to explain further. "One of my capos. He has a message. He found one of our men, beaten nearly beyond recognition. Sanders. He called Piero since he didn't have my direct number, and told him as soon as he got there that he had a message from the Profaci scum who'd jumped him and beaten him. They have Elisa. They want a meeting to negotiate their future in the city. They won't release Elisa until we comply. If we should choose not to…" Leone trailed off, and all around the room, those implications hit hard.

Sara shrieked. Her mother hushed her, but Maria's eyes were wide and terrified. Leone had gone pale, and even the old buzzard, Nevio, looked worried. Dario shuffled his feet beside me. He looked ready to restrain me if I reacted by doing something stupid, like throwing myself through a glass window and hitting the ground running on the way to find and butcher those bastards who had my wife.

I slowly shifted my eyes to Gastone. He'd been deathly silent since the call and my uncle's painful words.

He looked terrible. His coloring was entirely gray and chalky. His eyes were unfocused, probably due to shock. Suddenly, he let out a groan, clutched at his left arm, and slumped to his knees. He fell forward, face-first to the floor, before anyone could catch him.

"Call our doctor!" I yelled, rushing forward.

I reached Gastone first, before anyone else had even moved. In the background, I heard people yelling, feet thumping, commands being barked, and something else about a doctor again. I grasped Gastone's suit jacket, wrapped my arms around him, and carefully turned him over. His lips were flapping, and his eyes were open, dull and glazed over, but his skin was that same sickening shade of gray. There were flecks of spittle at the side of his mouth, running down his chin.

I jammed my fingers into the juncture of his neck, relieved when I found an erratic, weak pulse. Our surgeons would get there faster than any ambulance, I knew, even if this was something we could have sought out a regular hospital for.

"Hang on!" I commanded roughly in the ear of my former enemy. "We have good surgeons. They're on their way. You have to hang on for them. For *Elisa*!" Gastone didn't respond. His eyes rolled up, but his pulse didn't change below my fingertips. "We'll find her!" I swore. "We'll find her, and I swear to you, I will make each and every single one of them pay. If they've harmed her or not, they will answer for what they've done. I swear it on my life."

Gastone let out a wheezy breath, like he'd heard my oath and would hold me to it, even should he die. I realized, with terror, that that was a very real possibility. The pulse grew weaker beneath my fingertips.

I could not fucking let him die. I couldn't let Elisa be taken and then discover her father had died from the shock and horror of knowing that his only child was in danger, possibly hurt. As I gathered Gastone into my lap to support his head, my fingers steady at his neck, I closed my eyes and promised Elisa, wherever she was, that I'd find her, and that somehow, I'd save her father, too.

# Chapter 30

## Elisa

It was impossible for me to know how many hours or days I'd been imprisoned in the tiny, windowless room where I was being kept. I'd woken with a throbbing pain in my head. The dry, bitter taste in my mouth was hardly as bad as the metallic burn of regret that had settled in.

I couldn't change what had happened, though, and that made it worse. All I could do was wait. Wait in the minuscule room with a bare bulb in the ceiling that flickered erratically, sometimes plunging the room into darkness for moments at a time before it buzzed back to life. The place was more of a cell than a room. It had a cold, concrete floor, no windows, thick walls, a metal door, a barely working toilet in the corner, and a musty smell that made me believe I was being kept underground.

A few hours after the chloroform had worn off, I'd tried pounding on the door. Screaming for release. *Threatening. Begging.* There had been no response. I had no idea how many hours I'd been in that room before the door had cracked open and some thug had thrust in a tray with a plastic bottle of water and a few pieces of dry bread.

That's all I'd gotten, once every twenty-four hours or so. At least, that's what I'd guessed the regularity of it was. I had no real way to tell time. No sun rising or setting, no stars and no moon. I'd had three meals, so I figured that I'd been there for at least three days.

I'd have thought sleep would be impossible, but I had little else to do, and it was only during my sleeping hours of oblivion, curled into a corner of the room on the hard floor with no blanket or pillow, that I found any relief or release from my terrified thoughts and the weight of my worries.

I worried about my family. They'd be distraught at my having been taken. I worried about John—that he'd do something rash to try to get me back and be hurt in the process. I worried about our men, too, thinking that they'd get in the line of fire and that one or more might be killed and it would be my fault. I kept going over and over the last things I'd said to John, too. How I'd hit him and called him a Neanderthal. If I never saw him again, that's what I was going to have to live with. What if something happened to me? He'd blame himself, and I doubted he'd ever forgive himself, either. And Mary had helped me, so she'd blame herself, as well, which bothered me more than I could say.

I sat in a corner of the room, curled into myself. The floor was cold, but I didn't have the energy to stand up and keep the damp from crawling into my legs and settling into my bones. I'd gone through every emotion from hope to despair. Now, hungry, exhausted, cold, sore, and worried about those I loved, I was somewhere near hopelessness.

To keep myself from falling into that black pit, I thought about that night on the couch when John had apologized to me for what he'd said. How he'd opened up and shared the darkest parts of his life with me. I treasured the moments that we'd danced, playing that time over and over again in my mind. The way he'd ordered pizza for Sara when she'd been crying in my arms. That day seemed like it was a thousand years ago. But I clung to it now, and to those moments when I'd realized a tenderness in John that I wouldn't have thought could possibly exist.

When I'd first met him, I'd thought that he was beautiful on the outside, but with the terrible beauty of a man who had no soul. I'd been wrong. So wrong. He had a soul. He had a heart. It was probably a good one, too. I'd caught just the barest glimpses of it in those raw, unguarded moments that he'd shared with me. Would I ever get to see that again? Would I have the privilege of getting to know my own husband, to know

284

and return a tender touch, to one day fall in love and be treasured in return?

Or was I sitting here thinking all of these thoughts too late?

I dropped my aching head into my hands and blinked hard to clear the tears that were rising to the surface. What good would crying do? I'd cried so many times since I'd been taken that I'd lost count. Not a single tear had helped my family find me or swayed my captors into setting me free.

The tears hovered on my lashes anyway, and were there when the metal door at the far side of the tiny room squealed open. I jerked my head up, dashing the backs of my hands quickly against my eyes. I refused to give these bastards the satisfaction of knowing how close I was to being beaten.

A powerfully built, middle-aged man stepped through, and I gasped without meaning to. I knew this man. This was the one I'd told John about. That horrible man from lunch! I'd later found out his name when I overheard someone talking to him... what was it? Peter? Piedro? No, that wasn't it.... *Piero*, I finally remembered.

As soon as I recalled his name, the floodgates of fear unlocked inside of me. I literally trembled at the sight of him. John had said that he trusted this man, but he'd been planning to tell his brother to keep an eye on the bastard. To track him? Had he done that? Yes, if he'd said he was going to, then I knew that he would have kept his word. Which meant that this man was even more dangerous than anyone suspected. Did anyone know he was a traitor?

I shuddered at the man's appearance, and up close I realized his face wasn't disfigured, not exactly. He had a jagged scar along his jawline. It was old, since it stood out silvery white against his darker skin. When he smiled at me—a horrible, leering grin—I shivered at the missing teeth. The dark gaps made that grin much more sinister than it would have been otherwise.

"You don't know me," Piero said, circling around to the other side of the room. He didn't close in on me, but the evil he threw off was like a stench seeping from his pores. It permeated the room. "But I do know you."

I shuddered again, but held my head high and tried to hide the fear growing in the pit of my stomach like an iceberg. If he even saw the tip of that fear come to the surface, he'd know there was so much more hidden below. Evil men like this, men who were hardly human, fed on their ability to instill fear.

"I've been so very close to you all this time. Close to John for years. *Years.* I've been a trusted member of the Colombo family, and all this time, *decades*, I've been betraying them."

My heart stopped in my chest. This guy was clearly deranged. I could tell, just by looking into his eyes. They were blank where there should have been... *something.*

"I spent years proving myself to the Colombo don, but he repeatedly refused to move me up the ranks. He was satisfied with having me as his soldier, his attack dog, his *rabid* dog. I was no better than an animal on a leash. He didn't want that moving up. He didn't want to lose such a good, faithful soldier. A soldier who would do anything for him. A soldier who could make anyone disappear."

Fear bit hard at my nerves, nibbling them until they were raw. *A soldier who could make anyone disappear.* He could make *me* disappear. He'd already taken me. And I knew he was a killer. The kind of man who killed and didn't think twice about ending a life. What more did I matter, compared to anyone else he'd previously disposed of?

"The best part is this," he went on. "Here you are, and you have no idea how I've changed your life. Yes, you. I can see that you have your doubts, but take a good look at me, the man who stamped a permanent imprint into your life without you even knowing it. I wanted to prove myself to the Colombo don, and the best way to do that was to take out an enemy. Not just any enemy, but the head of a rival family. A powerful rival. Unfortunately, things went wrong. It wasn't your father who died in that car, but your mother."

I reacted without thinking. "You're lying! My mother died in a car *accident!*"

Piero grinned evilly, revealing those missing teeth and the brown stains at the bases of a few others. "Is that what you were told? I'm sure your father would have wanted to lessen the sting. He told you it was an accident? He was right. It *was* an accident. I *accidentally* killed the wrong Gambino. It was supposed to be your father getting into the car, but he worked late that night. You weren't with either of them—probably with some sitter. *She* got in the car, went to start it, and *bam!*" The bastard pantomimed the cloud of an explosion with hands that had spilled so much blood. "It was game-fucking-over for her. Of course, I regretted it, but there was nothing to be done for it."

It was like there was an explosion in the room itself. Something sharp and brutal detonated behind my eyes. My head snapped back with the impact and my body was flooded with a surge of energy. Fury gave me strength. This evil son of a bitch had killed my mother, and now he was here laughing about it. Throwing her death in my face. I reacted before I could think. Adrenaline burst inside of me, rushing through my veins and spurring me to action.

I burst off the floor and rushed at the bastard. Piero was a big man, though, and unfortunately, he saw me coming. When I lunged for his throat, throwing myself at him with my hands extended like claws, he dodged to the side. Fast as a real attack dog, he whipped out his weapon and struck me across my forehead with the butt of his gun.

I sank down to the floor, a sick pain twisting my guts and taking the place of the adrenaline that had been coursing through me just a second ago. I moaned and grabbed at my head. My hands came away sticky with bright red blood. The pain hit a second later, biting through me and gnawing at my bones until I thought I was going to be sick from it. The room smelled sharply of metal.

"Oh no, you little bitch. You *will* sit and listen. I'm not even halfway done yet. You haven't heard my crowning glory."

I had no choice but to obey. I knew that I couldn't stand. Blood bubbled between my fingers and dribbled slowly down my arm in a bright red rush. I wished that I could pass out. I didn't want to hear any more of this. I didn't want to sit there and have this pain eat away at me. The pain from the cut on my forehead. The pain from my lacerated heart.

Yet, the words continued, spilling out and burrowing their way into my ears like insidious worms even though I didn't want to hear them.

"The Colombo don—you never did get the pleasure of meeting him—was furious when he found out about the botched hit. He didn't want a war on his hands and, of course, a hit like that put him in a bad light. Everyone looked at him like he was the guilty party just because he was the enemy. He might not have been in town at the time. He was off on one of the many vacations he thought he had a right to take instead of working like the rest of us. He thought he was a god. So far above all us mere mortals who toiled away under his boot. He thought he could squash us at any time. The only thing he cared about were his brats and that whore of a wife. He traveled all over the fucking world with them. Just because he was gone at the time, though, that didn't put him above suspicion. He could have given the orders. I thought there'd be a bloody war between the two families, but somehow your father was convinced to leave it alone."

I barely managed to raise my head, but I stared the asshole down anyway. He was on one hell of a power trip, and I wanted him to see that I was no longer afraid of him.

He ignored me and went right on with his little tale of vengeance. Clearly, he reveled in it.

"I killed them, too. John's parents. The don and his wife. This time, I made sure I didn't botch the job. I thought for sure Leone Colombo would see my worth and make me the underboss. The next in line for the don of the family. It was always my plan, my fucking right, after years and years of loyal service, that I should be next. It should have been me leading the Colombos. We would have *taken over* this city. We wouldn't have cowered in the wake of our fucking enemies. We wouldn't have sought a bullshit peace. We would have been an empire. *My empire.* I wouldn't have been weak like Leone Colombo. But no. Instead, the idiot trained his child nephew to take over the position.

"And I couldn't kill the brats without raising suspicion. I couldn't take out Leone. He made sure someone was always watching. The old man is paranoid. Over-careful. It's probably the only reason he's still alive, but you'd better believe I plotted my revenge. I've been informing against the Colombos for years. I work on the inside. They trust me. They see me as a *loyal soldier*. A capo who would still do anything for them. They didn't even suspect it. *All. These. Years.* All these years, I've been giving away their secrets to the highest bidders. All their shipments that went missing, their jobs gone wrong. It was me who cost them, every little bit of it."

The man's face twisted with a sadistic expression that was probably joy.

Bile crawled up my throat. I wanted to vomit just from having to look at Piero, but I still didn't tear my eyes away. I was no longer trembling. I'd promised myself that I wouldn't be afraid. Hearing about my mother's death had banished that fear. It wasn't terror flowing through my veins now. It was a desire for vengeance. I had never imagined myself taking a life, but in this moment, I would have watched the light dim from this monster's eyes with pleasure. More, I would have made it happen if I could have.

"I took you because you're stupid and weak," he continued with a sneer. "You're the fastest way to get to John and his dumb brother, and when they're dead, I'll go for Leone next. Your father will follow, and then I'll be the head of both families. Gambinos and Colombos. I'll run this entire fucking city. They have no idea that, all along, the man who could bring them down was in their own ranks. They were so worried about the Profacis, who are nothing better than an eager ant. I fed them information. I was the one who urged Flavio to make a move. While both families were distracted by such a small inconvenience, it left the door wide open for me to do what I'd planned. To make *my* move. You've all been stupid and careless, and that will be your downfall."

Knowing it was true made my throat swell with bitter emotion.

I had been careless. It was my own fault.

Piero eyed his gun and then turned those terrible black orbs back to me. He slowly raised his hand, leveling the gun right at my head. I stared him down, refusing to look away. I would not cower before him, even if this was the moment of my death. It didn't even seem real, and the shock of it gave me strength. I felt like I was just in a dream—that, any minute, I would pull myself awake and none of this would be real. The gun felt like a toy, this man just being the product of the worst that a nightmare could throw at me.

The room spun as I stared down the barrel of that gun.

I knew it wasn't a toy. This wasn't a dream, but it all felt so surreal.

Piero moved his finger to the trigger. Something that felt very much like panic exploded in my chest, but I bit down hard on my tongue to keep a cry from escaping my lips. I would not make a sound. If he was going to kill me, I would keep my dignity. It was the only thing I would never let him take from me, this monster who had taken so much already.

So I waited, my chest heaving, blood dribbling from my forehead into my eyes, the scent of metal already hot in my nostrils. Bile flooded the back of my throat.

Surely, though, he wouldn't. Not now. How could he? He'd lose whatever leverage for which he'd taken me in the first place. All of the leverage he'd have over the Colombos and my own family. That had to have been his reasoning for going after me.

The shot never came.

Suddenly, raised voices echoed from somewhere else in the building. A commotion. Shouts. And then a loud pop that I knew was gunfire.

Piero let out a growl of frustrated rage, and I squeezed my eyes shut and braced for the impact—that last thing I would ever feel or hear—but it never came.

Instead, there were heavy footsteps, and the door opened and slammed shut.

I was left alone.

Alive.

At least for now.

I concentrated hard on the noise I could hear going on above me. Something was happening. Was it John? Was it my father? Had our families finally found me? If they had, they'd done it at exactly the right time. A moment later, and I might have been lying on the floor in a pool of my own blood.

But I couldn't allow those thoughts or the terror to creep back in. I needed to stay strong. I needed to be smart and get myself out of here alive before anyone else got hurt.

I knew that, no matter what, I would find that man, that monster who had taken my mother and John's parents, and I would make him pay. I would make him *suffer* for the hurt he'd caused. For the lives he'd snuffed out. For the innocence he'd banished forever.

There was no place in the world for people like him.

He'd promised to be my family's downfall. The Colombos' downfall. Well, now I would be his. I'd find a way, no matter how unlikely it seemed right this moment.

Wiping the blood from my forehead and out of my eyes, I got to my feet. I was stronger than I'd thought I'd be, and I never wavered as I walked to the door. I meant to pound on it. To make myself known. To let someone, anyone, know I was down there. What good was a rescue if my family couldn't find me?

The first strike of my fist against the door made it rattle strangely.

I let out a gasp, and my hand fell to the knob. It turned easily beneath my sticky, bloodied fingers.

It had been left unlocked.

# Chapter 31

## John

*Finally.*

Fucking finally, I was able to do something.

One of our men had *finally* gotten a location. He was a good soldier, and an even better tracker. If someone didn't want to be found, Shane was our man. He hadn't failed in the past, so I trusted his word.

The first tip-off had been when the tracker on Piero's car hadn't moved in hours. That had made it obvious that he'd figured out we were tracking him and ditched the car. Sure enough, we found it parked in a narrow alley in the territory Piero was supposed to be canvasing.

After everything that had happened, everything I'd seen and heard, I found that I wasn't shocked to discover Piero had indeed betrayed us. I just wished that I'd trusted my instincts after Elisa had been taken and gone to find him myself, even when he'd made it appear earlier that he was doing his job. Even though everyone trusted him. I'd known something was off, I'd known it in my gut, and I should have acted.

Piero had made a vital mistake, though. He'd had one of his men, whoever he was working with, make a call from the same neighborhood where Elisa was being held. Shane had tracked the call as soon as it had come in. The asshole had been on the line long enough, making his demands for a meeting, so that Shane had gotten a bead on the location right away. He'd left the house soon after Gastone had collapsed, promising that he'd go scout ahead of us and send word back before we moved out in order to make sure we weren't walking into a trap.

Gastone had been taken to the hospital on the advice of our surgeon—a heart attack wasn't a gunshot wound, so there was no real explaining to do—and a chunk of his men were keeping watch, circling the hospital.

Leone was agitated, and I'd had to argue with him to keep him where he was. He didn't go out into the field like a soldier. He argued that, normally, neither did I, but we both knew this was a special circumstance. He couldn't have held me there in his house if he'd fucking chained me to the ground.

I had waited until Shane felt certain of the house where the call had been placed. He couldn't be sure Elisa was there, but he'd confirmed that there only seemed to be four or five men in the building. It wasn't Profaci territory.

We moved out as soon as I knew I wouldn't be bringing my men to their own slaughter. I rode with Dario, following our men. A line of black vehicles sped along behind us. We looked like a goddamn funeral procession, and I thought about how fitting that was. Up ahead, Carlo Gambino drove like a madman, as eager to free his niece as I was. He had a few of the Gambino soldiers with him. It was still a relief to me that it was mostly our men, men who I knew—had worked with, and trusted—at my back and covering my front.

It felt like it took us forever to reach the sketchy neighborhood in New Jersey where Elisa was being held, but at least we had the cover of darkness. I was certain she was here. I felt that certainty deep in my gut. Every single house on the block looked vacant. It seemed like a good place for squatters and addicts to gather. The kind of neighborhood where no one asked questions about men dressed in black stalking an abandoned house.

I kept going over that call. The call that was supposed to have been placed by the Profacis. If they'd wanted to take Elisa, they might have brought her here, to an area we wouldn't have been likely to find her in, but it just didn't make any real sense. They were smarter than any of this suggested. The only thing I could figure out was that they were being set up. By Piero. That he wanted us to think it was them, or think that they were involved. That he wanted us distracted by them in order to keep our attention focused away from him.

Fuck the funeral procession, I realized as our men swarmed the block—this all looked like a goddamned FBI raid with all the black vehicles involved. We weren't circumspect, but then again, I wasn't trying to be. I wanted Piero and whatever men he had in there to see me coming and know they were about to meet their end. They'd fucked with our family. With our allies. Acts of war would be repaid in kind. I wasn't about to sneak up on them. I didn't need the element of fucking surprise. The Profacis, if it was them, thought they were well hidden out here in this decrepit area, outside of New York. That was surprise enough. And if it wasn't them, that was fine, too—we'd take out whoever was responsible for all of this and be glad to have done it.

My blood pulsed through me wildly and my heart beat hard enough to tear out of my chest. As soon as Dario stopped the car, I flung the door open with my Glock palmed and ready. Our men spilled out, closing in on the house. Ahead of me, Carlo Gambino shot me a look. I nodded back. Dario was at my side in the next instant, a pump-action shotgun extended in front of him.

I would have loved to have had grenades with us. Pulling that pin and blowing this whole fucking neighborhood to smithereens would have brought me a delight that I'd never experienced before, but I couldn't take that chance with Elisa inside. Just because we'd been told what house they were keeping her in at one point, that didn't mean they hadn't shuffled her over to another property.

We circled the house, surrounding it completely before the men inside made the first move. Shots tore through the swirling inky night, bullets whizzing past and thunking into the sides of cars, punctuating the stillness with deafening blasts.

Our men scattered, some hitting the ground and some running for cover behind other buildings, cars, and trees. I ran with Dario, diving back behind his car. The sides were armored and the glass was bulletproof. I moved around the bumper, eying the big bastard in the window of the house. He was up, confident in his position. Even through the near black of the night, my shot was clean. A spray of red erupted from the guard's head.

Bullets whizzed around me and I ducked back, flattening myself up against the car.

"Fucking hell, right?" Dario grinned at me. "This is a fine welcome."

"Don't do anything stupid. For god's sake, keep your fucking head down."

"I saw that. Nice shot."

"Yeah, but who knows how many there are?"

Our men returned fire from their positions. Windows shatters and metal screeched. There were dull thuds of wood exploding. There were the yells, too. High and low. Dull. A throaty roar. Screams from the injured. The silence of the dead. I wasn't worried about them hitting Elisa. There was no way the bastards would have been careless enough to keep her within easy reach. She was far too valuable, and I knew these men weren't that stupid. Reckless, maybe. Desperate. Following the orders of a man who was far too confident in his ability to bring us down. Still, they weren't stupid enough to give up their bargaining position. I just hoped that we hadn't arrived too late.

"Fuck this!" Dario yelled, as if he could read my mind. He clutched his gun and studied me. "We need to get in there. We can't give them time to move her or do... something else. You'll cover me?"

"What? No! Jesus Christ, stay where you fucking are. That's an order!"

Dario never had been very good at obeying anything I said. I wasn't surprised when he crept around the side of the car. I scrambled into position, tearing my other Glock out. He charged forward, shooting like a madman as he rushed the house. I did what I could to cover him— picking off another guard with a headshot, putting a bullet into the chest of another. Dario left a bloodied trail of carnage in his wake. Our men saw his mad rush and, when Dario reached the house and kicked in the front door, they followed.

I ran after my brother, unwilling to let him go into that fucking house alone. I passed Carlo Gambino, who stuck close to my back after I went by. Shots zipped past us, the pops echoing through my ears. I realized that, at any second, one could slam into me and that would be it.

I burst through the open doorway just in time to see Dario put a slug straight into one of the goons' heads. The man slumped over. I hit Dario's back, both of us breathing hard.

"You crazy motherfucker," he said to me, as if I was the one who'd charged fearlessly through gunfire, blazing my way inside.

I turned as our men poured into the house. It was dark inside, nearly impossible to make anything out. There were bodies strewn about, and darker pools of black blood congealing around them. The silence was as deafening and as threatening as the gunshots had been.

I motioned to our men to search the rooms. If Elisa was there, we would find her.

"Is anyone injured?" I asked under my breath, hoping like hell that the answer was no.

There was a grunt from behind me. I turned sharply to see Carlo sticking his hand under his jacket, near his stomach. When he pulled his hand away, even through the darkness, I could see the horrible plum-hued liquid on his fingertips.

"Fuck." I ran over to him while our men covered us.

I ripped his jacket off and studied the wound. It was leaking blood at an alarming rate. A gut shot. The dark red stained the black shirt below the wound, pressing it wetly to his body. His pants were rapidly becoming soaked.

"You need to get back to the car. Come on."

"No." Carlo shook his head. His hand covered mine, moving it away and pressing down hard with both of his. "No. Not until we have Elisa."

"Carlo, you're hit! If you don't get out of here now and get to a hospital, there's no chance! Do you understand me?"

He nodded slowly, eyes blazing like a wild animal on the hunt. "I do. I understand. I understand that my niece is in there somewhere and I won't leave until I get her back." His eyes met mine, and I had to swallow thickly, because his burned with a primal need to take back what was his. He was like an old lion. Even injured, he would still go down attacking.

I let my hands fall away and I returned the nod.

I thrust my way to the front despite protests of the men around me. Elisa was my wife. Not theirs. I *would* find her.

I rushed forward along with my men, but the house appeared empty.

I stalked forward anyway, thinking she had to be here. "Look for a basement or a cellar. Something beneath the house. They have to have something built here."

Further into the dank darkness, I sensed a movement to my right. I lunged before anyone could shoot. The man was large, but I was faster. I shoved my gun into the base of his skull as I wrestled one arm around his shoulders. Dario shifted through the black, his gun trained on the fucker's head.

"Tell us where she is," I commanded.

The man stayed obstinately silent.

"I won't ask you again. Tell us, or you can eat a lead sandwich."

The man breathed hard, his nostrils flaring. Spittle formed at the side of his mouth. His eyes swiveled to the side, and I imagined he could see that I was serious. If I wasn't, Dario certainly was, along with any one of our men at our backs. In a moment, he realized that there was no way out of it for him. No chance of escape.

"Downstairs," he finally hissed.

"Thanks." Dario ripped the bastard out of my hold and let out a blast that sent the goon sprawling back a few feet to slump on the floor.

I didn't have time to take in the carnage. I kept moving, pushing forward. Where the fuck was the door?

"Over here!" Carlo's voice was strained, growing weaker.

I whirled and saw him clutch at something. When he pulled it, the blackness yawned down like a gaping maw.

"Fuck, we can't go down there without a light!" Dario protested. "That would be suicide."

"Now, you want to talk to me about that?" I retorted. "We can't use a light or they'll see us coming. But I agree, going down in the dark is just as bad. They'll hear any movement."

"What do we do, then? Shoot first?"

"I'll go down. You cover me."

"No." One of our men, Donnie, clasped my arm. "I'll go. We can't risk either you or your brother. I'll take Mike and Ricky. Follow us when we've cleared it."

I shook my head and pulled away so that I could charge forward anyway, determined to get down those steps before anyone else. I wasn't going to waste time arguing. If Elisa was down there, I had to get to her. My whole body felt like it had been dipped in a vat of caustic chemicals. I felt like there was a wild animal thrashing just below the surface.

*Whoompf.* The air rushed out of my lungs as Dario slammed me into the nearest wall. He kept me pinned as Donnie held up his hand and signaled to the black-clad figures behind us. They rushed down the stairs ahead of us. I held my breath, expecting a burst of gunfire, but the house remained ominously silent.

Had we cleared them all out? Were they regrouping now, on their way to ambush us?

I knew we had to act fast. I couldn't wait.

"Get off of me!" I growled at Dario, and he finally obliged. I pushed him aside and charged the wooden stairs, my gun extended. It was basically like going in blind until a light flared on, further into the concrete space. My eyes burned at the single bulb. Donnie stood underneath it. He gave me a look, but crept on. Dario hit the floor behind me, followed by three more of our men.

The basement was one big open area with some framing here and there—not much more than posts to hold it up and an occasional space sectioned off, but the house was big enough that I wasn't seeing all of it. Not in the dim light and with the labyrinth of cheap walls along the sides of the main space. There was no sound but our movements, though. If there had ever been a furnace down there, it was long fucking gone, the space was so cold and damp. I was honestly surprised that there was any electricity at all in the building.

We crept on silently, our boots crunching against the dirty floor and our heavy breathing being the only sounds. I moved swiftly past a section of framing. A shadow caught my eye and I turned my head. My breath punched out of my lungs in a single shot.

*"Don't. Fucking. Move."*

I stared down the barrel of a 9mm.

*Piero.*

I slowly lowered my gun, dropping my hands down to my side. I didn't call out. No one else had seen me in this grungy corner yet. The framing was open to both sides, back and front. Piero was leaving his flank open, which just proved that he was desperate for escape. He'd use me as a human shield if he had to. He'd train the gun on me until our men stood down.

'You know you won't make it out of the city," I said in low tones. "Even if you manage to get out of here."

"So sure of yourself. You who worked alongside me for years and never knew that, all this time, I was feeding your enemies information. You never even figured out that I dumped that car in an alley. You didn't think I had any idea you were tracking me? *Pathetic.* You and your brother." Piero's evil grin gleamed through the dim lighting.

"I suspected," I confessed. "Leone assured everyone that you were loyal. He believed in you and trusted you. When one of us puts you below ground, though, I guarantee you'll go straight to wherever the universe decides that traitors should go."

"Traitors?" Piero hissed. The gun never wavered. He was too composed to give himself away in a fit of anger. I knew there was no chance that I'd be able to get under his skin. "Look at yourself when you speak of *traitors*. I was loyal to the Colombos for decades, and no one gave me a chance. Not your father. Not your uncle. Certainly not you. You even promoted your idiot brother to capo! He would have moved to underboss when the time came."

*Un-fucking-believable.* "So, that's what this is about? Power? Jealousy? Moving up in the world? You had everything! You had a good position. You had money. Weapons. Cars. Men beneath you. Was it really so important to be at the top?"

Piero's lips curled back. "Enough. Put your gun on the floor. Slowly. Kick it over to me. Make one wrong move, and you won't be making another."

I did as he asked, bending at the waist to put my gun on the concrete. As I bent, though, I saw a flash of a movement behind Piero, through the other side of the framed wall. I took extra time setting my gun down, and that was all it took.

A shot rang out, the sound skittering and ricocheting through the empty area.

I jumped back as Piero's body hit the ground in front of me. The bullet had torn right through his skull. A red pool spread out from the body like an encroaching tide.

There were shouts, and my men gathered around me. Dario was there first. He stared at the body. "Be smarter about where you call from next time, you motherfucker," he ground out.

I stepped away, walking around to the other side of the wall. The blackness was nearly complete on the other side, where a bare bulb in the center of the open wood beams running across the ceiling couldn't reach.

My throat went bone dry. My palm started to shake. I had my Glock back in my hand, and it vibrated at my side.

She looked like a ghost. White. *Stark white.* Congealed blood on her forehead, matted in her hair. Twin tear tracks racing silvery streaks down her cheeks. Huge eyes shining like emeralds that the darkness couldn't dim.

"Elisa," I choked.

"John!" She dropped the gun from her hand and ran at me.

She hurled herself into my arms and I held her—stroking her hair, trying to assure myself that she was real. I pulled back finally, but only to look at her head. I ran my thumb around the edges of the gash, but she shook her head.

"I'm fine," she whispered. "Just, please, I want to get out of here." Her eyes dropped and she let out a gasp. "Your shoulder."

Her hands flew up to examine me, and when her light touch hit me, I flinched. I felt the burn and my flesh started to throb as the anesthetic of the adrenaline started to fade. I looked down, angling toward the light. My shoulder was soaked, and Elisa's fingers came away red.

She carefully removed my jacket. When she unbuttoned my shirt, her fingers were agile. She checked the wound in my shoulder, biting down hard on her lip.

"It went right through. We need to find something to tie it off, though. You're bleeding a lot. Something clean."

"Use the jacket."

Elisa did, tying the arms around my shoulder so tight that I couldn't keep a hiss of pain from exploding from between my clenched teeth.

"Sorry." She gave me a funny look. "You guys came wearing suits?"

"I didn't realize I was supposed to stop off at home to get changed."

"How about bulletproof vests? How about—"

"How about I get you home?" I cut her off. "It's only me and Dario dressed like we're heading to the fucking office. The rest of the guys had their gear."

"We are going to have to have a serious conversation about this," Elisa said. She was remarkably composed for someone who had just been kidnapped, and who had just shot a man point-blank in the head.

I shook my head to anchor myself, but I needed to know one more thing. "Did they...?"

She read my face for the rest of the question and offered a small smile. "No," she promised, shaking her head. Her blonde hair was a mass of knots and dried blood, but still, some strands swirled around her face at the hard movement. "They never did anything to me. Just kept me locked in a room down here. Piero..." She pointed at the body. "He hit me when I attacked him, after... after he came in and told me all these terrible things. All of it. He... he was... he betrayed you."

"Shh. I know." I wrapped my good arm around Elisa's shoulders. I steered her away, out into the light where my men were waiting. Our voices had obviously carried, but no one had intruded on our moment of privacy.

Dario was waiting for us ahead of the others. He took off his jacket and wrapped it around Elisa's shoulders. She looked at him gratefully, and then let me lead her toward the stairs.

"He ran out when he heard the shots and the shouts upstairs. He left the door open behind him," she explained as we moved, seeming to need to get it all out at once. "There was a shot down here. That man, I think he shot the goon that was guarding the door. I have no idea why. It was a stupid thing for him to do because that's where I got the gun from."

"He wanted to escape." I led Elisa over to the stairs. "He knew that we'd found them and he didn't want any witnesses. They wouldn't have let him go. He knew it would be a blood bath."

As soon as my foot hid the bottom tread, one of my men called out the all-clear to us. They'd already secured the building and the wider area around the place.

I was thinking about Elisa. I was so focused on her and her needs, on the sheer joy I felt at having her alive and well at my side, that I forgot all about her uncle until we got upstairs. A few of my men had flashlights trained on us, and Carlo was there leaning against the wall, his hand over his side. Someone had given him an article of clothing to stanch the blood.

"Carlo!" Elisa cried. She broke free from me and ran to her uncle.

Carlo wheezed heavily when he saw her. "Thank god," he hissed. Blood bubbled out between his lips when he spoke.

"No!" Elisa sobbed. "No! Uncle… please. We have to get you to the hospital." Elisa's hands flew, inspecting the bullet hole, but I thought she knew what she'd find before she even moved the blood-soaked clothing and Carlo's hand away. "Come on! You should have been on your way there by now!"

"Look after your father," Carlo wheezed. He looked fondly at Elisa. "Sara. Maria. Love you, Elisa." His dark eyes landed on me. "Take care of him, too. You're where you were meant to end up."

"No!" Elisa screamed for the third time. She pressed down hard on the wound. "You're going to the hospital and you're going to be fine!"

Carlo looked over at me as my men came rushing to his side. They took over for Elisa, putting pressure on the wound, and helped him through the house, but still he insisted on hobbling along.

Elisa seemed frozen in place. Her hands were stained with her uncle's blood. I walked up behind her and set my hands on her shaking shoulders. "Come on. It's not safe here. We have to go before the Profacis regroup. Flavio is still out there. He's the one giving the orders. This whole block is probably owned by them, but it doesn't look like it's been used in some time. Probably why they figured we'd never find you here. I'm not taking the chance that someone didn't call the cops after hearing all those gunshots. We need to move."

Elisa still didn't move, so I gathered her up in my arms and held her against my chest.

Dario appeared and stepped in front of me. Our men surrounded both of us, and I walked right out the front door, straight to the backseat of Dario's car. I positioned Elisa and got in beside her. Then I wrapped my arms around her and she began to sob, clutching at my shirt.

I wished I could erase the horror of the night, but I couldn't. I could only promise myself that, in the future, I'd keep her safe. No matter what the cost.

I couldn't even begin to process what could have happened to her. What Piero could have done.

Dario slid into the driver's seat and, flanked by two other black cars, we sped away. The sounds of sirens were already wailing in the distance. I knew the rest of our men would get clear. I craned my head sharply, and I could already see smoke billowing up into the sky from down the block. My men were quite adept at covering our tracks. This was one hell of a track to obliterate, but I had no doubt that when the cops finally got to sift through the wreckage of that house, they'd find the charred remains and assume it had all been due to a drug deal gone wrong. A turf war, and one disgruntled drug lord leaving a message. It would never get as far as dental records or proper identifications. If it did, it wouldn't be traced back to us. My uncle would see to covering us and protecting us the way he always had. He had powerful men in his pocket, and powerful men had a way of making things disappear.

My arms tightened around Elisa. I barely felt the pain in my shoulder. The radiant joy at having her back beside me was tempered by the death of her uncle, which I felt sure was coming. She sobbed silently against me. I knew that she'd cry until her tears ran dry. I only hoped that, by the time we made it to whatever clinic Dario was driving us to, we'd have good news about her father. I couldn't bear to think of the ways that the grief of losing him would permanently scar her.

# Chapter 32

## Elisa

I remembered how I'd felt when my father announced I'd be marrying John.

I was numb. The world around me seemed like it was muffled in cotton. I felt nothing, and the world moved by in slow motion.

Now, I felt everything so acutely. The sharp tang of pain. Relief so sharp that it was like a blade itself.

I was sitting on the sterile, hard black bed of the clinic where John had brought me. The doctor had just finished putting a neat row of stitches in my forehead when John got the call that my uncle was in surgery and was expected to be just fine. The bullet had missed almost everything vital, and the blood loss had been curbed just in time. It had all looked much worse than it actually was.

Another doctor had patched up John's shoulder.

*John.* John, who hadn't even realized that he'd been shot in his crazed, urgent need to get to me. John, who had shot and fought his way in to get to me. John, who could have died trying to free me.

They'd packed his wound, the two doctors at the clinic, but he'd insisted that he not leave my sight. I'd sat and watched—detached, but not from a medical standpoint. After he'd been done, he'd stood guard while the doctor had placed the neat little stitches into my forehead. I imagine they were absolutely perfect, since John had glared at the man with enough menace to melt metal.

*"Elisa?"*

I snapped out of my trance. My eyes met John's. How could I ever have thought those eyes were all ice? They danced a bright indigo that bordered on purple, dark and huge under the clinic's fluorescent lighting.

I realized that the doctor was finished. He was stripping off his white latex gloves, cleaning up the bloody gauze and instruments.

"There's something I have to tell you," he said, caressing my cheek with the back of his knuckle as soon as the doctor vanished from the room.

I was transported back to the alley that day. The first time that his hand had ever gripped mine. I'd thought then that they were stained with blood. Now, I knew it was the blood of my enemies. John would do anything to keep me safe.

It turned out, maybe I'd go just as far to save him.

I'd shot a man. Shot him in the head and watched him topple over.

And I was glad.

I'd thought that no person could be wholly evil, but I'd been wrong. That man had taken so much from me, and from John, as well, and I'd burned with vengeance. I'd been entirely rational pulling that trigger. Unswayed by the insanity of emotion. There'd been no haze of red, no bloodlust, no madness. And now, I didn't regret it. Now that it was over. It was over, and I still felt completely detached from what I'd done. Would it ever sink in? Would I have regrets later?

*No.* Not regrets. I might feel something else, but not that.

I blinked when I realized that John's eyes were bright with worry.

I thought again about what my uncle had told me. He'd obviously thought he was in serious trouble back at that house. So had I. He'd told me that I was where I belonged. He'd asked me to take care of John. That had mattered to him.

I'd hear those words for as long as I lived. And I'd honor them. I knew what he'd meant. *Learn to love him.* Carlo had thought he wasn't going to make it, and that had been what he'd chosen to say.

John stared into my eyes, hesitating before he spoke. "I don't want you to think that I didn't tell you because I was trying to keep secrets from you, or that I was withholding information. I knew that we had to get cleaned up first before we'd be able to visit. Do you understand?"

I didn't, but I nodded, holding my attention to John even as my mind tried to wander again.

Worry lines creased his brow. He bent and ran his lips over my forehead, below the stitches, as though I was the one who had lines that needed to be smoothed away. Did I? God, I couldn't imagine what I looked like right now. My worry was entirely for John, my invading thoughts only of my uncle. I'd never once considered what a mess I must be. John didn't look at me that way, though. There was a new softness to his face, to his eyes and his lips, that I had never seen there before. It showed far, far more than just the relief illuminated in his eyes.

"I've started to—when you were taken.... I..." He blinked at me, unable to finish what he'd been saying, but I knew. I'd thought about it endlessly when I'd been locked in that room.

I reached up and set my hand on his. His words had faltered, and I had none of my own to replace them with.

He shook his head. "That... I... that wasn't what I meant to come out."

I understood. He wanted—no, *needed*—to tell me something. Something important. "What is it?" I asked when I found my voice, and with it, some of my strength. I was going to need it, I knew. I'd grown up a Gambino, and now I was a Colombo. I could be myself with John, be vulnerable and let him see the truth, but right now, my family needed my steel will to push forward.

"It's... please don't panic. I know you're already upset about your uncle. I don't want you to take this the wrong way."

My heart fluttered with the exact emotion John had told me not to feel. Panic. As if either of us could command it. I could feel my throat tightening.

John took my hand and clenched it hard between his, chafing my fingers as though they were frozen and he could rub life back into them. "It's your father. When you were... gone... we received a call from the Profacis, requesting a meeting. They threatened action if we didn't agree."

307

"You mean they were going to do something to me."

John nodded slowly. "That's what they threatened. We don't know what they would have done, and I'm so fucking thankful that we didn't have to find out. When your father heard their threats, he collapsed." I sucked in a breath as John rushed on, trying to reassure me. "He was conscious the whole time. Our doctor arrived, and we all knew he had to go to the hospital. He's very comfortable now. He's alert and he wants to see you. He knows that you're safe and that you'll be there as soon as you can. He's okay, Elisa."

"What?" I gasped, the news finally sinking in. "Why didn't you tell me? How could you not have taken me…" I trailed off, realizing it was obvious why John hadn't told me before now, and just as obvious why he couldn't have taken me straight to the hospital. I couldn't arrive in a hospital covered in my own blood, smelling like gun smoke and quite possibly spattered with the blood of the man I'd killed.

"The clinic has a shower in one of the staff bathrooms. I've already asked Dario for a change of clothes for both of us. He'll be here shortly. We can clean up and I'll take you right there."

"John?"

"Yes?"

"Why… was there… was there going to be a meeting?"

He frowned at me so fiercely that my breath caught. "The man we had tracking you found where they were holding you before it ever came to that. Shortly after your father was taken to the hospital, we got word. We moved right away."

"You should have taken time to—"

"There was no time. I swore that I'd blast through hell itself to get you back." John's voice wavered, and I realized how close he was to losing control. There was rage there, but sorrow, too.

My eyes stung with unshed tears. "I'm sorry," I whispered. "If I had just listened, none of this would have happened."

"It wasn't your fault. They wanted something to use against us. If it wasn't you, it could have been Sara or your aunt, or even Dario or myself.

We all moved around freely enough, thinking that we were safe. It was our job to ensure it, and we failed."

"Don't say that."

"You're right." John gently lifted me down from the bed I'd been sitting on. "There's time to talk later. Right now, we need to get cleaned up, and then I'll take you to see your father."

I nearly collapsed with relief. I wanted to thank John. I wanted to find my voice and tell him the thousand things I'd thought while sitting in that room. I wanted to tell him that we should start over. No more fighting. No more misunderstandings. Just us. Together. Learning how to care *for* each other. Learning how to care *about* each other. Growing and falling and loving.

That's what I wanted. I wanted a future that was peaceful. A future where I didn't have to worry about the people I loved getting hurt. If that wasn't possible—and, in truth, I'd grown up knowing for a fact that the way our families lived made it almost certain that safety could never be guaranteed—then I wanted to make every minute of what time we had count.

John understood. I think he knew just by looking at me that something was different. That I was different. He opened his arms and I fell into him. I nestled against his soft shirt, listening to the beating of his heart below. It was a glorious sound. A sound I hadn't been sure that I'd ever hear again. I let his arms enfold me, and hold me so tight that I could barely expand my lungs enough to steal a breath. He needed this as badly as I did, and that meant *everything*.

I still needed to tell him everything that Piero had said. There were so many hard moments coming for us, but wrapped in John's arms, I felt like I'd have the strength to face them. To find the words. To find the will to be strong for my family. To finally live the life that I'd been born into. To have the courage to let my guard down and learn how to love. I realized that John might need a lot of help with that, too. He'd had a hard upbringing with no parents, devoid of so much as a gentle touch. I knew that I'd find a way to be patient, above all.

"John?" I whispered.

"Hmm?" His breath was warm against the crown of my head.

"Save another dance for me? In our living room?" It might have been a corny thing to say, but John obviously didn't care.

"Always," he responded huskily. "I promise."

***

The second I saw my dad in that hospital bed, wires and monitors all over the place, I rushed to him. He was propped up in the bed with pillows behind his back. And although was very pale, his eyes shone brightly, even if there was still an edge there, which I guessed to be the very naked fear for me that he hadn't yet shaken off. He was alert, though, and the smile that arched over his lips when he saw me made my heart ache.

I was careful when I sat on the edge of the bed and leaned into his arms. They were still the strong arms of my dad, even though he trembled slightly with the fatigue of what he'd been through.

Even after a shower and a change of clothes, I knew I couldn't hide my face. It was still swollen from weeping. I felt like my entire life was swollen with grief, but I drew strength from my dad's warm chest. His heart still beat on steadily beneath my ear, and I was so very glad that he was alive.

"Elisa," my dad whispered thickly. That's all he could say, it seemed. Just my name.

I pulled back and looked into his face. Saw the utter relief, and so much love. I knew then that my father had bruises that went deeper than the flesh, just as I did. How many times had he lived through this? The loss? The violence? It hadn't just been my mother, I knew. How many of our men had he seen buried over the years? But we both bore scars now. And while I might have one on my forehead for the rest of my life, the real grief was carved deep in both of our souls.

My dad caressed my hair. He studied the line of stitches. And then he said everything that I needed to hear.

"I love you so very much, Elisa. I always have and I always will. My life wouldn't be what it is without you in it. You have always been the bright spot in my life, especially after your mother died."

I didn't even bother to blink back the burning tears. "I love you, too," I choked out.

My dad raised his eyes and slowly looked behind me. I glanced behind me, as well. John was standing in the doorway where I'd left him when I'd run to my dad. He looked shy, and there was a new tenderness on his face that I'd never seen there before.

"Great loves don't always start as great loves. Sometimes they take time to build," my dad whispered in my ear before he released me.

"Thank you," I said, so softly that I wasn't even sure if my dad would hear me. I brushed at my eyes and stood shakily.

John stood where he was and I stood beside my father's bed. He'd never lost that shy smile, and I had the urge to hug him, too. Not just hug him, but *include him*. To teach him what the love of a family meant. Yet, I knew that would be too much, too soon, so I offered him a shy, tender smile of my own.

"You go on home now. You've been through a lot," my dad said. Even from a hospital bed, he could still be commanding.

I wanted to protest, but my dad silenced me with a stern look. I knew I could visit again tomorrow, and he was right. I had been through a lot. We all had. I really needed to rest.

I said my goodbyes, and then I let John take me home.

I didn't even remember blinking until we walked into our home. The very same home that I'd escaped from a few days earlier. Mary wasn't there to greet me, but I knew that I'd see her in the morning. I hoped that she didn't think that what happened had been her fault in any way, just because she'd helped me. We'd have to make sure to reassure her on that.

John's hand was at my back suddenly, and I welcomed his hot touch. He led me down the hall and pushed open the door to the guest room. I shook my head slowly, but he just blinked at me and led the way inside. He peeled back the covers and I climbed in, still fully clothed.

I half-expected him to leave me there like that. My throat constricted with panic, but John somehow knew I needed him. He flipped off the lights and silently crawled in beside me.

Neither of us said anything. The bed was big enough that we weren't touching. Both of us were still in our clothes.

There were still so many things I needed to tell him, but I knew that I'd need time.

I shifted closer, reaching through the sheets until I found John's hand. I wrapped my fingers through his, and then he opened his arms and pulled me up against him gently, tucking me in against his side. He was warm. He smelled good, too, like *himself*. His presence was more than comforting.

I knew that he couldn't take away the pain I felt, or even do anything to ease it. Only time could do that, and I would never ask him to take that burden on. Just having him there next to me, his body sheltering mine and his breaths hot on my hair and forehead, helped.

I had missed him. I had missed him so much. More than I'd ever thought possible. I'd missed the warmth of him. Missed his touch. Missed his *presence*. I'd missed the goodness that he didn't even know he had and probably didn't even believe in. I'd missed his smile and his laughter. He had hardly offered me either, but I knew that he would.

John wasn't the enemy. He'd never truly been the enemy.

My body had known that before my head. I had never trusted it, but maybe it had been the wiser of the two all along when it came to John.

I twisted and reached up, wrapping my arms around John's neck. I pressed myself so tightly against him that I barely gave my lungs room to expand and contract. John's arms wrapped me up until he was all around me, his hands at my back and shoulders, his chest enveloping me. His entire being cut off all of the noise in my head so that, when I closed my eyes, there was just silence.

Silence, and us.

312

# Epilogue

# Elisa

"How are you feeling tonight, wife?" John's rich, smooth voice enveloped me as soon as I slid into the passenger seat of his car. I did up my seatbelt, and then he pulled away from the curb where he always parked.

Since I'd been taken, he'd insisted on giving me a driver for small things like errands, but he always made sure that he was the one who drove me to work and picked me up at the end of my shift.

"Okay." Since he was driving, but I still craved contact between us, I settled for taking his hand and gripping it.

"So, extremely nauseous?"

John knew me too well. I bit down on my bottom lip and nodded.

"Do you want me to make you another appointment? The doctor mentioned that medication you could try."

I shook my head. "No," I reassured him, "don't worry. I'll be fine. Just have to make it another month and it should let up."

He glanced over to me quickly, frowning. "But you're sick. *A lot.*"

I squeezed my husband's hand. "It's okay. Lots of women get morning sickness. It's actually a good sign of a healthy pregnancy."

John squeezed back. I wanted to ease his worries, so I smiled warmly at him. When he reached a red light, he turned to me and offered that small I loved so much.

"All right. I just want to make sure you're okay. I don't like seeing you in pain."

"No one ever died from an upset stomach."

He rolled his eyes. "You're a nurse. Don't use statements like that."

313

So touchy when it came to me, but I couldn't really complain about that. I could see how worried he truly was. I reached over and caressed his cheek. "It's okay. I'm fine. *Seriously*. I haven't even thrown up once! I just feel yucky and tired, and that's perfectly normal. I have a great doctor—you've seen to that. We've heard the heartbeat a thousand times, too." I removed my hand from his cheek and set mine over my heart. "And my own is going strong, at the normal rate. I promise that everything will be fine."

John nodded. The light changed, and he had to concentrate on traffic in front of us. Even at seven at night, it was thick. "I'm going to insist on you seeing another specialist soon. I was doing some research, and I think that's for the best. The doctors we employ don't normally deal with... with pregnant women."

I laughed. "No. They just deal with gunshot wounds and other traumas."

The corner of his lips turned up. "So, you agree?"

"Whatever will put your mind at ease."

"It puts my mind at ease having you here with me right now."

I sighed, but it was the happiest kind of sigh.

It turned out that my husband, beneath all those gruff layers, was actually quite romantic. Two months ago, when I'd found out that I was pregnant, he'd actually cried when I'd told him. Real tears. He was thrilled, but scared to death. I think we both were. Just like all parents. Our life was also more dangerous than that of most; even if I did work at a care home for senior citizens, John was still very much involved with the family business. He might not be the head of it, since his uncle was still in excellent health, but that didn't make his position any safer.

As a result, we didn't take a single moment for granted. My uncle's brush with near death, John's parents being taken from him, my own mother murdered, my father's heart attack... it all taught us that life was very precious. Bringing a child into our world was a hard thought.

I wasn't sure that we would have chosen to have children, and certainly not this soon, but when I'd found out that I was indeed pregnant, our thoughts had shifted to our future family and we'd both begun to plan for that. Together.

I had been on the pill—I certainly hadn't lied about that!—but I'd had an infection that I'd had to get medication for. I hadn't even thought about it messing with my birth control, but obviously it had. I was a nurse, and still I'd blanked on that possibility.

When I'd realized I was a week late, it had been the first thing I'd thought about.

John was amazing. When I told him, he swept me up in his arms, and then came the tears of joy. He promised to protect me—to protect us both. He'd pulled up my shirt and kissed my flat belly before he spread his hand over that space protectively.

I'd never forget those moments.

"So, work was uneventful?" he asked now.

"Yup. Thank goodness."

We'd had some incidents at the care home earlier in the month, where a few of the residents had managed to break out of the facility. It had been traumatic for the staff who'd been on at the time. I hadn't been at work that night, but losing someone who has dementia and could get seriously hurt outside of our facility was not a thing any of us wanted to contemplate. Thankfully, George, Iris, and Florence had all been found relatively quickly, just six blocks away, and no one had been hurt.

Having missed the interview at the hospital, I hadn't gotten the job I'd thought to be my dream job at the time, but I'd applied at other places and ended up where I was meant to be. I loved each and every one of the residents I worked with.

"You're tired?" John asked.

My shifts were from seven in the morning until seven at night. The way the care home worked, I never had to work at night. I just had my regular twelve hours during the day, while the night staff came on after me. It was nice, not having to work odd shifts. It helped me keep a regular schedule and meant that I had more time to spend with John. When I'd gotten the job, I had thought, ironically, that I'd once wanted to work night shifts so that it would take me out of the house and away from my husband.

I couldn't imagine that now.

Simply, I was happy. *We were happy.* We were so blessed, and we knew it. After I'd been kidnapped, we really had worked on getting to know each other and learning how to love each other. We'd found that we both loved reading. John enjoyed Shakespeare and many other authors. And while he liked reading biographies, true crime, and mystery, he did occasionally read something that I'd recommend, which was mostly historical fiction. He even sometimes pretended to enjoy it. We hadn't had a single fight over stupid things. Or important things, either. While we sometimes argued, it was always less of a fight and more of a controlled stating of our feelings, and we'd work it out without either of us getting angry or hurt.

We both loved going out for dinner, too, so we'd made it a point to work on becoming foodies, or whatever they called that propensity. John had taken me to shows, ballets, plays, and even operas. He enjoyed it, too, most of the time, even if he barely let it show.

We hadn't told anyone about the baby yet. When I got to be three months along, we'd let everyone know. I couldn't wait to tell Sara and my aunt. Not to mention my dad. My uncle. Even Dario and John's Uncle Leone would probably be pretty excited. Mary would be thrilled, though I suspected she already knew. We were becoming close now, and she'd become a little bit like a mother figure to me. She often joined us for shows, or she went with me when John just had to tap out. Ballet wasn't his favorite, but Mary and I adored it.

"No. Sorry." I shook my head, pulling myself out of my thoughts. "What did you have in mind?"

"Starved?"

"I really can't tell with the nausea, but I think so. I could handle something light, if you're hungry."

"Sushi?" John suggested, but he grinned at me. He knew very well that I couldn't eat that. As soon as I'd told him I was pregnant, he'd gone and printed out the world's longest list of foods which I could and couldn't eat. He'd gone out and bought a boat-load of decaf coffee, put all the wine and alcohol in the house away, and absolutely forbid me from ever eating deli meat again. I loved him for all of it. And for everything else he did, and everything he was.

316

"Hard pass. How about a burger?" I suggested.

"Unhealthy."

"What about cravings?"

"What about our favorite? You could get the chicken wrap you like."

"Mmm. Chicken. Okay, you're on."

"But no sprouts."

"No."

"And no feta."

"You're right." I never even bothered going against John's rules about food. I didn't tell him that most of the things on those lists were just suggestions and that people could choose how careful they wanted to be based on their own body and health. I just followed what he said because it put him at ease. Because I seriously loved him, and he had enough to worry about as it was.

"Okay." John took the next left and rerouted us.

"Now that you mention chicken wraps, I *am* hungry."

John took my hand again and threaded our fingers together. I loved that he did that. That he always had to be touching me. Even if we were just doing something like sitting and watching TV, reading in bed, or cooking together in the kitchen, he found every excuse to brush my hand, tuck my hair behind my ear, or touch shoulders or legs. I loved that, too. Very much.

I loved a lot of other things, as well.

Like John's warm body wrapped around mine every single night. How he called me during my lunch break, each and every time I went to work, to make sure I was doing okay. How he sometimes sent flowers or a new book for me when I was at home. How he liked to surprise me with a new place to eat or tickets for some show or event. He always let me put my cold feet on his. For a man who really hadn't had a lot of love growing up, he'd learned very fast how to be a good, caring, and kind husband.

And I had to say, my father adored him. He saw how John treated me, and that was enough to win him over. Actually, my whole family loved John. He was a part of us. I might officially have become a Colombo, but both of us would always be welcome with the Gambinos.

317

"You know," John mused, his fingers tightening on mine. He turned to look at me, since we were stopped at a light again. "I truly adore you. Did you know that?"

I smiled as I felt myself flush. "Yes."

"I might even love you. Just a little."

"Just a little?"

"Well. More than the entire world. More than anything on this earth. That kind of just a little."

I grinned until it felt like my entire face would crack with the expression. "I might love you just a little, too. I might even love your weird colorful underwear."

"I bought a new pair. They're bright green with bananas on them."

"Oh," I hummed low in my throat. "I can't wait to see them."

"Soon," he promised with a smooth smile and a wink that made my blood heat up. "After dinner."

"You're wearing them right now?"

"No. I bought them and left them at home on the bed. But if you'd like, we can play a guessing game about what pair I do have on. If you guess right, you can take them off of me."

"What if I guess wrong?"

"You can take them off me then, too."

"Ha!" I laughed, my heart swelling with so much love that I could barely contain it. "Sounds like a deal."

***

Such. Love. Overflowing, abundant love that is always ready. So ready to spill over. That's how I feel when I look at my children. A son and a daughter. Twins. I carried these babies in my body. I grew them from nothing more than a speck, and now they're here, six months old, each with their own personality. They've given me more than I ever thought possible. They've challenged me, frustrated me, overwhelmed me, and given me more joy than I ever thought it was possible to know. Often, I find myself bleary-eyed from lack of sleep, annoyed by the tiny things, half crazed by the raising of two tiny humans, and then I just stop and look at them and all of that washes away because I know what a wondrous miracle they truly are.

I pull the blanket up over Aiden's tiny chest and do the same for Rose. For once, they remain sound asleep, but then, it's only been an hour since John and I gave them their bottles and settled them down for the night. They're notoriously hard to settle. They refuse to sleep apart from each other, so they're in the same crib together. Personally, I think they do this to play tricks on me. Maybe they like to sleep together because it's more fun that way. They can easily keep each other awake, or wake each other up more often.

I stayed with them for half an hour after we put them down, just to make sure they really settled. They always fall asleep better if there's one of us in sight, even if they're together. I hovered over their crib, humming love songs, even though my voice is terrible, and they loved it in the way that they do with all things right now. Unconditionally.

I'm their mother. Right now, I'm their everything. They'll always be that in my hearts. My world. My everything. My joy. My reason for living. My light. My life. My loves.

I can't really blame the sudden waterworks filling my eyes and trickling down my cheeks on pregnancy hormones. It's been six months. I didn't have enough milk to nurse the twins, so I've been bottle feeding from the start. After I healed from the birth, I got my cycle back almost right away. I'm kind of back to being normal, as far as my body goes—at least

319

normal compared to how it was before I got pregnant. Maybe I can't blame it on pregnancy hormones, but my body has changed, and not just on the outside. I now have mother hormones. As a nurse, I know there's a more scientific word for it, but that's what I like to call the rush of overwhelming love and that knowledge that I would do anything for my children, even defend them with my last breath, if I had to.

I lost my own mom when I was young. I remember her though, so clearly. I know that I look like her—my hair, my eyes, my facial features. I'm glad that I got to carry that on with me. My twins look more like John, with their dark hair and their blue eyes and their olive undertone, but I'm just fine with that, because they're perfect. Did I mention that already?

"Goodnight, my loves. Sweet dreams, sweet babies." It's what I say to them every night, and it makes me smile because I know that I'll be back in here within a few hours, saying the same thing, blowing them each a kiss.

I leave the room, shutting the door tightly behind me in an effort to block out any sounds that might startle them awake. John has the room wired up with security cameras. Baby monitors didn't cut if for him. We can watch the twins from every room in the house. A lot of security systems don't have sound, but this one does.

I know that John is locked away in his study, catching up on work. With John entering into politics, as well as trying to stay on top of running the family business, which he's mostly steered toward more legit enterprises, he's been busy. Oh, right. On top of all of that, he's been raising two babies for the last half a year. It's been a ride, let me tell you. Maria, John's live-in housekeeper turned nanny, is amazing with the twins. She helps me out so much. Without her, I would probably have lost my mind. When John gets home, we give Maria a break and he helps me out. It's still a lot, but we would never think of hiring an official nanny. I know how John doesn't trust anyone as a rule, and when it comes to his children, he's every bit of the growly, protective, fight with his life kind of parent that I am myself.

In the kitchen, I pour myself a glass of water and lean against the counter. John and I have been so busy that to say that our love has been a little bit... uh... neglected would be a huge understatement and then some. I smile to myself when I think about the package that arrived in the mail this morning. John was at work and when Maria got the mail, she'd set it on the counter in the kitchen. I blushed scarlet when I realized what it was, even though the packaging was totally discreet.

*Is it too soon?*

I did wash it this afternoon, tucking it into the washer with the rest of the laundry when Maria wasn't looking. I had to race her to the laundry room when the wash cycle was finished, just so I could pilfer it out of there before it hit the dryer and probably shrunk to the size of a doll's outfit. Maria had cleaned our en suite bathroom the day before, so I hung it discreetly in the glass shower to dry. Before John got home, I folded it and put it in the bottom drawer of my dresser, hidden away beneath a mountain of socks.

I finish my water, leave my glass on the counter, and head to the bedroom. Even thinking about that folded up garment makes me feel naughty. I haven't felt that way in a while. Pregnancy, while an incredible experience, was a little bit rough. Carrying twins can be kind of painful. There isn't a lot of room in one body for two new people to grow. I know that I'll never look the same either. I might have lost most of the baby weight because I work out in order to have more energy and to feel better and stay healthy, but still. There are marks that weren't there before. I feel like I'm always going to have extra skin where I shouldn't. I might have bigger boobs now, which is a bonus, but I also feel like my hips and bottom are not so bonus worthy. It's hard to act sexy when you don't feel sexy.

I know it's not fair to John. He's been nothing but supportive, protective, loving, nurturing—all those things I was so amazed to find out he could be. I can't count how many times he massaged my back and my feet when I was pregnant. He was there for every second of my labor and the birth, and he was better than all those nurses combined. After, he was so patient and so helpful. I know that people call their husband their rock or silly things like that, but John has been a freaking mountain for me to cling to in all the changes. He's been steady and solid and strong.

I love him more now than I ever have.

I slip into the bedroom, kneel in front of the dresser, dig through the socks, and pull out the costume I ordered. I'm a nurse by trade, and when I look at the white and red outfit in my hand, I actually snicker out loud. I ordered it because I thought John would think it was funny. I strip out of my jeans and T-shirt and fit the ridiculous costume over my head. I have to tug to get it on, but once it settles into place, it doesn't feel too tight. It wasn't cheap, and it is well made. I still feel like I'm going to look absolutely ridiculous, but when I walk over to the floor-length mirror, I'm pleasantly shocked.

*Holy. Shit. Is that seriously me?*

I don't look like myself. My blonde hair falls in waves down my back. My face is a little bit fuller now, but in a good way. My lips part as I slowly turn from side to side, taking in the way the costume flatters my full breasts, even without a bra on. The thing is so short it barely covers my bottom, but it does outline my now slim waist and curvier hips. I look… I look… *sexy*. I look beautiful. Daring. This was supposed to just be a joke, but part of me wanted it to be something more. Something spicy. John deserves this. It's been six freaking months since I gave birth, and it was probably at least four months before that where I was so uncomfortable and big with the twins that I hadn't really wanted to do anything. That doesn't mean that things haven't happened. I mean, we've had sex, but it's been exhausted sex at best. I don't want to say routine, because I don't think it could ever be routine with John, but it's been— well—decidedly mild, if we're going with the spice scale.

I give myself one more once-over, spinning around to study myself. I know that my smile has turned into a grin, and nope, I'm absolutely not ashamed of how happy and excited this silly thing makes me.

I just wanted to try it on, but now that I have, I'm not going to take it off. I mean, not alone, at any rate. I creep down the hall, tiptoeing quietly, as every mother learns how to do. I actually hold my breath until I'm well past the twins' room; everything is quiet. I feel even more

322

daring, like I'm being sneaky. Like a spy. Maybe I went with the wrong outfit. I have to clap a hand over my mouth to keep my laughter from bursting out.

John's door is open a crack. I don't knock. He doesn't need me to. When I used to do that, he'd always roll his eyes and tell me that wives get special no-knocking privileges that no one else gets.

God, have I mentioned how much I love my husband?

John is bent over a stack of paperwork. He's concentrating so intently that he doesn't even see me come in. I know he hears me, but he doesn't look up. I know it's only because he's so tired and he knows that I'm the only one who would disturb him, so he feels safe enough not to be overly alert. The fact that he trusts me beyond anything makes my heart swell.

My pulse kicks up when I slip behind John. I set my hands on his shoulders and bend to whisper in his ear. "I hear you're not feeling well."

He grunts and still doesn't fully turn. He must be even more exhausted than I thought. "What's that?"

"Definitely not feeling well. Not as alert as normal." I slip my hand to his forehead. "Hmm. You feel a little warm."

"Elisa, what?" He finally cranks his head around and his breath catches. His eyes go wide when he sees what I'm wearing. "Oh," he rasps. His gaze roves hotly over my body and I watch as his pupils grow, eating up his icy blue eyes which I love so much. "Oh," he whispers again. "I—I see. Yes. Yes, I do think that I need a nurse. Badly."

# John

Good lord, I've never seen my wife look so… alluring. I can't believe she's wearing a tiny white nurse costume with a little red cross on the front. It's absurd, almost like something I'd dream up, or a wild fantasy of sorts, but I'm not about to complain.

"Do you like it?" The uncertainty in Elisa's voice, that little catch, stabs me in the chest.

"Good lord god, yes I like it. I more than like it." I twist around, getting out of the desk chair. Elisa's cheeks turn a beautiful pink as she blushes.

"I—I thought that maybe—that we should spice things up a little."

I grasp her waist, dragging her closer. "I'm sorry I've been so busy."

"It's not that," she whispers. "It's hard, all the changes. Work. Changes to the family business. The twins. I wouldn't trade it for anything, but I think we've both been so busy with everything, we haven't had proper time for us. I want to make some."

"It would be even better if we started a trend. Always us time in the evening."

"I'd like that," Elisa purrs.

The fact that my wife either went out—no, she must have ordered this thing costume online, because there's no way she'd have a driver take her and the twins to a place where she could actually buy something like this—the fact that she took the time to pick something out for me makes me want to throw her onto the desk, scatter my carefully piled up shit everywhere, and ram into her so hard that she can feel me for days. In a good way. I would never, ever hurt Elisa.

Also, the fact that she ordered this for us makes me want to participate in making this special, so throwing her anywhere and ramming up into her isn't on the docket for tonight. At least not the first go-round.

I do haul her up against me, since my blood is thrumming so hard in my veins I can barely think, and my dick is so hard it's drilling through my pants. She tips her face up, grasps my shoulders, and pulls herself flush against me. All her curves melt against my hard planes, exactly as they should, and I lower my mouth to hers. I haven't kissed her like this in a long time. This time I don't know hold back. I let her know exactly how hard it's been to hold myself in check. To keep myself under control. I let her have the full force of my desire for her as our tongues glide over each other, as I suckle her swollen lower lip into my mouth.

I lose myself in that kiss and she comes to me, getting lost in me as well. She's delicious, like fresh air and a spring rain—and whatever, I don't care if that's corny, because it's the first thing I think of, and I love those smells. My balls throb and my erection stabs into her stomach. God, I want to be buried inside of her, throbbing inside of her. I want her to feel every hard inch of me, take every hard inch, and know how much I want her.

"On closer inspection," Elisa pants against my lips, "I find that your kisses are quite—up to par. I don't think there's anything lacking there. I think I might need to perform a full examination. Without clothes on." Her hands tuck at my belt, freeing the buckle quickly. The button and the zipper on my pants follow suit, and then she's tugging everything down.

I'm just as frantic, my hands pushing and pulling. After my pants and boxers are off, Elisa grips the buttons of my shirt—I'm still wearing an expensive dress shirt from work earlier today—and tears the edges so hard that the buttons rain down over the floor. Those little plink, plink, plinks are the sexiest sounds I think I've ever heard.

Elisa rakes her hands over my chest, her nails scoring my pecs, trailing down to the ridges of my abs. I don't hesitate to take my straining erection in her hand. She wraps her fingers around me and strokes me from my engorged head to the base of my shaft. I pump my hips into her touch, letting out a long hiss of pleasure.

"Hmm," she says in her best business nurse tone. She looks up at me. "I think this is definitely a problem that I know how to fix. A very fucking hot kind of problem."

"How should we do that? Fix it?" I'm enjoying playing along with this more than I thought I would.

"Well…" Elisa croons.

She releases me, steps into me again, tangles her fingers in my hair, and tugs my face to hers. I blister her lips with a kiss as I grab her ass, kneading my fingers there as I ram her up against my aching dick. Aching is a severe understatement. If I was any harder, I might need medical attention for real.

"Yes?" I groan against her mouth. I kiss her chin, her neck, her shoulders, sinking my teeth into the soft skin, not enough to mark her, but just enough to make her cry out in surprised delight.

She rakes her nails over my chest again and a streak of lightning jolts through me. My cock bobs between us, soaking her costume, I'm sure. Goosebumps break out on Elisa's harms, so that the hair stands on end. She's enjoying teasing me.

I palm her breasts, which are fuller than they used to be. I'm gentle, but when I lower my head and claim her sweet, arched nipple right through the thin fabric, I use my teeth until she whimpers. "Are you going to tell me what treatment you recommend?" I switch, doing the same to her other nipple until the white fabric is nearly translucent and her nipples are hard enough to cut through it.

"I think that the best thing for you to do would be to bury your cock in my cunt. I want you to fill me so fast and hard that I feel like I'm being torn in half. I want to feel you in my stomach. I want you to fuck me until I can't breathe, until I can't stand, until I—"

"That's quite naughty, nurse," I rasp. I feel like someone just took a nail gun to my dick. Graphic, but accurate in the pain level I'm currently experiencing. I grab Elisa's hips and turn her, tilting her over the edge of the desk. When I slide my hand up her thigh, I find her already soaking wet, sweet beads of moisture trickling down her perfect, silky legs.

I let out a groan that rocks through the study. Elisa had the foresight to shut the door behind her, lucky for me. I don't want to spend another second away from her. Honestly, I don't think I could wait another second, even if I wanted to. I push up the hem of the costume, which is already so short that it nearly shows the rounded swells of Elisa's ass cheeks, but when I push it up and see that she's not wearing any panties, not even a thong as I suspected, my knees nearly buckle. I run my hand over her swollen folds, glistening with tiny beads of her arousal.

I don't know what possesses me—maybe the pain and the fact that my balls are two seconds away from detonating, but I grip my cock and pump it with my fist. Elisa turns and watches me over her shoulder, eyes wide with surprise, but then dark with excitement. I keep going, keep pumping my dick like that. All it takes is a few more long strokes before I'm coming, my hips pumping forward, in hot jets, all over Elisa's round peach ass, all over her bare, glistening pussy. I come in hot strands, coating her, glistening and slick. I come over her costume, over her ass, over her thighs. She lets out a gasp and arches back into me when I take my hand and smooth myself into her skin, rubbing my come over her, massaging her, making her pussy wet and slick with it.

After having the twins, we both decided that our family was complete. We might change our minds in the future, but for now, we have two beautiful, healthy children, and that's more of a blessing than anything we could have imagined. Elisa has an IUD in, so if we ever change our minds, we can. I'm not worried at all, massaging my come into her pussy, pressing my fingers up inside her tight passage. She moans, grasps the desk, and bends over further.

"You're so beautiful," I groan. "Do I tell you that often enough? Do you believe it when I say it? That you're perfect? That you'll always be perfect?"

She hesitates and tenses. "Yes," she finally whispers. "Sometimes I doubt it, in my own head, when I see how my body looks now, but when you say it, I always believe it."

328

I withdraw my fingers and spank her ass lightly. "You better always believe it. Whatever voices there are inside your head, whatever doubts, you can tell them to fuck off. You will always, always be perfect to me." I use the heel of my hand to cup her pussy before I spank her lightly there too. She writhes against the desk.

"Yes," she pants. "Okay. I believe you."

"Always?"

"Always."

"Now, should I see about that cure? I think you might be right. The problem hasn't solved itself." My dick is just as hard, pounding just as furiously, the tip as red and swollen as it was before I jacked myself off all over my exquisite wife.

"Yes," she whimpers. "You should definitely try out the method I mentioned. I think it might work."

I grasp her hips and fit the head of my cock to her entrance. I enter her with one long, hard thrust that steals the breath from both our lungs. Her hips roll back, bucking into me as I do what she asked me to do, splitting her in half, filling her so that my balls slap against her ass cheeks with every brutal thrust. She bucks back into me while I fuck her, her hips writhing up and down, pumping against me. Her fingers scrabble at papers on my desk, sending some of them flying. Through it all, she lets out the most delicate little moans, short panting whimpers, sharp sounds that threaten to tear me apart almost from the first thrust.

I thrust hard, wildly, filling her over and over, the sounds of our bodies slapping together, the smell of sex ripe in the room, until her walls start to clench around me.

"John, yes, god…" Elisa pants. She sends another stack of papers flying and I even though I had everything carefully organized, I don't give a single fuck.

Her slick inner walls grip my dick, the waves of her climax so powerful that they milk a second release from me. I groan out Elisa's name as I fist her hair in my hand and tug her head back so she can watch me fuck her hard until I can't hold out a second longer. I spill myself deep inside of her, the spasms so hard they threaten to tear my whole body apart.

"Holy shit," Elisa whispers after. She's collapsed against my desk, her hands splayed out in front of her, her cheek pressed into a pile of messy papers. She's so hot with that naughty costume rucked up around her waist, her beautiful round ass exposed, that even if I wasn't still hard inside of her, I'd be hard within a few seconds.

I slowly withdraw, plucking her up from the desk and drawing her close, holding her in my arms. "That was—that was very much needed," I tell her as I kiss her forehead. "Thank you."

Her cheeks get that wonderful pink tinge she still gets when she's embarrassed. And pleased. She kisses me softly, then tugs down her costume. She steps back and holds up a finger to her lips as she pretends to think. "Oh dear. I think that I might be coming down with something now, but I think I have the cure. Let's see. A warm bubble bath with my husband sounds like the perfect medicine."

I imagine Elisa, riding my dick in a tub full of sudsy water. Or Elisa, naked, her legs thrown over the edge of the bathtub while I fuck up into her from beneath her. *Christ.*

I grab my pants off the floor, because I should be semi-decent when I walk out of here just in case Maria is ghosting the halls, which she doesn't usually do, but still. I slip into them, then I wrap my arms around Elisa. I lift her and carry her down the hall, into our bedroom, into the en suite bathroom with the big tub.

"I don't think we have any bubbles," I say, with some amount of regret, even though I've never wanted to have a bubble bath in my life. "You might have to settle for a normal bath."

Elisa grins at me and when I set her down, she walks over to the vanity and produces a bottle. "It's a good thing the shop I got this costume from also had some other treats available online."

"What else did you get?"

She winks at me before switching on the water and pouring in a good dollop of that delicious cherry bubble bath. Yes. For her, I will go around the house smelling like fruit. I'm perfectly fine with that. If Elisa demanded that I bathe in floral-smelling stuff every single morning, I'd gladly do it for her, even if the rest of the world thinks I'm crazy.

"You'll just have to wait and see. I might have another surprise or two waiting in the bedroom for us."

"Any surprise that involves you is a good one. Thank you." I have to thank her again. For all of this. She gave me a family of my own. She's given me a remarkable life. She's given me two wonderful children. She's loved me, when I had no idea that love was possible for someone like me. She's taught me that I myself have an unending well of love inside me.

She sways against me, kissing me hard, before she pulls away, peels off that tiny little nurse outfit, and steps into the bath. She waits for me, stands there until I peel off my pants and join her. I sink in and she settles against me, in my arms, right where she's always belonged.


The End

# Thank you so much for reading Bound by Honor!

If you liked it, please consider leaving an honest review, I would be so grateful. Your support is the lifeblood of authors and provides us with the feedback we need to give the readers exactly what they want. I read each and every review.

Your support means the world to me.

# Who's Next?
## Read the Bound by Danger excerpt below

# Bound by Danger
## An Enemies to Lovers Mafia Romance
## (Born in Crime Book 2)

# Blurb

*What happens when gasoline meets a spark?*

**Sara** - *I'm done with guys for good, even though my uncle and my mom can't wait to marry me off to some charming mafia connection who they think is good for me. He's supposed to be the prince to my mafia princess. But Dario Colombo? Notorious playboy. Bad boy. The guy never takes a single thing seriously. I've kissed enough frogs to know he's no mafia prince. But this would all be a lot easier if he wasn't so damned good-looking.*

**Dario** - *Settling down with one woman, a white picket fence, two-point-two kids, and a dog was never my version of happily ever after. But everything changed when my brother John married Gastone Gambino's daughter to ensure peace between our families. That's when Sara Codutti, a fierce and fiery mafia princess, enchanted my soul and my heart. I will make her mine at all costs. This time, I have to get it right, which would be easier if everything else wasn't going to so wrong.*

# Chapter 1

# Dario

"Do you have something else you'd rather be doing?"

Sure, I could say, I'd rather be driving my classic '67 Mustang Shelby, drinking beers with the guys and talking about our college glory days because they really were the best, or cutting into a prime rib dinner. And yet, answering in the affirmative would likely guarantee that the beautiful Brazilian model lying half-naked in her bed never asks me for a repeat performance. Also, it would probably earn me a kick in the nuts. I'll always take a hard pass when it comes to damage to the family jewels, so I search my brain for the more appropriate response.

"No, of course not."

Julia Santos winds her long, tanned legs through the black silk sheets of her bed. Black silk makes me want to gag, but it obviously doesn't bother her. She crooks a finger and stares at me enticingly. Making intentions clear, her tongue runs over her full and shiny red bottom lip. "Then come here."

I'm still wearing all my clothes, minus a suit jacket. Normally, I would have stripped them off by now, but *normally*, I'd also be a few whiskeys into the night. Maybe, after all these years, I'm finally doing what my family has always hoped I'd do. Growing the fuck up. It's possible, I guess. This past year, I've worked hard. I've built up my own business and carved a name for myself in a family where everyone will always have cause to remember it—because I'm a Colombo. Unfortunately for me, I'm the little brother, and I've never taken things as seriously as my older brother, John, does.

The past twelve months have changed quite a bit for me, though. I have my own warehouses now, and I do a good business. It turns out, when people talk all that bullshit about finding what you love and doing it and it never feeling like work... well, they might actually be right. And the thing is, I love cars. Always have, always will. When I die, I hope they bury me in an expensive Italian import with all of my riches and light the thing on fire. Maybe that's too Viking-esque, but at least those guys knew how to live and how to do death right. And hell, if my family did that for me, I could see everyone having a good time. Funerals should be fun, right? They shouldn't be somber and mopey with everyone wearing black and crying their eyes out. They should be a celebration—because you lived and you excelled at it, and because the people celebrating your life hope you're a lucky motherfucker, and that your light or your bits of energy or whatever the hell you want to term it all is going to a better place.

Anyway, I do have other things on my mind tonight, besides Julia's lovely legs. Namely, what my men are doing at the moment... because it's been two hours since they've bothered to check in with me, and it's a Friday night.

Friday nights don't ever stay quiet for long.

Spoiler alert: My family doesn't actually operate on the right side of the law. Expensive cars don't come cheap. Unless you're me, that is. Then, they do, because they're stolen and stripped down, their serial numbers ground off, all to be repainted and sold to some lucky bastard overseas who has enough balls and enough pull to be able to get such a vehicle in hand and drive it like the proud owner of a legit, quarter-million-dollar car. Most of the process all gets cleaned up nicely so that people don't ask questions. Which they don't, because that would result in a bullet in their head; better to accept and be satisfied with the under-the-table cash they get from my uncle's men. Profits and pay-offs—always a good way to keep mouths shut. The money that filters down to me enables me to purchase legit nice cars. *Imports. Classics.* You name it, I have it. Not in every color, though. I only drive them in black. If they don't come that way, they get painted.

And yes, I probably have one for each decade after 1910. Doing what I do, I'm definitely on the receiving end of the cash we make, and that has some perks.

"Darian!"

Would it kill Julia to get my name right?

I drop down to my knees. Not obediently—because god knows I've never been that—but when I hook my hands around Julia's thighs and tug her down the bed, she doesn't protest. She has on a rhinestone thong, unquestionably over the top. Hard to tear off with your teeth without chipping one. Julia Santos is truly gorgeous, though. Six feet tall, endless curves, and full breasts. Fake full breasts, it's true, but they're the expensive kind of fake that you wouldn't know aren't real unless you touch them. All that, plus dark hair, liquid brown eyes, tanned skin, and full lips. She's the complete package.

And right now, all she's wearing is a white blouse, no bra on underneath, and those fucking rhinestone panties.

She spreads her legs artfully, my hands along for the ride as she plants her feet on the edge of the bed. I can smell her arousal, and I'm sorry I was distracted before. I have every intention of making it up to her.

Until my phone vibrates in my back pocket. And I take my hands off of her.

"Are you fucking kidding me?" Julia asks, visibly pissed when I put it up to my ear.

I put a finger over my lips to shush her and then speak into the phone. "Yeah?"

"Boss. We adopted a new kitten tonight. Taking it home. Thought you might want to have a look. I know how much you love... *pussies.*"

Subtlety isn't Marco's strong point, but unlike my brother's ex-number-one man, Marco is loyal. He doesn't go around doing frame-up jobs, getting us all worked up about rival families doing shit they didn't do. And another thing, Marco would *never* kidnap my wife...

though, then again, would I have one? The point is, Marco would never sucker-punch me below the belt because he's a piece of shit who's held a grudge against our family for some petty grievances for the past, oh, three decades. That was John's number-one, not mine. So, yeah, I can handle a few pussy jokes. And Marco's odd insistence that we refer to stolen cars as cats. I can handle that, too.

"On my way," I tell him now.

I hang up and nearly catch a kick to the nuts—I knew I should be worried about that—from Julia as she scoots up the bed and shoots me a death glare. "You're leaving?"

"Sorry. It's not you. It's business."

Her eyes nearly roll right out of her head. "Do you have any idea how many men would want to be in your position right now?"

I nod slowly just because I don't want to offend her. Earlier tonight, I may or may not have been having dinner at Emelia & Salt, an expensive five-star French restaurant without the fancy French name. I was talking business with an associate who knows someone who knows another someone who might want to order a few cars. I noticed Julia sitting a few tables down, and she kept giving me looks all night. Eventually, I ordered a bottle of expensive wine and had the waiter deliver it to her table. She was dining alone, but I'm not sure if she wanted it that way or if she was stood up. I'm guessing the former, because apparently there's a line of people who will take my place right now.

But tonight, it was me who paid for her dinner, including the wine. I asked her if she'd like a ride home, too, since I was sober and she looked like she could use a ride, just to be safe. That's when she asked me up to her penthouse condo. It looks a lot like mine. High up, with a lot of glass, modern art, and expensive furniture. Plenty of useless space that's empty because neither of us do a lot of living in our spaces, not the way most people do in their homes.

"I really am sorry," I tell her now. But that's as far as it goes—no need to give her the wrong signal, after all, promising to make it up to her and all that jazz. What's the point? I have zero plans to go the route of monogamy, deflated manhood, and whippings anytime soon. Unless they're the kinky kind of whippings. Normally, I would say that's not my flavor, but who knows? I might be up for it one night out of the week.

"No, you're not. I can tell." Her pride is wounded. Julia snatches a sheet and wraps it around herself, glaring daggers at me. "No one has ever turned me down before, Dario."

Ahh. So, that's it. She's used to getting what she wants.

"Sorry. I'm sure you have someone more willing. Call them up. That call was business, and I can't pick and choose when I go. I'm not at the top of the food chain. Not yet."

Her eyes narrow and sparks of hatred practically leap out of them. Good thing nothing in here looks overly flammable. We might have been in real trouble.

"You think you can toy with people. Do whatever you want to them. Have your moment, have your fun. *Use. Use. Discard.*"

Taking a look in the mirror to make sure she hasn't left any smudges of makeup, I shake my head in denial, but my voice gets harder. I don't need to deal with this shit after how nice I was to her tonight. "Nope, Julia. That's not my MO. I have lots of moments, but so do they. I guarantee this would have been a lot of fun, but duty really does call. There isn't much *discarding* involved." Jesus, she's seriously stung by this. I'm also glad I had the sense not to fuck her on the kitchen counter, within reach of sharp objects.

Julia huffs. "Show yourself out."

"So, I take it you won't be calling me for a rain-check?"

She laughs a strange, not at all funny kind of laugh that gives me chills. I'm starting to think that if I had pulled off those panties, I would've found a stick wedged up her ass. I'm glad I'm not the one who has to stay and yank it out. In fact, Marco's getting a bonus tonight for saving me from some serious trouble. I'll buy him something nice. A watch or flowers or something. Maybe a new set of black, shit-kicker boots. He's serious about his shit-kickers. With Marco, shit often gets kicked to a high degree.

341

Julia makes a sound in her throat as I snatch my black leather suit jacket from the floor and shrug into it. I didn't do any further undressing. There are no stray items to be located.

"Sorry," I toss over my shoulder as I stalk out of her expansive bedroom with the floor-to-ceiling windows. Yup, it's so similar to mine it's slightly creepy. "Really."

"Fuck you!" she yells at my back.

I show myself right out the door, down the elevator, and out the lobby of the building that rises up straight into the night sky. I always thought living near the top of a building like this was scary when I was a kid. Then? I grew up, got rich, and bought a penthouse condo at the top of a building taller than this one. All those whiny people who say we become what we dread are probably right. Except they don't tell you that, usually, it's a lot of fun, and you'll surprise yourself and find that you don't have any fears about it at all when you get there.

I crank open the door of my Mustang and slide into the black leather driver's seat. I'm one of those people who likes a real key to stick in a real ignition—not that push-button shit—and sliding the metal home, twisting it just so to hear the growl of four hundred and twenty horses come to life… that's the best part.

I tear off through the now quiet street. It's only just after nine. Though no part of New York ever sleeps, traffic isn't as thick as it usually is, which means more open asphalt for me.

The warm and sultry July air rushes through the car's open window. I also love that feeling of cranking a window down instead of hitting a button and letting a motor do it for me. That's the point of classics, as I keep telling John. They're *classic*.

It's quite a drive to my warehouse in the Bronx, but there's nowhere else I'd rather be and nothing I'd rather be doing. Driving gives me a sense of freedom that I don't have anywhere else in my life right now. Driving fast. Driving slow. Driving somewhere in the fucking middle. Whatever.

I lean back, breathing in the smells of the city as they rush into the car and listening to the roaring purr; this Mustang handles so well, she's

342

like an extension of my own body. For a second or two, I think about Julia in her bed, like she was back at her condo with her lush body on full display for me. Nope, there's absolutely nothing else I'd rather be doing than driving right now.

Normally, I pay attention to every single detail, but tonight I'm overconfident. People like to tell me it's a bad habit of mine. I was at least careful to make sure that no one followed me to the warehouse, and I slowed down and obeyed the fucking traffic laws when I got close, so that I wouldn't draw undue attention. And it sure seems like I was careful enough when I get there. When I park the car and get out behind the warehouse, the night is filled up with the usual kinds of night noise you'd expect from any big city. Sirens far off in the distance. The blast of a horn even farther away. The reverberation of all kinds of different engines— vehicles, compressors, air conditioners. The hum of the million and a half people who call the Bronx their home all going about their business.

I spot Marco's car parked about twenty feet from the back entrance. Next to it are a few cars I recognized as belonging to my men. I assume they're all inside waiting for me.

Nothing sounds off. Nothing looks off. Nothing at all seems off.

I stalk across the stretch of crumbling asphalt that used to be a parking lot and walk up to the metal door at the back of the building. It's an ugly thing, though in this industrial part of town, it's just the usual signal of another old warehouse being used for storage after times were hard and the previous owners packed up and left.

I've installed good security and a passcode on the door. I punch in the seven, the two, and the eight. I'm reaching for the four when something slams me up against the door so that I pitch forward, my face breaking my fall. My cheekbone grinds against cold steel, and it takes me a full damn minute to register that I feel nothing. No pain in my face, no pain in my shoulder… no pain at all.

Until I hit the ground. Then it bursts over me the way a forest fire erupts—a spark catching dry tinder, only to make for a violent blaze that eats up everything in its path.

343

When I bring my hand up, my fingers come away sticky and red.

Through the shock filtering through the red-hot fire sticking my shoulder with red-hot daggers, I have one clear thought. *Holy mother of fucking god, there's a bullet in me.* That's followed up by another, far more terrifying thought. *It was meant as a warning, or someone has terrible aim.*

Either way, I know that sitting here with my back to the door and a stupid look on my face isn't going to help me. I force myself to my feet, even though I nearly puke all over my shoes to do it. I hit the fucking four on the number pad since the whole attack has probably gone down in less than twenty seconds. It's only my mind that thinks it's been an eternity—specifically, the asshole parts of my brain responsible for receiving and transmitting pain signals. Thankfully, the code hasn't reset itself. I've also been told that I'm a lucky asshole most of the time, and I guess that's the case tonight. I've always thought it wasn't true, because everyone knows what happened with my knee in college and how that shot my dreams of pro football to shit, but as I pitch forward and hear the door click shut behind me, I'm willing to accept that maybe everyone was right. That bullet could have lodged in my lung, heart, throat, or in my melon. But it didn't. Also, they waited until I was out of the Mustang to shoot, so that's a bonus. Scrubbing blood out of a classic car would be a real bitch.

That's the last thought I have before shit gets fuzzy. I see Marco rushing toward me, panic in his eyes, and then the lights go right the fuck out.

# Chapter 2

## Sara

"My god, I can't tell you how good it is to see you. I was getting worried."

I'm already walking into the penthouse condo as my cousin Elisa laughs in response, stepping back from the door. Looking around, I think how it's a nice place, but not Elisa's style. It belonged to her husband prior to the two of them even meeting, and she moved in after they were married. Which wasn't her choice, by the way, but she's happy now. I can tell. She has this whole crazy glow going on. That could also be the pregnancy hormones since she's *very pregnant* with twins. Although, maybe five months along on someone not carrying two lives looks a little less obvious? Either way, I'm no expert on pregnancy or pregnant women, but I personally think Elisa looks more like she's gone a month past her due date. I feel seriously bad for her, too, because I can't imagine being her size and knowing I have about four more months left to go.

Elisa grins at me, though, and steps up to wrap her arms around me. We both laugh when her belly makes it impossible for me to get even halfway there.

"It's a good thing I have long arms," Elisa jokes. She steps back as she twists her long blonde hair around her hand and then flicks it over her shoulder. She has gorgeous green eyes that I've always been a little jealous of, and they're sparkling with amusement at the moment. "I'm sorry I've been MIA. Between work and doctor's appointments and all the other stuff?" She flicks a hand as though to indicate this big cloud of "other stuff" hanging in the room. "I've been really freaking busy."

"Too busy for your favorite cousin who also happens to be your best friend?"

Just then, John Colombo, Elisa's husband, stalks into the room. "Too busy to remember to take her pre-natal vitamins," he says pointedly.

"Good lord," Elisa mutters, "you're right." She face-palms herself as John walks past, gripping her shoulder quickly as he does—as if in support. He really has turned out to be a good husband to her, from everything I've seen. The condo is open-concept, of course. The kitchen is to the left, and John's headed there. He picks up a bottle of vitamins, shakes out one that's approximately the size of a horse tranq, fills up a cup of water, and hands both to Elisa.

I shake my head as she pops it into her mouth and swallows it back like a champ. Then I look to John, raising an eyebrow at him. "Jesus, man. Do you shake the bottle out and count 'em every single morning, or can you just tell that she didn't take it by glancing at her?"

"I checked the security footage, actually," John mutters.

My mouth drops open, but then I realize he's kidding.

"He just knows me." Elisa says this like she's annoyed, but she's so in love that it's sickening. She gives John a sappy look as she passes the empty water glass back, and he returns the same sort of look back.

It's amazing to me that these two used to hate each other. Our families were kind of sworn enemies, but then John and Elisa were forced to get married because Elisa's dad, who's our family Don, made an alliance with the Colombo Don—John's uncle. They got married, hated each other for a bit, and then decided to get on with things and fall in love despite their start. Maybe some hate sex was involved.

I'm just guessing on that little tidbit, though.

Of course, there was also some drama with Elisa getting kidnapped by some asshole the Colombos trusted—a guy in their own family, too. He was a real prick, and no one was sorry when he met the business end of a bullet to the head. John got Elisa back after that shot, and I think they both realized that maybe they didn't hate each other after all. It must

346

have been around that time, at least, because a few months later, Elisa told everyone she's expecting twins.

So, yeah, it's been a crazy ride.

Their place has a great view of downtown Manhattan, and I follow Elisa over to the massive leather sectional at the far side of the room. The couch isn't very comfortable, but I imagine it'll get replaced soon. I'm pretty sure Elisa is using the whole "we're having babies soon, so we need more space" argument to convince John to move. Or, if she isn't already, she will be soon. She's way more of a classic, comfy, homey-home kind of person than one who'd want this somewhat uncomfortable extravagance for her family.

Homey. That's the kind of house she grew up in. After she moved out of her dad's place, my mom and I moved in. Elisa's mom—my Uncle Gastone's wife—has been dead for a long time, and he was visibly lonely after she moved out. It's worked out perfectly because my dad's actually in prison, which is another long story. Racketeering, unfortunately. My uncle couldn't get him off and he went away. He *still* has nine years to go on his sentence, so it made sense for us to get rid of our condo and move in with my uncle. My mom's been a lot happier, and I suspect she feels a lot safer there. She also gets to look after her brother—make sure he's eating properly and all that—so that's one less worry for her. Because yeah, she's *that* type. You come to her table hungry or she'll worry about you for weeks.

"When are you going on maternity leave?" I ask as soon as my butt hits the hard-as-a-rock leather surface.

Elisa glances at John, who's busy in the kitchen. He's pulling out pots and pans, and I'm hoping he's going to get something delicious going. Did I mention he can cook? He might have been an enemy of our family, but Elisa kind of hit the jackpot with this guy—if you go for his ultra-serious type, admittedly, which I really don't. But anyway, it's after seven, and I'm starving. If he's cooking, I'll eat. Meanwhile, I look back to Elisa and repeat my question.

"Soon," she says vaguely, and I get the impression that this is a contentious issue between them. "I know my own body," she declares loudly. Yup. Contentious. "Anyway. How's volunteering at the shelter going?"

"Oh. Right." I forgot I haven't told her much about it. "It's good, and it gets me away from the house, which is *huge* right now. Mom and Uncle Gastone, even Uncle Carlo, are all trying to marry me off as soon as possible. Find me a good Mafia don or underboss or whatever. It's pretty gross. And I guess I could do what you did and apply for jobs even though she doesn't want me to, rock the boat and all"—I poke her shoulder for emphasis—"but that seems like an awful lot of headaches right now. Maybe later."

Elisa sighs. "I'm sorry, Sara."

What I just said is a big *maybe*, and we both know it. I'm not the type to rock the proverbial boat of my Mafia family. Elisa walked her own path. She always made it pretty clear that she didn't want to have much to do with what our family does. Gastone let her have her way, too, even though he didn't like it. Yeah, he fought her about nursing school, but he paid for it anyway. Elisa is his only child, after all, and he could never deny her anything. She graduated last year and works as a nurse now. She always swore that she'd go legit and not marry into the underworld, but I guess it was a trade-off for her, and she could see her dad wanted to build a truce with John's family. It worked out.

For me, it's basically always been understood that I'll take the family route. I didn't go to college. I've never even been allowed to have a job. And I don't have a car either, though I did insist that I get my license. My uncle's men drive me wherever I have to go, but they think of me having a license as a last-ditch safety measure, and I think of it as one little sign of freedom, however small.

John bangs a pot in the kitchen, then mutters an apology. It wasn't a matter of protest, and although he can hear our conversation, I'm sure he feels no need to echo Elisa's sentiment of apology. As the Colombo underboss, second behind his uncle, he gets it.

I look back to Elisa and shrug. "Just because they want me to do it doesn't mean it's going to happen. I keep telling them I don't want to even date right now. Not yet. I had enough with—" I cut myself off there, but Elisa knows who I'm speaking of, and I'm training myself to not even say my ex's name. The guy was an asshole. We dated for two years, and then I found out he was cheating on me. He happened to knock up the poor girl and now they have a kid. Which sucks for her. And the kid. I try not to think about it.

"But it's been a year since you broke up," Elisa says quietly. "I can see how they'd be getting anxious to line up dates for you. Please tell me that they're at least being subtle?"

I snort. Elisa knows her dad and my mom too well. "Nope. They keep throwing out names. My mom keeps using the word 'duty' around me. Always *duty* this and *duty* that."

"At least you won't be brokered for peace." Elisa wrinkles her nose at John.

"Hey!" He fills up a pot with water. "That worked out well enough for us."

"But it could easily have not worked out!" she shoots right back.

"It was always going to work."

"Oh. Right. I forgot your animal charm can't be denied."

"Jesus," I mutter, "I feel like my ears are bleeding."

Elisa and John just grin at each other. Finally, John goes back to preparing whatever he's making. I really hope it's pasta. I freaking love pasta. I know everyone says carbs are the devil, but I've never subscribed to that myself, and I'm making out all right. I might not look like a model, but I still think, carbs included, that I'm at least a seven on the ratings scale. I could make myself an eight if I dyed my hair blonde like Elisa does. It would go well with the whole olive undertone thing I have going on, but I've always liked my hair natural. Plus, I know that, when it's as dark as mine, there would be killer breakage to deal with, and I've been growing my hair forever.

"Anyway, tell me about the shelter," Elisa urges me.

"Right. So, it's nice. It's a non-profit. I just volunteer, which makes everyone in the family pretty happy since philanthropy is important to the reputation. I really do like it, though. It gets me out of the house, and you know I've always loved animals. Mom is against getting a dog and your dad would flip out if I even said the word *goldfish*—"

"I know," Elisa giggles. "It sucked never being allowed to have a pet."

"Yeah, exactly. So, the shelter's a good place for me. There are tons of dogs and cats there. I get my fill of kitty cuddles and puppy love whenever I get to volunteer. I've been making sure I go at least three times a week, and more when they're busy. It's nice to get out and have something to do. Especially now that I'm single. I mean, don't get me wrong, I want to stay that way as long as I can, but I never have an excuse to leave the house unless I'm volunteering. Mom's always telling me I'm shopping too much or walking too much, but what else do I have to do?"

"Mmm-hmm," Elisa says. "I know how it is."

"There's this guy at the shelter..." I trail off, because talking about him was not the plan. But now it's too late, just from the look on Elisa's face which appeared the second it popped out. I've said too much. Elisa's giving me this excited look that says she really wants me to not be single anymore. It makes me feel slightly nauseated, truth be told, and I rush to explain. "I mean, *not that way*. I'm not into him, Elisa, really. He's just very nice. I've only been on a couple shifts with him since he started volunteering there last week. He seems cool, though. Like we could be *friends*."

That earns me a sympathetic look. Elisa's closer than a sister to me. She gets me in a way that nobody else does. We were both only kids, and growing up in our family, we stuck together. Then Elisa's mom died when she was young, and my mom basically filled that role for her. Anyway, Elisa knows I don't have a lot of friends. And even though she didn't want to be part of the underworld life, she was raised the same way I was. Our parents were always paranoid about something happening to us, about us slipping up and saying something about business, and so on and so forth. It didn't exactly make for us having a lot of people who were close to us—outside the family, that is.

"Well, I'm happy that you're happy there. I'm sorry I've been really busy," she adds. "When I go on maternity leave next month..." Elisa says loudly, and looks right at John. He stares at her, shakes his head, and grins. Elisa looks back at me and continues, "We'll have time to hang out more. I promise."

"And soon, I'll be an aunt—kind of—and I'll get to entertain myself with the world's most beautiful babies," I tell her. "I'll be sure I'm the best aunt, the kind that gives kids back when they're poopy or when they cry, or when they're difficult little beasts…."

Elisa laughs. "Oh my god. We both know you adore babies. And you're good with them. Not like me. I'm seriously going to have to learn some things real fast."

"Well, with two to look after, I'm sure you'll get a crash course."

She groans. "Everyone says that they're difficult the first year and then super-easy. We just have to get through that."

"Ha! Everyone says that because they don't want to tell you the real truth," I laugh. "Kind of like how people say that birth won't really suck so bad, but I'm sure it actually does. I mean, firing not one, but two human beings out of your—"

"Thank you!" John says loudly. "Do you want the spinach ravioli or the feta cheese?"

"Ew! Feta! Obviously," I reply.

"I can't have feta!" Elisa protests.

"Right." John looks like someone just shot him in the leg. He's gone totally pale in a way that would be comical if he didn't look so terrified.

I look back at Elisa, who's got a sort of befuddled look on her face. "He's worried he accidentally just about poisoned you," I point out.

With a little grunt of realization, Elisa stands up and walks over to John. She throws her arms around his neck and kisses him—like, really goes for it—before she gets the spinach ravioli out of the freezer. I assume it contains some kind of acceptable cheese. "It's okay," she assures him. "You're allowed to make one mistake, you know."

"I shouldn't forget things like that."

"As far as I know, you're human." She kisses him again. "Besides. You remember everything else. You're like a human Rolodex, if you remember what those things are. You're like… I don't know. The AI from the house thing that you installed. Anyway. You're amazing, and I love you."

They're always like this, so my gag reflex has had a lot of practice.

351

"Now," she says when she's sitting back down across from me. "Tell me all the good gossip from home, and all about this guy at the shelter. Tell me about dogs, cats, anything! I'm sorry I've been MIA for like eight days. I'll listen like you wouldn't believe and then you can forgive me for being a terrible friend. We'll eat, we'll watch movies, I'll make popcorn... I have ice cream, too."

I try to pout, but it doesn't work. "You're trying to buy back my favor with all the foods you know I can't resist."

She blinks innocently. "Would you hate me if I was?"

"Absolutely not," I say, no longer fighting a grin. "That's one peace offering I'll always agree on."

It's a good thing John is an absolute genius in the kitchen, because Elisa really can't cook. It's because of him that we get to have a good meal. I laugh more than I've laughed in a very long time. Afterward, Elisa cues up a movie. It's Friday night, so who doesn't love a good rom-com? There are thousands of good ones to choose from, but our favorite has to be *You've Got Mail.* I won't hear any arguments about that movie—it's just amazing. John goes off somewhere else in the condo, probably to see to work. Or maybe just to give Elisa and me some girl time. Either way, I appreciate it.

After the movie, we talk about Elisa's work, the shelter, and whatever gossip is going on at home and with the business—the stuff that I happen to know about, that is, which isn't much. She probably knows more than I do. I know John tells her just about everything. He's nice like that. I have to admit, he gets my stamp of approval when it comes to being a husband. I can only hope I'll be half as lucky as Elisa. I also hope my family sticks with the suggestion of letting me date someone first, and doesn't force someone on me like what happened with Elisa. I also know that her dad wouldn't have made her marry someone he didn't think was a good man. He never would have done that, no matter what was going on with family stuff.

After I'm fresh out of juicy information and Elisa doesn't have anything else to tell me, we break out the ice cream and watch a second chick flick. I'm sure some people would judge me for it, but if you ask me, maybe what everyone needs is a good cry once in a while. *The Notebook* should be at the top of everyone's list of favorite movies that give you hope for humanity and also break your heart. And since I know it's getting late, I send my mom a text, letting her know that I'll be spending the night at Elisa and John's condo. John and Elisa's guest bedroom is always open to me.

"Well…" I pause the movie as the end credits start to roll. My face is still wet with tears. Who doesn't love a sappy chick flick on a Friday night?

Elisa looks like she's two seconds away from breaking down again herself. She bawled openly ten minutes ago, when the dude in the movie died, even though we'd already seen this movie probably twelve times. Now, she can at least blame it on the pregnancy hormones. All I can blame for my penchant for sobbing over movies is… well, I don't even know. My own sappy personality?

I always say I don't believe in love, let alone that true love crap, but secretly, maybe I want to.

Elisa stands and flicks on the lights. She brushes at her eyes. "Goodness. Yup. The hormones are settling in hard."

"I think we need more ice cream."

"How about deep-fried pickles with honey dill dip?"

I stare at her, fighting the urge to laugh. "That's very specific."

"I know. Cravings, I guess." Elisa rubs her hand over her very prominent belly. She's wearing a cute, dark blue maternity tunic and leggings. She looks adorable. I imagine that, if I was in her position, I'd look more like a bloated whale.

"Okay," I tell her bravely. "I'm down."

Elisa produces her phone, and she must have had this particular craving a lot lately, because she either has the number memorized or has freaking added it to her contacts list. She puts the phone up to her ear, and I can hear it ringing.

All of a sudden, though, someone pounds at the door. No way are pickles that fast.

The condo has a lobby, so whoever's out there freaking got past the glass door, the security at the front, and also had to put in the code for the elevator. Either someone is very good at being bad, or it's someone we know. John materializes out of nowhere. He's very good at that, too, but I still startle at seeing him go by in such a blur. Dressed in black, he moves so fast that I wouldn't have known it was him if I hadn't known he was the only man in the condo with us. He has his gun out and pointed at the door before I can even take a breath.

I react on instinct, grabbing Elisa, who drops her phone.

I can hear the guy on the other end saying hello and something about Murphy and Patty's Diner over and over again. Not leaving her time to go after the phone, I make a run for it, dragging Elisa along for the ride down the hall with me. I know John's housekeeper, Mary, has her own room at the back, but I'm not worried about her. I know for a fact she has a lock on her door.

After I stash Elisa, I run to the guest room and grab my own Glock out from under the mattress. I'm what people in our kind of work like to call a mafia princess, but I'm no *princess* princess. My dad taught me how to use a gun when I was six years old. He wanted to know I could keep myself safe. My uncle gave me the Glock for my birthday last year, and though my mom just about had a heart attack when she saw it, it's the eighth one I own.

It might be fucked up, but I'd rather have the ability to protect myself than let someone take pot shots at me and do whatever they please.

I rush out into the living room, though if I haven't heard any shouts or shots by now, I figure everything is okay and someone just had to talk to John pretty urgently. Phones aren't always a safe bet. If I had a dollar for every time someone pounded down my uncle's door....

When I get to the main room, I still have my Glock in my right hand, ready to use the damn thing if I have to. Instead, I find John's arm wrapped around his brother, guiding him over to the couch. The guy's leaking a lot of blood. I tuck the Glock into the back of my jeans, knowing without thinking about it that I never even took the safety off. I can't say that I'm not tempted to use the gun here and now, however—at least a little bit. Dario is an obnoxious meathead at best, and a matching bullet somewhere benign, like in his foot, for instance, might do wonders for his odious personality.

I mean, not really, but sometimes it's nice to imagine things like that. I've always appreciated a good joke. Humor makes life tolerable. And it's how I deal with blood, too—in this amount, anyway.

"Fuck," I say under my breath as I watch John lay his brother out. The guy can't stay upright. "We're going to need Elisa for this."

"Bullet's still in there," John says over his shoulder. He's so calm, it's like he's saying that a spider dropped down his brother's shirt and needs to be extracted. Not a dangerous one, either. "We're going to need more than Elisa. They patched him up at the warehouse, but he's bleeding through what they packed on. Call our surgeon."

It's fucked up that I have the guy in my contacts, but I do. Or maybe it only makes sense, depending on how you look at it. Either way, I find myself dialing. I don't mind the sight of blood, but my stomach is churning. Dario might be a pain in the ass at the best of times, but he's still John's brother. Worse, if someone's taking shots at high-ranking members of the Colombo family, it means trouble for all of us.

I stand there while the phone rings. A puddle of dark red blood, darker than wine, is seeping onto the sectional where I was just sitting a few minutes ago. I guess I know now why John prefers real leather to something a heck of a lot more comfortable.

At least leather wipes clean.

# Chapter 3

## Dario

I've never bought into the "first time for everything" cliché, but maybe, just maybe, I'm now willing to admit this saying could be true. For example, I've never been shot before. Also, I've never seen Elisa's cousin, Sara Codutti, look at me with anything less than burning dislike. Right now, though, she's hovering over me like a dark-haired angel of mercy… and she actually looks worried. Her top teeth are sunk into a full, coral-hued bottom lip, turning it bright red as she works it over. She has a beautiful olive undertone, liquid brown eyes, and a cascade of thick dark hair that flows over her shoulders like it really is water. And while I've never seen her blush before—maybe since she has such a dark complexion—there are two red spots on her cheeks at the moment.

I'm slightly ashamed to admit there's a particular kind of woman who I find attractive. A type, so to speak. Tall. Toned. Busty. A tight, round hind end. That kind of thing. Hair color doesn't matter so much, but the women I usually go for are definitely of the model variety. I've never been one for the artsy, the waiflike, or the more real, everyday kind of look. I know that's an asshole thing to say, but I could be dying here, so I might as well admit it to myself if no one else.

Sara Codutti isn't a model. She's not tall. She's not overly toned. She's not busty, either, and from what I've seen, she doesn't have an incredible hind end. Her beauty is far less what you'd see in magazines and far more understated… in the way that, once you realize it's there, she's more than just pretty. She's incredible.

"We have to get that shirt off," she says, chewing on her lip and hovering over me again.

My vision is starting to go black along the sides and isn't very focused in front, but I can see how upset she is. She has long lashes, too. Really long lashes. I don't know why I never noticed that before. The thick fringe keeps hovering up and down as she blinks at me. All that blinking doesn't erase the worry she's making no effort to hide.

She starts unbuttoning the black shirt the guys had rebuttoned at the warehouse after they slapped on the bandages we got from the first aid kit. I'm a stubborn bastard, and I like to think I'm tough, so that was all I felt I needed before getting in my car and driving my own ass to my big brother's place. My plan? I was going to explain what had happened and hope that John would have a game plan. Instead, I'm lucky I made it here before I bled out all over the car. Or blacked out. But the blood worried me more.

As Sara's sure hands with those nimble fingers start working at the top buttons of my shirt, I gather enough of my wits to stave off the blackness and give her my most charming grin. "This isn't how I saw this going down, the first time you undressed me."

She rolls her eyes. "Jesus. You're always obnoxious, aren't you?"

"I can't help myself. Some women actually *would* call it flirting. I mean, foreplay."

"Some women are idiots." She tugs hard at the next two buttons and I let out a hiss of pain at the movement.

"And some men should know when to be silent and bite down on the pain," she adds, blinking. She moves more gently, though. "I swear I've had worse headaches than this," she tells me, going until all the buttons are undone. Her hands are cool and small, and feel like heaven against my fevered skin. "Good lord, he's soaked in sweat." Sara said that bit over her shoulder, though it wasn't news to me, and suddenly my brother's anxious face swims into view behind her.

He makes a noise in his throat that I don't like. "The surgeon will be here soon," he tells me.

I think I nod, but the blackness is getting harder to put off, and there's a deep pain that's getting harder to smile through.

"I should get Elisa," Sara comments quietly.

John barely glances at her, but answers, "I don't want to worry her."

"She's hiding with your housekeeper right now," Sara says. "I'd go get her if I were you."

John grumbles again and stalks off. I remember with a start that Elisa is pregnant, and that's probably why John doesn't want to scare her. Startle her. Worry her? That would be bad for her health, I guess. The baby's health. Of course, she's pregnant. I swallow down the confusion, hating how foggy my brain is feeling. That's more worrying than the pain. How could I forget something like that? My brain seems to be flickering on and off. Most people would tell you that's a common thing when it comes to me, but I usually have control over it. It's more of a selective shutdown so I can focus where I want. Focus isn't coming to me right now, though.

"I volunteer at an animal shelter," Sara informs me as her eyes track to the bandages at my shoulder. Her hand shifts upward, and I see it waver. Or, I think it wavers, but that might just be my vision. "The dogs are sometimes in rough shape when they come in."

I stare at her, trying to focus and follow what she's saying. "Are you... comparing me to a dog?"

Sara's fingers brush against the bandage on my arm. Suddenly, she disappears, and the blackness does a little dance across my entire field of vision. My head swims and my stomach doesn't feel right. My shoulder hurts like a thousand angry yellow jackets have hollowed it out, built a nest, and are ready to defend their home at any cost.

All of a sudden, Sara's back. She presses something to my shoulder, and that pressure is so painful it feels like getting kicked in the nuts, teeth, nose, and nipples simultaneously. I can't help groaning out loud. It might be a show of weakness, but I'll call it a win that I don't scream as she presses in harder. I thought she was an angel of mercy earlier, but now I'm doing some quick revision in my head. This is *not* mercy.

"The best thing about the dogs?" she comments. "They don't complain. They let you fix them up and they put all their trust in you. Even if they're afraid. Even the ones that have been hurt badly or haven't known a single moment of kindness. They're *tough*. They've *brave*. People could learn a few things from dogs."

Sara presses a little harder, and my stomach lurches as a new, fiery pain spreads through my entire body. I think there's a good chance I might vomit up the two-hundred-dollar steak dinner I had earlier.

God, that dinner seems like a thousand years ago.

I let out a groan that doesn't sound like me at all. I used to play football. I thought I'd go pro. I've taken some hard hits in my time, and I've also been in fights. Lots of fights. Growing up, I often used my fists to settle shit out. I guess it's been a while since any of that went down. Years. Jesus.

Fuck, this hurts.

"Maybe I should sit you up. Get this elevated. I think that would help with the bleeding."

I groan again.

"Where the hell is Elisa?" Sara mutters. "I'm not trained for this."

"You're doing all right," I grit out, suddenly very aware of just how much I don't want her to leave me alone. I grip her hand, surprising us both. "Help me sit up. I feel like I'm going to puke… and I think… it would be done much more neatly if I wasn't on my back."

Sara saws at her bottom lip some more. She looks uncertain. Meanwhile, I'm realizing how beautiful she actually is. How have I never truly noticed it before? And she's not only beautiful. She's brave. She's also probably right. If it was her with the bullet in her shoulder, she'd probably ask for something to bite on, a bottle of whiskey, and some tweezers. She'd go to town on herself, all without making a sound.

"You're right. That would be disgusting," she finally remarks, regaining some of her sass. She looks less worried, or at least she's doing a better job of hiding it.

She tucks those sweet, cool hands under my burning shoulder, and I get another surprise—she's stronger than she looks. I'm also weaker than I remember. Somehow, with a lot of struggle, grunting, lip-biting, cursing, and nearly tossing my cookies—that part's just me, not her—I end up vertical again. Mostly vertical. I sag against the back of the couch, letting it take all the weight I can't seem to support.

"You've lost a lot of blood." Sara sits down beside me. She presses the towel she got from the kitchen back to the wound, and a fresh wave of pain assaults me. Bile splashes up into my throat.

I take a breath, building up the will to speak through the agony I'm feeling and the urge to get sick. Mostly, what's holding me back from throwing up is knowing how much more pain I'll be in if my stomach spasms like that, but I also want to warn her again. "I might puke," I finally manage to say.

"That's okay. Just turn your head the other way so I don't wear it."

She's serious. I can't think of a single other woman who would get herself covered in my blood and then tell me it was okay to puke in front of her.

I want to laugh, but all I can do is groan. "Usually, when I'm half-naked, it's a lot more exciting." For some reason, I feel the need to put that out there. Where did my shirt go anyway? I hardly remember it being taken off.

"Oh, I don't know. Personally, I find this to be quite enough drama." She presses down harder on the towel, and I grimace.

"Oh my god!" a brand new female voice exclaims from somewhere distant. Elisa, I realize. *God, the black is starting to do its worst again.* "What happened?" she asks.

"Somehow, he managed to get himself shot," John tells her, his deep voice seeming to come from a distance. I wouldn't know since I've got my eyes closed, trying to keep the blackness from spinning. "It's highly inconvenient, given that I've told him we should keep things quiet while I'm trying to get into politics. You know. For the advancement of the family," John goes on. He's rambling, I realize. That means he's worried. Or that he doesn't care. Better it be the second one, I think as he continues. "So we can start doing more legit business. Start a brand new era. Politics is absolutely the best path. Even Leone agrees. Right, Dario?"

I open my eyes and glare at him. "Whatever. And I have no idea who… it was. Who shot me," I add, when I see the confusion on Sara's face. I'm making sense, right? Either way, I'm pissed now, that my brother finds it inconvenient that I could have been killed. "I haven't fucked with anyone. I've been behaving," I add, having to gasp for breath

for a second as Sara presses down on the towel again. "Taking things…
seriously. Keeping it quiet… like you said."

Fuck, was that my voice? I sound fucking weak.

The blackness is inching around again, and I try not to focus on it. To
think of something, anything else. I do have a track record for not taking
things as seriously as I should, including family business, but the last
year really has been different. I've been grinding it out, working my ass
off, and, yes, taking shit as seriously as serious shit can fucking be taken.
Serious as a bullet, mostly.

"But yeah," I groan. "Worry about your career ass-kissing and brown-
nosing… with city officials… instead of your own brother. Who's been
shot," I tack on sarcastically. I don't know if he understood that last bit,
though. I didn't scream, but those words definitely came out with as
much pain as meaning.

John grunts. It's the kind of grunt that says he doesn't like what he's
seeing—maybe the situation, maybe me. In the back of my head, I know
he's distancing, responding to the situation as a whole instead of me. It's
not my attitude, not the fact that I got shot, not that he knows that I'm
right about me behaving, about not making new enemies. The old ones
aren't doing much of anything lately, after all. We have a truce going on.

But for someone to take a shot, and hit the mark, at a member of our
family… that's serious shit. Nobody knows it better than me, I think,
and I have the uncomfortable urge to laugh even as a fresh wave of pain
hits.

"John!" Elisa whispers. "That's not helping. He's bleeding a lot. You've
called the surgeon?"

"Eight million years ago," Sara responds. She presses down hard again,
and I let out an undignified gasp.

"He should almost be here." John's information is more helpful.

Elisa sighs. "Good. Keep pressing that towel on. I'll get you a couple
of fresh ones. That one is just about sodden. I'll get some cold water and
towels to clean him up, too. You're okay with that, Dario?"

I blink. "Clean me up?"

"You're soaking wet," Sara informs me. "The couch looks like a rain
cloud just moved over it and is letting loose all its fury."

*Right. Blood and sweat. John must love this.* "Don't take my pants off," I tell her through a groan.

Sara chokes. "Why would I take your pants off?"

"Are they wet?"

"Ummm…"

"That's sweat. I swear." I drag in an inhale that hurts like hell because it makes my shoulder rise and fall, and then I catch the scent of fresh rain. I know it's laundry soap or shampoo, and that it belongs to Sara, but just for a second, I think about that rain cloud she mentioned, and how she might actually have the power to summon one. She smells that wonderful.

Truth is, right now, I've never been more humiliated. Here's this woman who I have just realized is beautiful, despite the fact that I've known her for a while and never so much as noticed her. A woman who isn't squeamish about blood or barf, and who came into the room wielding a Glock like an angry goddess when I walked through the door, a mafia princess in her own right. She's got her hands drenched in my blood, trying to stop it from draining out the rest of the way and killing me. She's here, trying to save my life. Oh, and she might think that, when I got shot, I pissed myself.

"Good lord," Sara mutters. She turns away from me and I notice Elisa is back. Or did I already know that? It seems like things are getting blurrier, more black swimming around the edges of my vision like sharks. I watch as Elisa passes over a larger towel. At least this one is black. Sara passes back one which is stained scarlet. It really is sodden, and for the first time, I'm legitimately worried that this is not good. As in, *the end* type of not good.

"What's good lord?" Elisa asks.

"He's worried about his pants."

"Why?" John's back now, too.

I groan. I don't know how this could get any worse.

Elisa sits down on the other side of me while Sara presses the fresh towel into my shoulder, hard enough to pack the wound. A new wave of pain nearly guts me. My head lolls forward and I gag, tasting something foul in my throat, but nothing comes up farther than that.

"Whoa, there." Elisa takes my face in her hands, and I try to focus on her. Her hands are cool, too. And she has a wet cloth. God, it's gloriously wet. And cold. She smooths it over my face gently before working it down my neck, then over my chest. This sponge bath of sorts is the best bath I've ever had in my life. The cold feels delicious, even through the pain. I know it's only because my skin feels like I've been thrown into an incinerator, but I'll take what relief I can get.

Everything goes black for a second, and then, suddenly, there's a man standing over me. I don't recognize him. The surgeon, I'm guessing. I try to raise my head, but it feels heavy. I swallow bile, and in another moment, I realize I'm freezing now. I close my eyes and let my head fall back, giving up on fighting off the blackness.

But then there are warm hands. Nice, warm, soft hands. They grip my face at either side. I open my eyes even though the lids feel like stones. I stare into a set of soft, gorgeous, big brown eyes. Her lashes are so thick. *So. Thick.*

"Hey," Sara says softly. "It's going to be okay. They'll pull the bullet out and stitch you up and then you can go back to being your annoying, arrogant, self-serving self. Got that?"

I try to speak, but just groan.

That warm palm pats my cheek. "That's the spirit."

I watch her back away to stand by Elisa, who looks agitated even though she's a nurse. My brother takes Sara's place beside me. His brow is furrowed all wrong. Hazily, I let my eyes move around the group, unable to really focus as I try to take it all in. Everyone is looking at me like I might actually be in real trouble.

I watch as the surgeon—who's a not very good-looking, middle-aged man—draws out a huge syringe and fills it up with something nasty looking. Anything going in a needle that big has to be nasty. He plunges it into my shoulder, and I let out a squeak that I'm immediately ashamed of, especially since everyone is watching, but then the pain starts to numb.

A second needle slips into my vein, this time in the ditch of my arm, and then everything numbs out completely.

\*\*\*

364

# Did you enjoy the preview of Bound by Danger? Then read on!

**READ BOUND BY DANGER TODAY**
**FREE IN KINDLE UNLIMITED**

# Acknowledgements

First of all, I want to thank my family for all the support and love they have always shown me, especially in difficult times. You are the most important people in my life.

I also want to thank my wonderful team. Without you, none of this would have been achieved. I am very grateful to have such professional people by my side, willing to help me with all of my requests. The success of any author comes from the work of many people.

Finally, I want to thank all of my readers; it is you who give me the greatest joy. I try to put all of myself into the novels I write, and your support is essential. If you had a good time reading this novel and it got you excited, I've achieved my biggest goal, and that makes me happy.

I am grateful for what life offers me every day, and I wish you the best.

Love and Hugs,

Kelsey

xoxo

# Keep in Touch

Never miss new release, bonus content or giveaway!
Enter your email address to sign up for my newsletter on my website and follow me.

**Website:** kelseydawson.com

**Facebook:** @authorkelseydawson

**Instagram:** @authorkelseydawson

**Amazon Author Page:** Kelsey Dawson

**Goodreads:** Kelsey Dawson

For personal inquiries, feedback or suggestion please email: **kelsey@kelseydawson.com .**

# About the Author

Kelsey Dawson is a best-selling author of Contemporary Romance and New Adult novels. She writes intense, sexy romance with strong heroines and dominant men who will do anything to capture their hearts.

Born and raised in New York City, Kelsey graduated with degrees in Creative Writing and Journalism. She still lives in the city today, with her husband, their daughter, and their Pomeranian, Romeo.

Working as a full-time mom and writer, Kelsey uses her free time for enjoying reading, keeping fit by going to the gym, salsa dancing with Mr. Dawson, and taking nature walks.

She can often be seen with a pocketful of discarded garbage, collected from one of her strolls, and she is an advocate of saving the planet in any way she can.

And while she likes to sip tea while she writes, she prefers a wine glass when she reads a good book.

CONTEMPORARY
ROMANCE

Printed in Great Britain
by Amazon

12639755R00220